Praise for Lucy Dillon

'A beautifully written story about friendship, trust and love. I adored it.' Milly Johnson on *One Small Act of Kindness*

'A book you'll read into the wee hours, full of warmth, love and bravery.' Lucy Robinson on *One Small Act of Kindness*

'Such a brilliant book. So satisfying and clever and deeply moving. I'll be passing it on to all my friends.' Sophie Kinsella on *A Hundred Pieces of Me*

'A thoughtful, romantic, bittersweet story' *Sunday Mirror* on *A Hundred Pieces of Me*

'A totally feelgood novel about the importance of living life to the full' *Sun* on *A Hundred Pieces of Me*

'I can think of few lovelier "me" moments than the joy of being curled up with a truly magical novel like this one.' Fiona Walker on *A Hundred Pieces of Me*

'Lucy Dillon's voice is gentle and kind throughout . . . perceptive and well handled.' *Red* on *The Secret of Happy Ever After*

'Witty, heart-warming and a very real tale of loss and redemption' *Stylist* on *Walking Back to Happiness*

'I loved this book! Heartwarming, real and entertaining' Katie Fforde on *Lost Dogs and Lonely Hearts*

'A charming, heartwarming, entertaining read' *Glamour* on *The Ballroom Class*

Lucy Dillon

one small act of kindness

HODDER

First published in Great Britain in 2015 by Hodder & Stoughton
An Hachette UK company

1

Copyright © Lucy Dillon 2015

A CIP catalogue record for this title is available from the British Library

Paperback ISBN 978 1 444 79602 5
Ebook ISBN 978 1 444 79603 2

Typeset in Plantin Light by Hewer Text UK Ltd, Edinburgh

Printed and bound by CPI Group (UK) Ltd, Croydon, CR0 4YY

Hodder & Stoughton policy is to use papers that are natural, renewable
and recyclable products and made from wood grown in sustainable forests.
The logging and manufacturing processes are expected to conform
to the environmental regulations of the country of origin.

Hodder & Stoughton Ltd
Carmelite House
50 Victoria Embankment
London EC4Y 0DZ

www.hodder.co.uk

For Jan and James Wood,
the kindest and best neighbours anyone could
wish for. Especially if the anyone is a scatty,
key-losing writer.

Chapter One

Arthur stared up at Libby, his beady eyes conveying what his elderly owners were too polite to say. Which was, 'You haven't got us booked in, have you?'

On the other side of the Swan Hotel's polished oak reception desk, Libby's hand froze as she clicked through the computer check-in system. He *knows*, she thought, staring back at Arthur. He *knows* that we have no record of any reservation, that we currently have not one room in a fit state to show to a guest and that I secretly don't even think dogs should be allowed in hotels, let alone on a bed.

The dachshund wagged his whippy tail slowly from side to side and tilted his head as if to confirm she was right. Particularly the bit about dogs on beds.

Libby blinked hard. It's a sausage dog, she reminded herself. Not a hotel inspector.

Although, as the hotel forums warned, you never knew . . .

'Two nights, name of Harold,' repeated Mrs Harold, shifting her handbag onto her other forearm. 'Is there a problem? We've been travelling since eight to get here.'

'From Carlisle,' explained Mr Harold. 'Three changes and a replacement bus service. I could do with a cup of tea, love.'

'I'm so sorry.' Libby tore her gaze away from Arthur and increased the warmth of her smile – the smile she hoped was covering up her panic as the upstairs rooms flashed before her mind's eye. She'd launched Operation Deep Clean two hours ago specifically *because* the hotel was empty, and now not one of the rooms had a bed in the right place, let alone a spotlessly smoothed set of pillows. She and Dawn, the cleaner, had moved everything so they could tackle the carpets properly; as Dawn pointed out, there was enough accumulated dog hair under the beds to knit your own Crufts. Libby pushed that thought away. 'My husband and I only took over last month,' she explained. 'We're still finding our feet with the booking system.'

Mr Harold coughed and awkwardly touched his salt-and-pepper hair, confirming the sinking suspicion forming in Libby's mind since she'd sprinted downstairs to answer the brass reception bell. 'I don't mean to . . . Is that something in your hair?'

Libby casually ran a hand through her blonde bob. Yup. It *was* a cobweb. A massive one.

'We're in the thick of renovating,' she explained, trying to flick it discreetly off her fingers. Maybe if Dawn moved one bed back and closed all the doors, they could get one room ready . . . 'Now then, where are we?' She willed the screen to stop messing her about. 'You're absolutely sure it was *April the twenty-fourth*?'

'Yes! I spoke at some length on the telephone to your receptionist. An older lady.'

An older lady. The penny dropped. 'Oh. In that case . . .' Libby reached under the desk for the battered reservations book, angling it so the Harolds couldn't see that Friday and Saturday's columns were untroubled by any bookings, whether in pencil, on Post-its or any of the other haphazard note forms employed by her mother-in-law, Margaret, who had only recently started writing down reservations at all.

'Donald and I never wrote anything down,' Margaret would insist. 'When it's your hotel, you just *know* who's coming.'

The problem was, though, thought Libby, scanning the book in vain, this wasn't Margaret's hotel anymore. It was *their* hotel: Libby's, Jason's and Margaret's. And at the moment, pretty much no one was coming.

The booking spreadsheet was just one of the ideas Jason had introduced when he and Libby had moved into the hotel to help Margaret after his father, Donald, had died very unexpectedly; however, like most of their efforts to make Margaret's life easier, she had taken it as a personal criticism. Jason's website suggestions hadn't gone down well either ('Your father wasn't at all convinced about the internet, Jason . . .'), nor had their ideas about making some rooms dog-free or putting croissants on the breakfast menu.

Libby's heart broke on a daily basis for Margaret, who seemed suddenly colourless and lost without jolly, sensible Donald, whom she'd nagged and adored for thirty-five years, but the Swan was in urgent need of attention. Both financially and hygienically. In order to get the deep clean started without a hurt Margaret arguing that most guests didn't share their 'paranoia about a dog hair or two', Jason had had to take his mother over to the big Waitrose for a leisurely morning's shopping, leaving Libby in charge of a hotel *and* a guerrilla cleaning operation. Not to mention Margaret's self-important basset hound, Bob, who was safely shut in the office. Libby wasn't even going to think about what he might be getting up to in there.

'Does it matter? You can't be full, surely?' said Mr Harold, looking around at the deserted reception. He made eye contact with the moth-eaten stag's head over the door to the lounge and did a violent double take.

Libby sighed. If Margaret was putting her foot down about the reservations book, it was nothing compared with her resistance to their plans to update the decor. Jason had grown up in the Swan and didn't mind the wall-to-wall thistlemania in the public areas, and Libby had rather enjoyed its gloomy charm when they visited a few times a year from London, but now their remaining life savings were tied up in the shabby, stag-infested surroundings, it made her twitchy. She wished there were some way she could persuade Margaret to let them get on with the revamp they'd agreed when they'd sold up and moved here for their own fresh start.

As it was, thanks to Margaret's reluctance and their own careful budgeting, she and Jason were doing it room by room, by themselves, in the evenings. The bedrooms were more Laura Ashley than Braveheart, and they'd spent the previous month stripping the busy pink paper from room four, replacing it with soothing dove-grey-painted walls and soft linens. Libby had made mood boards for the luxurious boutique look they'd decided the hotel needed if they were going to attract a bigger-spending clientele. Or any spending clientele, come to that. Jason and Libby's savings had just about managed to rescue Margaret from the clutches of the bank, but there wasn't a lot left over to rescue the hotel from the ravages of time.

Neither of them had done any DIY before – Jason had been a stockbroker; Libby had been a television researcher – but room four looked pretty good, considering. And she'd quite enjoyed watching Jason wielding a sander, with his sleeves rolled up and his fair hair dark with sweat. She'd always known him in his City suit, or his off-duty weekend wear. And it gave them time alone to talk. And to not talk, too, sometimes; just working alongside each other, worn out in a good way, knowing every scrubbed board or sanded windowsill was a step forward. Room four was the start of something precious, Libby reminded herself. Proof that fresh starts sometimes came disguised as horrible endings.

As if she could read Libby's mind, Mrs Harold said, 'The lady we spoke to over the phone said she'd give us a specially refurbished one. Room four? Arthur likes a firm bed for his back, and I understand room four has a brand-new memory-foam mattress.'

'Indeed it does! Room four is—' Libby started to address her reply to Mr Harold, then remembered that Arthur was, in fact, the guest currently sniffing the laundry bag and ... Oh lovely. Cocking his tiny leg against it. 'Room four, um, might still need a day or two's airing. Wet paint,' she finished, as convincingly as she could.

Arthur wagged his tail at her, but it cut no ice with Libby. Dog hairs weren't part of the plan, despite Margaret's stubborn insistence that dog-friendly rooms had been their trademark for years.

'I can give you a lovely ground-floor room,' she went on. 'With a garden view on—'

'What was that?' Mr Harold put one finger in the air and inclined his head towards the door.

'Could have been our cleaner upstairs,' said Libby. Dawn was getting full value out of the rented carpet shampoo-er; the water coming out was mesmerising them both with its tarry blackness. 'It's just this morning. We won't be disturbing you later on.'

5

'No, it was definitely something outside,' he said. 'Unless I'm losing my hearing . . .'

'I do sometimes wonder if you can hear a word I say,' muttered Mrs Harold to herself.

Libby stopped and listened. Nothing, apart from the sound of Dawn shampooing. And some ominous crunching from inside the office. She remembered, too late, that she'd left the nice biscuits in there. The ones that were supposed to be in the lounge, for guests.

'Did I just hear a car braking?' said Mr Harold.

And then they all heard something: the undeniable sound of a woman's scream. A thin, falling yelp that cut through the air.

Libby's throat tightened up. The hotel was on a bend, and the turning for the car park wasn't obvious, so cars slowing down to find it were in danger of being hit by someone coming the other way. The locals, of course, knew the road and so wouldn't – Margaret had assured her – need the safety mirror Libby thought they ought to install as a matter of urgency.

'I'd better go and see if everything's all right. Would you like to take a seat in the lounge while I check?' She slipped out from behind the front desk, grabbing her mobile as she went, and crossed the reception to open the door to the lounge. More tartan, more squashy sofas, but at least Dawn had cleaned in there already today, and Libby had replaced the pre-millennium *Country Life*s with some more recent magazines. 'If you and, er, Arthur would like to relax in here and help yourself to tea and coffee, I won't be a moment.'

The Harolds gave the stag's head a nervous glance and made their way underneath his glassy stare into the chintzy comfort of the lounge.

* * *

Outside, the bright sunlight shining through the trees made Libby squint, but the scene on the main road was all too clear.

A rough-and-ready farmer's 4x4 and a red Mini had stopped at strange angles, like toy cars abandoned by a bored child: the Mini was pointing up towards the banked hedge, and the Land Rover was in the middle of the road. There was no sign of a driver in the Land Rover, but a man was getting out of the Mini, looking shell-shocked.

It was his guilty expression that set a chill running across Libby's skin. Whatever awful thing had just happened was clearly reflected on his face.

'Are you all right?' she called. 'Do you need an ambulance?'

The man shook his head – he was about thirty, dark hair, stubble; Libby thought she should try to remember details in case she was later asked as a witness – and it was then that she saw what he was staring at.

A pair of bare feet on the ground, partially hidden by the Land Rover's wheels. Libby spotted a flip-flop, a plain black one, thrown across the other side of the road.

Her chest tightened. The feet were long and pale, a woman's feet, and the calves above them were speckled with tiny drops of blood from fresh grazes.

'I didn't see her,' the Mini driver was saying, rubbing his face in disbelief. 'The sun was in my eyes. She was in the middle of the road . . .'

Libby hurried round the Land Rover, where the driver was bent over a young woman's body. An older man, she noted, not wanting to look down. Grey hair, fifties, checked shirt and cords. Probably a farmer. Good. He'd know what to do. He wouldn't be scared of blood. Libby was very squeamish.

7

Moving to the countryside hadn't helped; there seemed to be a kamikaze amount of roadkill around Longhampton.

Don't be such a wuss, she told herself. Who else is going to help?

'Is she breathing?' Libby inched nearer. 'Is she . . . OK?'

The man winced. 'She hit the Mini, only just missed me. She went up his bonnet, then straight down onto the road. Head took a fair knock. Don't know if anything's broken, but she's out for the count, poor lass.'

The woman was curled up as if she were napping, her dark brown hair fanning out around her head and her denim skirt riding up above her bare knees. Her toenails were painted a bright candy pink, the only bold colour on her. Everything else was plain: dark skirt, dark hair, long-sleeved black T-shirt, even though it was a sunny day.

A startling thought flashed across Libby's mind: she looks just like Sarah. It was followed by a protective pang. She knew it wasn't her little sister – Sarah was in Hong Kong – but something vulnerable about her face jolted her. The creaminess of the skin, with the oak-brown freckles underneath. The long eyelashes, like a doll's. She leaned forward, forgetting her squeamishness, and put her fingers to the woman's pale throat.

The skin was cool under her fingertips, but she felt a pulse. Libby let out a breath and realised her own heart was beating hard, high in her chest.

'It's OK – there's a pulse.' She glanced up. 'Have you called the police? And an ambulance?'

'I'll do that now.' The man stepped away and went back to his car.

Libby couldn't take her eyes off the woman, but her brain

was clicking into gear, throwing up practical information to blot out the panic. She'd been on a one-day first-aid course for the hotel (thankfully mostly theory, not gory practice) and they'd covered the basics. Don't move her, in case of spinal injuries. Airway – clear. Good. There didn't seem to be any blood, though her grazed arm was at a funny angle, pale against the rough grey tarmac, crossing the white line.

The white line. Libby stood up with a jerk, signalling to the Mini driver.

'We need to stop the traffic coming round the corner. You've got warning triangles, haven't you?'

He didn't move, just carried on staring at the motionless body, hypnotised by what had happened, so quickly, in the middle of a perfectly normal morning. Libby would have stared as well, but she was too aware of every second ticking past for the woman on the ground. A lump the size of a duck egg was rising on the woman's pale temple, and the skin around her eyes was bruised. Libby tried not to think about what internal injuries there might be.

'Warning triangles – get them out, quickly! Do you want someone else to get hurt, crashing into your car?' She glared at him and he opened his mouth to speak, changed his mind and hurried off.

Libby bent down to hide her own shock. 'It's fine,' she murmured, putting her hand on the woman's shoulder. It had been something the first-aid trainer had said: keep talking, keep contact going, even if you think they can't hear you. 'Don't worry – the ambulance is on its way. You're going to be fine. Everything's going to be OK.'

Silence fell again, apart from the half-conversation of the farmer on the phone to the police dispatcher, and birdsong in the trees around them. Something this dramatic shouldn't be happening in such peaceful surroundings, thought Libby. In London, there'd be sirens by now, passers-by crowding round, opinions, people shoving in to help, or walk past. In Longhampton, there were just a lot of birds. Possibly a distant sheep.

It made her feel very personally responsible.

'Hang on,' she murmured again, trying not to see her younger sister in the woman's face. 'You're going to be all right. I'm not going to leave till you're safely in that ambulance. I promise. I'm here.'

What else could she do? Libby looked at the woman's bare feet and took off her blue cashmere cardigan to cover them up. This was a strange place for her to be, wearing flip-flops, she thought. There was no footpath along this side of the road, and the hotel was a bit of a hike out of town. Sometimes Libby saw walkers strolling past with dogs; there was a bridle path running through the grounds, one of the routes that made up the Longhampton Apple Trail, but she obviously wasn't on her way there – Libby knew from walking Margaret's dog that the paths were still muddy enough to need wellies.

Was she heading for the hotel? Libby looked around for a bag, but couldn't see one. And there was definitely no booking for a single woman in the hotel that night – although, if Margaret had taken the booking . . .

She checked her watch. Nearly ten to one. Jason hadn't said what time he and Margaret would be coming back. Margaret liked to spin out her trips to the big Waitrose: not only did she much prefer the superior-quality produce, but it gave her a chance to show off Jason, her successful financial-expert son, to the various committee friends of hers who also liked to make a morning of their shopping. Libby didn't want Margaret to be upset by the accident, but at the same time she didn't want the unsupervised Harolds to explore too far into the hotel, not with the chaos upstairs. It had been a stupid idea to do all the rooms at once, she thought, mentally kicking herself. A beginner's mistake – thinking like a home-owner, not a hotelier.

Libby sat back on her heels, ashamed of obsessing about cleaning logistics when the unconscious stranger might be seriously injured.

'It's fine,' she whispered, hoping the woman would hear her voice and know someone was trying to help her. 'It's fine. Not going to leave you.'

She hummed tunelessly, as much to calm her own rising panic, until she heard footsteps approaching. Libby's head bounced up, hoping for a reassuring figure in uniform or at least the farmer returning with an update. Instead, she saw Jason's broad frame striding towards them and relief swept through her like the sun coming out from behind the clouds.

Jason looked concerned but not worried – worrying wasn't his style. But as he got closer, he frowned and ran a hand through his blond hair – farmer's-boy thatch, as Libby used to tease him when they'd first met. It never looked quite right above his pinstripe suit, unruly and thick. Now, in his checked shirt and jeans, it looked fine. He'd fitted back in here as if he'd never left.

'Has there been a shunt? I saw the triangles up just before the turning to the car park, so we left the car and—' His eyes widened as he registered the woman on the ground. 'Christ! What's happened? Are you all right, babe?'

'No.' Libby rose to her feet, and wobbled. She felt light-headed. 'I mean, I'm fine, but I don't think she is.'

'Hey, come here. You're white as a sheet.' Jason hugged her to his chest, dropping reassuring kisses onto the top of her head while he rubbed her back, and Libby felt her shoulders relax. His touch was comforting; she fitted into him perfectly, the top of her head level with his chin. Thank God Jason's here, she thought, and realised how many ways she meant it.

Then, just as she was about to ask if Margaret had gone straight in to the hotel, Libby saw her mother-in-law carrying two bags of shopping. For a moment she looked like the old Margaret – fussy, filling her clothes exactly, bustling some-where – but the smile that had started on her round face slipped away as she took in the scene in front of her. In an instant she looked older, nearer seventy than sixty. She put the bags down and covered her mouth; her eyes, an unusual pale blue like Jason's, filled with horror.

'Oh my goodness.' It came out like a wail. 'What's happened?'

Libby wished she hadn't had to see this. It was only six months since Donald had collapsed in reception, then died from a massive heart attack before the ambulance arrived. Margaret had been alone. Overnight her confidence had vanished, leaving a twitchiness that could easily turn to fright-ened tears. Libby broke free from Jason's arms and took a step towards Margaret, blocking her view.

'I don't know. I didn't see it – I just came out and found those two cars and this lady on the ground. Don't worry – we've called an ambulance and the police are coming.' Libby glanced down as she spoke; it felt odd talking over the woman's body as if she weren't there. 'She's going to be absolutely fine,' she added, in case the woman could hear.

'Sounds like you've done everything you can.' Jason hovered

between his wife and his mother, unsure who he should be comforting first.

Libby gave him a nudge towards Margaret and muttered, 'Take her inside. There's a couple waiting in the lounge – can you deal with them? They're called Harold, and they say they're booked in for the weekend, but there's no record on the computer.'

Jason looked exasperated, but Libby shook her head. 'It doesn't matter. Don't make a big deal about it, but we need to put them somewhere. See if Dawn's finished one of the rooms. Or, we hadn't started the carpet in room seven – try that.'

'Is there something we can do?' Margaret called. Her voice was brave but plaintive.

'No, everything's on its way, Margaret. You go inside.' She glanced at Jason. 'Hurry up before your mother checks them in to room four. They've got a *dog*.'

His eyes rounded at the mention of room four. 'Say no more.' Jason squeezed her shoulder. 'But are you sure you don't want me to stay till the police get here? You've done your bit.'

Libby half wanted to let him, but she felt a strange reluctance to leave the woman. 'No, it's fine. I said I'd stay with her and I will.'

'What's she called?'

'Oh. I don't know.'

'Where's her handbag?'

They both looked around; there wasn't one in sight.

'I'll check the hedges,' said Jason, but Libby waved him away.

'I'll do that once the police arrive. You sort the guests out. And make sure your mother hasn't let Bob into the lounge again. I spent all morning hoovering that sofa. He should be *bald*, the amount of hair that dog leaves behind him.'

Jason opened his mouth to reply, but at that moment, in the distance, Libby heard the sirens tearing through the air, and the raw anguish on Margaret's face washed away any lingering worries about the bookings system.

The ambulance crew worked briskly around the injured woman, and as they were getting a stretcher ready, a police car arrived. Two officers began interviewing the drivers, marking off the scene and radioing instructions ahead.

The controlled activity felt reassuring after the stillness before. Libby walked up and down the road, looking for the woman's handbag, but couldn't find anything. After that, she wasn't sure what she was supposed to do. She wasn't involved and yet she didn't want to leave until she knew what was happening to the stranger. The paramedics had wrapped the woman in a blanket and strapped an oxygen mask over her pale face. She looked much smaller under the blanket.

'And did you witness the accident, ma'am?'

Libby jumped. A young police constable was standing right next to her. He had a local accent, with the stretchy vowels that made Libby think of tractors and fields and cider orchards. Jason's accent, sharpened by years in London, had already started to soften again, mainly thanks to the catching up he'd been doing in the Bells with his old mates, none of whom had ever managed to leave Longhampton for more than two years.

'No, I heard a noise from inside the hotel.' She gestured towards it. 'My name's Libby Corcoran. We own the Swan. When I got here, everything was just as you see it now.'

'And you don't know this lady?'

One Small Act of Kindness

'No, I've never seen her before.'

'Did you pick up her handbag?'

'I didn't see one. I've checked the hedges, but there doesn't seem to be anything. It might have gone through to the field.'

The policeman looked frustrated. 'I was hoping you'd say you'd picked one up. That's going to make things trickier. No ID.'

Libby was surprised. 'None at all? No phone? Have you looked under the cars?'

'We've searched the scene – there's nothing. And you're definitely saying you've never seen her before?'

'Definitely,' said Libby. 'Why do you ask?'

He frowned. 'Because the only thing the ambulance lads found on her was your address, in her pocket – she'd written it down.'

'*My* address?' The unexpected connection between them startled her. Why would this stranger have her address? They were miles away from Wandsworth.

'Yes.' The policeman seemed surprised by Libby's reaction. 'You did say you ran the hotel, didn't you?'

'Um, yes, of course, the hotel.' What was she thinking? That house wasn't hers anymore, anyway. Someone else was wafting around her gorgeous kitchen now. Someone else soaking in her roll-top bath. She shook her head. 'Sorry – I'm still getting used to the new job. We've only been here a couple of months.'

The policeman smiled politely. 'Thought you didn't sound local, ma'am.'

'If I had a fiver for everyone who's said that—' Libby began, then stopped, because she was going to say, 'I'd have enough to pay some bills.'

But the tingle of connection was still there: this dark-haired, bare-legged stranger had written down the name of the hotel, looked it up somewhere. She was coming to them. Another two minutes and she'd have been walking through the door and none of this would be a mystery. She was a stranger to Libby, but she knew Libby's name, Jason's name. The hairs on the back of Libby's arms prickled up.

'We don't have anyone booked in for tonight,' she said.

'She might have been calling in to enquire about work. Have you advertised for any staff recently? Cleaners? Cooks?'

'No, we haven't. We're not taking on any new staff.'

Far from it. When Jason had gone over the books, it had been touch and go as to whether they could afford to keep on both part-time cleaners.

'Maybe she was meeting someone at the hotel?' The police officer knitted his brows. 'A friend? A boyfriend?'

'Excuse *me*,' joked Libby, 'it's not *that* kind of hotel,' but then realised when the policeman's ears turned cerise that that was a townie joke too far.

'We don't really get spur-of-the-moment guests, and we don't do lunch or dinner, so there aren't many drop-ins,' she amended hastily. 'I'll certainly keep an eye on anyone arriving looking for her.'

'If you could call us, I'd appreciate it.' He started to take her contact details, and out of the corner of her eye, Libby saw the stretcher being loaded into the back of the ambulance. The woman was almost invisible under the blankets, apart from the fall of brown hair that reminded Libby of her sister's fringe, always getting in her eyes, and she felt a tug of guilt: she'd promised she'd stay with her.

'Should I go with her? To the hospital?' she asked. 'Will she be all right on her own?'

'It's kind of you to offer, but there isn't much room in the back of those ambulances, and they'll want to get her straight in for a CT scan.' The policeman's radio crackled and he turned to answer it. 'I've got your details – and if you find anything else, give me a ring.'

'OK.' Libby watched the ambulance's blue lights start up again and she felt cold inside, thinking of the grazed legs, the pink toenails. The flashes of colour on the pale skin. 'I just wish . . . there was something more I could do.'

'You've done plenty just by staying with her and getting us out as soon as you could' – he checked his notes – 'Mrs Corcoran.'

'Libby,' she said. 'It was nothing. What else are you supposed to do?' The other officer was looking at her now, standing next to the surly Mini driver, who was holding a breathalyser and trying not to cry.

'Plenty don't do anything, believe me. You'd be surprised. Now, then. Get someone to make you a cup of sweet tea, eh?' he added, patting her arm. 'The shock will probably hit you once you sit down. Don't always sink in at first. But you've done a good turn here today.'

Libby managed a smile. His kindliness, not the shock, was making her tearful.

The ambulance siren wailed, making Libby jump as it accelerated away. She watched until it vanished, then hugged herself tightly.

'We'll be in touch if there are any . . . developments,' said the policeman, and with the dip of his head on the word 'developments', the reality of what had happened finally did hit Libby, square in the chest, and a cold shiver ran through her whole body.

Chapter Two

The first thing she noticed when she woke up was the smell of antiseptic and coffee.

There was someone in the room with her. A woman. A nurse in blue overalls, checking the charts at the foot of her bed. She was frowning. When she moved, the nurse didn't stop checking the charts, but turned the frown quickly into a smile and said, 'Good morning!'

She started to say, 'Where am I?' but her throat was too sore and dry, and nothing came out apart from a croak.

'Don't move,' said the nurse. 'Let me get you a glass of water.'

It took the time between the nurse leaving the room and returning with a very cold plastic cup of water to process where she was: a hospital room, on her own, view over a half-full car park, heavy sheets pinning her to the bed. Her brain seemed to be moving extremely slowly.

How did I get here? she thought, and instead of an answer there was just a heavy black sensation in her head like a rubbery cloud, filling up where the answer should be. She felt that should worry her more than it actually did.

'There you go. Sip it slowly. You're probably still a bit groggy. Been out of it a little while, haven't you?' The nurse guided the cup into her hand.

She smiled back automatically, but felt something stopping her facial muscles moving. She reached up and her fingers touched bandages. Rough elasticated bandages on her cheek.

There were bandages on her head. How did that happen? What had she done? She lifted her hand upwards to feel where the bandages stopped, but there was a drip attached to the back and the thin tube caught on the blanket.

The nurse stopped her moving, gently but firmly.

'Don't touch the bandages. I know they must be itchy.' She slipped a blood pressure sleeve up her arm and started the machine. 'You've had serious concussion. Probably feels as if you've got the hangover to end all hangovers!'

Bad hangover. That felt about right. Her head was throbbing with the worst headache she'd ever had, as if her brain was too big for her skull, and her eyes felt sore and gritty, and the inside of her mouth . . . Rough. But there was something else. Something bigger at the edges of her mind, something that kept sliding sideways out of her fuzzy grasp.

She was in a hospital, but she had no idea how or why she'd got here. Everything was fine, but in an oddly synthetic way. As if everything was a little slow. A little far away, like a bad recording.

Why am I not panicking more? she wondered, and before she could speak, the nurse said, 'And you'll still feel woozy, with the painkillers.' She slipped off the sleeve. 'Blood pressure's fine. Well done. Can I check your pupils? Look over here . . . And here . . .'

She blinked as she focused on the nurse's finger, moving slowly backwards and forwards, side to side. There was a name badge: Karen Holister. She had short grey hair, black-rimmed glasses. Her face wasn't familiar, but her voice was. And as she followed the nurse's finger, the movement of her eyes felt familiar too. She didn't know why. A distant flutter of fear skimmed across the back of her mind like wind rippling across a deep lake.

'What happened?' It didn't sound like her voice. It was scratchy and faint. It ached to speak – not just her throat, but her head, her chest.

'You were in a road accident. You came in to A&E unconscious, and you've been under observation for two days. Don't worry – someone's been with you the whole time.'

Two days? Had she been here for *two days*?

She sipped at the cup to distract herself. The icy water hurt as it ran down her parched throat and increased the throbbing in her temples. Hung-over. Was this a hangover? Had she been so drunk that she'd blacked out? Been found somewhere? Nothing made sense.

'Was that why I was in the accident?' The words came out painfully.

The nurse took away the plastic cup. 'How do you mean?'

'Was I . . . drunk?' She probed in her mind for the details, but there was nothing, just darkness. A blank space. Like putting your hands into water and connecting with nothing.

'No, you weren't drunk. You were hit by a car.'

A car? Hit by a car. Again, nothing. Nothing in the memory. No ambulance, no pain, no panic. 'Where am I?'

'Longhampton Hospital. We put you in a side room because it's rather noisy out there.' The nurse was checking her notes, then checking the upside-down watch on her blue tunic top. 'The head injuries specialist will be along to check on you again very soon.'

'Longhampton?'

That wasn't right. Or was it?

The nurse picked up the notes from the plastic shelf at the foot of her bed and clicked her pen. She smiled. 'And now you're awake, maybe you can help us solve a couple of mysteries. First off, what's your name?'

She opened her mouth to speak, and then it hit her like a sheet of cold water, out of nowhere.

She didn't know.

The neurological consultant arrived a few minutes after eleven o'clock, followed by the same nurse.

The nurse was Karen, she reminded herself. Karen Holister. She could remember things *now*. *Now* wasn't a problem. It was just everything leading up to now.

'So, good morning.' He smiled, then pushed his glasses up his nose to study her notes. 'I'm Jonathan Reynolds. I'm from the traumatic brain injuries department. You are . . . ?'

'I told Karen,' she said, trying to sound calmer than she felt. 'I can't remember.'

The foggy black sensation in her head intensified, and underneath the artificial calm of the painkillers, she felt a distant wrench of panic. Hearing that made it real. And it didn't prompt a sudden flood of information, as she realised she'd secretly hoped it would.

Jonathan Reynolds murmured something to the nurse, who went to close the door. Then he took a seat on a chair next to the bed. He smiled calmly and crossed his legs.

'That must feel distressing, but please, don't worry. You suffered concussion as a result of your accident and it looks as if that's resulted in retrograde amnesia. Memory loss, in other words. It's really not uncommon. Things generally right

21

themselves in a short time frame. You had a CT scan when you were brought in and you didn't present with any significant neurological damage, which is a very positive sign.'

He had a relaxed manner, but she could tell he was watching her, his sharp brown eyes moving behind his glasses. She'd been here two days. They'd been watching her for two days. And she had no memory of any of it.

'Does that mean I've got brain damage?' she asked slowly. 'Or not?'

'Yes and no. The brain's a funny thing. I don't know how much you know about how memory works,' he went on, as if they were discussing the weather, 'but we store recent memories and remote memories in different areas of the brain. If you bang your head, or sometimes if you have a very traumatic experience, the connections are broken and you can't access things that happened in the recent past, but you can still remember things that happened when you were a child. Or things you've learned through lots of repetition, like walking or driving. All those things would seem to be fine with you so far. You can speak; you have coordinated movement. We just need to work out which parts of your memory have been affected and then see if we can't coax the rest out. It's very, very rare to lose your memory completely. So don't worry.'

'I don't remember the accident.'

'Well, that's not surprising. The good news is that apart from a few cracked ribs and some rather nasty grazing, you managed to walk away from it with nothing broken. You've got some spectacular bruises, mind you.'

She stared at him, cold under the warm blanket of the painkillers. He kept using phrases like 'good news' and 'positive

22

sign', but how could that possibly be true if she didn't even know who she was?

'But I don't know my own name.' Saying it gave her a physical tilt, as if she were on a rollercoaster that had suddenly dropped. She felt weightless, balancing on the edge of every second. 'I don't know who I am. How come *you* don't know who I am? Aren't there . . . records?'

The doctor (Jonathan Reynolds) turned to pass the question to the nurse (Karen Holister). She gave her a quick apologetic shake of the head.

'We're not quite at that police state yet. You didn't have any ID on you when you were brought in. We were waiting for you to wake up properly to tell us who you were.'

That didn't make sense. 'I had no ID? But what about my handbag?'

'You weren't carrying it. Or rather, the police couldn't find one at the scene.'

'No phone? Didn't I have a *phone* on me?'

'I know, it's quite incredible, isn't it?' He smiled. 'You weren't carrying a phone either. The police are going through their lost property, in case anyone's handed something in locally.'

'But no one's called looking for me?' Another strange sensation rippled through her: quick and shimmering, too quick to pin down. Her whole identity reliant on someone else, someone finding her, naming her. Bringing her back.

'Not so far. We're checking the missing person reports, obviously. But actually, we do have one thing,' said Nurse Karen. 'The police found this in your back pocket. Does it mean anything to you? I'm afraid the people at the address didn't know you.'

The nurse handed her a small Ziploc bag with a piece of paper in it.

An evidence bag, she thought, like on television dramas. I'm in a television drama. I'm the mystery woman. It felt as if they were all talking about someone else.

The paper was a page torn from a notebook, and on it was written:

Jason and Libby Corcoran, The Swan Hotel, Rosehill Road, Longhampton.

A phone number was scrawled underneath.

Disappointment rose up her chest, spiked with panic. It meant nothing. It wasn't a clue at all – more like the back of a piece of paper with something more important on the other side.

Is that my handwriting? she wondered. Neat capitals, very clear and precise.

'No,' she said. 'That . . . that's not bringing anything back.'

'No? No problem,' said Mr Reynolds. If *he* was disappointed, he didn't show it. 'What we're going to do to begin with is try to work out when your memory stops and starts, by running through some questions. Is that all right? Do you feel up to it?'

She nodded. What choice did she have?

'Don't think too hard about your answers. Just say whatever pops into your mind.' He clicked his pen and glanced down at his notes, but a thought pushed its way out of her before he could ask the first question.

'What have you been calling me? While I've been here. What name's been on my notes?'

She felt vulnerable, completely at the mercy of these strangers. The nurses didn't 'know' any of the patients on the ward, but they had names. They had an identity, the start of a conversation. Clues to who they were – an Elsie, a Camilla, a Natalie.

'We've been calling you Jo,' said the nurse kindly. 'Short for Joanne Bloggs. We were waiting until you were conscious so we could ask you what your name was.'

Her eyes widened. *Joanne*. I'm not a Joanne. But that's who I am now. That's who they've decided I am.

'Or if you didn't know, what you'd like us to call you,' the nurse (Karen) went on, as if that were completely normal.

They were both looking at her. Waiting for her to say what she wanted to be called. Who she wanted to be.

'Um, I don't know what I want to be called.' She struggled between wanting to help them and, at the same time, not feeling able to make a decision so huge.

'We'll come back to that – give you time to think.' Mr Reynolds (Jonathan) smiled. 'So, where do you live?'

'I don't know.'

'OK. Mum and Dad. Where do they live?'

'They don't.' It came out automatically; it was a fact, not something she felt. 'They're both dead.'

'I'm sorry. How long ago did they die?' It was conversational, but she knew he was aiming the questions carefully, pinpointing something technical, medical, within the soft emotional fabric of her life.

She squeezed her eyes shut as the thick pain in her head increased and the detail of the memory slipped away. It was there, but she couldn't get it. 'I don't know.'

'We'll come back to that,' he said easily. 'It's a good sign that it's there. How about you? Where do you live?'

She opened her mouth, but . . . nothing. She shook her head.

'Do you live here? Do you live in Longhampton? Or nearby? Martley? Rosehill? Much Headley?'

She shook her head again. None of those places sounded familiar.

'Don't think of a name. Just think of home. What can you smell? What can you hear?'

The blackness behind her eyelids thickened. She panicked, and then suddenly something made her dry lips move.

'I think . . . London?' It was a vague sensation of windows high up, counting red London buses. The smell of fried chicken and hot streets and a park with scrubby grass. Noise.

'London! Very good. Well, you're a long way from home, in that case.'

'Not recently, though,' she said, without opening her eyes, carefully probing the memory, trying to sneak up on something unawares so it popped into her mouth like a fact. 'I think that was when I was younger.'

'But that's a start. Do you live with someone? Are you married?'

She opened her eyes and glanced down at her hands, but they didn't help. No ring. No pale mark where a wedding ring would have been. No nail varnish, no bitten nails. Just average hands.

This is surreal, she thought, her head aching with the effort of it, that I'm looking at my body for clues to my life. What else would her body tell the doctors that she couldn't? Was it possible that she could be a mother and not remember, yet have a caesarean scar on her stomach? Had the nurses already looked, checking her naked body for clues while she was unconscious? Did they know something about her that she didn't?

The lurching, edge-of-a-cliff sensation swept through her again.

One Small Act of Kindness

Who am I?

'I don't know. I don't think so.'

'How old were you last birthday?' Mr Reynolds asked, and she heard herself say, 'Thirty,' without thinking.

'Good.' He sounded pleased.

But her brain was beginning to tick over now. 'How do I know that's right, though? What if that's just the last birthday I remember?'

'Possibly. But we know you're at least thirty,' he replied with the same conversational ease, glancing over the top of his glasses. 'I don't think anyone imagines their thirtieth birthday before they have to have it, do they?'

She looked past the consultant to the nurse. To *Karen*, she made herself think. 'Has no one called at all? In two days?'

Surely after two days someone would have noticed she was missing? If not a husband, then work colleagues?

Her chest felt tighter and tighter. What sort of person didn't have anyone to miss them? Or what if someone was missing her but couldn't find her?

'Well, we don't know that they aren't calling. You might be a long way from home. They might be trying local hospitals first.' Nurse Karen's eyes were brown and sympathetic. 'Don't worry – there's a good network for missing people. The police are on to it. *They*'ve called quite often to check on you – makes a change from investigating missing tractors and shoplifters.'

She looked down at her hands again. There was a long graze down her wrist, and a bandage on one palm where – she guessed – she'd scraped it along the road surface. Questions were rising now like dark birds from the back of her mind, set free as the sleepiness wore off. What if no one comes? What if my memory doesn't come back? Where do I go?

27

'Can you remember where you were last Christmas?' Jonathan Reynolds asked, and without warning a deep sadness filled her.

'No.'

Exhausted tears rushed up her throat, filling her head, flooding her gritty eyes, and she saw a movement – the nurse glancing at the consultant, the briefest twitch of her eyebrows suggesting this was enough. She felt grateful: the doctor was curious, and he wanted to solve the problem in front of him, but she was still struggling to get her head around the fact that she *was* the problem. However keen Jonathan Reynolds was to work out who she was, it was nothing compared with how much she wanted to know.

'I'm sorry,' she said. 'I can't . . . My head . . . it's aching.'

'Of course. I think that's probably enough for now,' he said. 'Rest is going to be crucial. We'll leave some paper and pens here, and if anything pops into your mind, just jot it down or call one of the nurses and let them know. I'll drop by later.'

Was that a test too? she thought. Whether I can still write?

She picked up a pen gingerly. Her fingers gripped it and she felt nauseous with relief.

'And please don't worry,' he said. 'Most patients with retrograde amnesia find that everything comes back after a day or two. Like turning the computer on and off again.'

She found herself mirroring his reassuring smile. But she didn't feel very reassured at all.

Chapter Three

Before Libby moved to Longhampton and began her new career as a semi-professional breakfast chef, she had had no idea that there was a right and a wrong way to cook bacon.

Or rather, there was 'a' way, and there was 'Donald's' way.

'That's it,' Margaret instructed from her perch at the kitchen table; despite Jason's insistence that they'd handle morning duties from now on, Margaret still got up most days to coach Libby in the art of proper breakfast preparation. 'Now put the press on it.' She nodded with approval as Libby dutifully pressed the bacon and the pan sizzled. Under the table – where he definitely shouldn't be, according to the health and safety guidelines Libby had been reading up on – Bob thumped his tail against the chair leg. It sounded like Morse code for 'Two rounds for me, please. No ketchup.'

'Did you know Donald had that press specially sent from America?' Margaret went on. 'After that wonderful trip to Boston Jason arranged for our anniversary. Oh, the bacon we had out there was *marvellous*.'

'Was it?' Libby checked on the toast. She did know. She'd heard about it so many times that sometimes she forgot that she and Jason hadn't actually been with them in the luxury Winnebago, but reminiscing seemed to bring back a flicker of the old Margaret, so Libby was happy to listen. She was still trying to work out how best to handle her mother-in-law's grief – the Corcorans were very 'No, no, let's just get on with things' sort of people – and this was as close as she got to talking about her loss. Libby was trying her best, but like a lot of habitual helpers, Margaret couldn't, or wouldn't, let her close enough to help. So if she wanted to talk, Libby didn't mind listening.

She mentally ran through Monday's tasks as Margaret waxed lyrical about the diner brunches, the magnificent fall leaves, Donald's daily calls to the hotel to check it wasn't burning down in their first ever extended absence. She and Jason were supposed to be starting room six that evening and Libby was looking forward to watching Jason wielding the wallpaper steamer. There was one major advantage to Margaret's refusal to come near the renovation process, she reminded herself, stifling an exhausted yawn. The privacy. And the steam.

'. . . missed Bob too much. You and Jason were so generous,' Margaret concluded with a sad smile. 'I'll never forget that fortnight. Such happy memories.'

'I'm glad. You two deserved a nice holiday.' Libby concentrated on pouring the egg into the fried-egg mould, another element of the perfect Swan Hotel breakfast, then added, because it had niggled her in every telling of the anniversary vacation tale, 'But you know Luke went halves with us on the trip?'

Luke was Jason's rarely seen older brother. The black sheep of the family, although Libby couldn't quite see why – he'd had a tricky adolescence, by Jason's somewhat admiring account, then joined the army, but now he had his own business installing burglar alarms and bespoke home security systems. Luke would have paid for the whole thing if Jason hadn't insisted on it being split equally, so instead there'd been some competitive flight upgrading, champagne in hotel rooms, the lot – the trip had ended up costing more than their own fortnight in Bali.

Libby tried not to think about Bali. The days of expensive foreign holidays were well and truly over now; what money they had was earmarked for turning the hotel into the sort of cosy haven people would spend two and a half hours driving out of London to visit. Her life now revolved around other people's holidays. Which was fine, she reminded herself. This fresh start had the potential to turn into a life that was actually better than the one they'd had to leave behind.

'It was Jason's idea, though, wasn't it?' persisted Margaret. 'He planned it all. He's always been *exceptionally* organised. He takes after his father like that.'

'Well, to be honest, Margaret, we all planned it – it was a team effort.' Libby's hand hovered over the toaster. Had Mr Brayfield in room two ordered white or wholemeal? 'I'd been researching a documentary about the Boston Tea Party for BBC Four, so I worked out the route. Luke sorted your flights. Jason's PA did a fair bit too – she spent hours on the internet finding you the right hotels! Can you remember, was it white or brown?' She looked up and saw Margaret was pouting.

'I know, dear, and we were very appreciative, but Jason had such a highly pressured office job,' she said. 'Donald and I were particularly touched he made time for us.'

Libby reached for her double-strength coffee. She was happy to indulge Margaret all day long when it came to Donald, but much as she loved Jason, currently snoring away in bed while she and Margaret handled breakfast, he was far from the perfect son of Margaret's fond imaginings. There was a *reason* they were here in Longhampton right now and not planning their next long-haul jolly. Besides which, Jason wasn't the only one with a highly pressured job: Luke had been just as busy, yet still unpicked a flight hiccup while on some job in Dubai.

Margaret's blatant favouritism had always been a running joke, but Donald wasn't here to tut gently at his wife. And now . . . well, Libby had never thought it was fair, the way Luke was left out. 'We *all* wanted you to have a good time.'

Margaret caught her awkward expression. 'I suppose so. And we *did* have a good time.' She smiled sadly. 'It was brown toast. And would you cut it into triangles this time, Elizabeth? Sorry to be a fusspot.'

'You're not being a fusspot,' lied Libby. 'You know, if you wanted to pop out with Bob for his morning walk, I can finish here . . .'

'Ah, well, I was rather waiting until Jason came down to ask about that.' Margaret poured herself some more tea. 'It's Bob's Pets As Therapy day and I was wondering if Jason could run us up to the hospital. It's such a highlight of the old dears' week, by all accounts, Bob's visit.'

On cue, Bob let out a long groan from under the table, accompanied by a noxious smell, and Libby had to turn to the fridge to hide her grimace of disbelief.

Bob – or Broadpaws Bobby Dazzler, according to the five-generation pedigree hanging in the downstairs loo – ruled the Swan Hotel with the sort of charming autocracy that reminded Libby of Charles II after success had really gone to his head. He'd been Bob when he'd arrived as a wrinkly puppy, but his imperious manner and ermine-speckled throat beneath a thick cloak of glossy black fur and expressive ginger eyebrows had led to Jason ennobling him to Sir Bob, then Lord Bob within a matter of months. Now King Bob was only a step away. Despite ignoring most house rules, sleeping anywhere he shouldn't and being very unreliable around butter, he had Margaret wrapped round his massive paw, as well as most of the guests, who wrote delighted compliments about their 'canine host' in the guestbook.

However, like quite a few self-willed, stinky people, what redeemed Lord Bob was his tireless work for charity. His visits to the local hospice and children's ward as Longhampton's most popular Pets As Therapy dog were lovingly documented in Margaret and Donald's Christmas cards, which often featured Lord Bob in his doggy Father Christmas costume. No matter what he got up to at home, in public Bob was a model of charm and obedience, and would put up with any amount of patting, petting and fussing, while looking tragic in a way only a basset hound could.

Libby took the milk out of the fridge and eyed him under the table. His rippling head wrinkles suggested he was eating something. Probably a rasher of bacon, since Margaret was also looking guilty.

'Where's he performing today?' she enquired.

'The old people's day centre.' Margaret's expression was almost as melancholy as Bob's. 'For some of them, it's the only affection they get, a cuddle with Bob. I would go myself, but that car park is so tight. I don't trust myself.'

'Oh, Margaret, don't say *that* – you're a great driver!' Libby put down the milk and went to give her a hug. It was Margaret's sudden lack of confidence that she found hardest to bear; it had been one of the things she'd most loved about coming home with Jason, the fizz of activity that had surrounded his mother. Phones ringing, lists being ticked off, people dropping in, orders being issued. Even Margaret's famous flower arrangements were a riot of colour and energy, her perky signature neck scarves knotted just so. She was so unlike Libby's own mother,

33

Diane (anxious, germphobic, now living with her second husband in Jersey), that Libby often told Jason the only reason she'd married him was for the in-laws. But now Margaret had even stopped driving, and instead got Jason to run her around.

Libby knew it wasn't just about the parking, and she didn't begrudge Margaret some time with her son, but this wasn't a good morning for Jason to disappear for hours. Apart from making a start on room six, he was also supposed to be finalising the accounts, which had been left in a worrying state; the accountants kept asking for missing receipts and Jason had been putting them off for weeks while he tried to find them.

Margaret submitted to the hug with a sigh, while over her curly head Libby kept a tentative eye on the egg, now with a lacy, golden-brown crisp edge. At least her fried eggs were almost at the approved standard.

'Tell you what,' she said, with a final squeeze, 'why don't *I* take you up to the hospital? I've been thinking about that poor woman who was knocked down on Friday – if she's still in, I'd like to visit her, make sure she's on the mend.'

The police officer in charge had phoned over the weekend to ask if anything had been handed in that might help them identify the woman; it seemed she was still unconscious, and not matching any missing person report. The idea of her lying there, nameless and disorientated, had haunted Libby ever since.

'Oh, that *would* be kind of you, Elizabeth.' Margaret brightened. 'But maybe Jason should come and—'

'My parking is great, even Jason says so. I learned to drive in Central London. And it's his turn to look after the front desk,' said Libby. 'Let's just hope nothing dramatic happens while *he*'s here on his own.'

* * *

One Small Act of Kindness

When Margaret and Libby arrived at the hospital reception desk with Bob, Libby had a glimpse into what life must be like for one of the Queen's ladies-in-waiting. Or possibly what it felt like to wear an invisibility cloak.

'Good morning, Bob, you handsome chap!' cooed Sonia, the ward sister, then said, as an afterthought, 'And you too, of course, Margaret! Thank you so much for bringing him in. I shouldn't have favourites but he's our favourite PAT dog. Aren't you?' she added, as Bob let out a groan, sat down, then lay down, the picture of regal tranquillity, his long, speckled nose between his paws.

'Bob!' Two more nurses had appeared from nowhere. 'We've been waiting for you! He's adorable,' one added to Margaret. 'We're always saying he's like a dog from an advert!'

'Yes, one of his relations is the dog on the Bonio box!' Margaret beamed. Bob was sporting his official Pets As Therapy jacket and wagged his tail affably as his public approached. He hadn't looked so affable, Libby thought, when she'd tried to remove the last slice of toast from him before they left. 'Ladies, this is my daughter-in-law, Elizabeth.'

Libby smiled and shook hands with everyone as the sister got their security passes ready.

'There you go – you're on Team Bob!' said Margaret, slipping a lanyard over her head; it had a photo of Bob on one side, and 'Official Visitor' on the other.

'Shall I take you through now?' the ward sister asked. 'Come on into the lounge. He's got a great turnout!'

And like a PA shadowing a very important rock star, Libby followed Lord Bob as he got up and waddled down the corridor, sticking closely to Margaret's side without any need for a cheese bribe. As if that were how he always went for a walk.

* * *

After ten minutes of reflected glory, Libby managed to excuse herself from the Bob love-in and went off in search of someone who could direct her to the mystery stranger. She'd walked down two corridors with no success, when she caught sight of the famous Tree of Kindness, its green leaves spreading over the wall between two snack machines.

She studied it with interest.

The Tree of Kindness was something she'd heard a lot about from Margaret, who described it as 'absolutely Longhampton'; it was a wall-high painted tree, covered in green handprints for leaves, and Post-it notes in the shape of flying birds, on which people wrote their thanks to strangers for the little things they'd done to help them. It was intended to celebrate the small acts of thoughtfulness that made life better for everyone and to inspire others – sending the 'birds' of kindness out into the community. Margaret said it summed up the spirit of the town in the nicest way. 'People care here,' she told Libby, at least four times a week. 'They look out for each other.'

It made for touching reading, Libby had to admit, angling her head to make out some of the messages.

Thanks to the teenage boys who carried my buggy up two flights of stairs when the station lift broke – you're a credit to Longhampton High School!

Thank you to the nurses who looked after my dad during his heart op, especially Nurse Karen, who did his lottery numbers for him.

Thanks to the knitting group for taking it in turns to bring me to the church hall when I broke my leg.

One Small Act of Kindness

There was surprisingly little stealth boasting on it, too. Libby looked in vain for any references to generous loans of holiday homes, or showing off about charity work, but it was mainly the snags of everyday life, smoothed over by a stranger's helpful action. It *was* nice, she thought. Nice in its fundamental decency. And nice to be reminded that giving a stranger twenty pence to put in a no-change parking meter could actually improve their whole day.

'Can I help you?' asked a voice behind her.

Libby turned. There were two receptionists on the information desk. One was on the phone, and the other wore a badge reading, 'Be patient. I'm training!'

'Yes!' she said. 'I'm looking for someone, but I don't know what ward she's in.'

The receptionist wriggled her fingers over the keyboard. 'That's not a problem. Have you got a name?'

'No. She was involved in a road accident outside my house, and the police have been in touch with me about trying to identify her.'

The receptionist's eyes lit up. 'Oh, you mean the mystery RTI woman in A&E?'

'Paula!' muttered her colleague, swivelling her eyes. 'No, sorry – I wasn't talking to you,' she added to whoever she was dealing with on the phone.

Libby glanced down and realised she still had on her security pass. She moved it so it half showed across the desk and as if by magic, Paula's fingers started clicking across the keyboard.

'If you go down into the Loughborough Wing, I think she's in a single room off Dean Ward. Ask at the desk when you get down there.' She peered at Libby more closely, but Libby decided it would be better to quit while she was ahead, and

37

before Paula's colleague could get off the phone to start asking questions, she was heading down the white corridors.

The 'mystery RTI woman' was in a room opposite the unmanned Dean Ward reception desk, and the door had been left open, wide enough for Libby to see the figure sitting up in bed.

Her face was almost as white as it had been when she'd been lying unconscious on the road, and the bandages on her head made Libby shiver at what might be underneath. The arms under the grey T-shirt had deep purple bruises, and her crossed legs were making a doughnut shape under the blankets, as she leaned forward, her pointed chin resting on her hands.

Libby wondered what she was looking at with such intense concentration. The woman was frowning as if she was thinking hard. Then suddenly she rubbed her face and blinked, and a look of intense sadness came over her, tilting the corners of her brown eyes downward.

Libby hesitated. Was she intruding? But there was nothing in the bare room – no flowers, no cards, no familiar things brought by the family to cheer her up. When Libby had had her gall bladder out, her room had looked like a florist's, with bouquets from Jason, her friends, Margaret and Donald, her sister, her old boss. She'd only been in three days, and it had been almost embarrassing in the end, endless lavish flowers arriving like she was at death's door, not recovering from a minor operation. Two bouquets had arrived after she'd been discharged.

Was this even visiting time? Was the woman up to receiving visitors?

Libby took another step back to see if there was anyone around to ask, but from the racket coming from another room, it seemed the entire nursing staff was occupied in dealing with someone who seemed very keen to discharge themselves. Two nurses were hurrying in that direction from another end of the ward and they didn't give her a second look.

When she glanced back, she realised her movement had attracted the woman's attention; she'd turned her head to see who was by her door and was now looking straight at Libby with a guarded curiosity.

'Hello!' said Libby. She thought of the thanks on the Tree of Kindness; there'd been at least *one* thank-you for hospital visits. 'Sorry, I hope I'm not intruding. I'm Libby. Libby Corcoran. I work at the Swan Hotel. I was a witness at your accident. I would have come with you, but there wasn't any room . . .'

The woman's forehead wrinkled. 'Thank you. Sorry – I can't actually remember a thing about the accident. I've got retrograde amnesia. And a lot of bruises.' She moved, then winced. 'Plus three cracked ribs.'

'Oh no! Sounds nasty. But there wasn't any . . . ?' Libby paused, making a vague gesture around her head, suddenly unsure whether it was appropriate to ask whether someone had brain injuries or not.

'No, no neurological damage. Well, apart from the amnesia. I was lucky, apparently. The bandages are because of some grazing. They had to shave my head to clean it out. I'll look a bit edgy when the bandages come off.' She pulled a face.

She was pretty, Libby thought, despite the hospital paleness – a firm nose, long dark lashes, small mouth, the freckles that'd reminded her of Sarah. Porcelain skin that bruised and blushed in a second.

She noticed Libby trying not to notice her black eye, and touched it self-consciously. 'It looks more dramatic than it is. I gave myself a shock the first time I went to the loo.'

Libby hadn't expected her to be so chatty. Maybe she was on painkillers. She hovered by the door, unsure what to do. 'Sorry – I didn't ask if you were up to having visitors. You must be tired. Should I . . . ?'

'No, please. Come in. I'd quite like to hear more about the accident, if you don't mind.' She gestured towards the chair by the bed and Libby noticed that there was something on top of the blankets: a notepad and a pen. The woman started to write, and she saw her name, **Libby Corcoran**, appear in neat black handwriting. Then, **Witness accident Swan Hotel**.

'Sorry,' the woman said, still scribbling. 'I'm writing everything down. Apparently this type of amnesia doesn't affect your basic skills, just recent memories. And in my case, randomly important details like my own name. I can't even introduce myself.' She glanced up and there was a painful vulnerability in her eyes that made Libby blink.

'Oh . . . So what should I call you?' She tried to process how that would feel, not to know what your own name was; she couldn't.

'The nurses are calling me Jo. Short for Joanne Bloggs, Joe Bloggs's anonymous sister.'

She said it in such a deadpan way that Libby laughed. 'Better than Ann O'Nymous, I suppose. The Irish amnesiac.'

The woman managed a half-smile, which suddenly dissolved into a scared frown. 'It's so weird, not knowing who I am. Or where I *live*. Or what my phone number is so someone can come and get me. Not even the police know anything. No one's reported me missing.'

'Really?' Libby struggled to imagine it. 'Can't you remember anything? At all?'

She pressed her lips together. 'I know my parents are dead. I know I'm at least thirty – that must have been a memorable party, but I don't know *why*. I grew up in London. But the rest . . . it's just blank. The consultant reckons that one familiar thing will trip it all back before too long – smells often do the trick, he says. Or music. Random things. This sort of amnesia doesn't normally last more than a few days.' She managed a smile that didn't quite reach her sad eyes. 'So, you know, fingers crossed.'

Libby raised her own crossed fingers. 'Well, maybe I can try to jog your memory while I'm here . . . Should I call you Jo? Joanne?'

The woman wrinkled her freckled nose. 'To be honest, it doesn't feel like me.'

'So you're not a Jo,' said Libby. 'What about Jenny? Catherine? Louise?'

'None of those.'

'Charlie? Jessica? Erin? Becky?' She paused. These were all the names of her old friends in London; she was mentally running through her Facebook list. It gave her a strange pang that she didn't want to examine right now.

'Is that what I look like? A Becky?' The woman raised her eyebrows in wry acknowledgement of how weird the conversation was. 'I always think of Beckys as being blonde. You could be a Becky.'

'Ha! Thanks,' said Libby. 'I wouldn't mind swapping my name for something more interesting. There were *four* Elizabeths in my class. I spent about a year when I was nine insisting everyone called me Philomena.'

'Really? Why? You don't look like a Philomena.'

'I think that's the whole point.' Libby ran a hand through her blonde bob, now grown out of its swingy precision cut into shaggier waves. She hadn't been to the hairdresser since they'd

41

moved. Jason had promised her he'd treat her to a cut in her old salon for her birthday; it seemed crazy now to spend what she had been spending on a haircut – to be honest, it had seemed crazy then, to Libby – but there was something embarrassingly addictive about walking out of the salon, all glossy and on a par with the 'village' wives in their Mongolian gilets and skinny jeans. Funny how you always wanted to be different as a child, then exactly the same as everyone else once you grew up. 'Back then I wanted to be a dark-haired, green-eyed Irish temptress. Not a nice girl from Petersfield.'

'If it's any consolation, you do look like an Elizabeth.'

'And what does one of those look like?'

'Trustworthy. Sensible. Utterly English.' The brown eyes squinted and Libby felt herself being assessed. 'But you're a Libby too. Libby wears interesting sandals and 1970s prints. Did your parents give you an unusual middle name?'

Libby laughed. 'Ha! No, I wish. My middle name's Clair. No "e". My parents thought they were being pretty crazy dropping the "e" off the end.'

The woman looked up from her notebook and gave her a cautious smile, the echo of what might be a wicked grin, Libby thought, when she was well. When she was herself again, and knew what sort of sense of humour she had. Somehow, that thought made her seem even more in need of protection than when Libby had found her lying unconscious on the road.

'Maybe it would help your memory if you choose a name you like,' she suggested. 'One you feel is you. Don't think too hard about it – hearing people call you it might trigger something.'

The woman tapped the pen against her mouth and thought. 'You know what,' she said, 'the name Pippa's just popped into my head. Pippa. But I can't be Pippa in real life, can I?'

'You might be.'

She frowned. 'I don't think so.'

'Go for it, then. It's better than Jo.'

'Ha! Yes . . . Would you mind passing me that water behind you? My throat gets very dry.' Again, there was a quick flash of that shadowy smile.

Libby passed the half-empty glass of water on the bedside table to the woman – Pippa, she guessed she should now call her. There *was* something Pippa-y about her. An old-fashioned arch to her eyebrows, which were pale for her dark brown hair. A sharpness to the cheekbones and the nose.

'Sorry,' she said. 'Do you mind if I write this down?'

'Not at all,' said Libby. 'Go ahead.'

Their conversation seemed to have brought some colour to Pippa's skin, and there was a pinkish flush now on her cheeks. She chewed her lip as she scribbled, absent-mindedly scratching under the bandage on her head with the other hand, absorbed in getting every detail down as they zipped through her mind.

Libby wondered what else she could do to help. It was funny how a complete stranger had homed straight in on the name Libby being right for her, she thought. *Libby wears interesting sandals*. She hadn't said so, but she'd tried on every other short version of Elizabeth – Beth, Lizzy, Eliza – but Libby had been the only one she liked. Because it did feel more her. A bit more interesting than the Elizabeth Clair that her parents seemed to want her to be.

She watched Pippa turn over a new page in her notebook and thought how easy she was to chat with, despite being concussed, and having no memory of the last few years. Libby didn't find it hard to talk to people, but most of her neighbours

43

in London had required a lot of background information and drip-feeding of shared interests before friendships had sprouted; Jason could banter matily about the markets and Chelsea to the men, but it felt as if there was an assault course of opinions to negotiate with the wives – schools, bags, diets, holidays – all requiring the right answer before you got to any real personal exchanges. Or maybe it was her, she conceded. Jason had told her she was mad, and recommended just 'having a big boozy night out' to get over it. Except none of them drank.

Libby had hoped the countryside would be different, but despite Margaret's Tree of Kindness, sometimes it felt it was the same story in Longhampton, just with another set of opinions – the new shopping centre, dogs on beds, hunting, thermal vests – and this time she had even less clue what the right answers were.

Philomena. She hadn't thought of that in so long. Philomena brought back hot Ribena, her red corduroy pinafore, the smell of suncream. Libby realised she hadn't told anyone that since Kirsty Little winkled it out of her at university.

Pippa had stopped writing and was staring at her, her forehead again furrowed with concentration. When Libby caught her eye she smiled apologetically. 'Sorry. It's just that . . . I can't help feeling I know you from somewhere. Do I? You seem familiar.'

'I don't think so, but I know what you mean,' said Libby. 'You don't feel unfamiliar to me either. Were you at Bristol Uni about fifteen years ago? History? Have you worked at the BBC? I was a researcher on factual entertainment programmes. Then freelance – for Thimble Productions.'

Pippa started to shake her head, then rolled her eyes instead. 'Well, I might have done. I can't remember, can I?'

'You know this is going to be your fallback excuse at parties for years,' said Libby, deadpan. 'You never need bother remembering anyone's name again. Oh,' she added, smacking her forehead, 'of course you had the address of my hotel in your pocket. Have they told you that?'

'They did. But that doesn't ring any bells either. Had I stayed there before?'

'Maybe. My husband and I only took over last month, though, so you might have done in the past but we wouldn't have met.' Libby racked her brains. 'Maybe your subconscious recognises my voice from the accident. It's clinging on to that as something familiar and making you think you know me.'

'Did you talk a lot?'

'Oh yes. There's nothing I like more than a captive audience. I barely stopped. I even sang when I ran out of boring chit-chat about how we're planning to create a boutique hotel, where Jason and I used to live in London, how we met on a train . . . I thought maybe you were faking waking up at one point. Out of sheer boredom.'

Pippa smiled, then a shadow crossed her face. 'I haven't said thank you.'

'What? Oh no, don't be daft. I just did what anyone would have done.' Libby lifted her hands and let them fall. 'I didn't even do that much really, just—'

'Not just the accident. Thank you for coming to see me today. I feel as if . . . as if I've been closer to who I am while you've been here. Does that sound weird?'

'No weirder than anything else. I can't actually imagine what it must be like.'

Pippa poked her finger into her hairline again, and scratched under the bandage. 'When I try to think directly about details

– my name, where I'm from – my brain goes blank. It makes me panic, then everything goes more blank. Plus the doctor or the nurse is standing there, so that's more pressure. The more I want to remember things, the tighter my head feels. But while we've just been chatting . . .' She scrunched her nose up, trying to find the right words. 'I feel as if it's all *there*, just *outside* my head, not inside. But it's reassuring. I feel as if it's still there.'

'Good,' said Libby, because she didn't know what else to say.

Pippa smiled and Libby was touched by how sweet the smile was: trusting, despite the awfulness of her situation. 'It's kind of you to come and talk to someone you don't know.'

'I'm glad it's been of some help. But I bet the police will be here any moment with someone to get you. Your husband, going mad with worry!'

Pippa stretched out her bare hands. 'No rings. Don't think there's a husband.'

'Your boyfriend, then,' said Libby, then realised that wasn't guaranteed either.

Well done, Libby, she berated herself.

'Or girlfriend,' she added quickly. 'Or friends? I mean, who knows? Who knows who's going to walk through that door looking for you? It could be a celebrity! It could be . . . anyone!'

They looked at each other and Libby thought she caught the faintest hint of fear in Pippa's face. Or maybe it was just the light.

'Who knows?' said Pippa, and smiled. This time, thought Libby, the smile wasn't quite as certain as before.

Chapter Four

Room six was a double room with a perfectly proportioned sash window framing a storybook view of the rear garden and its lilac and apple trees. The garden was about the only aspect of the hotel that didn't need an overhaul, thanks to Margaret's obsession with her borders; the velvety lawn was edged with a kaleidoscopic array of hundreds of flowers Libby didn't know the names of, and wasn't allowed to pick for displays unless Margaret was supervising.

If Margaret's gardening was a kind of silent, non-talking therapy, then so was Jason and Libby's DIY. Initially, when they were still stumbling through the smoke and debris of Jason's departure from work and Donald's death, Libby had thought that even if they couldn't talk, they'd be together and that'd be enough, just working towards a common goal again, but after a shaky start, they did talk. They talked more than they'd done since they'd first started dating in London, when Jason was a graduate trainee and Libby had been a junior runner, earning less per month than he did per week. Something about being equally hopeless at DIY bonded them; they discussed paint, website ideas, the impossibility of training Lord Bob, Jason's memories of Donald, Longhampton. The only thing they didn't talk about was the one thing they needed to: the unfortunate chain of events that had led them from Wandsworth to wallpaper steamers in the first place.

Libby stood back from the section of wall she'd managed to strip and massaged the side of her neck with scuffed knuckles. Jason had made a start, but there were several layers of paper to work through: a bland, spriggy print giving way to Laura Ashley Regency stripes from the 1980s, giving way to a psychedelic sunflower pattern that must have sent guests to bed convinced they'd eaten something very magic mushroomy in the 1970s.

She closed her eyes and visualised the images from her room six Pinterest board, trying to project them into the empty space. No tired wallpaper, no swirly carpet. Just plain, restful French-grey walls. A thick rug in a striking accent colour: turquoise or mustard, soft under bare, sleepy feet. Generous, blackout-lined curtains in biscuit linen, tied back with heavy gold swags. A new Vi-Spring bed, draped with a goosedown duvet and proper feather pillows, a velvet coverlet.

A warm feeling spread through Libby: Jason was right, this was going to be more than OK. They were on a budget, but Libby had insisted that they kept back enough money from the house sale to do the finishing touches properly. They were what people noticed. The right details were what would take this neglected hotel from being nice enough to something special.

She opened her eyes and stared at the ragged bedroom wall, with a few patches of wallpaper still clinging obstinately to it, and the warm feeling dipped. It was just going to take a long time – but they knew that already. Libby had project-managed the extension on their London house – she'd been made redundant from the production company in a round of cutbacks and Jason had suggested she take six months off to supervise the work – but she was starting to realise just how good Marek their builder's team had been. And also what a brilliant organiser Marek was. And how fast his men worked. And, despite being a very competent researcher, how little managing she'd actually had to do of that project.

Libby's yearning for her airy kitchen with its architect-designed skylights and smooth ivory wall of cupboards was interrupted by the sound of her mobile ringing.

Her friend Erin's photo smiled up from the screen: funny, enthusiastic Erin, her fashion buyer neighbour from St Mary's Road, with the Boston accent and the big American fridge and the twins, the Beans.

Libby winced. She was supposed to have called Erin by now. Erin had posted a few times on Libby's Facebook page, asking – no, *demanding* – to see photos of the hotel, but something had frozen inside Libby and she'd made excuses not to. She wasn't proud of herself, but since the Swan didn't have a website, Libby had let her London friends assume that the Swan Hotel was basically Babington House but nearer Wales. Everyone had looked impressed – Libby had never been to Babington House, but they all seemed to go every other weekend – and she didn't want them to see the reality until she'd got three rooms up to scratch.

It wasn't that she was ashamed of the Swan, just that while the shock of Jason losing his job was still fresh, she'd reframed their house sale/downsizing/good life as a deliberate life choice. It had made her feel better about it. And her circle of friends were . . . Libby searched for the right word to describe her circle of friends. 'Judgy' made them sound awful. They weren't bad people; they were generous, cultured, sociable. But they were . . . Actually, yes. They were judgy.

Erin wasn't, though, thank God. She claimed, being American, she had no idea what to be judgy about, and that it was a good job she had Libby there to explain the social difference between a lounge and a sitting room to her. She was stylish, but in an easy, unlabel-conscious way. Very early on, while Libby was outlining the various neighbourhood feuds over a bottle of wine, she'd confessed that since she and Jason had moved into the area, she never knew what to wear. Libby wasn't really into clothes, whereas everyone she knew in the book-group-and-barbecue gang did a lot of 'fashion singular' talk – one of them even had a 'school runway' blog. Erin had promptly traded an evening's babysitting for a styling overhaul, and coaxed Libby in and out of changing rooms until she didn't look, or feel, like an unemployed arts researcher anymore. One afternoon with Erin had given Libby a confidence way beyond what she'd put on her credit card, plus a proper friendship. As she told Jason afterwards, when someone's seen you trapped in a bodycon dress, there aren't many secrets left.

Meeting Erin had been the turning point for Libby in that new house. It had been Erin who'd tipped her off that if she bought one new handbag per year, she'd always have something she could talk to Rebecca, Marian and Helena about. And from that Burberry seed, friendships had grown. Sort of.

Libby grabbed the phone before she could change her mind. It wasn't Facetime. Erin couldn't see the shambolic wallpaper. 'Erin! How nice to see your face on my phone!'

'Hey, stranger!' Erin sounded pleased. 'Did you call while we were on holiday? It's been *weeks*! It's not like you to go so long without a catch-up!'

Libby could hear the shrill laughter of the Beans playing in the background and knew exactly where she was: the play-ground in the corner of the park, with the red swings in the shape of ladybirds, and the cricket pavilion tearoom that did coffee-and-walnut cake. Their old haunt.

'Sorry. Things have been mad.' She turned away from the wall, forcing a smile onto her face as a longing for that lost life, going on without her, cut into her chest. 'I keep meaning to ring, but there's never enough time to settle in for a proper chat.'

'Of course. It must be crazy! Sorry – I'm being selfish *and* nosy. We just miss you, is all. Are you run off your feet? Tobias, get off that, honey. It's not safe . . . We're in nanny-on-holiday crisis mode here! You're going to have to give me staff-manage-ment tips!'

Libby tried to remember what she'd told Erin about the staff situation. She probably hadn't mentioned that it was just her and Jason, Jason's mother when she felt up to it and Dawn and Peggy cleaning on different days.

'So, come on, I want to know everything!' said Erin. 'Are you redecorating? Did you do your mood boards? How are your plans for the spa?'

At the leaving lunch, after three glasses of wine and a tense conversation with Rebecca Hamilton about her four-week Body Holiday in Mustique, Libby had spontaneously invented a holistic spa she and Jason were going to build behind the hotel. *Everyone* had wanted to come to the hotel then. Or so they'd said.

'I think we need to spend a while getting the feel of the place before we start any major work.' It was so tempting to unload to Erin, but Libby knew she couldn't. She owed it to Jason to keep any teething troubles to themselves. Positive, she reminded herself. New start.

'Hurry up, will you? I'm dying to come visit – you're going to make it *fabulous*. In fact, I was talking to my friend Katie about you. Remember Katie? The features director at *Inside Home*? I told her she should send one of the travel freelancers, Tara, to review the Swan when it's done. I gave her that whole pitch: boutique hotel, slice of London in the countryside, cute family business backstory . . . She *adored* the hook of you and Jason going on a hotel adventure together!'

Libby didn't know whether to be thrilled or terrified. A journalist. Coming to the hotel. A journalist. From *Inside Home*.

'Did you? Thanks, Erin. That was really kind of you.'

'No problem! I thought it'd help your relaunch profile, right? When *are* you planning on relaunching? Wasn't it just a refresh, apart from the spa?'

A chill of excitement and panic rippled through Libby. 'It might take a few months . . .'

'Perfect! Christmas issue! Romantic winter getaways in the UK. You've got a log fire there, haven't you?' Erin made a noise of extreme envy. 'I *love* country hotels. I think they're one of my favourite things about the UK. That and John Lewis.'

Libby couldn't concentrate: as she turned to the window, she'd spotted a crack, previously hidden by wallpaper, and it seemed to be running all the way up towards the ceiling. Had that been there the previous night? Jason had dismissed her suggestion of getting someone to look over the place before they bought in ('Mum would know if it was falling down'), but since they'd started work, she'd spotted a few problems that she recognised from their last house: damp spots, cracks, creaky floors.

'So shall I give Katie your details,' Erin went on, oblivious to Libby's frown, 'and you can set up a good time?'

'Um, yes!' The idea of a travel writer checking in to the damp, dog-hairy hotel as it currently stood made Libby's blood run cold, but what Erin was offering was a major lifeline. A *major* lifeline. Magazine coverage in exactly the market she and Jason needed to attract if they were going to turn the hotel around – you couldn't buy publicity like that. Well, you could, but they couldn't afford it.

It was a target, she told herself, her pulse fluttering in her throat. A target would focus them. Start thinking like confident hotel owners. No one knows you're making it up as you go along if you don't tell them.

'Erin, you're a star,' she said, gratefully. 'That'd be so fantastic. We can totally recreate Christmas in September for her – we've got a *gorgeous* log fire.' Libby recast the lounge in her head, stripped of the tartan carpet, done out in sisal flooring with generous Harris Tweed sofas huddled round the fireplace. A better fireplace. A reclaimed one from somewhere. Candles, holly, mulled wine in goblets. 'We're planning to hold wine tastings, and winter teas, with hot toddies and my mother-in-law's family-recipe fruit cake. There are some lovely walks around here . . .'

Libby had no idea if there were lovely walks around Longhampton – she'd only been on the one that led down to the town, round the back of the hotel – but it was in the countryside and wasn't that the whole point of the country? Open spaces where you could get cold and wet, and then come inside to recover over a glass of wine.

'Oh, you know, Libby, I so envy you,' Erin sighed. 'I was telling Pete about it – we're thinking about following your lead and doing something similar.'

That brought Libby to a guilty stop. 'Really?'

'What you're doing – it's such a dream. Getting out of the city, building your business . . . Don't tell anyone, but I've been looking at fixer-upper hotels in upstate New York. It's my new secret Pinterest board.'

'God, Erin, why would you do that?' asked Libby. 'Pete's just been promoted!'

Erin's husband, Pete, ran a graphic design agency; in comparison to the other couples they knew – most of whom were bankers – the Douglases were fairly normal, in that they only went on two foreign holidays a year, plus Easter skiing, and Pete was from Wolverhampton.

'I know, but I barely see him these days. By the time he gets in from work, the Beans are in bed and I'm shattered . . . Sure we go on some nice vacations, but it's the time you spend together that's precious. You and Jason are right to put your relationship first. I love that he resigned the big-city job to build this hotel with you and his mom. That's so him! Well, it's so you too.'

Libby tried to make her face smile so Erin couldn't tell her eyes were squeezed tightly shut. 'Yeah!'

Erin didn't know about Jason's 'resignation' from his firm, or what he'd done to give his bosses no choice in the matter. She didn't know that the money from the sale of beautiful 24 St Mary's Road had first gone to clear some stomach-turning debts, then Margaret's mortgage arrears. And only then were they able to put what was left into the renovation account.

Jason and Libby had a great relationship, yes, but Erin definitely didn't know about the rows that had made Libby say things she was horrified to hear coming out of her own mouth. The things sweet-natured, everyone's-favourite-husband Jason had spat back at her still made Libby's skin crawl in the middle of the night. Those words had been said in anger, and they'd both cried and apologised, but it had spoiled the clean, fresh happiness of their relationship, the simple ease of it up until then. A tiny dark part of Libby had been almost relieved when disaster crashed into their life; no one, she felt, deserved to be as unequivocally happy as they'd been. Could you be *too* lucky? Had they had all their breaks upfront, in those rushing, love-filled early years, when money and breaks flowed in and flowed out like water, and London felt like living in a film, a collage of late-night champagne and black cabs and Sunday strolls?

Libby stared at the crack in the wall. She hated not being completely honest with Erin, but no one knew the whole truth. Not Margaret, not her parents (God almighty, definitely not her parents), not her sister. Just her and Jason. That was part of their punishment, dealing with it, in exile from everything they'd known.

Well, everything she'd known. This was Jason's home.

'But the main question is,' Erin went on, still excited, 'when can *we* come stay? I've told Pete we need a weekend in Longhampton as soon as possible. And when I get back, I'm going on a big PR mission for you! You are going to be turning guests away once I'm done telling everyone!' she finished, in the cartoon American accent she always put on when she was taking the mickey out of herself.

'Course,' said Libby weakly. 'We're just ... When we've finished a couple more rooms?'

'Just tell me when I can pack my party dress!' she said. 'Oh my God, that reminds me – did you see the photos from Rebecca's birthday party for Otis on Instagram?'

Libby had to bite her lip hard: she had. She couldn't stop

Lucy Dillon

tormenting herself with late-night viewing of her old friends' social media pages, 'liking' things while wondering if they even noticed she wasn't there.

'What was that, hon?'

Libby realised she'd let a moan slip out. 'Sorry, nothing. Um, just talking to the dog.'

'You've got a dog? That is so cool! Every country hotel needs a dog. What kind is it?'

On cue, Lord Bob came slinking out of a bedroom he shouldn't have been in, and when he saw Libby glowering at him, his double take made his ginger eyebrows shoot up into the folds around his ears.

'A basset hound,' she said, still giving Lord Bob the stink eye. She refused to fall for that 'love me' expression he pulled on everyone. Once she gave in to him, her battle against bedroom dog hair would be lost. It was her line in the sand. 'My mother-in-law's. He's a liability.'

'Aw! I love basset hounds!'

'You wouldn't love this one,' said Libby darkly, as Lord Bob gave her one last glance, then waddled towards the stairs and airily started to descend. His white-tipped tail swung gradually out of sight. 'He's spoiled rotten, and he weighs about five stone, so you can't argue with him. He pretends to be asleep until you open a bag of crisps in another room and suddenly he's there. And he smells. I spend half my life hoovering up dog hair, and the other half chasing him with the Febreze.'

Erin laughed, as if Libby were joking. 'Hey, I bet he's no less messy than my kids, and the day care's cheaper, right? But listen, tell me about your poor mother-in-law. It's been what, six months now? How's she getting—' There was the sound of distant wailing in the background, one child, then two. Erin groaned. 'Tobias! *Tobias!* I told you what would happen, didn't I? I'm so sorry, Libby, I have to go. There's been an incident.'

'Don't worry.' Libby tried to keep the disappointment out of her voice. She'd just started to relax into the conversation and now it felt as if a door was closing, leaving her on her own somewhere very quiet.

'I'll ring you again,' Erin promised. 'Tobias, I am not joking, mister . . . There's so much we need to catch up on. Like, have you joined a new book group?'

'Ha! No! Apparently I need to go for an interview for that, and not even Margaret can—' Libby started, but Erin was going.

'I'll text you,' she was saying. 'We'll fix a time for a proper chat and—Tobias! Sorry. Bye, Libby!'

And she was gone.

Libby realised she hadn't told her about the accident, or the stranger who'd been heading for the hotel.

Typical, she thought, probing the crack with a cross finger-tip. Of all the things she *could* have told Erin about, it was Lord bloody Bob who got most of the airtime.

Erin's phone call – and her wallpaper scraper breaking – meant Libby spent the rest of the afternoon in the hotel office, trying to plan a timetable that would get them on track for a journalistic visit and a late-summer relaunch.

Doing the decorating themselves was cheap and surprisingly enjoyable, but if they carried on at this rate, it'd be well into the following year before they finished. Libby twirled the pen round her fingers as she stared at the calendar on her laptop. That clearly wasn't going to work. And she couldn't get that crack out of her head. The hotel needed sorting out *properly*. Guests noticed things like cracks and creaks. Then they wrote snotty reviews on TripAdvisor about them.

'Hey, babe, what are you up to?'

Jason swung into the office with a couple of B&Q bags and a copy of the evening paper. He'd gone out at lunchtime 'to look at some new doors' and hadn't been back.

'Where've you been?' Libby frowned, ready to nag him about vanishing, but then he reached theatrically into one of the B&Q carriers and dropped a twisted paper bag from the town bakery in front of her. An Eccles cake. Her new favourite.

'I never stop thinking about you,' Jason informed her solemnly. 'Even in the sandpaper aisle. What have you been doing while I've been out?'

Before she could speak, he came round to the desk, wrapping his arms around her and nuzzling the side of her neck, and Libby melted inside, as much at the small thoughtfulness of the cake as the instinctive way Jason knew just where to kiss her. He was trying, she told herself. And he loved her whether she ate carbs or not, unlike Rebecca Hamilton's husband.

'I'm making plans,' she said. 'Where've you been?'

'B&Q for more DIY stuff. And town.' He pulled a chunk off her Eccles cake and ate it over her shoulder. 'Amazing how many of the old shops are still there. And there are some good new ones. Two delis! Who'd have thought it? If you'd told me Longhampton would have stuffed olives when I were a lad, I'd have laughed. And asked who Olive was.'

'Erin phoned,' said Libby. 'She's got us a brilliant lead for some PR, but we're going to have to get real about the redecoration timetable. Oi!' She slapped his hand away as he went for more cake. 'Can we talk about it tonight? With your mother? I think we're going to have to bite the bullet and spend some money on proper decorators.'

Jason broke off a large chunk of pastry and popped it in her mouth at the same time as he said, 'Can we do it tomorrow? I'm out tonight.'

'What?' spluttered Libby, through the pastry. 'You're supposed to be on reception tonight. It's on the rota! The one we promised we'd stick to?'

Jason pulled his 'forgive me' expression, the one that made his blue eyes appealing and boyish. He didn't look thirty-five generally. His 'forgive me' expression brought him down to about ten. 'Sorry, I forgot. Chopper's asked me to the pub for a beer.'

'Chopper?'

'Mike Prosser.' He did a sort of mime that was evidently supposed to jog her memory. 'You know Chopper. Mike! The Chopper!'

'The only Mike I know is Mike Adams,' said Libby. 'Our dentist. He was more . . . the Gummer.'

'Ha!' Jason laughed and pointed at her. 'Funny girl. Didn't you ever meet Chopper? You must have. He's a legend.'

'I have never met Chopper. It sounds like I'd have remembered.'

'Oh, well, maybe you didn't. We played rugby together. Year above me at school, first guy I knew who could down a pint in one. His dad had a farm near Hartley, and we used to go there to—'

'Chop wood?'

'Exactly.' Jason grinned with delight. 'Anyway, I saw him in town this afternoon. Invited me out for a drink – couldn't really say no.'

Except you could. Libby's chest tightened and she had to concentrate not to let the sensation spread. What is this feeling telling me? she asked herself, as their counsellor used to say. Or had said, in the two sessions they'd managed to go to before the house was sold and they had to leave.

I'm annoyed Jason's already bending our agreement about sharing jobs?

I'm jealous that he's got friends here and all mine are in London?

Or is it that Chopper is going to be some sort of reckless rugby idiot who'll end up getting Jason pissed and then he'll be useless for most of tomorrow, as well as out of action tonight? When I'd hoped I'd be watching him steam wallpaper with me?

Libby stared at her hands on the keyboard of her laptop. Her nail varnish was chipped from the wallpaper stripping, and she hadn't had time to redo it. A flake of tangerine paint had wedged itself under the diamond of her engagement ring, an Edwardian one from an antique shop in Brighton that still made her think of a bedraggled Jason proposing in the rain on the London Eye, because he'd lent her his coat when the heavens opened. It wasn't a huge diamond. It predated his promotions. She'd never wanted to change it, despite pressure from her new friends to upgrade.

'Aw, Libs, you're not mad, are you?' He hugged her. 'Don't be mad. I won't be late back. It's just a pint – he's a lawyer now, probably a good guy to know.'

With an effort, she reshuffled the thoughts in her head. Maybe Chopper had a wife. Maybe Mrs Chopper could be someone she could have coffee with. Someone who could tell her where to get her hair cut round here, or which garage wouldn't rip you off because you had an offcomer's accent.

'Why don't I come too?' she said brightly, spinning round in her chair. 'Just for half an hour or so, say hello. I'd like to meet your old friends. Why don't we book a table somewhere nice and do some research for the hotel information packs?'

'Ah.' Jason's expression changed. 'Thing is, I'm going to join in with the training session, then go on to the pub after.'

'*What* training session?'

'At the club,' he said, too casually. 'They're a couple of men short for next season. Mike wondered if I fancied making up the numbers in the training squad. See how I get on.'

She widened her eyes in disbelief. 'What for? Not the rugby team?'

'No, the flower-arranging team. Ha, ha! Of course the rugby team.'

'But you haven't played rugby since . . .' Libby tried to remember. 'Since before we got married. Have you forgotten how that went? You swore you'd never play again after you got that black eye before my sister's wedding.'

Jason made a dismissive gesture. 'There hasn't been anywhere for me to play in London. Anyway, it's different when you're playing with your mates.'

'But that was fifteen years ago, Jase. How much wallpaper stripping are you going to be able to do with a crocked back?'

'It's not like I've been sitting around.' Jason looked affronted. 'I'm not unfit, Libby. I did that 10k.'

Libby bit down on what nearly came out of her mouth. The 10k had nearly killed Jason, on his City diet of strong coffee, booze, late nights and stress. He'd done it with the most spectacular hangover known to man and only sheer bloody-mindedness – and the sponsorship money, and the competitive non-training in the office – had got him over the finishing line. One of the things she loved about Jason was his refusal to go back on a promise, but not when the personal costs were that high.

'What? You've got that look on your face, Libby.'

He was staring at her in a way he never had in London, not even when they were thrashing things out after he was sacked. Defensively. Libby looked straight back, and felt the row building. She hated how it came out of nothing. That downward spiral that they could never get off these days once they started. It always led to the door of a very bad place, and although they never went through the door and into the heart of what they were thinking, they got close enough to see it. The silence was worse than the row. It told them both they were scared of what was on the other side.

'So you're saying that after a hard day's work, I can't even go out for *one beer*,' he began, with a martyred expression that looked very Margaret-ish to Libby, but she didn't have the energy for a big argument. She ached in places she didn't know existed.

'Fine,' she said, raising her hands, 'but for God's sake, don't break anything.'

'Sure, not until the rooms are all finished,' he said. '*Ma'am*.'

Libby wasn't sure how much he was joking. She got up and walked to the window to open it, not because it was particularly hot but because she needed to shake off the mood in herself.

'What? It smells of dog in here,' she said, when he looked questioningly at her.

Jason folded his arms. 'What's up? Come on.'

'*I* don't know anyone to go for a drink with, Jason. And I'm knackered.' Libby tried to keep her voice level, but now the euphoria of Erin's call had worn off, and the reality of what they had to do was sinking in, she felt limp. Minimal sleep, cleaning, scrubbing and smiling all day, struggling with figures, soaking up Margaret's despair: it was taking every ounce of energy she had. 'How am I going to meet people when I'm working here and everyone our age is either too busy for new friends or on the school run? It's not as if there's any chance of me joining *that* anytime soon, is there?' Her voice cracked at the end. She hadn't meant to go that far.

The surliness melted from Jason's face. 'Oh, Lib.' He stepped closer to her, holding out his arms with an apologetic murmur. 'Come here, babe.'

Libby resisted for a moment, then let him hug her, rocking her from side to side. His touch always made her feel better, his smell, his solid warmth.

'I'm sorry if you feel like that,' he said softly. 'You just seem to cope so well with everything.'

She didn't say anything. She didn't trust herself.

'How about I suggest a get-together?' he went on, his breath in her hair. 'I'm not sure what Chopper's situation is at home, though. He got married to Steff Taylor while I was at uni, but I don't know if they're still together. I didn't like to say, "How about dinner with my lovely wife?" if he hasn't got one. You know what I mean? You've got to tread carefully till you know what's what.'

'I suppose.'

'I'll find out,' he went on. 'Tonight. Test the waters. Then maybe set something up for next week?'

'I need to make friends too, Jase,' said Libby. 'It's easy for you – you've already got friends here. I miss . . . *being* a friend.'

'I know. I want you to be happy. I do.'

They looked at each other. If it is just us, Libby told herself fiercely, it'd be fine. Me and him. We've known each other a long time, we're not like those whirlwind couples who marry and have two kids in the space of a year and wake up one morning and realise there's a complete stranger lying next to them.

But if he turned back into a man she didn't know, a man he'd been before . . .

'We'll talk when I get back,' he said. 'Promise.'

And then he kissed her forehead and went off to find his gym kit. Whistling.

Libby didn't remember Jason ever whistling in London.

Chapter Five

Pippa woke up on the fifth day and immediately tried to pin down what she'd been dreaming about. She'd been somewhere . . . Near the sea? With friends? A dog? It had been windy. She'd been happy. That happiness lingered on in her mind like an echoing sound, lifting her inside. She'd felt weightless, and her skin was warm, clouds dancing behind her closed eyes.

Her hand reached out for her pen, but the more she tried to recall the details, the faster the dream slid away from her, leaving her staring at the traces of dawn light outlining the blackout curtains of her room.

This was the first morning she hadn't woken up and thought, How weird – I dreamed I lost my memory. This was the first morning she'd woken knowing that the current version of herself, Pippa, started and finished in this hospital room. There *was* a before, but the bridge between it and her had gone, and until someone appeared to lead her back over it, the before might as well not exist.

A clammy sensation crawled over her skin, as the memory faded and the morning's reality sharpened up in its place. If someone didn't appear, as they hadn't so far, all she had were the clothes she'd arrived in. No money, no home, no phone, no qualifications, no CV, no idea who she was beyond that very moment. Nothing.

Pippa jerked with panic, suppressing the involuntary sob that rose up inside her throat, and focused on her breaths, keeping them shallow on account of her aching ribs, counting to four, over and over, until the first sounds of the ward waking up made her feel less alone. While she breathed, she ran through everything in her mind, hoping to catch some stray fact that had slipped unnoticed through the blankness in her mind, like a cat returning soundlessly from a night out.

Her head was hurting . . . less than before? The drip had been taken out of her hand, which had a bruise like a purple-green pansy where the needle had gone in. Her ribs ached more. Maybe because the painkillers had worn off overnight.

Pippa knew that three of her ribs were cracked, on the left-hand side, over her heart. Probably, the doctor had said, pointing at the hairline traces on the bones, from where she hit the car. The wing mirror, maybe, he'd suggested, and she'd nodded, trying to supply the mental image of it, and failing. It could have been the wing mirror. Later on, he'd shown her the multicoloured scan of her brain, and she'd thought how weird it was that the specialist could see inside her head but couldn't extract anything useful from it, or nudge it back into cooperation.

Four weeks, he reckoned, for the ribs to heal. Until then, lots of painkillers and rest.

And his name was, prompted a voice in her head. *His name was . . .*

His name was Dr Shah. Dr Suveer Shah. She was in Dean Ward, in the Loughborough Wing. The nurses were Bernie and Karen in the daytime, Sue and Yolanda at night. The head injuries specialist was called Jonathan Reynolds. He'd been to see her every day she'd been awake (three), running through the same questions, and some different ones, trying to work out where her vague memories stopped, but not managing to press whatever the magic memory-reset button was to access the rest.

'Don't worry,' he said, giving her the same optimistic smile each time he left. 'You're processing new information fine, and there's nothing presenting on your scans to suggest the memory loss is going to be anything other than short term. You might never recall the accident itself, but when your brain's ready, I'm pretty confident the rest will come back.'

'Pretty' confident. Pippa noticed that he never said 'completely'.

PC Canning had been in also, to 'update her on the investigation', but the facts she could remember weren't enough to go on, and no one had come forward from the small mention of her accident in that week's local paper. He was polite, but Pippa pounced on every tiny clue available to her, and she could tell he too was curious as to why no one had come for her. His pity made her feel ashamed, and scared. It clearly wasn't normal. She wasn't normal, something about her situation wasn't normal, and she didn't even know why.

In the meantime, she wrote everything down, partly out of fear of waking up to find the last few days had been wiped, and partly to give herself something to do. She'd asked Bernie, one of the day nurses, if there were some magazines or a book she could borrow, and Bernie had sighed and said she'd check, but it probably wasn't a good idea to strain her eyes, and wouldn't she be better just taking it easy and resting? As if reading were some sort of chore.

Pippa had stared at her notebook and written down, *I like reading*.

That was who she was. Whatever was written in her notebook.

Ninety minutes and two almost perfect full English breakfasts later, Libby and Margaret were heading up to the hospital with Lord Bob freshly brushed in the back of the car, ready to bring comfort, affection and a meaty tang of dog breath into the lives of Longhampton's elderly folk.

Jason, who was still walking gingerly after his training session, had been left to check out the two guests in room four, with instructions to offer them a complimentary breakfast voucher if they so much as mentioned the poached egg. Libby's poached eggs weren't quite as reliable as her fried ones, and the Pattersons had the look of people who liked to write scathing reviews of disappointing eggs on the internet.

Almost as soon as she'd pulled out of the hotel car park, Libby found herself stuck behind two horses whose riders seemed to be having a leisurely conversation. They clearly weren't, Libby thought, discussing the huge rush they were in to get to town.

Next to her, Margaret fidgeted in her seat, which immediately put Libby on high alert; Margaret liked to save difficult conversations for a time when Libby was trying to concentrate on something else, like chopping onions or maintaining a steady speed of ten miles per hour behind two enormous hunters. One of them was swishing its tail in a manner that made Libby worry for the bonnet of the car.

'Jason tells me you've invited a journalist to put us in a magazine,' she said.

Oh. Just that? Well, that wasn't too bad. Libby relaxed.

'Yes! Well, I didn't invite her, exactly. One of my friends

recommended she came to check us out. When we're finished decorating, of course.'

Margaret made the noise she always made, the one that indicated she understood the need for decorating but didn't completely agree with it. 'A friend from London?'

Libby pulled out to see round the horses, but there was no way past. 'Yes. Erin. She's American, works a lot with stylists and magazines. We used to share a cleaner. She's lovely.'

'You need some friends around here,' said Margaret, as if Libby had somehow decided against the idea. 'Why don't you think about signing up for the PAT rota yourself? It's such a good way of meeting people. I mean, it's easier for Jason – he has old friends he can pick up again. You need your own girlfriends.' She paused, then added, coyly, 'If you had a little one, or two, you could be meeting people every day on the school run.'

Oh, *that* was what she was leading up to. Libby gripped the steering wheel tighter. Margaret had never been one of those mothers-in-law who dropped massive hints about grandchildren, but lately she'd noticed a few comments creeping in. More sighs at adverts for nappies, more wistful observations about how adorable Jason had been as a toddler. How she'd be around to help, now they were all living together. How her friends loved being grandmothers, how it had given them all a new lease of life.

Libby pulled herself up before the irritation could take hold. She knew she was being oversensitive. She and Jason *wanted* to have a baby. But what with one thing and another, any plans in that direction had moved down the priority list, beneath the hotel, their finances, supporting Margaret in her bereavement . . . Libby needed things to be solid. She didn't want to visit her own broken-up childhood on *her* children. And more than money, she and Jason needed to get back that trust.

'Is that something we might all look forward to soon?' Margaret enquired.

'Not *right* now,' Libby replied, still trying to see round the horses. 'We have to get the hotel sorted first, don't we?'

'Oh.' Margaret gave a little laugh. 'I rather thought, with the country air, and more space, and less stress, you and Jason might—'

'Whoa, too much information, Margaret!' said Libby.

Also, less stress? *Less stress?* Sometimes she wished Jason had shared a few more details of why they were actually here with his mother.

'I'm sorry.' Instantly, Margaret's hands folded in her lap, a prim barrier. 'I just wondered.'

'Jason and I would love to start a family soon, but we want everything to be right.' The road was finally clear. Libby indicated to pass the horses. Slowly. 'You know what hard work running the hotel is. We need to get a system up and running, generate some more new business. This is a big change for us both – we're still learning.' She glanced across, trying to frame it as generously as she could. 'We need you passing on your hotel wisdom, Margaret, not tying you up with childcare!'

'Oh, you seem to be managing very well. I'm not sure I'm doing anything. I'm not the one in charge anymore, am I?'

Libby knew deep down this was true; she knew Margaret knew it too. It was awkward.

'I'm sure it'll happen soon,' she said, not wanting to upset her, *or* promise anything. 'And you'll have a world of good advice to give us there too.'

The hands unfolded and folded again, making the eternity

rings glitter. 'Young people today seem to need everything to be perfect.' There was an edge of peevishness in her voice. 'When Donald and I moved here, Luke was a tiny baby and Jason was on the way, and we just got on with things.'

'Yes, well . . . Jason and I have had a difficult year. I'd like to get that behind us first.'

'More difficult than my year?' Margaret turned her head; her pale blue eyes were silvery with tears. 'A bit of good news would be just what the family needs, I would say.'

Guilt swept through Libby. 'I'm sorry, Margaret. You've had an *awful* year. But this tip from Erin is good news, honestly.' She racked her brains for some more good news, then remembered something Jason had told her the previous night. 'What about Luke? Wasn't Jason saying he'd won some award for his company? Some enterprise recognition?'

Margaret knitted her fingers together. 'So I hear. Of course that's good news. But business isn't everything. If Luke had spent less time with the company and more time with Suzanne over the years, he might have had someone to share his success with. Poor Suzanne.'

'I know, it's a shame it didn't work out for them.' Libby didn't think there was a lot of poor Suzanne about it. Not from what little she'd seen of her. Luke's ex-wife was an army medic, a tough cookie with honours to prove it, and the marriage hadn't lasted long; she and Jason had stumbled on them outside the registry office arguing about who was going to drive to the reception. 'But if they weren't suited, better that they still have the chance to meet someone else . . .'

'Suzanne was Luke's chance to settle down and grow up. And he threw it away,' said Margaret, with a finality that Libby didn't feel able to argue with. 'So, did you say you were going to see that accident lady?' she went on, in a conversation-changing tone.

'Yes, I am.' She should have known better than to try to change the conversation to Luke. 'You see? I'm meeting new people. I've got a new friend there.'

And she pulled away from the horses just as one of them dropped a series of dung balls down the winding road.

Pippa was making a list of names beginning with 'L', trying to jog her memory when the nice daytime nurse, Bernie, put her head round the door, her pale red eyebrows raised in fun. 'Are you up to seeing a visitor?'

'Yes! Who is it?'

At last, she thought, anticipation fluttering in her stomach, someone's come! It was closely followed by a darker flutter. What if it was a boyfriend, or a husband, but she didn't recognise him? How would she even know if it was a friend?

It didn't matter. Someone had come to see her! Someone who might have answers.

Bernie's face fell, seeing her excitement. 'Sorry, love, it's not . . . It's the lady from the accident. Lizzy?'

'Libby,' said Pippa.

'Just testing you,' said Bernie with a wink.

'Hello!' Libby peered round her. 'I was passing, so I thought I'd pop in and say hello! I'm sort of sorry to find you still here . . .'

'Still here,' said Pippa. 'Going round and round like an unclaimed suitcase on the baggage carousel.'

'Oh, I always think they're the most intriguing suitcases,' said Bernie. 'They're . . . mysterious! Now, would you ladies like a cup of tea?' Pippa knew she was trying to make up for the disappointment. The ward was understaffed and Bernie rarely had time to make a cup of tea for herself, let alone visitors. Bernie was kind like that; it was in her notebook too. She planned to stick a thank-you for Bernie's extra teas on the Tree of Kindness in the foyer when she left; the nurses had let her walk down that far the previous day for exercise and the messages of thanks had made her quite tearful. Although she *was* still on quite strong painkillers.

'Ooh, yes. That'd be lovely,' said Libby before Pippa could say, 'No, it's fine – don't worry.'

'So, how are you feeling today?' Libby folded herself into the chair by the bed. 'Any developments?'

'Nope. Not unless you count some new bruises that have come up.' Pippa showed her the ring of purple circles round the top of her arm.

'Ouch.' Libby winced. 'Well, to take your mind off things . . . I thought you might need some reading matter.' She rummaged in her shoulder bag.

Libby's bag was an expensive one, Pippa noted: soft plum leather with brass fittings and a swing tag. The sort of tag that was supposed to say something about the owner, although she didn't recognise the brand and so wasn't sure what that was. Libby looked like the sort of person who'd have the 'right' bag, though: stylish but not too flashy, not stupidly expensive. She reached for her pen to add it to the book, but stopped herself.

Libby had a page in Pippa's notebook – **Libby Corcoran: Swan Hotel, married, just moved here, thirty-ish, no children.** Together with Libby's smooth accent, and her chunky honey-and-gold highlights and her leather ballet flats, and now the bag, Pippa guessed that the hotel must be pretty posh.

So why had *she* been heading there? Had she been meeting someone? A shape formed at the back of her brain, dark and definite, but immediately slithered away, leaving a cold spot in its wake.

'Here you go – you can give them to the waiting room if there's nothing that takes your fancy.' Libby offered her a stack of glossy magazines. 'I thought they might prompt a memory – if you see a dress you've got, or come across a feature you've read before in the hairdresser's?'

'That's really kind. Thank you.'

'Oh, it's no bother. I get them for the hotel lounge.' She flipped through the pile. '*Vogue*, *Red*, *Vanity Fair*, *Cosmo*, *Country Life*. I didn't know which magazines you read, but—'

'But I don't either. So that's fine.'

Libby started to apologise, then saw Pippa was joking. She grinned, and her face suddenly looked much less grown-up. Less grown-up than the smart bag and the ballet flats, somehow. More Libby. More kooky sandals.

'Well, I don't think I read *Country Life*.' Pippa gazed at the covers spread out on the blanket and recognised, to her relief, some of the famous faces – Judi Dench on *The Lady*, Kate Moss on *Vogue* – but other women seemed blandly anonymous. Just smiling, blonde, pretty. Panic rippled through her. How much memory had she lost? How many years?

'Should I know her?' She pointed at *Heat*'s cover star, a dark-haired woman scrutinising her stomach folds in a straining bikini.

'Hmm.' Libby frowned at it and shook her head. 'Nope. I have no idea who that is . . . Oh, she's in *Made in Chelsea*. Do you watch that? I don't. Ha! Maybe this isn't such a great idea. I'm going to feel like I've lost my memory too at this rate.'

Pippa laughed as Libby clucked in self-reproach. 'I'm so sorry,' she said. 'That was in bad taste.'

'Don't worry. Least it means I've got a sense of humour.' Pippa met her gaze and smiled until Libby looked less embarrassed. She thought Libby had a sympathetic, expressive face, one that revealed every emotion passing across her mind. Her eyes widened and crinkled when she smiled or frowned, and her hands moved constantly as she talked, covering her mouth, tucking her hair behind her small ears. Going on what Pippa had seen so far – two visits, a thoughtful present, friendly conversation – Libby seemed like a good person. She gave off a sort of wholesome helpfulness.

'Maybe we should do a quiz?' Libby suggested, examining the magazines. 'Work out ...' She peered at the cover of one. '"What's Your Romcom Relationship Style?"'

'What's my *what*?'

'No, really. Look ...' She showed her a photo spread of some actors whom Pippa wasn't sure she recognised.

But then all the magazine covers seemed peppered with urgent questions, none of which Pippa knew the answer to. *Are You a Control Freak? What's Your Relationship Age? Are You Your Own Best Friend?* If someone was here who knew me, she thought, they'd probably say, 'Yes, you're a *total* control freak. Remember how many different colours you painted the sitting room before you got the right green?' Or they might laugh and remind her how she'd have to ring round all her mates before she could decide on what to wear on a date.

That was how you knew who you were. A lifetime of episodes and anecdotes and tests and moments, confirmed and catalogued by friends. And if they were gone – the friends, and the memories – how did you know who you were without having to start all over again?

'I don't know if I can do that,' she said, and this time her voice cracked.

'Oh, you can,' said Libby. 'They're not Mensa questions.' She started flipping through the pages. 'I'll do it with you. I love being told what personality I've got. They never say, "Oh dear, you're a psychopath." It's always variations on nice.'

Pippa settled back into the pillows. There was something restful about Libby's good-natured bossiness.

'First question. "What's your ultimate must-have in a relationship? Is it (a) romance, (b) trust, (c) humour or (d) passion?"'

'Shouldn't all four of those be must-haves?'

'Hmmm. Yes, probably. But which is the most important for you? And don't think too much about it. I don't think whoever wrote this did.'

Pippa weighed the options up in her mind. 'I'd say . . . trust. I think you have to know exactly who you're with. You have to trust them in order to be yourself.'

'Oh, I like that.' Libby circled it. 'OK, I'm going for . . . romance. If you don't have that, then you might as well just have a flatmate.'

'How did you meet your husband? Was that romantic?'

Libby smiled and rolled her eyes. 'Yes, it was, actually. We used to get the same train into London every day for work, and I'd noticed Jason, and Jason had noticed me, but you know what it's like – we never said anything. I fancied him so much I was sure he could feel it across the carriage. Then one day, he got on at a different door, so we were squeezed up together. The train stopped suddenly and he spilled his coffee all over himself – I mopped him up with my *brand-new* scarf before it could stain his suit.' Pippa noticed Libby's cheeks were flushing as she spoke, and a nostalgic smile was lifting the corners of her wide mouth, as if she couldn't think about it without being there again. 'Ruined my scarf, obviously. He insisted on taking it away with him to have it cleaned, and later sent me a new one with some flowers . . . And it sort of went from there.'

She had gone very pink and young-looking. Rosy, like a milkmaid.

'That's very sweet,' said Pippa, but her brain was whirring as it always did now when someone fed it new information.

What did that say about them? Libby was spontaneous? Jason was clumsy? They were both quite shy? It wouldn't matter what happened in the future, that memory would always link them, a gold loop round that shared moment, joining their lives together from that point. And now she was in that memory too. That was what linked everyone together. Memories. Memories of conversations.

Pippa ached. Other people now had memories of her, when she didn't. She'd been cut loose, existing in their minds, not her own. 'How long have you been together?' she asked quickly, to stop herself thinking anymore.

'Nine years. Five-year wedding anniversary coming up!' Libby looked as if she was going to say something else, then stopped, blushing. 'Enough about me. Question two! "Would your ideal hero live in (a) a castle, (b) a Manhattan apartment, (c) a Georgian farmhouse or (d) a Parisian garret?" Don't think too hard.'

'Georgian farmhouse.'

Libby raised her eyebrow. 'Are you trying to pick Mr Darcy here?'

'No, I just don't see myself in a Manhattan penthouse or a French attic. Or a castle.' So that ruled out certain lifestyle choices, she reasoned to herself. I'm a traditionalist. I'm not a traveller.

'I'm going to go for the farmhouse too.' Libby circled the answer, neatly completing an 'O' round the letter. 'There's something very romantic about fireplaces, men warming their breeches by them. And I *am* trying to choose Mr Darcy, by the way.'

'He's your ideal man?'

'Yup. I like a man of quality, taking charge, being honourable. I kept making Jason wear big white shirts to fancy-dress parties until he got the hint. Refuses to learn to ride, though, sadly.'

They carried on going through the questions. Pippa felt she was learning more about Libby than she was about herself: Libby happily showered details of her life, of Jason, what she liked and didn't, and Pippa realised she envied her for knowing the answers, for having those memories to throw around.

Eventually, Libby concluded the final question and started to tot up the scores. She did, as she predicted, get Mr Darcy, and looked pleased to have her personality confirmed.

'And your ideal hero is . . .' Libby turned to the other page. 'Jack Dawson from *Titanic*. You want someone you can laugh with as well as fall in love with. Someone loyal and faithful you can rely on, but with a sense of fun.'

'But what does that say about me?'

Libby considered. 'It says you're the sort of person who's independent but likes having an equal partner. You're not easily pushed over. And presumably if the opportunity arises, you're happy to get your kit off and be painted like one of those French girls.'

'Thank you very much,' she said. 'Sounds ideal.'

'So now we know who's coming to get you,' said Libby, with an encouraging smile. 'We just have to wait for him to turn up.'

'How do you know someone's coming?' Pippa asked.

'I'm *sure* there's someone's looking for you right now,' said Libby, and her sunny face reflected her certainty. 'I just am. And if there isn't, there will be soon.'

Pippa smiled back, but something flickered inside that wasn't quite as sunny; a few dark moths fluttered among the pale butterflies of anticipation.

Chapter Six

Erin's journalist friend, Katie, phoned on Wednesday morning, enthused at length about the 'charming' hotel and the romantic adventure Erin had described to her, and by the time the call had ended, Libby was buzzing with excitement and had agreed that Tara, the freelancer, should come to stay at the beginning of September.

Which was four months away. Sixteen weeks.

Or, as she put it to Jason, '*Sixteen weeks!*'

Jason's response was succinct. First he said, 'You are absolutely amazing, you networking genius!' and kissed her so hard they both ignored the ringing of the reception phone for two lots of rings.

Then he said, 'We need to call Marek. Time to get the professionals on the case.'

Even though she'd suggested getting decorators in, Libby couldn't help feeling a bit disappointed, hearing it from Jason. 'Do we? I told Katie what a romantic experience it was, that night we stayed up till three, getting the paper off and listening to talk radio.'

Describing their DIY therapy to Katie had reminded her what fun it had been. How much they'd laughed, what a sense of achievement she'd felt seeing the room come back to life. And, added a quiet voice, they were going to be so busy from now on, when would they get those hours to themselves? Was every evening going to be spent 'keeping Margaret company', watching *Poirot* reruns and nodding when she told them how Donald had read every single Agatha Christie novel?

Jason had pulled her close. 'It *was* a romantic experience,' he said, practically, kissing the tip of her nose. 'We had it, and we can treasure it, and we can talk to this journalist about it, and if you want to bond with the builders finishing it off, that's fine with me. Just don't ask me to scrape off any more of this wallpaper. It's only a matter of time before I have someone's eye out with something.'

A smile forced its way through Libby's disappointment.

'Be realistic. We're not really cut out for DIY, are we?' he went on. 'Don't disagree with me. I saw you reading the instructions on the paint can. It's *paint*. There's only so much it can do.'

'But can we afford Marek?' Marek was the best, she knew that, but he was expensive. Libby worried about money. She couldn't help it. 'Shouldn't we ask about local firms?'

Jason had looked very serious. 'I think what you should be saying at this stage is, "Can we afford *not* to get Marek in?"'

And with that her resistance crumbled. Already Libby could see the smooth, professionally improved version of the hotel appearing around her and a weight lifted from her shoulders. The relief surprised her.

Jason kissed her again, and before she'd had time to say, 'Don't you remember how much Marek cost in the end?' Jason was dialling his number.

Libby didn't know what Jason had said, or how much he'd promised to pay, but somehow the following day, just before lunch, a familiar black van crunched onto their gravel drive.

Margaret had just escorted Bob on his walk and Libby was relieved she wasn't going to be around for the builder's visit – Marek had quite a pragmatic way of talking about houses that she knew would have Margaret springing to the defence of her Highland scenes and rag-rolled office. He'd been pretty brutal about her kitchen, and she hadn't even liked it that much herself.

Libby hurried over to the residents' lounge, where Jason was up a stepladder changing the dusty light bulbs in the big chandelier; it was down to five bulbs now, which flattered the cobwebs but wasn't ideal for reading.

'Marek's here,' she said. 'Have you done the list?'

'What list?' Jason started to come down and Libby steadied the wobbly steps.

'You said you were going to make a list of things we need doing. So he quotes on everything.'

'Ah, no, sorry. Didn't get round to it – I was sorting out Mum's phone.' Jason pushed his hair out of his face. 'Do we need a list? Marek knows what he's looking at.'

'Did you have time to work out the new budget?' Libby gave Jason a calm look that hid a flicker of inner nerves. This was where she had to show she trusted him. Fresh start. Total honesty. No loaded questions.

'Yes,' said Jason, equally calmly. 'I worked out a budget.'

'With new en suites included?'

'With new en suites.'

They looked at each other, and Libby asked the question she'd have preferred not to ask, but knew she had to. 'And we definitely have enough money in the account?'

'Yes,' said Jason, his pale blue eyes locked on hers. 'We definitely have enough money. Now, you said they were here?'

They went out to the front porch to welcome Marek, who was walking up the gravel accompanied by his sidekick, Jan the electrician, both in shades and black polo shirts, a vision of pure London amid the floral backdrop of the hotel's hydrangeas. Excitement fizzed inside Libby's chest. The frantic wallpaper and dismal lounge were vanishing before her eyes, without so much as another splinter or sandpaper burn.

When Margaret saw how well they worked, even she wouldn't mind the changes, Libby told herself. It'd be finished and lovely before she even had time to get her disappointed face on – and didn't Donald appreciate quality workmanship? He'd want to see his hotel back up and running, the way it had in its heyday.

'Aye aye, the Reservoir Dogs are back,' said Jason under his breath.

'Don't call them that,' murmured Libby. 'I'm pretty sure that's not the look they're going for.'

'I'm not so sure ... Morning, guys – hope the journey up wasn't too bad,' said Jason, holding out a hand.

'Hello, Jason, Libby,' said Marek, and the memories rushed back at her: the long, hot summer of Radio 1 from eight till five, unearthing festering coffee mugs, and the smell of dust and Lynx and Ginsters pasties. Six months she'd spent camping out in one room while Marek and his merry men ripped half the house to pieces and put it back together again, seemingly with fifty per cent more light and air. No one had ever walked into that house afterwards and not marvelled at how gorgeous it was, as if clean light filtered in through invisible windows. And now he was going to work his magic on this place.

'Hello, Marek!' she cried, and only just stopped herself adding a kiss.

Silent Jan managed a hint of a smile and Libby felt a warmth towards them that she'd never have believed she'd feel at the height of her own building work.

'Can I get you something to eat or drink?' she asked. 'Cup of tea?'

'That's very kind, Libby,' said Marek, taking off his shades to rub his bloodshot eyes. He worked insane hours and ran an undisclosed number of super-efficient building teams, all sporting his company's logoed polo shirts. 'But can we make a start? I need to get back to quote for a job in town this afternoon. It's further from London than we thought . . .'

'Ha!' she said. 'And not just in motorway terms! What?' she added, seeing Jason give her a reproachful look.

'It's three hours, tops,' he said.

'And about twenty years!'

'Libby . . .'

'I'm just making sure Marek knows that although we're a long way out of London, we haven't gone all green wellies and floral borders,' she said brightly. 'We want the Swan Hotel to have the same high standards as the top hotels anywhere. It's going to be the best hotel in the county.'

'I can smell something.' Marek lifted a finger and sniffed analytically. 'You have damp?'

'Or drains,' said Silent Jan, uncharacteristically moved to speech. Libby winced: it must be something he found particularly revolting.

Jason sighed. 'No,' he said, with a 'Don't say, "I told you so"' sideways glance at Libby. 'It's the dog.'

'You have dogs? Inside the hotel?' Marek looked even more horrified than he had been at the thought of damp.

'For the moment. It's something else we need to discuss.' Libby smiled. 'Now, shall we start at the top and work down?'

'So,' said Jason, when Marek's black van had disappeared round the corner several hours later. He let the word hang between them like the smoke from a starting pistol. The hotel suddenly seemed quiet without the steady background noise of rasping tape measures, short bursts of intense Polish discussion, Marek's phone ringing every three minutes and Jan's increasingly anxious *hmmm* noise every time he found evidence of Donald's enthusiasm for amateur electrical engineering.

'So,' said Libby. She wanted Jason to speak first, in case she'd read the situation wrong and the shimmering vision she'd glimpsed was all in her head. Marek had made it seem so possible, turning her Pinterest inspiration pages to reality there in front of her, just with a few minutes' scrutiny, and one or two radical and expensive suggestions about plumbing.

They stood on the stone porch of the hotel, framed by the stone pillars like the original Georgian owners, posing for a portrait in front of their country estate.

'This would be a nice photo for the website, us on the front steps,' she added. 'Maybe have Bob in here. If he could stay still.'

Jason glanced at her with a wry smile. 'For the website? Shouldn't we get the damp fixed first?'

'No, we need to think beyond that. Write the perfect pitch, then build it.' Libby breathed in, enjoying the freshness of the air after the stuffiness of the over-furnished hotel. It was the first spring day with a touch of summer in it, and the air smelled green with leaves and grass.

Jason slung an arm around her and she relaxed into his chest.

They stood like that for a moment or two, enjoying the sparkles of splashy light in the mossy fountain that filled the turning circle; Libby imagined the shiny Austins and Fords that must have dropped off party guests in the 1930s. Before it was a hotel, when it was still the home of a prosperous country family.

She turned her head to bury her nose in Jason's clean blue shirt, inhaling his familiar smell: Hugo Boss, and washing powder, and the spice-warm masculinity of his golden skin, the combination of sexy and comforting that had clicked with something in her brain the first time she managed to get close to him, on that commuter train. She'd spent weeks wondering what he smelled like, from across the carriage, what his skin would feel like under her fingertips. Now she knew. It was exactly as she'd imagined.

'It feels more real now, doesn't it?' he said, and she felt the buzz of his voice deep in his chest. 'The hotel, I mean.'

'What? It's always felt real. You just haven't been getting up to do the breakfasts like I have.'

'No, real as in I can see Marek getting on with this.' He shook his head, as if he couldn't believe his own stupidity. 'We should have called him right at the start. Four weeks for the decorating, a week or so for the general stuff . . . We should be ready to reopen by the beginning of July at the latest. Get some practice in so we're up to speed when this journalist comes.'

We *are* thinking the same things, Libby thought, relieved. 'Is it good that Marek can start so soon? Shouldn't he be booked up for months?'

'Well . . . he's the ringmaster, isn't he? He's got teams working for him.' Jason leaned back against the stone pillar and blew air out of his cheeks. 'Marek's not the cheapest, but we know him, and we don't know any builders round here. And we need someone good, and quick.'

He spoke casually, but Libby knew he was dropping tiny warnings. This wasn't going to be cheap. This was going to raise the stakes. This was going to take them back into a situation where money would have to be discussed, big sums of money that they didn't have anymore. They no longer had the safety net of Jason's huge salary, or the safety net of their own undented confidence.

Can we do this? she thought, and her positive mood wobbled for a second. Wouldn't it be easier to scale down their ambitions, keep the avocado bathroom suites, learn to live in a smaller, quieter way? Margaret would be happier with that.

Then she looked up at Jason, watching for her reaction with guarded hope in his eyes, and she knew he wouldn't be. She wouldn't either. They needed to achieve something new, and better. And working towards a shared goal – wasn't that something that would rebuild their marriage?

Jason wanted to prove she could trust him. She wanted to prove that she was willing to. There were *lots* of good reasons to take a chance on themselves.

Libby took a deep breath. 'How much does Marek reckon it's going to cost?'

Jason didn't reply immediately. He stared out at their cars parked by the rhododendron bushes and chewed his lower lip. He did that when he didn't want to say something; it was a tic Libby had learned to spot at parties. He'd rarely done it with her.

'How much, Jason?'

'We always said that if we were going to do this, we should do it properly.' He spoke slowly. 'If we've got a vision, for something that's our own . . .'

'Then we should go for it.' Libby's breath quickened in her throat. 'It'd be a false economy to make half the hotel really nice and leave the rest shabby – people would notice. And we'll make the money back, when we're full of guests.'

'We certainly will. When your amazing website's lured them in.' He slipped his arms round her waist. 'And your amazing breakfasts. And your luxurious bedrooms. And you in the reception, making everyone feel special.'

Libby blinked, as the hard edges of the task ahead peeked out from underneath the euphoria: how much there would still be to do, after Marek had finished and gone. The hotel would look fabulous, but *they*'d have to drive it, every folded towel, every promotional idea, every fresh smile for a new guest when they were feeling dead on their feet. Those snitty TripAdvisor reviews would be about *her*.

'What?' Jason pulled back to look at her properly. 'You look freaked out. It won't just be you doing all that – I'll help.'

'Too right you will. No, it just dawned on me what we're taking on. I've never done something like this, where it's so . . .' She searched for the right words, wanting to sound realistic, not negative. 'Where everything we do is so open and obvious. How well we do, how hard we work – there's nowhere to hide. I've always been more of a back-room person.'

Jason tilted up her chin, so she could see his face. His eyes were bright, and he looked energised for the first time in months.

'But that's what I *want*, Libby,' he said. 'I've spent the last ten years moving money that I never saw, trading things that didn't even exist. This is real. This is going to be something we can look at and think, We did this. When guests leave looking all blissed out because we've got the best beds in the county, or when someone comes up from London and books to come back because it's the best experience they've had . . . *we*'ll have done that.'

'I know,' she said.

'And I *am* going to make this work, Libby,' he said fiercely. 'I promise. This is going to be the best thing that could have happened for us.'

He looked so hopeful that Libby forgot her follow-up questions about the finances, the mortgage, the staff. Jason had lost a lot of things when he'd lost his job, but the thing she missed the most was his sense of purpose, that bounding enthusiasm that she'd liked so much about him when they'd first met. Now he seemed more like his old self, it made her own excitement sharper and safer. Libby hated nagging him, chivvying him about rotas; it reminded them both of the days after the sacking, when she had literally had to force him out of bed each morning.

'Yes,' she said, wrapping her arms round his neck. 'One day we'll talk about this moment, when the Corcoran boutique hotel empire began.'

He grinned. 'Brilliant. Now we just have to tell Mum.'

Libby tried to put a cosy spin on the meeting in the cluttered office by bringing cake and tea along, but Margaret sat at the heavy partners' desk as if she were facing a firing squad. Bob lay at her feet, occasionally sniffing the air in case any cake found its way to floor level.

Jason outlined the revised building plans, and Libby showed her the mood boards, and the bathroom catalogues Marek had left for them to choose from, and the colours they'd be using, all of which were met with a faint smile and murmurs of 'Lovely.'

The main change to the plans, Jason explained, was that they'd be putting in new bathroom suites, rather than repainting what was already there.

'But I don't see why we have to,' protested Margaret. 'What's wrong with what we have now?'

'Nothing's wrong, but it's time to update them,' said Libby tactfully. 'Guests like a bit of luxury – white baths, lovely shiny taps, a powerful shower.'

Margaret glanced at Jason, looking for support. 'As long as everything's clean, what does it matter whether the bathrooms are fashionable or not?'

'They do need updating, Mum,' he said. 'I read a few comments in the guestbook about stains on the baths, and when Libby had a word with Dawn, she said they can't *get* them any cleaner.'

'Then we need to look into better cleaning products.' Margaret's jaw tightened. 'Those baths are top of the range – they were extremely expensive.'

'I'm sure they were. But in when, 1983? That's over thirty years ago.'

'No, it's—' She stopped. 'Oh. I suppose it is.' She blinked. 'Thirty years. Goodness.'

Jason took advantage of her temporary distraction. 'The thing is, Mum, guests expect different things now, and we've got to find some new business. This feature's a great shot at some national exposure. It gives us a target to aim for.'

'I don't like the implication that what we currently have is *beneath* anyone's target.' Margaret's chin rose, to Libby's surprise. She hadn't seen Margaret argue this hard against the decor before. 'I appreciate things aren't up to ... to London standards, but we've been ticking over fine, in our own *unambitious* way, for a few years ...'

'Oh, Mum. It wasn't a criticism.' Jason stopped and Libby could see him deflating, his earlier bouncy mood dissipating under his mother's reproachful gaze.

'Of course it's not a criticism. What Jason means,' Libby said quickly, 'is that you've always said the hotel's in need of some TLC, and this is a good chance to spend money *once* and get everything ticked off. Decoration, any repairs, any maintenance – Marek can sort it out in one go. It sounds like a lot, but really, once you see it, it'll just feel like ...' She scrabbled for a comparison, because actually, she *did* want to effect a massive change. Libby wanted the place to be unrecognisable, from the mangy stag's head up. '... like when you get a new pair of glasses and it takes a day or two to get used to them,' she said. 'And then you wonder why you didn't choose that style years ago.'

There was a long pause. She felt the pressure of Jason's foot against her ankle under the table, a silent *thank you*.

Eventually, Margaret's defiance slipped away. 'Well, clearly you've already put a lot of thought into this project. There's not really a lot I can add. I'm sure you know what you're doing.'

'But we *want* your input, Margaret,' insisted Libby. 'It's your hotel too.'

Too late, she wondered if that 'too' was wrong. Margaret let out a long breath through her nostrils. Nuts, thought Libby. It was.

Chapter Seven

No one's coming to get me.

Pippa's eyes snapped open. The words were so clear that for a sleepy half-second it felt as if someone had spoken them into her ear. *No one's coming to get me.* That brutal truth had been floating behind her thoughts for days now, while she'd managed to cover it with other things, but now it was the only thing in her head. No dreams. No drifting, unfocused memories, slipping away in the light. Just cold, helpless fear.

No one's coming to get me. I have no name. I have no home. I have nowhere to go, nowhere to start.

Pippa's head filled with white noise, pinning her to the bed and making her heart thrash painfully in her tightening chest, while her mind raced round and round like a mouse, frantic in a humane trap. She stared at the ceiling, trying to go through her routine of exploring her memory for fresh fragments, but fear blocked out all thoughts. Seven days. Seven days and no one had missed her. Fine, so there wasn't a boyfriend beside himself with worry. Fair enough. She could be between boyfriends. But no family? No workmates? No flatmates? No one?

It frightened Pippa, deep in the pit of her stomach. Who *was* she? She didn't *feel* that she was reclusive or unloved or unpopular in some weird way. She got on fine with the nurses, and she'd even had a laugh with Libby Corcoran – Libby, a total stranger who'd come to see her twice now, and stayed over an hour each time. Where were her friends? Was she a shy person, outside this room? Had she had some epic falling-out with everyone she knew? Had she jilted someone? Had she just got out of prison? Run off with someone's husband? Was that why she'd been heading to a hotel – she'd left her home?

She stared at the bright strip of sunlight around the curtains, as the sound of the swing doors heralded the arrival of the first shift, and the familiar noise brought her panic down a notch. Prison was a bit melodramatic. And she didn't *feel* like an offender or an adulterer. But who knew? The possibilities were too big to comprehend. She could literally be anyone. Without a past, without memories, how would you know what you were like? The magazines Libby had left were full of features encouraging readers to make a fresh start – 'Reinvent Your Wardrobe!', 'Transform Your Love Story!' – but that was only fun if you knew what you were changing *from*. Pippa felt sick.

The nurses had suggested various reasons why no one had turned up to claim her, all of which felt very plausible, but they still weren't quite as reassuring as they probably hoped.

'Ah, they'll be on holiday,' was Bernie's favourite. She had a thing about holidays, Pippa had noted in her book; she monitored everyone's time off like a hawk. 'Won't they turn up here with a tan and presents for you, and feeling terrible that they've been sunning themselves all this time?'

Karen, the other daytime nurse, lived alone, miles from her family in Scotland, so her theory was that Pippa probably had an enviable independent lifestyle, which was nothing to be ashamed of. 'I'd have to be in hospital for a month before any of my family noticed I was missing,' she said, punching the pillows hard as she rearranged them behind Pippa's aching ribs. 'Over Christmas. And they'd only report me missing here if they were short for a shift.'

It was kind of them to be so quick with explanations, Pippa thought, but what if she really was as friendless as she seemed? She'd have to face it when her memory came back. As the morning sun got stronger outside, she finally allowed herself to think the thought she really had been trying to ignore. With every satisfactory blood pressure test, every reduction in her pain meds, every inconclusive chat with the head injuries specialist, who said she was perfectly fine, apart from this memory loss, it loomed closer and closer.

Where was she going to go when they discharged her, if she didn't know who she was?

Pippa lay back on her pillows and closed her eyes tightly, willing the morning to stop. Willing to slip into another deep sleep and wake up with her memories all back.

At lunchtime, Scottish Karen put her head round the door. 'You've got a visitor.' She smiled encouragingly and Pippa hoped it was Libby, but it wasn't.

The woman standing behind Karen wasn't someone she recognised, but she seemed pleasant: a middle-aged woman in a flowery summer dress, with a navy short-sleeved jacket on top and comfortable sandals that suggested she spent most of her day on her feet. Her hair was wispy and blonde, pulled back into a small bun that revealed her earlobes, weighed down with a gold hoop earring on each side.

Pippa scanned her face for familiarities – were those eyes

like hers? Could she be an aunt? An old friend? A landlady? She was surprised to feel a flicker of nervousness, not relief.

'Hello . . . Pippa,' she said, and as the lady's eyes dropped to her file, to check her details, so did Pippa's heart.

She didn't know her. She was another stranger, being nice because she *was* nice, and also because it was her job.

Pippa managed a hopeful smile. 'Hello.'

'My name's Marcia, and I'm from social services,' she explained, sitting down on the chair by the bed, without asking. 'The police have passed your case on to me now, as you're not a missing person, and there's no record of your DNA on their system.' She paused and smiled. 'Which is a good thing!'

As Marcia spoke, she opened the file on her knee; it was thin and had only a few pieces of paper in.

Is that me? thought Pippa. Is that all I am? Of course it is. I'm starting from scratch here. I'm only seven days old.

'Social services?' she repeated.

Marcia saw the panic in her face and made a soothing noise. 'Because of the nature of your head injury, someone needs to keep an eye on you once you've been discharged by your medical team. Normally the hospital would release you to a family member, but as that's not going to be possible until your memory comes back and we *find* you a family member, it falls within social services' remit.'

'Oh,' said Pippa weakly.

'I'm sure it's just a temporary measure,' said Karen robustly. 'You could be fine by this afternoon, in which case . . .'

They let the thought hang in the air. *And if she wasn't?*

'I'll leave you to it.' Karen made to go. 'Press your buzzer if you need me.'

'So . . .' Marcia uncapped her pen and glanced at her watch.

Pippa noted that she hadn't even removed her jacket. This obviously wasn't going to be a long visit. 'I've been advised by your consultant that as far as he's concerned, you're physically ready to be discharged. He wants you to maintain regular contact until your memory is fully recovered, but that can be done via appointments. There'll be a support pack that will have all the info in it.'

'I can't stay here?' Pippa asked. Her voice sounded more desperate than she wanted it to.

Marcia made a quick, sympathetic 'Sorry, no' face. 'Unfortunately not. As you can imagine, there's a lot of pressure on bed space. Here and in the psychiatric ward.'

The psychiatric ward. She flinched. 'Of course. Yes.'

'So, what I'm going to do,' Marcia went on, taking out a pamphlet and circling some phone numbers, 'is give you our hospital discharge protocol for homeless people—'

'I'm not homeless!' Pippa stopped, shocked. To all intents and purposes, she was. Where was her home? She didn't know. And anyway, just because you didn't *feel* like a homeless person didn't mean you couldn't be one. She could be anything. Homeless. Divorced. A mother. What hole had she left in someone's life? Or hadn't she left one?

The unanswerable questions swarmed into her head again, and a shrinking feeling of being at the mercy of total strangers clutched her stomach. She half coughed, half gasped.

Marcia reached for the water by the bed, concerned. 'Do you need a moment? Would you like me to call the nurse back in?'

'Sorry.' Pippa tried to gather herself. 'It's just . . . Sorry, carry on.'

'I've managed to allocate you a room in some emergency accommodation in a women's hostel just outside Hartley. It's only a temporary arrangement, as again, we're pressured for space right now, but Mr Reynolds seems confident that it shouldn't take more than a few days for your memory to come back, so ideally you won't be there long term.'

Hostel. The word conjured up images of drug addicts, frightened women hiding from abusive partners, locked doors, people crying at night. Lost people.

'It's not as bad as it sounds,' Marcia reassured her. 'It means you'd have some contact with people on a day-to-day basis. In case your medical situation changed suddenly.'

There was a noise over by the door and they both looked up, expecting to see one of the doctors with a flock of medical students (Pippa was something of a star attraction for the neurologists) or a cleaner. But in the doorway, in her black jersey jacket, was Libby and she was almost hopping from foot to foot, trying to contain herself.

'I'm sorry to interrupt,' she said, 'but you're not really going to send Pippa somewhere on her own, are you?'

Pippa felt a wave of relief rush through her at the sight of Libby's face. The plain jacket, shoved up at the elbows. The huge plum bag. She clung to each familiar thing as if it could anchor her.

'Are you family?' Marcia looked hopeful.

'Um, no . . .'

'Libby was a witness to the accident,' Pippa said quickly. 'She's been visiting me.'

Could she ask to go home with Libby? Was that too much? Was that going beyond kindness?

Libby took a confident step into the room and perched herself on the spare chair with a smile, ignoring the officious way Marcia covered up Pippa's case notes.

'I know it's rather unusual, but this *is* such an unusual set of circumstances . . .' Pippa noticed that Libby's accent had suddenly gone more London, more assured, as if she was used to talking her way around situations and settling things. 'Might I suggest that Pippa stays in our hotel, if it's just a short-term arrangement? She was on her way there at the time of the accident. It could be that something about the place triggers a memory. We're not busy at the moment, and rather than going into a hostel . . .'

She glanced at Pippa and Pippa knew from her eyes that the word 'hostel' had given her the same shudder.

'That would be an option,' said Marcia. 'Although obviously there are no funds to meet hotel bills . . .'

'That's not an issue,' said Libby firmly. 'And my mother-in-law has been on the hospital volunteer committee for years, so we can arrange for transport to the appointments too. She's up and down to the hospital a few times a week. As am I. With our Pets As Therapy hound. You might have met her? Margaret Corcoran.'

Marcia's face lit up. 'You're Bob's owner?'

Pippa didn't think she'd ever been so grateful to someone in her life. It made her feel almost childlike. The sense of having been saved from a shocking drop, snatched at the last minute by someone on a trapeze, made her dizzy with relief.

'In that case . . . if you're sure you don't mind?' Marcia's shoulders lifted with the air of someone whose workload had just halved in front of her.

'Of course not. It's what I hope someone would do for me,' said Libby. 'If I was knocked down and didn't know who I was, or where I was, I'd like to think someone would be decent enough to look after me till I knew what was going on.'

'That's a very Christian attitude. Have you got ten minutes now? I'll need to do some paperwork,' said Marcia, but Pippa could see her pen moving across the page, and she knew that she was already thinking about the next homeless stranger, the newly free bed.

She looked up at Libby and mouthed, 'Thank you.'

'No problem,' Libby mouthed back, and smiled her unworried, generous smile.

'Jason, it's me. Listen, I need to talk to you about something. Quickly.'

Libby glanced around the foyer, but there was no sign of Margaret or Lord Bob. She reckoned she'd be able to smell Bob before he appeared, or tell by the wave of public adoration coming from afar. And she wanted to run this by Jason before she mentioned it to Margaret, just to make sure she got in there first.

'If you're ringing about Marek,' he said, 'I've got good news—'

'I'm not ringing about Marek.' Libby juggled the facts in her head, trying to work out how best to explain it, but realised there wasn't a right or wrong way. It was what it was. What else could anyone do?

'It's Pippa,' she said. 'The hospital want to discharge her, but they can't send her home because she still doesn't know where she lives. And no one's come for her. I arrived just as social services were going to send her to a *hostel*.'

There was a pause at the other end. Libby thought she could hear the clicking of a mouse. Was Jason browsing the internet while she was talking to him?

'A *hostel*, Jason,' she repeated, in case he thought she'd said hotel. 'Where social services put battered women on the run from their partners, and methadone addicts and all sorts.'

'I know what a hostel is,' he said mildly. 'And for the record, I'm not sure Longhampton is a festering pit of domestic violence and crack addicts, but go on.'

'Go on? Well, what do you think I did?'

'You said she could come here.'

'Of course. She doesn't know anyone else. The look on her face when I said she could stay . . .' Libby bit her lip, thinking about it. Pippa's undisguised relief made it much more real, somehow – that absolute defencelessness of having to trust whatever people said to you because you really didn't have an option. Pippa was the first person she'd truly clicked with in Longhampton, but even if they hadn't, wouldn't she still want to help?

'Well, I guess we owe her a bed since she was coming here anyway,' he said. 'Do we know how long it's likely to last?'

'What, the amnesia? Not long, hopefully. But the doctors want her to be around people, which, again, is ideal because we're there all day.'

'And you're sure she isn't some sort of confidence trickster who'll never leave?'

'Sorry?' Libby realised she'd walked towards the Tree of Kindness without thinking. A quick glance along its boughs reminded her that putting someone up for a few nights wasn't a lot to do for a person in need – not by a long shot. There were two new birds up, thanking volunteers for donating bone marrow to a child and for reading *A Tale of Two Cities* to someone's dying mother. A lump came to her throat. 'Jason, she's got retrograde amnesia and cracked ribs! That's a hell of a lot of effort to go to for a few free nights in a hotel.'

'I didn't mean—'

'It's not as though we don't have room. If it's the money you're bothered about, I'm sure she'll be happy to settle up once her memory comes back.' Libby didn't even mean that, but something prodded her to say it. 'Or we can invoice social services,' she added. 'They probably won't leave a TripAdvisor review, though.'

Why was he being so mean? This really wasn't like Jason, she thought. Normally he'd have been offering to drive up here to collect them before she'd got the words out.

'Are you all right?' she asked. 'You sound grumpy. Is the Nespresso machine broken?'

'I'm just . . .' She heard a groan and could imagine him running a hand through his hair. 'Sorry, I've been looking at the accounts. Marek's going to send a prep team to get cracking on Monday, but he needs a starting payment by the end of today and I'm trying to see what I can move around. Nothing's adding up, unless I've . . .' The reception phone started to ring, a strident, old-fashioned peal.

'Oh God, I hate that bloody thing,' growled Jason, and he really *didn't* sound like himself.

'Answer that,' she said. 'I'll be back in a minute anyway – I need to grab some clothes for Pippa. She's only got what she was brought in with.'

'Have you told Mum?'

'Not yet. I'm waiting for Lord Bob to finish his afternoon performance.' As she spoke, Libby heard the skittering of claws on corridor tile and Margaret and Lord Bob appeared round the corner. Bob was doing his public show prance, the one that made his jowls swing adorably and his apple bottom sway from side to side. The nurse was clearly charmed, inclining her head to take into account the five-foot height difference.

Libby watched them approaching and started to gather her bags together. 'She's here now. See you soon,' she said, and hung up.

Margaret didn't need any persuading at all about having Pippa stay for a few days. In fact, she seemed astonished that Libby felt she even had to ask.

'But of course she must come to us,' she said, before Libby had got to the explanation about the homeless shelter. 'What a question! That poor girl, all on her own. Awful. *Awful!* I hope you said "yes" straightaway.'

'I did.' Libby checked in her mirrors before pulling out of the parking space and jumped, as she always did, when she saw Lord Bob's head looming through the gap between the back seats and the boot. His tongue was lolling and he was panting with the effort of being calmly entertaining for an hour. If he'd been a rock star, thought Libby, he'd have a damp white towel draped round his thick neck. And possibly shades. He was making up for lost time by releasing all the flatulence he'd been holding in while the patients had been stroking his velvety ears.

'I've been thinking about her, wondering what she was coming to see us for,' Margaret went on, sounding more like her usual self than she had for ages, now she had something to organise. *Someone* to organise. 'And of course, she must stay with us until her memory comes back. Donald wouldn't even have given it a second thought. We need to look after her. Did you get all her discharge forms? And her appointments?'

Libby shot Margaret a side glance on the pretext of turning out of the hospital car park.

'Yes,' she said. 'I'm glad it's OK – I hoped you wouldn't think it was an intrusion.'

Margaret's hands – which Libby used as a sort of visual barometer – stopped moving in her lap. 'Sometimes it's good to be reminded that people are worse off than you are. Just because I'm still . . . still very much missing Donald doesn't mean I can't feel sorry for other people's troubles.'

'Of course not!' Because that was, actually, exactly what Libby had been thinking. She went red.

Margaret was looking straight ahead, at the sights of Longhampton passing before them. 'Anyway, it'll give me something to do, while you're dealing with these builders. We should pop her in the spare room – it'll be quieter in there. Away from all the mess.'

'Well, you're the best nurse I ever had,' said Libby. 'I never wanted to leave when you were looking after me and my broken leg.' Two weeks' bed rest in the spare room, and enough Heinz tomato soup to fill a bath. Her own mother would never have taken such good care of her, or let her have a bell by the bedside to ring for toast.

Maybe this was a good thing, she thought. Someone for Margaret to fuss over, other than Jason, or Bob.

'I must admit I'm rather intrigued by the mystery of it.' Margaret settled back in her seat. 'A few people have asked about the accident – if we know what happened. Oh, look, Norman Jeffreys. Hello!' She leaned forward and waved back at someone heading into the car park, pushing an ancient man in a wheelchair. 'Hello!' She sighed. 'Poor old thing. No, apparently, it was Veronica Parker's nephew who was driving the Mini. Callum. He's already been up for careless driving, and his wife's left him twice. Not that we ever mention anything at

Mothers' Union, but we do worry about Veronica. Have you met Veronica?'

'Um, librarian Veronica?' Libby tried to remember who Veronica Parker was and where she fitted on Margaret's complex social chart. Even in London it had never occurred to her that you could judge people on what they grew in their gardens. (Roses: good. Red-hot pokers: bad. Gnomes: beyond the pale.)

'No! That's Vanessa. Veronica was the church organist who was *asked to leave.*'

'Can anyone have a secret in this place?' asked Libby, only semi-joking.

'Not really.' Margaret waved at someone else heading towards the hospital. 'The vicar,' she added, before Libby could even ask. 'Reverend Jackie. Very nice lady. Did you see how some anonymous person – Janet Harvey, I believe – thanked her on the Tree for taking her cat when she went into the home? Heart of gold.'

Libby murmured agreement and turned onto the main road towards the hotel. She didn't really need to have her own act of kindness put on the Tree: it'd be all round the town before poor Pippa was even through their door. Along with poor Pippa's mysterious circumstance, no doubt.

Chapter Eight

The Corcorans' flat had two spare rooms: Luke's old room up in the attic and the official guest room, in which Libby had rested her broken leg while working her way through Margaret's Georgette Heyer collection. Despite being on the small side, it managed to house a pine double bed, a pine chest of drawers topped with a small pine vanity mirror, a pine wardrobe and a pine clothes stand, as well as a thick crop of Highland stag paintings. Every time Libby stepped into the spare room, she had a powerful urge to paint everything white. That and drink tomato soup.

Jason was oblivious to the pine, but then he didn't seem to mind that their room – his room – was unchanged from the day he'd left it, including the football posters. Libby was pretty sure that the chest of drawers Margaret had cleared out before they'd arrived had still had his boxer shorts folded in neat blue-and-white rows.

'I'm sure she'd be better in the attic than in here,' said Libby in an undertone as Jason shucked off the old duvet cover, and she peeled the pillowcases. 'She'll wake up every morning thinking she's in World of Pine.'

'You can't put a guest in the attic.' He shook out the pillow-cases from Margaret's neat bundle – plain white linen, tied with red ribbon to indicate a double bed. Singles were yellow, king size blue. 'It's full of junk.'

Libby paused with her hands on her hips. 'How come your room's been cryogenically preserved in its original state, but Luke's attic's now a dumping ground for all manner of tat?'

'Because I sometimes come home, and Luke doesn't,' Jason retorted. 'And there is a lot of tat to be stored, as you may have noticed.' He finished stuffing the pillowcases and threw a fresh duvet cover over the bed. 'Duvet, go!'

They began hunting for the duvet corners with practised speed; it always cheered Libby up, their bed-making routine. It was a chore she'd hated for years, so Jason had challenged her to see how quickly they could get it over and done with, like F1 mechanics servicing a pit stop; now, hundreds of duvets later, they moved in a rhythm, back and forth, smooth and shake. The teamwork of it was satisfying, and watching the concentration set on Jason's face made Libby want to laugh and kiss him at the same time.

Libby had never told any of her London friends about the duvet routine, not even Erin. She knew how much *she*'d roll her eyes if someone told her they'd turned bed-making into a private joke. It was appallingly twee. But it was nice. Libby had dreaded that the nice, twee habits she and Jason had built up would vanish when things collapsed; it meant more to her than she could express that they still did this.

Libby shoved her duvet corner into the cover's corner, pulled it down in time with Jason, then looked up to see him grinning triumphantly at her.

'Getting slow,' he said.

'You've got longer arms.'

'No, I'm just naturally skill,' he replied, airily. 'And,' he added, 'Dad used to give me and Luke fifty pence for every duvet we changed when he was on laundry duty. Soon get quick when there's up to four pounds at stake.'

'You never told me that.'

'I'd forgotten till I came back. It was fine until Mum found out. Then she put us on a flat rate.' He wrinkled his nose, remembering. 'She said she wanted it to be fair, but I think she thought Luke was quicker than me. He wasn't,' he added. 'But he used to get the money back off me at poker afterwards. The cheeky sod.'

Libby smoothed the cover and straightened up. 'What *is* your mother's problem with Luke?' she asked. 'I mentioned that award the other day and she managed to get in a dig about him and Suzanne. I mean, I understand he was a handful, but what did he actually do? Set fire to the dogs' home?'

Jason ran a hand through his thick hair. 'Nothing like that. It's Dad, I guess. Stressing Dad out. Mum blames Luke for Dad's high blood pressure.'

'Really? But when did he leave home? Nearly twenty years ago?'

'Oh, I know – it's nothing to do with Luke. Dad worked sixteen-hour days trying to keep this place going; he liked his cheese, never exercised – that was why he had high blood pressure. Mum just doesn't want that to be the reason.'

'So, what *did* he do?' Libby didn't like pushing Jason to talk about upsetting things – she knew Donald's death had hit him hard, even though he'd insisted 'Dad would've wanted us being strong for Mum, not sitting around being miserable for him' – but the gaps in her knowledge of his family were starting to feel uncomfortable now she was living in their house. 'I need to know, Jase. I worry about putting my foot in it with your mother. I don't want to upset her, especially not with . . . you know.'

He sighed. 'Luke wasn't bad, but he had some dodgy mates. Nothing major – bit of fighting, bit of covering up for the older lads. Set fire to a few things. He put Dad in some awkward positions when we were growing up. Dad was on the council, chaired various charity committees, magistrate . . . Luke didn't give a toss. It got to the point where Dad couldn't have got him off the next charge, which was when he joined the army.'

'But once Luke was in the army, he did all right, didn't he?' Libby tried to piece it together with the Luke she'd met: quietly spoken, sharp-eyed, sharp-boned, with an air of tightly wound energy. Like Margaret, funnily enough.

'No, he did really well. But that's not what people like to gossip about, is it? Not, "Ooh, I hear Luke Corcoran's been made a captain." It's all "Ooh, who'd have thought Donald Corcoran's lad would be up for joyriding." God love Longhampton, but there's not a lot else to talk about. Mum probably blames Luke for Dad never being elected mayor or chief mason or whatever it was that she thinks he ought to have been.'

'Donald as mayor? Did he want that?' Libby's memories of Donald were of his quiet affability, not his political ambitions. He'd carved the Christmas turkey in exactly equal slices by the dresser, while Margaret had done all the flamboyant business with the flaming puddings. 'I can't imagine your dad doing all that civic-duty stuff. Although, I can totally imagine . . .' She trailed off, unsure if it would come out right.

'Mum as lady mayor? Yeah, I can too.' Jason pulled a wry face. 'Most of her wardrobe was designed to have a great big gold chain of office over the top.'

'You should see her up at the hospital with Bob, chatting with everyone, knowing everyone's name – she would have been great as a mayor,' said Libby. 'What am I saying? She still *would* be. She's barely sixty. Why doesn't she do it now? Has she thought about joining the town council? I know she's still coming to terms with being on her own, but she's got so much to offer in her own right, not just as Donald's wife. I don't think she realises how much people admire her round here.'

She didn't add, 'And it'd stop her getting wound up about the hotel,' but she could tell Jason was thinking it too.

He shook his head. 'Mum's old-fashioned. I think she liked the idea of it being her and Dad.'

'I know.' Libby saw Jason glance down, wrong-footed by the memory, and reached over to grab his hand. 'I'm sorry, Jase. I miss him too.' And she did: the hotel was different without Donald. He wouldn't have seemed out of place in a pre-war cricket line-up, with his neat grey side-parting and trusting gaze. A million times nicer than her own quick-tempered, manipulative father. 'I only married you on the understanding that you'd end up like your dad.'

'Thanks. Something to aim for, I guess.'

'What did he think about Luke?'

'How do you mean?'

'Well, your dad never did all this flinching and eye-rolling that your mother does. I don't even remember him saying a bad word about Luke.'

Jason squeezed her hand and dropped it, gathering up the discarded sheets. 'No, Dad was always a lot more chilled about Luke than Mum was. Maybe he took a "boys will be boys" view about the stuff he got up to.'

'Did he think he'd grow out of it?'

'Something like that. I mean, it seemed shocking at the time, but looking back, it was just your average adolescent drunken behaviour. I guess they were worried about where it might lead, not what it was.'

'Understandable, really, when you consider the perfect little brother with the top grades, on the rugby team with his great hair.'

She was expecting Jason to rise to the bait, but he didn't. He stared blankly at the fresh bed, as if he was reconsidering the answer to that question. 'Actually, Luke could have played for the county, but . . .' He shrugged. 'He wasn't allowed to go for trials, because he was on detention at school. And after that, he skived games.'

'Maybe he didn't want to be compared with you.'

'Don't know why – he was streets ahead of me. I was all right. I was fit. And I turned up to the practices. But Luke played like he wasn't scared of anyone. He had this immense way of tackling, given he wasn't a big lad.' Jason looked up with a twinkle in his eye. 'Funnily enough, Chopper was telling me a story about Luke the other night. It was some match the town team had a few years back – you know, the proper Longhampton RFC team, not the school. They'd lost a couple of players on a stag do. Luke had been in the club bar before the match with his mates – he knew everyone – and Mickey Giles, the captain, wanders in and asks him if he has size-ten feet, as a joke. He said he did, so Mickey chucks Luke some spare boots and asks if he wants to sit on the bench to make up the numbers.'

'And he went on and scored the winning try.'

'Not just the winning try but two tries on top of that.' Jason raised his shoulders, then dropped them. 'I'd never heard that story until the other night. Luke never told me. Mum probably didn't even know. But it's a great story, isn't it? Pulling on his boots and playing. And then just sloping off into the night.'

'On his motorbike.'

'He didn't have a bike. He had a Vauxhall Nova.'

They gazed at each other over the smooth white duvet, as the scene unfolded in Libby's imagination, collaged from family photos and her current Thursday-morning reading of the local paper to learn about her new adopted town. She pictured wiry Luke, a slight figure in mud-streaked shorts, the ragged roars of the scrubby rugby ground down by the station, with its sidings advertising car body shops and local scrap dealers, the blokeish camaraderie afterwards and the mutterings. Luke Corcoran. A wrong'un who tackled like a man twice his size.

Libby hadn't seen Luke since his unfortunate wedding to Suzanne. If Jason had a healthy blond farmer's good looks, Luke was the opposite: smaller, darker, hollow-cheeked, handsome in a watchful, brooding way. If Jason had told her Luke and Suzanne had met in the special forces, not the Mercian Regiment, she wouldn't have been surprised. Maybe they had.

'You know, it's weird,' said Libby. 'We've been married nearly five years and I still don't feel as if I know anything about Luke at all.'

'Welcome to the Corcoran family,' said Jason, and chucked her the used bed linen.

Mr Reynolds didn't get round to Pippa until nearly five, and she was starting to worry that he'd changed his mind about discharging her.

Libby hadn't come back either, and that worried Pippa even more. Everything balanced so delicately on what other people decided; it made her stomach lurch every time she heard someone coming down the corridor towards her room.

In the end, they both arrived at the same time, Libby with a bag of clothes, and Jonathan Reynolds with some forms, some leaflets and a nurse holding a bag of prescription medication.

'We'll see you next week,' he said, once he'd run through the discharge procedure and the exercises he wanted her to do to coax back her memory. He tapped the forms with his pen. 'Things will be mending, even if you can't feel it. It's always fascinating to see how different patients' recovery arcs are. Hopefully those vague memories we managed to touch on will slowly knit together with more over the next few days. Don't worry if you never remember the accident, though.'

'I'm glad to be fascinating,' said Pippa, 'but I'm kind of looking forward to being normal again.'

'I'm sure it won't be long.' He looked round. 'Ah, your friend is here. Very good. I'll leave you to it.'

Once he and the nurse had left, Libby came in, bearing a bag. Again Pippa thought it said more about Libby than the clothes inside did: it was a big yellow one from Selfridges, the stiff paper kind that had obviously once held a pair of boots or a large handbag. Interesting that she'd kept it, not chucked it away.

'I brought a few things,' she said. 'I thought we were roughly the same size.'

'I don't know about that!' Pippa laughed. 'You're much thinner than me.'

'Do you think so? I'd say you were smaller, if anything. We're about the same height, but . . .' Libby didn't seem to be being overly modest.

Pippa looked down at her own wrists. They were thin,

knobbly. And her arms were also thinner than she felt they were in her head. She felt bigger than this.

Could you do that? Could all those ridiculous Hollywood films have a grain of truth – get knocked unconscious and wake up in someone else's brain? Sometimes her dreams felt as if they were someone else's, but not while she was having them, only when she had a tangential reminder about them during the day. Hers and yet not hers.

Pippa shut her eyes tightly. Things were definitely starting to move behind the dark curtain in her head, as if her brain was trying to fit things together. Slowly, piece by piece. And yet nothing firm. Nothing she could close her hand on.

'I just brought some loose yoga things,' Libby went on, 'so it doesn't hurt your ribs. There's a vest and a wrap top, and whatever.' She pulled some grey jersey things out of the bag and draped them on the bed. 'There. See what fits. It's quite warm outside. Summer's on the way!'

'That's so kind,' she said, touching the soft fabric. As she moved the top, she saw Libby had discreetly hidden some underwear in the folds, a pair of knickers and vest with a shelf bra inside. Thoughtful.

Libby smiled, pleased. 'No problem. I just thought earlier the only thing that made me feel halfway human when I had my gall bladder out was my cashmere pyjamas. Anyway, I'll let you get changed and I suppose we'll make a move. If you're ready?'

'Yes, all signed out.' Pippa pointed to the pile of papers on her bedside table.

They looked at each other, conscious of the oddness of the situation.

Why do I feel I can trust Libby? Pippa thought. What is it

about her that makes me relax, as if she knows me? Is it because she seems to trust me, whoever I am?

I hope she can trust you, said a voice in her head, and she pushed it away.

Libby drove like she talked: quickly and enthusiastically, and with a disregard for amber lights.

'. . . so touch wood, the builders will be arriving at the start of the week. I'll try to keep things quiet for you.'

'Please don't worry.' Pippa stared at the scenery as they drove through Longhampton; none of it was familiar. 'I don't want to be in the way.'

'You won't, honestly. We don't have enough guests at the moment for anyone to be in the way of anything.'

They were leaving the town now, heading away from its red bricks and charity shops, out towards the fields and trees of the countryside, but before they'd gone much further, Libby went quiet and slowed down.

'Do you . . . ?' she began. 'I mean, this is . . .'

Pippa saw the painted sign indicating the Swan Hotel was up ahead and she realised that this must be where the accident had happened. The bend, the road, the big trees overhanging the road, the stone wall running alongside on the left . . .

She racked her brain for a memory, but there was nothing. Not even a worrying blank, just nothing. Without speaking, she shook her head.

'Probably a good thing,' said Libby, and indicated to turn into the car park.

The Swan Hotel was nice but somehow smaller than Pippa had imagined from Libby's bag and accent and general appearance; it was a solid, ivy-covered, three-storey Georgian house, with four ground-floor large sash windows, two either side of the front door.

Not smaller, she corrected herself, as she got out of the car, but warmer. Friendlier. Tweedy and cosy, rather than the slick London boutique-style place she'd assumed it'd be.

'It's all a bit of a mess,' Libby went on, escorting her over the gravel drive. 'And I warn you now – my mother-in-law seems to have this fantasy that the hotel is actually in the Scottish Highlands, so if you're allergic to tartan, you'd better hold your breath.'

Someone was waiting at the front door, standing between the pillars: a small, brown-haired woman in a tweed skirt and beige jumper. As they came nearer, she lifted a hand in welcome and smiled.

'Hello, Margaret!' called Libby, then added, 'Oh, watch out, Pippa – he's a licker . . .'

A low-slung dog came trotting out from behind Margaret and made straight for them, a black basset hound with ears that nearly touched the ground. He headed for Pippa, but she wasn't scared; a funny feeling of comfort came over her, and she bent down, cautiously on account of her sore ribs, and let him sniff her hand with his leathery nose. She could feel the air moving with each powerful sniff; it was a curiously intimate sensation, the dog analysing her in ways she couldn't know, drawing his own complex conclusions with each inhalation.

'Hello,' she said, as the huge black nose inspected her fingers, then her arm. The white-tipped tail swept from side to side happily. 'Who are you?'

'Lord Bob Corcoran, but you can call him Bob,' said Libby. 'Or You Bloody Animal, which is what I call him. We're great friends.'

Pippa stroked Bob's majestic head and gazed into his funny-sad face. 'You are a very handsome man,' she told him, and his deep brown eyes seemed to smile.

'Blimey, that is the calmest I've seen him outside the hospital,' said Libby. 'You obviously smell of the PAT ward. He's automatically therapising you.'

'No, I'm good with dogs,' said Pippa, without thinking. When Libby didn't reply, she looked up, to see her pointing a knowing finger, her face wreathed in smiles. 'What?'

'You're good with dogs. That's a memory, right? A memory!'

'Oh yes.' Pippa stopped, her hand shaped to the curve of Bob's skull. 'It is.' She tried to pin it down – which dog? When? A childhood dog? A friend's? A recent one? – but the sensation slid away.

Libby looked pleased. 'Margaret will love that – Bob bringing your memory back. She's already convinced he's a better therapist than most of the nurses. Margaret! This is Pippa. Pippa, Margaret.'

The older lady had approached across the gravel and now she held out a hand. 'Hello, Pippa. So pleased you've made it here at last. Just a week late, eh?'

There was a twinkle in her eye that surprised Pippa; she hadn't expected it, after the way Libby had spoken about her mother-in-law. For some reason, she'd been expecting someone older, sadder. This lady was quite spry and friendly, her outfit toning, and finished with a scarf.

'Thank you very much for letting me stay,' she said. 'I'm so grateful.'

'Not at all! You're most welcome, Pippa. Come on in. I've made some tea.' Margaret gestured towards the hall with a gracious sweep of her hand and Pippa found herself being drawn in.

The dog, Bob, followed Margaret into the hotel, and Libby and Pippa trailed after them both. Pippa's first impressions of the place were borne out when she got inside: the place smelled like someone's grandparents' house; the air was musty with potpourri, and dark polished furniture, and dusty carpets, and slightly saggy sofas that dogs had been napping on when they shouldn't. The sort of hotel you'd book into for a wedding nearby, one that served a huge English breakfast and had old copies of *Country Life* going back to the 1980s.

The reception was dark – the rampant tartan Libby had warned her about wasn't quite as bad as she'd expected, being limited to the Black Watch carpet – but it was cosy, and old-fashioned. A good-looking man in a blue checked shirt stood behind a polished oak reception counter, deep in discussion with someone on the phone – an old black phone, which fitted the country-house style. He was cradling his head in his hand, one elbow on the counter, and he was drilling a pen into the side of his head. When they came in, he stood up and made 'Sorry, sorry!' gestures at the phone.

'Absolutely, Marek . . . No, won't be a problem. Eight o'clock . . . OK, listen, I'll have to go . . .'

Pippa guessed it must be Jason: he was so exactly what she'd expected Libby's husband to look like that it made her wonder if maybe she *had* been here before. He was tall, broad-shouldered and handsome – blond hair, lightly tanned face, an even white smile that suggested he'd worn braces as a teenager.

The reception area seemed to close in as Pippa stared at him, trying to pin down the strange sense of having seen him before, until she had to look away when his smile grew a little fixed. He *was* familiar, she thought, her heartrate surging.

Wasn't he? That face was somewhere in the jumbled, locked filing cabinets of her memory, but she didn't know where, or how, or . . .

Exhaustion caught up with her and she felt Libby's arm round her waist. Steadying her.

'Tea!' she said, and led her through to the lounge.

Chapter Nine

The builders arrived on Monday morning at eight o'clock on the dot, while Libby was coordinating two poached eggs and some toast for the nice Irish couple in room four (no dog), and Jason was restacking the dishwasher according to his preferred formula, while trying to stop Lord Bob pre-cleaning the plates.

'The cavalry is here,' Jason announced, peering out of the kitchen window. 'Blimey, Marek's sent an entire unit.'

'Let me see.' Libby put the timer on the windowsill and came to look.

They watched as the building team disembarked from the black van parked up next to their Irish guests' hire car – the only one in the car park apart from theirs. Libby felt a frisson of excitement mingled with a shiver of trepidation. Something about builders' ability to reduce a room to bare-bricked chaos within minutes, leave it naked and vulnerable for weeks on end and then restore it apparently overnight, with the added frisson that they could leave at any moment for a 'rush job in Beckenham'.

'How did they get so many of them in there?' Jason marvelled, as one builder after another emerged from the back, all wearing Marek's black polo shirts. 'It's like a circus van of builders.'

'How many has he sent? Seven, eight, nine . . . Blimey.'

Jason reached for his checklist, room by room, of the work they'd agreed on. 'I hope at least one of them speaks English. This would be a very good time for Pippa to remember she's some sort of translator.' He took a last slurp of coffee. 'Is she up yet?'

'No, she's sleeping.'

Pippa had slept most of the weekend, which Libby thought was probably a good thing: she still looked exhausted, with dark circles under her eyes, and big bruises, now turning a sickly yellowy-green, on her pale skin. Despite being in some pain from her ribs, she'd been a model guest, making endless conversation with a pleasingly perked-up Margaret about her garden (and her dog, and Longhampton, and Donald, and all the other things Jason and Libby had had to hear a lot of) and had offered to help Libby and Jason shift furniture out of the bedrooms, in preparation for the workmen's arrival.

Libby had said no, of course. 'But you must wander around,' she told her. 'See if anything comes back to you.'

Later, on her way to make everyone some tea after a hard afternoon moving old beds, Libby had spotted Pippa tucked up on a sofa in the residents' lounge, busily writing things down in her notebook. Her dark head was bent, and her legs were curled underneath her. Lord Bob was sprawled up against her slim calves, using them as an armrest. Pippa didn't seem to mind, and occasionally her hand would reach out and absent-mindedly fondle his big ears.

I wonder what she's writing, Libby had thought. What's she noticing about us? And the hotel – what's she seeing here? Libby hoped she was doing her best impression of a confident manager, but when Pippa looked at her with those perceptive brown eyes, she worried that the real Libby was showing through: the Wandsworth wife who didn't quite fit in with the others, the hotel owner who didn't totally understand VAT. Something about the squint of concentration in Pippa's expression, her need to extract the tiniest clue from everything in order to work out who *she* was, made Libby more conscious of herself at the same time.

She's not writing about you, Libby had told herself sharply. She's writing about herself, who she is.

And she'd pulled on a smile and poked her head round to offer Pippa some tea.

'I said I'll go and see to the builders,' Jason repeated, as if talking to a very old or very deaf person.

'What? Sorry, I was miles away.'

'I know. Imagining your beautiful new bathrooms?' He handed her the mug to put in the dishwasher – his faded Longhampton FC one. 'Or trying to work out how many boxes of builder's tea to get at the wholesaler?'

'Something like that,' said Libby. She grinned, unable to contain her excitement. 'It's really happening, isn't it?'

Jason grabbed her arms and gave her a swift, soft kiss on the forehead as he went. 'Exciting times, Mrs Corcoran! Our hotel!'

Libby smiled, and her earlier trepidation vanished under Jason's infectious enthusiasm. *Our hotel*.

Libby spent the morning in the office, sorting through a drawer of unopened paperwork that had come to light when Jason was dealing with the accounts at the weekend, and at eleven, Pippa knocked on the door frame, her brown hair still damp from the shower.

'No,' said Libby, before she could speak, 'there is nothing you should be doing to help. Apart from sitting in that chair over there and making me a cup of coffee every half an hour. If you want to tell me every so often you can't hear a thing going on upstairs, I'd appreciate it.'

'Are you sure I couldn't . . . ?'

'Sit,' she insisted. 'Please.'

'Let me make some fresh coffee,' said Pippa, spotting her empty mug on the pile of council tax arrears, and the machine on the filing cabinet. 'You look like you could do with some.'

They'd barely got settled down again – Libby to the paper-work, Pippa to her notebook – when Jason came in, and something in his manner set Libby's nerves jangling. There was no smile in his eyes, and his mouth was set; that morning's exuberance had vanished behind a very grey cloud of visible stress.

'Libby, can I have a word?' he said. 'I need to ask you some-thing.' He glanced between her and Pippa. 'Um, it's about the building work.' He gestured with his head towards the door, and the hotel beyond.

'What? Now? This minute?'

'Yes, now,' said Jason. 'If you don't mind.'

Libby pushed back her chair. 'Won't be a second, Pippa,' she said. 'If the phone rings, can you answer it and take a message?'

She followed Jason out into the reception, but he carried on walking towards the empty lounge. 'What's up?' she said. 'Has Bob been doing his own redecorating work upstairs again?'

'No.' Jason checked there was no one in the lounge, then perched on the arm of a big chesterfield sofa. Libby hesitated, then sat down opposite.

'Jason? Are you all right? Is everything OK?'

'Everything's fine.' He smiled, but he didn't seem entirely relaxed. Then he ran a hand through his thatch of hair and her heart sank. 'Babe, I need you to do us a favour.'

'OK,' said Libby slowly. 'Go on.'

'You know you said that we might be able to ask your dad to invest some money in the business?'

At the words 'your dad' and 'money', Libby's heart sank even further. 'In an emergency, maybe. Not as a choice, though. I'd rather look into selling a kidney. There'd be fewer strings involved.'

'Really? Even if it was a proper investment? Now he knows we're going to be featured in a magazine and will be *the* boutique hotel of the area in six months' time?' He frowned. 'You're his daughter. This is a family business.'

'And that,' Libby replied, 'shows how well you know my dad.' For a couple who'd been together as long as she and Jason had, they still had a lot to learn about each other's families. Or maybe up until now they'd been able to stay a good distance away from them.

'Bear in mind we're talking about the man who still jokes' – she added air hooks to the word 'jokes' – 'about how my sister should pay back her university fees after she dropped out of college with an eating disorder after her parents' acrimonious divorce? Sarah doesn't live in Hong Kong for no reason, you know.'

'Well, fine.' Jason looked chastened; he liked Sarah – they'd spent part of their honeymoon in Hong Kong. 'But it depends how much you want to refit the en suites.'

That brought Libby up short. 'What? I thought you said we had enough to do all this?'

'I did.' Jason rubbed his chin. 'And we do. But the estimate's suddenly gone up by another fifteen grand. I've just spoken to Marek's foreman and he says we need to redo the plumbing if we want the new showers to run properly – that damp Marek could smell is coming from the old pipes leaking. Finding it and fixing it's going to be another week's work minimum, plus materials. On top of that, I spoke to the bathroom suppliers and they want a deposit before they'll put the order for baths through.' He turned his hands over helplessly. 'You know how little we've been taking, so some cash has gone on day-to-day costs, and the bulk of the house equity's tied up in other accounts. We need cash *now*. This week.'

'Oh.' Libby felt a stab of guilt: she had gone slightly over-board with the baths, but they were going to be a feature, something that would sell the whole hotel. 'Can't we talk to the bank? Can they do a short-term loan?'

'I'd rather not go to the bank. We've only just got things back on an even footing there. And I'm not sure they'd lend us what we need that quickly. They've seen the books.' Jason fiddled with the dried-up head of a thistle in one of the flower arrangements, then looked up at her. 'They're not very risk-happy out here.'

'I know. I was in that meeting.' The bank manager had been an old friend of Donald's. He hadn't exactly told them they were idiots for wanting to renovate the Swan, but there was a lot of bushy-eyebrow-raising and muttering about ambitious London folk he'd known make terrible losses, over-investing in country pubs in the area. They'd assured him that there was no way they'd be making those mistakes, oh no.

'Although . . .' he paused, and his voice when he spoke again was different. More guarded, but at the same time, more confi-dent, 'there is another option.'

'Which is?'

Jason's eyes warned her not to snap. 'Darren called me last week.'

'Darren from Harris Hebden? I didn't think you were still in touch with those guys.'

Jason hadn't exactly been marched through the office with his desk contents in a box, but the lack of a typical boozy leaving-do hadn't gone unnoticed. He'd had lots of friends at work. Everyone had loved Jason at Harris Hebden. Up to a point.

'Course I'm still in touch with Darren. And Tim. I worked with *those guys* for seven years.' He crossed his arms defensively. 'Anyway, Darren called the other day to give me a heads-up on an oilfields deal he's putting together. Quick turnaround, low—'

Libby didn't want to hear any more. Her hand flew up to stop him, before she even knew what she was doing. 'No, Jason, please. Don't. You promised. This is our future. Your *mother*'s future.'

'There's no need to be dramatic,' he said tetchily. 'Darren wanted to help me out, that's all. It's not a risky deal – he's getting into it himself. And he's got four kids.'

'But you *promised*.' She could hear it now, in her head: Darren – nice guy but a wide boy and proud of it – offering a taste of the old excitement, the easy multiplication of imaginary cash, all done with a click of the mouse at the right moment. And Jason, she knew, would have found it hard to say no. That had been his reputation in the office: his instinct for an opening.

Libby had loved how good Jason was at his job: he had the perfect blend of pragmatism, diligence, client skills and sheer luck. In the time they'd been together, he'd grown from an eager trainee into a seasoned, confident operator, the golden country tan turning into a Verbier and Maldives glow. He often explained what he did, but she'd never completely understood the markets: Libby's mind worked with people, faces, anecdotes, not figures. At first, its ever-shifting rewards and shocks, rising and falling like a powerful, international tide, excited her, then frightened her; then she'd taken it for granted.

And now the tide was licking at their toes again here. In the place they'd come to escape its seductive ebb and flow.

Jason rolled his eyes, an impatient gesture Libby hadn't seen in a while, and without warning, the physical taste of the day he lost his job flooded back: the fresh-paint smell of their new kitchen, Jason at the table, his face bloated, eyes scared, his loud tie halfway down his shirt looking sickeningly like a Hermès noose, the sour tang of the wine she'd drunk at lunch with Erin repeating in her throat as she struggled to understand his broken half-sentences. The truth about his own trading slipped out painfully. It was only when Libby logged into their online banking and saw her modest savings account had been wiped to zero that the extent of Jason's gambling suddenly sank in. Those few thousand had been real, in a way the bonus nest egg had never been, and they were gone. No job, no salary. No salary, no mortgage. No mortgage, no house ... ? And then the ripples had spread from Jason's laptop to their home, to his office. And then finally to their happy, careless world, washing everything away.

They'd gone from a flat in Acton to a villa in Wandsworth almost overnight, and Libby had worried that their new world could vanish just as suddenly; then, almost as soon as she stopped worrying, it did.

Jason opened his mouth to speak, and the thought filled

Libby's head like a shout. No. That is not coming back into this life.

'You promised me,' she repeated. *Don't shout, Dad shouted.* 'It's the only thing I asked, that you wouldn't take any more financial risks.'

'I hear what you're saying, but I think you're over-reacting. This is a few grand, Libby. And I know what I'm doing – I'm not some spare-room hobbyist with his PC and his copy of *Investing for Dummies*.'

'It doesn't matter how much it is – the stakes are totally different now! We can't afford to lose.' She fixed her gaze straight at him, willing him to understand that it wasn't just about the money. 'I need to know exactly where I stand. With our finances, with the hotel . . . with you.'

It was the first time since they'd left London that she'd brought up his sacking and their debts. After that surreal afternoon, they'd dealt with the immediate fallout in a kind of efficiency trance, not unlike the brisk to-do list that had got Jason through Donald's funeral a few months earlier. What they hadn't talked about, not properly, was what the betrayal had done to their relationship, once the floods had receded and they were left, exhausted and suspicious, surrounded by wreckage, with everything changed. Jason had been ashen with shame; Libby hadn't wanted to kick him when he was so down.

But we need to be able to talk about this kind of thing if our marriage is going to work, she thought. Jason had always been so sensitive to her feelings; why couldn't he see how this bothered her? Libby knew on one level he was right – the deal probably would work out – but this was about Jason listening to her, rebuilding her trust, or else she'd never be able to stop worrying when this new life, with its risks, might all collapse too.

'So what's the answer?' he said flatly. 'You don't want to ask your dad. You won't let me speak to Darren. We can't go to the bank. Your mum has no money; neither does mine. We *need* to pay for this plumbing – it's not an option. And we need the money *now*. This week.'

'Why don't we ask Luke?'

Jason looked twitchy. 'You know why not. Mum made a huge deal about only working with us in the hotel. She doesn't want Luke involved. And we don't have time for the painful Family Talk that would entail . . .'

Libby took a deep breath and tried to order her thoughts. Already she felt bad about challenging Jason on the one area of their marriage he'd always managed so well. At least, for most of their marriage. Maybe I'm making this worse, she thought glumly. I've forbidden him to trade, the one way he had of earning, I can't support us, and we need the money for the hotel, for our new start together.

'Right.' She readied herself. 'I'll speak to my dad. Do you think we should email him a proposal first?'

Jason's face registered surprise, then relief. Libby didn't want to look too closely at the relief. 'I don't think there's time. Marek wants the starting payment today, and I've got to pay the bathroom suppliers.'

There was another long pause, and Libby felt as if the hotel were looming over them both, its heavy hand on their shoulders. The ticking clock, the smell of the old carpet, the endless dusty wood wherever she looked.

She pushed her hair behind her ears. 'Fine. But we have to prioritise repaying him even if it means eating nothing but porridge for the next year.'

Jason reached for her hand. Libby let him take it and he

slowly raised it to his lips and kissed the back of her fingers, keeping his gaze fixed on her.

'What?' she asked.

'Thanks,' he said. 'I know this is a big thing for you. I appreciate it.'

'If it's what we have to do . . .' Libby didn't expect the ripple that ran through her, as if they were both standing at the edge of a cliff. This was it, from now on. Every time they made a decision, it seemed to raise the stakes one more notch. But it would be worth it, she told herself. This was a future built on something solid.

She squeezed his fingers. 'Just go and make me a strong cup of coffee. No, actually. Make me a gin and tonic.'

'So,' said Colin Davies, when he picked up the phone on the second ring, 'it's not my birthday, and it's not your birthday, so how much do you need?'

Libby reminded herself that her dad always started phone calls like that – it was the joke of his friends that he was 'plain-spoken'. Normally she was only ringing for a dutiful monthly catch-up, but now she had a favour to ask, she felt even more on the back foot. When she was a teenager needing a pocket-money advance, he'd made her feel like one of his useless junior solicitors asking for a raise; now she was a grown-up, he made her feel like a teenager.

Still, if he wanted to be plain-spoken, she could be too.

'Hello, Dad,' she said. 'Is this a good time to chat? I was hoping I could ask you something about the hotel.'

'Ah, so you do want something. Well, out with it. I was on my way out to the tip.'

'Right.' It sounded as if he'd just had words with Sophie, her stepmother. Arguments in the Davies household were often punctuated with some ruthless recycling, one of the reasons her mother had finally filed for divorce: the junking of their wedding albums. That and the demands for receipts and teabag reuse and the screaming rows. 'I'll get to the point. Jason and I are making some substantial upgrades to the hotel over the next few months and—'

'You want Daddy to pay for them.'

'No, not at all.' Libby gripped her pen and stared at the figures Jason had given her, as well as the handy phrases she'd jotted down. Her mind tended to go blank during conversations with her father. 'We just need a sort of bridging loan, to get some initial renovation work underway. Obviously we'd pay you back with interest, and a fixed repayment time frame.'

She hoped he wasn't going to push her too hard on those details. Not that Libby didn't want to pay the controlling sod interest, but she didn't put it past him to 'test' her on the technicalities. Since he retired, on his generous civil service pension, he'd got even more into investing; it was one of the reasons he and Jason used to get on so well, and he'd shamelessly squeezed Jason for share tips. Not that they'd had many of those conversations latterly.

'Sounds very official,' he said. 'Would it be easier if I talked to Jason about this? Without wishing to be rude, Libby, you've got your mother's brain when it comes to figures.'

'No, Jason's dealing with the builders right now. I'm happy to discuss this with you. I'm an equal partner in the business.'

And a graduate who had an enviable media job until two years ago and did manage to pay off the one credit-card debt every student racks up . . .

Colin let out an amused noise that made Libby squirm, even though she angrily told herself not to.

'How much are we talking about, then?'

She glanced down at Jason's notes and told him. The sharp intake of breath would have been the same had she said twenty quid or two million.

'That's quite a substantial sum, Elizabeth. What are you doing, gold-plating the taps?'

'No, just some overdue updating. We're bringing the hotel into line with modern expectations, so we can start marketing to a broader clientele. When we've got things going, we're looking into wine tastings, small weddings, maybe a spa . . .'

'Not my sort of place, then.'

'Of course it'll be your sort of place!' Just be interested. Please. Stop trying to come out on top.

He chuckled. 'With the best will in the world, I doubt it. And is there a reason you're approaching the Bank of Dad and not the actual bank? This is definitely for the hotel, and not some personal debt you'd rather not go into?'

'Of course it's for the hotel.' Libby's nails were digging into her other palm. 'I thought you might enjoy being involved in our new project.'

This is mad, she thought. Surely the normal way for this conversation to go would be for the father to phone the *daughter* to offer to help her out of the financial crisis her reckless husband had got her into? *Let us tide you over. Let us help you get back on your feet. You're being really brave and we're proud of your fighting spirit.*

Although that assumed the father was aware that the daughter was in financial crisis. Colin was yet another person under the impression that she and Jason had downsized for the love of hotel-keeping. Libby knew she'd never have heard the end of it if he'd had the full story, and somehow, once the shabby truth was laid out, it'd probably have ended up being her fault, somehow – ditzy Libby who hid credit-card statements for one credit card, ten years ago.

After a long pause that he'd learned from television talent shows, Colin cleared his throat. 'Fine,' he said. 'Let me have a think about the amount I'd be willing to advance you. But for heaven's sake, Libby, don't think you can make a habit of this. If you're going to go into business, you've got to be scrupulous with money. Scrupulous and honest. I'm surprised Jason hasn't been through all this with you.'

'He has,' said Libby, through gritted teeth. 'And thanks, Dad. I really appreciate this.'

As she put down the phone, her skin still crawling with the shame of begging her own father for help, Jason appeared at the door. He was carrying another large gin and tonic, and when he saw she'd finished the conversation, he came in and handed it to her.

He didn't say anything, but raised an eyebrow.

'He's going to lend us some money,' she said, and before Jason could cheer, she added, 'And just so you know, I am never, ever, *ever* going to do that again. So please, spend it very wisely.'

'I will,' said Jason. 'Well done.'

Libby sank her nose into the glass and took a long drink. She totally understood now why her mother had formed such a close personal relationship with the drinks cabinet.

Chapter Ten

'Well, this is most time efficient,' said Margaret happily, settling into the front seat of Libby's car while Libby and Pippa heaved Lord Bob and his various accoutrements into the boot. 'Fitted in very nicely, didn't it? Your hospital appointment, Pippa, Bob's therapy session and Elizabeth's PAT assessment with Gina.'

Libby concentrated on reversing round the builders' van, parked in the most inconvenient place on the drive. She was glad to be getting out, even if it was to ferry everyone back up to the hospital. After only three days, the hotel was fully under siege to Marek's black-polo-shirted army. All the rooms bar the one they'd renovated were emptied of furniture and shrouded with dust sheets, and wheelbarrows full of wallpaper peelings and piles of dust were rolling steadily down the plastic-sheeting aisle, through the reception and out to a skip that had arrived overnight.

Jason was excited about the skip. He'd already thrown some of their own junk into it, just because he could. 'Just think,' he'd told her, as they stacked the breakfast dishwasher, 'if we were back in London, that skip would already be half full of everyone else's crap by now.'

'Is that what it's come to?' Libby had asked. 'Celebrating the fact that we get our skip to ourselves?'

'You've got to take your pleasures where you find them, babe,' Jason had replied with a beatific smile. Just as Margaret had brightened up now she had Pippa to feed soup to and fuss over, Jason had been in a much-improved mood ever since Colin had transferred £20,000 into the hotel bank account the previous night. He'd vanished into the office and started doing all sorts of calculations, emerging much later with a revised timetable of deliveries and a bottle of wine from the hotel cellar to celebrate.

Libby wasn't so sure he ought to be celebrating. She had a feeling the shoe still had to drop on her dad's generosity. Something about it made her uneasy.

'Ah, don't be grumpy. Just think of your baths. They're on their way!' Jason grinned, and Libby reflected that while she felt more ragged every day, between the tan, the rolled-up sleeves and the two nights a week – at least – he was spending either training or down the pub with his mates, Jason had the look of a man on holiday.

'Why don't we award ourselves a coffee and a slice of cake afterwards?' Margaret went on. 'There's a lovely café in the High Street that's very dog-friendly – I don't suppose you know it, Pippa?' she added, over her shoulder.

'Not yet,' said Pippa politely.

'Have you been, Elizabeth?'

'I haven't really had a lot of time for visiting cafés,' she said, then, because she didn't want to sound martyred in front of Pippa, added, 'But I've been meaning to try out some of the places in town. I'm updating the welcome pack for the rooms – did you know some of the pubs and cafés we're recommending guests eat at have closed down?'

The nice Irish couple had told her that. So had one less nice couple on TripAdvisor.

'Really? Oh. That's a shame. Then we *must* go to the Wild Dog,' said Margaret. 'I insist. Bob's treat.'

'You could do a special guide on your website for the canine guests,' said Pippa, from the back. 'Where to take your owner for a walk while you're staying at the hotel, finishing in a café where you can both get something to drink.'

'What a charming idea!' exclaimed Margaret. 'Did you hear that, Bob?'

'Maybe Bob could write it?' Pippa suggested. '"Lord Bob's Dog Guide to Longhampton."'

What? That was *too far*. Libby glanced in her rear-view mirror to catch Pippa's eye and saw the innocent glitter in it. Pippa was hunched in the small back seat, with Lord Bob's head stuck through the headrests next to her. Bob didn't look conspiratorial. He was drooling unconcernedly onto the back of Margaret's seat. Libby was very glad Jason wasn't there to see.

Pippa opened her eyes in a 'What?' expression. In the five days she'd been staying at the hotel, she'd started to look more like how Libby assumed she did normally: pink-cheeked, cheerful, even mischievous. Pippa seemed determined to help, in whatever small ways she could. Cups of tea, phones answered and messages taken, a well-timed comment that defused a touchy atmosphere.

It made it all the more baffling to Libby that there weren't hordes of friends missing her – but apparently the police still hadn't managed to connect her with missing person reports.

She returned the smile. 'What are you seeing the consultant for today?'

'Not the consultant, some other therapist,' said Pippa. 'She's going to try hypnotherapy, to see if that helps.' She looked doubtful. 'It might work. I feel things are getting looser – you know, like when a tooth's coming out? One good session might do the trick.'

'Fingers crossed, dear,' said Margaret, and Libby murmured in agreement; even though she wasn't in a hurry to lose her company in the hotel, she obviously wanted Pippa's life to restart properly.

Libby parked in a space allocated for visitors and set about wrangling Bob into his official Pets As Therapy harness. Today, to please Margaret, she'd agreed to undergo an assessment as a PAT dog companion, so she could take Bob up there when Margaret was indisposed. Which Libby privately hoped would be never.

He gazed nobly into the middle distance as Libby adjusted the straps and permitted himself one atrociously pungent pre-performance fart, which the three of them pretended not to notice.

'You'll be a good boy for Libby, won't you?' Margaret instructed him. 'No pulling or messing about. Not that you would.'

'Yes, you tell him, Margaret,' said Libby. 'No carrying on, Bob.'

'You've got the emergency cheese? If he needs distracting?'

Margaret insisted Bob understood English. Libby knew he only spoke the language of cheese. She patted her pocket. 'Cheddar *and* Stilton.'

'And I'll be there, of course. In the background. But don't let him get too close to Bert Carter. He smells of cats.' Margaret dropped her voice. 'Even now.'

Libby nodded and tried to remember who Bert Carter was. The idea of today was that Margaret would introduce her to the volunteer organiser, Gina, who would then watch her with Lord Bob as he offered himself to the patients for patting, tickling and chatting, to check that she had him fully under control at all times. Libby was the one under assessment. Bob's credentials were impeccable.

Pippa gave Bob a quick ear scratch, then stood up.

'Where shall I meet you afterwards?' she asked. 'My appointment's at half twelve and I guess it'll be an hour or so.'

As she said that, a shadow passed over her face and Libby patted her arm. 'Don't worry, we'll wait. You've got my mobile. If your appointment finishes early or overruns, call me. And call me if you want me to be there with you – I don't mind.'

'It's fine.' Pippa managed a smile. 'I don't want to cut into your dog time.'

Libby glanced at Margaret and Bob, now both ready for the off. 'No chance of that,' she said.

Gina, the PAT coordinator, was not the mad old dog lady in a hairy fleece Libby had assumed she'd be. Instead, she saw a woman a few years older than herself, with a short dark pixie cut, warm brown eyes and a solemn greyhound with white spots sprinkled delicately over his grey haunches like snowflakes. Like Bob, he wore a bright yellow Pets As Therapy coat, but underneath it Libby could make out a colourful embroidered martingale collar round his broad neck.

They made a stylish couple, she thought. Maybe you *could* have a dog and not be condemned to a life of fleece.

Lord Bob greeted both Gina and the greyhound as if they were at a smart canine cocktail party: gentle sniffs, casual wag of the tail, 'You sit . . . No, you sit' routine, which the greyhound lost by sitting down first, with an elegant sigh.

Gina shook Libby's hand and a kind-hearted smile lit up her face. 'Thanks so much for volunteering,' she said. 'It's wonderful what a difference a PAT visit makes to the patients – it seems to take them somewhere else. And Bob's such a favourite. They'll be thrilled if he has an extra helper!'

They glanced over to where Margaret and Bob were talking to an elderly man with liver-spotted hands and rheumy eyes. When Bob approached, Libby saw the man's face suddenly engage, and he leaned down to touch Bob's brown-speckled nose, mumbling animatedly to him, although the words weren't clear. Bob gazed solemnly up at him, his tail sweeping in a gentle, friendly arc as if in response to the man's babbling.

'The nurses tell me Ernest barely moves most of the day,' said Gina. 'He just sits and stares out of the window. But when Bob or the other PAT dogs come round, something clicks on inside him. Talks about the dog he used to have when he was a boy. Comes out with some lovely stories.'

Libby laid her hand on the greyhound's narrow head. He went very still, but let her stroke the soft skin behind his ears. She noticed one of his velvety ears was shorter than the other, as if a piece was missing.

'Who's this?' she asked.

'This is Buzz.' Gina touched his neck and he leaned into her without turning his head. 'Buzz is really my own therapy dog. I adopted him about two years ago, when I was going through a bad time. Well, we were both having a bad time, weren't we?' She scratched behind his short ear. 'We got through it together. There's something about dogs – they live in the moment, so you slow down too and appreciate the small things. And they're lovely company.'

'That's what Margaret says,' said Libby. 'Bob was a great

comfort when my father-in-law died. I can forgive him quite a lot for that,' she confessed, in an undertone. 'Bob was there when my husband and I couldn't be. I think those big ears probably mopped up a fair few tears.'

Gina nodded, as if she understood. 'They listen in a way humans can't. And they never try to give you advice. Buzz listens for some of the kids at the primary school. He's a reading dog.'

'He can read?'

She laughed. 'No, the kids read to him. Shy ones love it – he puts his paw on the page they're reading from. He loves it too. That's what's so great about this programme: everyone seems to get something from it. Buzz had a horrible start in life, but now he's happy, it's as if he wants to give something back by coming along and doing this. I helped him and now he's helping other people. And the hospital's been very good to me too, so we're both paying it forward. Anyway, shall we make a start? Margaret? Would you like to bring Bob over so Libby can take the reins?'

'Of course!' Margaret approached, with Bob at her side, and passed his lead to Libby, as if handing over a ceremonial baton.

Bob looked up at her, and for a second, Libby thought he was about to do something naughty, just to test her. But instead he wagged his tail and stared at an old lady in a nearby chair, who seemed eager to stroke him.

'So, Libby, I'm going to have a boring chat with you while you keep hold of Bob,' said Gina. 'Just to check you've got him under control when nothing interesting is happening. Is that all right?'

This isn't remotely awkward, thought Libby, feeling various

hooded eyes turning towards her and Bob. But she smiled brightly and said, 'What would you like to talk to me about? I can do lots of dull topics. We've got builders in the hotel at the moment. Would you like me to talk to you about dust sheets? And tea?'

'Ah, my specialist subject,' said Gina, making a mark on her clipboard. 'There is literally nothing you can tell me about builders that I haven't learned from personal experience.'

'Are you having work done too?'

'No, I'm a project manager – I spend my entire working day trying to get hold of them. Plumbers are the worst. If there's anything you ever need to ask about builders, including my very controversial top-ten list of local cowboys to avoid, just let me know.'

'Jason hasn't engaged cowboys.' Margaret leaned forward. 'My son is project-managing the renovations and he's hired a team who've worked on various Duchy properties in London.'

Gina glanced between Margaret and Libby. 'Ooh. Really? Posh.'

'Very posh.' For someone who hadn't even wanted the renovations a week ago, Margaret now seemed surprisingly proud of them, Libby thought. Of course, if *Jason* had engaged them . . .

'I don't think Marek has sent the Duchy team to steam off our wallpaper,' she said.

'Margaret, I think to give Libby a proper test with Bob, it might be better if you popped out for ten minutes,' said Gina firmly. 'Why don't you go and get a coffee?'

'Are you sure?'

'If you wouldn't mind?' said Gina. 'We all need to concentrate. Now, Libby,' she said, once Margaret had left the room, with just a few backward glances and waves, 'who would be a good person to chat to?' She glanced around the room. 'Oh! Have you met Doris?'

'Is she the lady who used to be the housekeeper at the Swan?' asked Libby. 'Margaret's mentioned her a few times, yes.'

'She's a character.' Gina raised her finely plucked eyebrows. 'I think Margaret and her husband inherited her with the hotel. She's got plenty of stories about what guests used to get up to in the bad old days. Come and have a chat with her now. She likes Bob. And she'd love to hear what you're doing to the place, I'm sure.'

Libby steered Bob across the day room towards a paisley-covered wing chair by the window. It was only when they were nearly next to it that she realised the chair was occupied by a tiny woman with a pale face, wrinkled like a walnut and topped with a swirl of white hair. She was wearing a turquoise dress and very small lace-up shoes, and she was gazing absorbedly into the middle distance.

'Hello, Doris,' said Gina. 'How are you today? Are you up to having a chat with us?'

The old lady's head turned and Libby was aware of a very sharp pair of pale green eyes fixing on her, then looking down at Bob. The gaze softened noticeably when it reached Bob. 'I'm middling, Gina. As well as can be expected with my lungs. Hello, Bob. Who's this you've brought with you today?'

'I'm Libby Corcoran,' said Libby, offering her hand to shake.

Doris had begun to lean down to offer Bob a pat on the head, but at the mention of Libby's name, she straightened back up to give her a proper look.

'Corcoran? Are you married to one of Margaret and Donald's boys, then?'

'I am.' Libby smiled.

The old lady regarded her. 'Jason, I expect.'

'Yes. How did you know?'

Doris pursed her pink lips. 'You're handling Margaret's precious dog. You'd have to be Jason's wife to do that.'

'It's an honour I'm very aware of,' Libby agreed.

'Libby and her husband have moved back to help Margaret out,' Gina explained. 'Said you had a few stories about the Swan that'd make her hair curl!'

'Now that I have!' But before Doris could elaborate – and she seemed to be relishing the prospect – a nurse came up pushing an empty wheelchair.

'Sorry to interrupt, but I need to steal Doris here away – time for your appointment with the hairdresser! Are you set?'

'Oh, shame! Literal hair curling. Another time, then,' said Gina. 'Now, how about going to talk to Gordon?'

Reluctantly – because she'd rather wanted to hear what Doris had to say about the hotel, and Margaret – Libby adjusted her course and her warm smile for the next elderly man in need of Bob's serene presence.

Pippa sat on the chair in the waiting room with a plastic cup of water and tried to process the last hour.

She couldn't remember much about the hypnosis – ha! Irony! – but Kim the therapist had told her not to worry about that. Her gentle voice had been encouraging, and Pippa had managed to turn off her brain until pictures began to float into her mind of their own accord. It was like being walked slowly along a path that was familiar, if a bit blurry; sometimes, when she tried to get more specific, the ground fell from her feet, leaving her scrabbling and panicky. Then Kim's voice had brought her back, giving her solid factual handrails to grip: the hotel, Libby and Jason, the names of the nurses who'd looked after her. Facts she could trust.

They'd talked through school, her friends, her parents, other things she couldn't remember but which she'd apparently spoken about. It was only when Kim tried to get more recent that the blankness rose up again like a curtain.

'Can you remember the last birthday you celebrated? Maybe you were in London. Maybe you were with friends . . . or a boyfriend?'

The curtain bulged inside Pippa's mind, a sense of something behind it, pushing to be seen, but when she tried to pin down what it was, it fell away out of her grasp.

'Relax,' Kim had said, but the harder she tried, the blanker her brain felt. It made her panic. Then the session had been wound down and she was back in the darkened consulting room.

Pippa sipped the cold water from the fountain, so cold it made her temples ache. Had that been progress? Were the invisible links in her brain starting to click back together? Kim had written a lot down, and assured her that it might all suddenly spring back when she woke up one morning, or if she had that one breakthrough memory, but when Pippa tried to think about what she'd remembered, she felt really, really tired.

Tired, and wary. Even though Kim had been encouraging, Pippa couldn't quite share her positivity. The darkness was stirring, but something about it made her heart flutter in her chest, hard and quick. If she was being honest, Pippa wasn't sure whether she wanted to know what was behind that curtain. Whatever it was, her body didn't seem to want her to remember. And that had to mean something.

Back home, a pleasant peacefulness had fallen over the hotel, the builders having left for the day. It was a warm, light evening and Margaret went out to the garden to do some weeding, while Jason settled himself on the sofa to watch a football match.

Pippa and Libby sat in the kitchen with a glass of wine to celebrate Libby's new status as approved PAT volunteer, talking and flicking through interiors magazines and discussing decoration ideas until at eight o'clock, Jason appeared in the doorway.

'Can someone take Bob out for his constitutional? I don't want to miss the second half . . .' He was already inching backwards.

'I'll go,' said Pippa, pushing back her chair.

'No, I'll come with you,' said Libby. 'Now I'm his official handler. Come on,' she said to Lord Bob, who was affecting sleepy oblivion on the kitchen sofa. 'Out you go.'

No response.

'Come on,' said Libby. 'Is he ignoring me? I mean, is that a sarcastic sleep?'

'Watch this,' said Pippa, and broke a piece of biscuit in half. She said nothing, but put it on the floor just by the side of the sofa where Bob was.

They watched for a moment, then another; then the edge of Bob's nose twitched in the air. Without opening his eyes, he moved his head, locating the biscuit; then, like an omelette being slid out of a pan, he slid precisely off the sofa, snaffling the biscuit as he went, ending up by Pippa's feet, where he shook himself awake. The tremor ran along his long body, finishing with a rapid flick of the tail. The ears were the last to stop shaking.

'You have a knack,' said Jason admiringly. 'Must have had a dog in a previous life.'

'Or even this one,' said Pippa, and felt a strange twitch inside.

They walked out of the hotel, and Libby was about to turn out of the gate towards the footpath that ran behind the building when Pippa felt an impulse to turn the other way. She'd driven past the scene of the accident but hadn't actually stood there since it happened, and suddenly she had an urge to see it.

'Can we?' she said. 'I feel like I want to walk down there.'

Libby stopped trying to drag Lord Bob out of a patch of nettles and looked concerned. 'Are you sure it wouldn't be upsetting?'

Pippa shook her head. 'I want to see. I feel as if something's . . . something's starting to come together. I can't explain.'

There was no pavement, just a grass verge, and they walked slowly down it, listening out for cars, until they reached the spot Libby said she'd found her. Pippa was listening to her own instincts too, trying to feel any flickers inside, but there was nothing, until she heard Libby shout, 'Wait!'

She'd stopped a few metres back and was holding out her hand. Something glinted on her palm: it was a silver shape, a pendant in the form of an 'A', with a strand of broken silver chain still attached.

'Look!' she said excitedly. 'Is this yours? Could it have come off when you were hit by the car?'

Pippa walked back to her and picked up the 'A'. As she touched the cool metal, a shapeless thought bulged in the back of her mind, bigger and bigger, while at the same time a pin-sharp memory appeared, not in her head but somewhere in her chest. The two spread up and out and merged until it wasn't so much a visual memory as a feeling coming back to her, flooding her whole body: of being loved, of being given something precious. She closed her eyes and felt hot tears fill them as she let the memory submerge her.

Of feeling absolutely happy between her mum and her dad, in a booth in a pizza place. The best birthday ever.

'My birthday.' Her voice sounded miles away; she didn't know where it was coming from. 'My mum and dad gave me a special necklace.'

She smelled the pizza, Dad's wool jacket that smelled of their terrier, who sometimes travelled in his pocket, Mum's going-out perfume. A first grown-up birthday lunch, just her and Mum and Dad. *No washing-up!* An ice-cream sundae with two sparklers and the most exciting box in the world, with a white ribbon round it.

'Pippa?' She heard Libby's voice and shook her head. Something was moving up, up, up in her brain, coming into focus, words pushing onto her lips.

'*Pippi*,' she said. 'Dad used to call me his little Pippi. Not Pippa. Pippi Longstocking. I had plaits. Mum used to plait them for me before bed.' She couldn't bear it; somewhere in her chest, somewhere behind her head, she felt the sleepy sensation of Dad's warm weight as he sat reading at the end of her bed, his voice softening, softening as she drifted into sleep, secure and loved. His voice low and clear as if he were speaking to her now.

Night-night, Alice.

It wasn't a voice; it was a feeling in her heart. Tears streamed down her face as a powerful longing swept through her like a gale, rattling her chest, her stomach. It was so real, so physical. The longing to climb into her own head and be in that moment again, with Dad, with Mum just outside the door, waiting to put out the light.

God bless, Alice.

The images were jumbling now, one slipping into another as her memory shot them across her mind. Mum giggling as she Incy Wincy Spidered her fingers up Alice's freckly arm, sun hot on their skin, her short red nails like glossy ladybirds. Alice ached to stretch out and touch her, hug her, one more time, a yearning so hard it took her breath away.

Alice. Alice. She was somebody. She existed. She had an anchor in the world, a past, a history. She was Alice Robinson.

I'm not lost, she thought. I'm Alice. But the relief only lasted a second before the images faded, stuck in their short loop, and pain caught up with her. Dad was gone. Mum was gone. A cold, thin ache wound round her heart, spreading up into her head, as she lost them all over again. The memory was all she had, that look of love, that feeling of warmth and belonging – she'd never touch them, or tell them her secrets, or have fresh memories to replace these.

Alice closed her eyes, desperate to stay in the memory, not see the rough hedgerow, the roadside of the present. Was not knowing this better than the pain of knowing it?

She was someone, but she was no one's. There *was* no one trying to find her. No one. She hadn't realised until then how much she'd secretly hoped there would be.

Alice looked up and saw Libby's excited grin turn to horror when she saw her crumpled, bereft face.

'Pippa?' said Libby. 'Pippa!'

'Alice,' she managed. Then suddenly, she was being crushed into Libby's chest and hugged tightly, and she let herself go at last and cried for the parents who would never come and get her.

Chapter Eleven

Alice and Libby stood for a while by the side of the road, not speaking, until Alice managed to smile through the hiccups. Libby put her arm round her waist and they walked slowly back to the hotel, Bob following obediently on his lead for once.

Libby's concern was touched with barely concealed excitement. 'Now you've got a name, we could be taking you home in the morning!' she said, in her comforting 'everything will be fine' manner. 'Ten minutes on the internet and I bet we'll be able to find out all sorts.'

Alice nodded, but didn't know what to say. Emotions were flying back and forth in her head too fast for her to explain how she felt. She was relieved that her memory was obviously starting to mend, even if it broke her heart to remember and lose her parents like that, but under the relief were other, darker questions.

Why hadn't *everything* come back?

Was her brain prioritising memories? Could it choose what to repair, or was it random?

What if only half her memories were there? Would she have lost half of herself, half of her experiences, half of her life? What if she met people who remembered things about her she couldn't?

And why couldn't she remember anything more recent, like why she was here? With these people who were strangers, but familiar?

Alice shook her pounding head. Stop it, she thought. Stop thinking.

But she couldn't. The idea that her brain was repairing itself freaked her out: the invisible electrical impulses shooting back and forth, mending the bridges, reopening flashes of information? How would she ever know what she was unable to remember . . . if she couldn't remember it?

Alice felt as if she'd got her name back, but not enough else. She was unbalanced, still half in that aching moment, half anxious for the next unexpected lurch forwards.

Libby was too excited to notice her quietness as they pushed open the doors to the reception, the dark furniture shrouded in dust sheets. She took off Lord Bob's lead, shooed him away towards the flat, then took Alice straight into the office.

'You start searching the internet,' she instructed, opening up her laptop, 'and I'll make you a drink and tell Jason the good news.' She clapped her hands. 'Oh my God, I'm so pleased for you, Pip— Alice!' She made a face. '*Alice*. Must get used to that! Do you think we should ring the hospital?'

'It's ten past nine.' Alice couldn't face more questions. More analysis. 'I think it can wait till morning.'

'Yes, of course. You never know, now this has started – you might have a lot more to tell them by morning!'

It's a game to her, Alice thought, smiling back automatically. The final part in a television drama, the happy conclusion.

Libby left, and she faced the laptop, the bland screen that could tell her things about herself she didn't know. Her stomach churned. Come on, Alice told herself. Be brave. What can be worse than remembering your parents are dead?

Alice's fingers hovered over the keys, but she couldn't make them move. After what felt like no time, Libby returned with Jason, and together, they started searching for her life on the internet, while Alice watched, her shaking hands clutched round a hot mug of sweet tea. But it soon became clear that it wasn't going to be that easy.

For a start, there were nearly two hundred thousand results for 'Alice Robinson' on Google. None of them, she noted, were newspaper reports searching for a missing friend.

'Is this you, on LinkedIn?' Libby asked, pointing to the first entry.

That Alice Robinson was about the right age, but she was a political analyst who'd won several industry awards and had qualifications coming out of her ears. For a moment, Alice wished that *was* her, but she knew it wasn't.

'I don't think so. I think I'd remember being that dynamic.'

'You'd also be a long way from home if you were.' Jason pointed out the New York background.

'Ha! Oh yes. I'm glad you're not her, actually. She doesn't look as if she's got many pairs of flip-flops in her wardrobe.' Libby glanced up. 'You were wearing flip-flops when you were run over. You don't remember? In the hospital bag?'

Alice blinked. 'Oh yes.' She'd got so used to wearing Libby's clothes; they fitted her and, more to the point, suited her so well she'd almost forgotten they weren't hers. Her own clothes were somewhere else. Waiting for her, in a wardrobe, every item a clue to her personality.

Libby was clicking on, and on. 'Don't worry – there are loads more Alice Robinsons. Can you remember what sort of job you did? Did you work in an office? Can you remember what you studied at university?'

Had she gone to university? Alice dutifully closed her eyes and tried to picture herself at work. Odd images came back now, as if they'd never been away, but with bits missing – no sound, a blur where names were. It was as if one solid fact had linked another, and another, giving each a foothold in her mind where they'd slipped away before. A crammed Tube carriage at rush hour. Aching feet in stiff court shoes. The wet smell of London at night, summer-evening drinkers spilling from a pub onto the pavement, taxi lights glowing yellow in the dusk.

'I worked in the City,' she said slowly. 'In an office? I can't remember which company.'

'Forget work – start with Facebook,' suggested Jason. 'You're bound to be on there. I bet your page will be full of mates wondering where you are.'

They scrolled through pages and pages of Facebook entries, but Alice's face didn't appear in any of them. As they clicked from one chunk of results to the next, trying to joke that she was *bound* to be on the next page, Alice was aware that Libby was getting more flustered and embarrassed.

'Well, that's interesting,' said Jason, as they came to the tail end of the Alice Robinsons. 'You're not on Facebook. Are you sure you're not in some sort of witness relocation programme? Or are your security settings really, really tight for some reason?'

'Would I remember if I were in MI5?' said Alice, only half joking.

'It doesn't necessarily mean anything,' said Libby quickly, shooting a glare at Jason. 'Plenty of people aren't on Facebook. Teachers, or policemen . . . I don't go on it much myself these days,' she added. 'People get very competitive about it, don't they?'

'You're definitely Robinson?' Jason tapped a pen against his teeth. 'Would you have forgotten getting married? Or changing your name?'

'No.' Her head felt tight and dark again. 'I don't know. The more I think about something, the harder it gets to work out what I'm remembering, and what I'm wanting to remember.'

Libby looked up from the laptop, then closed the lid with a firm click. 'Sorry, Alice. We're being selfish. You've had a huge shock . . . remembering about your dad and your mum. Do you want to leave it for tonight? Your brain might recover better while you're in sleep mode. So to speak.'

Alice managed a smile. She could tell Libby was dying to carry on, but it had been a long day and she wasn't sure she had the strength to think *and* deal with what might emerge now. Fragments were flashing at the back of her mind like fireflies, bright enough to give her a jolt, not staying long enough to examine them properly.

Dad's scratchy fisherman's jumper. Dark blue. Elbow patches.

Mum's red leather bag with the clip like a barrel and the pockets with sweets behind the zips.

Dad, she thought. Mum. It was as if intense love were shining a torch into the blackness, picking out these precious memories. Another wave of sadness made her feel painfully alone.

Libby saw it and rested a hand on her shoulder. 'Time for bed,' she said. 'Tomorrow's another day.'

And who knows who I'll be when I wake up? thought Alice.

★ ★ ★

On Friday, after Libby had dealt with the hotel admin, then walked Bob, then had a testy conversation with Margaret about the 'somewhat intrusive level' of the builders' radio, she settled into the office with Alice and finally got to use some of her rusty research skills. She tried to be tactful, seeing Alice's anxious fidgeting each time they uncovered a fresh nugget of information, but it felt good to use her brain again – Libby hadn't realised quite how much she'd missed her old job.

By the end of the afternoon, they'd found Alice's A-level results, from a girls' grammar school in Bromley, and a Google Earth location for two flats she'd lived in after university, but no photographs or anything more recent than five years ago, when she'd sponsored someone to jump out of a plane dressed as Superman. From that, they worked out that she must have been working as a PA, temping in various legal firms across London.

'It's a start, isn't it?' said Libby encouragingly. 'Maybe you can get in touch with the— Oh, hello!'

'Hello, ladies!' Jason had strolled in wearing jeans and a rugby shirt, with a gym bag over his shoulder. He looked in a very good mood. 'Just to let you know I won't be around for supper tonight, so don't bother making anything for me.'

'Oh?' Libby was disappointed. 'I was going to do a fish pie to celebrate Alice's news. Your mum's going to teach me the "right" way to make it.'

Jason frowned. 'But your fish pie's great.'

'I know,' said Libby. 'But I think she enjoys teaching me how to do things her way.'

Alice glanced between them, sensing the mood. 'Don't go to any bother for me, Libby. You've already done so much. I'll take Bob upstairs for his supper, shall I?' She got up and slipped out, Bob following behind, tail aloft.

Jason and Libby watched with surprise.

'He didn't look that well trained when I was dragging him out of the rhododendrons earlier,' Libby observed, impressed. 'Anyway, so where are you going tonight?'

'She said the magic word "supper".' He swung the bag onto his other shoulder. 'It's just rugby practice. I've got keys to the front door, so you can lock up for the night whenever you want.'

'What time's the practice?' She glanced at her watch. 'It's only five now.'

'It's six till eight, but we'll probably have a drink or two in the clubhouse after. Did I tell you about the new clubhouse?' Jason did 'jazz hands' to convey his excitement. 'It's new! It has guest ales as well as Stella! They've got a chef who just does pies! And – get this – an actual purpose-built ladies' loo!'

'Brilliant!' Libby didn't know why she felt jealous; she didn't even like rugby that much. Maybe it was that her fish pie was being outgunned by a new loo. 'So when's ladies' night?'

'Sorry?' He dropped his jazz hands and looked wary.

'Now the rugby club has ladies' facilities, when are the social nights that ladies can attend? I wouldn't mind an evening out. Meet some fellow rugby widows?'

'To be honest, Lib, I think they only built it for equality-legislation reasons.' Jason pretended to look appalled. 'Most of the wives steer well clear. They've still got those 1970s-style Big D peanut cards behind the bar, and it's only semi-ironic.'

Libby forced a smile. 'I can cope with sexist peanuts, if it means having a date night with you. I miss our date nights with the wallpaper steamer. And there's a whole world of entertainment out there in Longhampton, apparently.'

'I know, babe. But you really wouldn't want to come to the clubhouse. Why don't you and Alice go out somewhere?'

Something about the casual way he said it caught on the rough edge of her tiredness. Although the hotel was hardly busy, someone had to be around in the evenings in case of enquiries or to deal with the few guests; Libby had argued Margaret should be excused from evenings, so she could keep up with her friends as much as possible, but that didn't mean Jason could land her with every shift now his social life was picking up.

'When?' Libby put her hands on her hips. 'I can't really plan if you just waltz off whenever you feel like it.'

'Didn't I put it on the calendar?' It wasn't convincing. 'I need to be there for practice – it's only a small club; you've got to show willing. And afterwards, well, half the team's on the council or in business round here. A few pints are worth loads of phone calls . . . We're oiling the wheels of commerce.'

'Fine. Just don't . . .' Libby hesitated, then, since the mood was now distinctly tetchy, ploughed on. She hadn't said anything after Jason had staggered in after the last night out with the lads, in case it was a one-off. 'Just don't go overboard this time.'

'Meaning?'

'Meaning, last time you decided to "oil the wheels of commerce", you didn't surface until ten, and I had to do breakfast and the laundry change on my own. This isn't like the office – I can't put your day on hold until your hangover clears. We need to go to the cash and carry first thing tomorrow. I don't mean to nag,' she added, well aware that she *was* nagging, 'but . . .'

Jason made placating hand gestures. 'I hear you. I won't be late. I'll just get a couple of rounds in and then I'll be back. What? What are you looking at me like that for?'

It was out of Libby's mouth before she could stop it. 'Just don't go overboard on the round-buying either. I got the credit-card bills this morning and we're nearly maxed out.'

Oh God, why did you say that? she asked herself crossly. But she already knew the answer: the fact that she couldn't get that conversation with her dad out of her head, coupled with finding the bar receipt for the last night out in the back pocket of Jason's jeans when she did the laundry. Jason had, it seemed, left his card behind the bar and paid for the entire team to get wasted. And they were rugby players. They liked a challenge.

Libby had always adored Jason's generosity. He was the opposite of her dad in so many ways. But they couldn't afford that open-handedness now, and she hated having to curtail his nature – more than that, she hated having to be the one to remind him. He should *know*.

'Anything else?' asked Jason. 'Don't stay out late, don't get drunk, don't spend too much money? No, wait. You missed don't have any fun.'

They stared at each other and the air between them felt thundery with the row they could have, or avert.

This is how strong marriages grow, Libby reminded herself. By working through tough patches.

'I don't enjoy feeling like your mum,' she said quietly. 'But this is hard enough already without making things harder for ourselves. Isn't it?'

Just apologise. Just acknowledge why I'm really hurt. How humiliating it is for me not to be able to trust you.

Jason sighed and put down his kit bag. 'I'm sorry, Lib,' he said. 'I hear what you're saying. Take the evening off. You need to relax too.'

She didn't answer.

Jason stepped closer and slid his arms round her, resting his cheek next to hers. He pressed his lips against the soft skin behind her ear; it had always made Libby's insides turn to water, and now, right on cue, she felt herself melt. She looked down at the strong arms circling her shoulders, and, despite her tension, she relaxed into them.

At least we still have this, she thought. At least this didn't evaporate with everything else.

'You'll never know how much I appreciate you going with me on this,' he murmured. 'But you've got to trust me – money comes in and it goes out. Sometimes you have to spend it to make it. It's what happens in business.'

Libby wanted to believe that more than anything. She rested her nose on his arm and breathed in the smell of Jason's skin. The comfort of his hug was blocking out any irritating small voices in her mind.

'I don't want to stop trying to make *us* work because we're making the hotel work.' There, she'd said it.

'Me neither, babe. The hotel will work *because* we're making us work.' Jason squeezed her. 'I won't be late back. If you promise to be in the bath at exactly half past ten . . .'

Libby pulled away. 'Make it ten,' she said in a seductive murmur. 'Your mother's going to be out until half ten. The Soroptimists' spring party, apparently.'

Jason paused by the door, then jiggled his eyebrows. 'In that case, I'll be back by half nine. See you later, gorgeous.'

Libby blew him a kiss and listened to him whistling happily as he let himself out through the stag-infested reception, fading back into silence as the front door closed.

With Margaret and Jason both out, Libby spent the evening in the office with Alice, where they could listen for the phone but get on with something useful at the same time.

The something useful was brainstorming marketing ideas

from one of Libby's many how-to guides to the hospitality industry. She had to hide them in a filing cabinet, since Margaret seemed to take the stack of books as a slight on her thirty-five years' experience, but Libby needed the practical reassurance of lists and goals. She and Jason didn't have a clue about business management, and every question she asked Margaret was now met with 'Donald used to . . .' which was understandable, but not very helpful.

Alice was an easy person to bounce ideas around with, and after filling pages of Libby's notebook with offers and special weekends, they stopped at half eight for something to eat. Since she'd had to abandon her fish-pie treat, Libby ordered a pizza from the new pizzeria in town, under the pretext of checking it out for guests. She and Alice had, after all, done more work in two hours than Jason and Margaret had done all day.

'Did any of those details we found today jog your memory?' she asked, passing Alice some kitchen roll to wipe her fingers.

'Nothing that's much help.' She looked sad. 'I keep wondering why I'm not on Facebook. I mean, then at least I could work out what sort of person I am from my friends.'

'I don't know if you *can* work out who you are from your Facebook friends,' said Libby. 'It just tells you who you've met.'

Facebook was a touchy subject for Libby. Erin and the others often posted on her page – lots of 'Hi, hon!'s and tagging to photos of parties she hadn't gone to – but she couldn't bring herself to reply, given that their hectic lives of toddler yoga and Goa holidays rolled on, while hers . . . didn't. She checked it every day, often late at night so no one would spot her on there, but she'd only posted two photos of Margaret's garden, the one unequivocally good bit of the hotel. Even then, she'd had to wait for the drizzle to clear up.

Jason thought she was being ridiculous, but Facebook made Libby feel weirdly defensive. No, actually, she thought, it *wasn't* weird. It was her newsfeed: looking at it made her wonder how much she and the Wandsworth 'girls' really had in common. Erin was lovely, but the others, though perfectly nice, had never been the sort of people Libby felt she could tell secrets to, not with any confidence. If she'd had kids, she sometimes thought, there might have been a real connection, a bond made out of private, awkward, less-than-perfect confessions, but the one time she'd tipsily admitted that her entry for the summer street party wasn't, in fact, Margaret Corcoran's ye olde family lemon curd recipe but Lidl lemon curd decanted into a plain jar, the ensuing tumbleweed meant she'd thought twice about any soul-baring. (Erin, thankfully, had roared with laughter.)

Urgh, The Lemon Curd Incident. Libby's face burned, as it always did when she remembered it, and she realised Alice was scrutinising her. Then, because Alice's lack of judginess made it easy to say what she felt, she said, 'I keep telling myself that Facebook is all edited highlights, but when we're working hard here, and on a budget . . . you don't always want to see how amazing other people's lives are, do you?'

'True.'

'And real friends are real friends,' she went on. 'Not people who've clicked on your profile and added you to get their numbers up.'

'I know. But it's like a paper trail, isn't it? Of who you've been. What freaks me out,' said Alice slowly, 'is what if I never meet someone who knows me again? Those years I can't remember, they've just . . . gone. Even if I trace all my old school mates, they're in London. What am I doing here? Have I just . . . lost the person I've been for the past few years?' She blinked, lost, and Libby felt bad about her own selfishness.

'No! Your memory will come back. And of *course* you've got friends, and of course they'll find you. But you can start again, if you have to. You can make new friends – I mean, look, you've made two new friends already, me and Jason. Everyone has to reinvent themselves when they move. You're just a bit more . . . extreme than that.'

As she said it, Libby realised she hadn't exactly taken her own advice on that score. Two months in and the only new friend she'd made had literally been brought to her front door by a careless driver.

Alice picked at her pizza. 'I'm so grateful to you two, but I can't stay here forever. How can I get a job with no references and no bank account? No National Insurance number? It's going to look so dodgy.'

'We can start tracing all those things now. And you've got a job here whenever you want.'

'Really? You don't have to say that.'

'Of course! You're already a better receptionist than the last one Margaret had. By which I mean me.'

Alice smiled at Libby, and Libby's throat tightened at how relieved she seemed. 'Thanks, Libby. You've been so kind . . .'

There was a crash out in reception and they both jumped, and listened. It sounded like something being knocked over.

Libby put down her pizza. 'It's probably Jason, back early. I don't think Margaret would be crashing in like that. Unless she's fallen over the dog.'

'Where *is* Bob when you need him?' said Alice. 'Some guard dog he is.'

'Who's in room four? Mr Harrington? I suppose he might have tried to get into the lounge for the papers.' Libby slipped her feet back into her shoes. 'I'll go and see.'

As she went out into the reception area, she saw movement over by the door and heard a male voice whisper, 'Shhhhhh!' far too loudly.

It was Jason. He always lost his volume control when he'd had a few. Libby braced herself for the display of puppyish affection that was heading her way. Jason's tolerance for drink was about four pints, although he was capable of putting back a considerable amount more than that.

On the one hand, he'd come back in good time for their rendezvous in the bath, but on the other, she thought, irritated, it sounded as if he'd be sleeping in it. Still, at least she hadn't wasted her last two centimetres of decent bath oil on him.

Jason was clinging to the door frame and smiling cherubically. The lights were still on, and the pale dust sheets made the room even brighter. His blond hair was plastered to his head, as if much beer had been spilled on it. There was someone else with him – one of his mates, in a red hoody under a leather jacket, was half supporting him, half holding him up.

Had to be another rugby player, Libby thought; he was a good six inches shorter than Jason, but was wiry enough to keep all thirteen stone of inebriated idiot upright.

She was about to go over to relieve him of his wobbly prisoner when Jason suddenly bent over the brass umbrella stand and started making the same dramatic retching noises Lord Bob liked to make after eating something dodgy in the park.

Oh, you're joking, she thought. How come Margaret never sees this?

'Man, I'm feeling really—' said Jason, in a very strong

Longhampton accent, and then threw up noisily into the umbrella stand. While Libby was still staring, open-mouthed, by the reception desk, Jason straightened up, wiping his face with the back of his hand. He grinned gormlessly at his mate, who said nothing, but let out a long sigh.

'Better in there than on the carpet,' said Jason. 'And least I didn't do it in the taxi.'

'That wasn't a taxi, you weapon, that was my van,' said the friend, and pushed his hoody back off his face with a weary hand. As he spoke, Libby realised exactly who it was, even though it had been a while – Luke.

Luke always made Libby think of the moody guitarists in the indie bands she'd liked as a teenager – he was wiry and hollow-cheeked, and looked like he could knock out a stage-diver without breaking rhythm. His eyes were the first thing anyone noticed about him, not because they were beautiful and blue, like Jason's, but because they had an intensity that frequently made Libby glance behind her to see if someone more interesting had suddenly walked in.

'Luke?'

He turned, and when he saw her, he groaned.

'Oh shit, I mean, hi, Libby. I was going to try to get Jase upstairs and into bed without bothering you.'

'Not into my bed, I hope. That's not the kind of surprise a girl likes to come across late at night.'

He turned his palms up in acknowledgement. 'Good point. Plan B was to stick him in the bath. Easier to hose him down in there.'

They both looked over at Jason, who had sunk to his knees and was hanging on to the umbrella stand as if it were a life raft.

'How much has he had?'

'Ten pints!' Jason raised an unsteady hand. 'T . . . en! Or twelve!'

'Four, I'd imagine,' said Libby. 'If that.'

Luke ran a hand through his dark hair; it was longer than it had been the last time she'd seen him. Then it had been almost army-short, but now it was long enough to fall into a half-quiff over his forehead. 'Six, I reckon.'

'Well, thanks for carting him home,' she said. Luke never said much, and she found herself gabbling to fill the gaps. 'How did you find him?'

'I called into the clubhouse to meet someone about a job and he was there.' Luke nudged Jason with the toe of his trainer and Jason let out a groan. 'He was pretty far gone by the time I arrived. You're out of practice, mate,' he added for good measure.

'You are not my keeper,' slurred Jason. 'If I want to have a drink with the lads, then I don't need my big brother telling me—'

Whatever else he was going to say was lost in another bout of retching.

'What a catch,' said Libby.

'Anyway, since I was there, I thought I'd better bring him back. Bit old for Mum to come and get you, aren't you?' He directed the comment towards his feet.

Jason mumbled incoherently.

'Well, thanks for risking your own van to do it. I didn't know you were around,' said Libby. 'Where are you staying? You know we've been here since the beginning of March?'

'So I gather. I've been back and forth, meaning to give you a ring, but you know, Mum . . .' Luke shrugged. 'Listen, I don't want to sound rude, but I think we'd better get Wonderboy up the stairs before— Oh, hello.'

For a second, Libby wondered if Margaret had come back; Luke had straightened up, and was smiling uncertainly towards the office. Good, she thought. Now Margaret can see what Jason's really like after a few jars, instead of intimating that I always make a fuss about nothing.

But Luke's smile was different. He looked pleased but uncertain. Surprised, even.

Libby spun round and saw that Alice had appeared and was staring at them with the same ambiguous expression on her own face. It was an expression Libby had seen a lot over the past few days, while she was reading magazines, while they were doing quizzes, while they were talking. Alice was trying to remember something. Trying really hard.

Finally, Luke spoke.

'Alice!' he said. And then he smiled. As if he knew her.

Chapter Twelve

Alice stared at the man holding Jason up on the other side of the reception and a shapeless thought pushed in the back of her head, trying to get through the wall of blankness.

She didn't *know* him, but he . . . wasn't unfamiliar. Libby had called him Luke, and something in her head had gone, *Oh yes, of course. Luke*, but no more than that.

He knew her. He'd said her name, but the way he was looking at her confirmed it. Luke was the first person she'd met who actually knew who she was, and she'd met him here in the hotel she'd been heading for.

Alice's throat went dry.

He took a step closer, frowning at her lack of response, and the quick movement of his gaze over her face was familiar too: the sharp, attractive eyes, almost black under his strong, straight eyebrows. A hank of brown hair fell over his brow and he pushed it back to see her better, revealing a small tattoo on his wrist: an apple.

Luke.

Alice felt a tug inside. He looks really pleased to see me, but he's confused, she thought, reading his angular face. And he knows *me*. He knows who *I* am.

'Alice?' he repeated. 'It *is* you, isn't it?'

'Yes. It is,' she said. 'But . . .'

Luke had started to step nearer, but now he stopped, confused. A bit hurt? 'Are you all right?'

'Luke. You're Jason's brother,' said Alice slowly, focusing on the facts she could rely on. New facts, not old memories, she reminded herself.

His frown deepened, making his face harder suddenly. 'Yes. Isn't that why you're here?' He stared at her, his dark brown eyes seeing a 'her' she didn't know, and Alice felt an urge to say the right thing, even though she didn't know what that could possibly be.

'Do you two know each other?' demanded Libby.

Luke seemed to be waiting for Alice to speak, and when she didn't, he said, 'Yes, we do.'

'Well, *how*?' Libby made an impatient noise. 'Come on! This isn't a *Miss Marple*! You don't have to spin it out!'

'I know Alice from the pub ... The White Horse in Embersley.' He glanced between Libby and Alice, surprised that she wasn't offering the information herself. 'Why? What's happened? Alice?'

Alice couldn't speak. Luke looked hurt. Why did he look hurt? What had she done? How did he know her? Was he her friend? More than a friend? Her stomach clenched.

'Alice was in an accident outside the hotel, about a fortnight ago. She lost her memory, and so we brought her here until she remembers where she lives,' said Libby. 'Sorry, Alice,' she added, over her shoulder, 'speaking for you there. Are you all right? You've gone very pale.'

As Libby had been talking Alice had seen shock sweep Luke's face, only for it to vanish as soon as it appeared. He was good at controlling his expressions, unlike Libby. Since the memory loss Alice had become eagle-eyed when it came to seizing on tiny reactions, clues to things she didn't know, and at the mention of an accident, his expression had set, as if different thoughts were going through his mind, not the blurted 'Oh my God!' reaction other people had had.

He knows something about me, she thought, out of nowhere, and felt another shapeless thought rise and fall unseen just out of reach.

'Are you all right now?' he asked, stepping away from Jason's wobbling form. 'What kind of accident? Were you hurt?'

'I was hit by a car. Two cars. I don't know what happened. It's all—' Alice's knees suddenly turned to water, and white spots appeared in front of her eyes. She staggered and reached out for the edge of the reception desk. Before she knew it, Libby was there, her arm round her waist.

'Careful!' she said. 'I think we should get Alice upstairs. She's still on medication.' She glanced across at Jason, slumped over the umbrella stand, his head resting peacefully against the rim. 'Luke, you bring the drunkard, would you? Use a shovel if you have to.'

Alice tried to walk, but Libby was stronger than she looked, and gratefully, she let herself be guided upstairs into the kitchen.

Across the landing in the bathroom, the sounds of Luke manhandling a groaning Jason into the bath could be heard, and Alice was thankful for the momentary break. She put her head between her knees, and her mind swirled with darkness; nothing useful appeared. No memories of Luke, just a sense of anxiety. Libby put the kettle on, then crouched down in front of her chair.

'Are you all right?' she asked in a worried undertone. 'You really have gone white.'

'I'm fine.' Alice touched her ribs. They were aching where Libby had helped her up the stairs. 'Just . . . awkward, when people know you but you don't know them.'

'Awkward?' Libby realised she was joking and rolled her eyes. 'Is Luke a friend of yours? Can you remember the last time you saw him?'

'I don't know,' said Alice. 'I . . . No, I don't know.' She was scrabbling around in her mind, but whatever was there darted out of reach. 'Has he mentioned me? Do you think *he* told me to come here?'

'He hasn't mentioned you, but we're not all that close. He hasn't been here himself for months. Literally, months. I probably said, he and Margaret don't get on. Last time I saw Luke was . . . two years ago? At his wedding?'

His wedding. Luke was married. Alice felt a strange shimmer run across her insides. Not a memory, a deeper reaction.

'Goodness me, what on earth is going on?' The skittering of claws on tiles indicated that Margaret and Bob had returned from the Soroptimists' party. Margaret was looking smart in her floaty floral dress and pearls; Bob's self-satisfied expression suggested he'd had a lot of illicit vol-au-vents. 'There is *the* most appalling smell in reception, I thought . . . Alice? Are you all right, dear?'

'She's fine,' said Libby, as the sound of more loud heaving reverberated from the bathroom. 'Unfortunately, I can't say the same for Jason.'

'Is Jason ill?' Margaret's face creased with anxiety. 'Has he eaten something that hasn't agreed with him? He's always been funny with mushrooms . . .'

'He's drunk something, more like.' The kettle boiled and Libby stood up to make the tea. 'Don't worry, Luke's with him.'

'*Luke?*' Alice watched Margaret's anxiety turn to annoyance and caught the slight answering hunch of Libby's shoulders. She tried to read the dynamic that had sprung up: both Libby and Margaret had gone blandly polite. 'I didn't know Luke was coming.'

'Neither did we. But Luke rescued Jason and brought him home. He's not sick; he's just revoltingly drunk,' she added. 'But the good news is that—'

'I should go and see if he's all right.' Margaret put her handbag down on the table. 'Jason's not a drinker! Do you think one of his friends spiked his drink? You read about these things . . .'

'Yes,' said Libby, deadpan. 'I think they spiked his drink – with a lot of alcohol. And poor Jason drank it.'

'Do you? Oh.' Margaret pouted, getting the joke. 'I'm not sure it's something to make light of, Elizabeth. People can have serious reactions to excess alcohol.'

Glancing between them, Alice caught an irritation in Libby's eyes, a biting of her tongue.

'He'll be fine, Margaret,' said Libby. 'I've seen him much worse than this. But as I was saying, the *good* news is that Luke—'

'Luke what?'

Their heads swivelled to see Luke in the doorway, drying his hands on a hand towel from the bathroom. It was pink, and looked wrong in his strong hands.

'Hello, Mum,' he said. 'You look nice – have you been out?'

Alice watched as he tried to keep his attention fixed on his mother, but when his eyes slid sideways to her, they met her own gaze and a shiver ran through her. But without a memory to cross-reference, she didn't know whether that shiver was a good one or a warning one.

'The Soroptimists' party,' she said, taking the towel off him and leaning in as he dutifully kissed her cheek. It wasn't the affectionate bearhug that Jason usually gave Margaret; they were both stiff, and cautious, as if they wouldn't be doing this without an audience. 'This is a surprise. You should have phoned.'

'Wasn't planned – I was going to drop round tomorrow. So you know, I've put Jason to bed in the spare room,' he added to Libby, as she handed him a cup of tea. 'Left the door open in case he needs us, but I think he's out for the count.'

'Oh.' Margaret had started to move towards the door to check on Jason. 'Alice is staying in the spare room.'

Alice blushed as they turned to her. 'It's fine,' she said quickly. 'I'll sleep on the sofa for tonight. It's no bother.'

'No, Alice, absolutely not. You mustn't, dear.' Margaret looked concerned. 'Your ribs . . . Maybe Libby could sleep in the hotel and you could have her bed, just for tonight?'

'Please, it's fine,' said Alice, seeing Libby's eyebrows shoot up behind Margaret's back. 'Honestly.'

'We'll work something out,' said Libby. 'It's a hotel – it's not like we don't have a lot of spare rooms. Now, Luke, sit down – *far* more important is that you tell us how you know Alice!'

Margaret was halfway out of the door, but she froze. 'What?'

'Luke knows Alice,' said Libby. 'Don't you?'

'How?'

Luke turned his mug round in his hands. 'I was staying at a pub in Embersley a few weeks ago, while we were working on a couple of jobs in the area, and Alice worked there.'

'A pub! In Embersley! Can you remember?' Libby glanced at her, eagerly.

She shook her head. 'Not really.'

'I'm going to check on Jason,' Margaret announced, as if

insufficient attention had been paid to his condition. 'See if he needs anything.'

'Good luck, Margaret, but I think he'll be snoring by now,' said Libby without turning round. She stirred a couple of sugars into a mug of tea and passed it to Alice.

Luke pulled out a chair and slid into it. He'd taken off his hoody and Alice automatically noted his well-worn jeans, the narrow thighs beneath, the soft line on his sinewy bicep where his arms went from pale brown to a deeper tan. And the apple, inked in green on his wrist. Familiar? Not familiar?

'So,' said Libby. 'Tell us about this pub – is it a nice one?'

'Yes, it's very nice. It's a countryside inn with rooms upstairs and a good weekend roast. It's by a river, with ducks in the garden.' The ghost of a smile flickered on his face. 'Bloody noisy ducks.'

He glanced at Alice as he said it and seemed disappointed when nothing registered on her face. Had they joked about it?

'And . . . have I worked there long?' she asked, wishing she didn't have to ask.

He gazed at her, then looked down; she couldn't see his eyes. 'A year? We didn't exactly swap CVs.'

'Details!' demanded Libby. 'Anything! The randomer the better!'

'Ah . . . what can I tell you . . . ? You're good at darts, better than my lads, anyway. You were going to apply for a better job than pouring pints. You were very good at pouring pints, by the way. Are,' he corrected himself. Self-conscious. 'You *are* very good at pouring pints.'

'I'm sure I still am. The doctor said that kind of skill doesn't just go away with a car accident,' she said, and Luke finally looked straight at her and smiled – suddenly he seemed younger, less serious. He met her gaze dead on, with a direct, honest look that seemed to see right inside her head.

Then he said, 'And you live with your boyfriend somewhere in Stratton,' and Alice's heart did a funny plummet-skip.

She had a boyfriend. It wasn't Luke.

Stupid, she thought. If he was her boyfriend, he'd have kissed her. She'd have known him. He'd have come for her before now, found her, looked for her. She struggled with a knotty mess of reaction she couldn't untangle. She couldn't find a start to it.

'You've got a boyfriend – I knew it!' Libby was saying, delighted, and Alice nodded.

This is good, she told herself. She *did* have someone who cared about her. She wasn't totally alone. She wasn't completely unlovable or just out of prison or rehab or something. She was normal.

'And what, um, what's he called?' she asked. And immediately thought how 'un-normal' it was to have to ask a stranger what your boyfriend's name was.

'Gethin. Don't know the surname.'

'Gethin,' she said slowly, trying to hear any echoes it made in her mind.

'Whoa! What kind of a name is that?' asked Libby. 'Gethin?'

'Welsh, apparently,' said Luke. 'You tried to teach me some Welsh at some point, but I'm afraid I've forgotten it.' The quick, sharp smile. 'Can't blame that on an accident, I'm afraid.'

Gethin.

Alice tried to summon up a memory of her voice calling that name. Her mouth formed the shape, silently, imagining herself murmuring it in his ear, speaking it into a phone, writing it on a card, but nothing would come. But he was telling her she had. She must have done.

'That's fantastic news!' Libby's face was bright with excitement across the table. 'I *knew* you'd have a boyfriend. Didn't imagine he'd be Welsh, but . . .'

'What did you imagine my boyfriend would be like?' Alice asked. 'Jack from *Titanic*?'

'I don't know! I thought he'd be a nice local boy called Jamie or Ryan or something.' Libby made vague shapes with her hands. 'I saw you with a policeman, for some reason. There goes my career as a top psychic, eh? Are you *sure* you don't know a surname, Luke?' She reached for her phone. 'We can Google him. How many Gethins can there be round here? We can get an address! Alice, you could be home tonight!'

Luke didn't answer her; he was playing with his mug of tea, turning it round and round in his hands.

'What does he do? Gethin?' asked Alice. The facts were stacking up now, but they weren't making a bridge to anywhere in her head, or triggering a memory. Was it because she was pushing too hard? Of all the things she wanted to remember, it was the face of someone who loved her. Who knew her.

Luke shrugged. 'I don't know if you ever said. I assumed he must be in IT or something. But then,' he added, 'I didn't really ask. I wasn't interviewing you for a job; we were just chatting in the bar.'

Just chatting, thought Alice. Really?

'And' – Libby leaned across the table and put her hand on Alice's arm, an apology for interrupting – 'sorry, but I have to ask this – it's doing my head in – you found all this out in the space of one round of drinks, Luke?'

'No, I was staying in the pub. I was fitting some security systems in the area – two jobs, a private house and an office block. My team was working around the builders, so we were moving between the sites, and the pub was somewhere in the middle. We ate in the bar most nights. Alice did a few evening shifts – you know what it's like here. You get chatting to guests.'

'So I guess Stratton must be near there, then,' said Alice slowly. 'Near Embersley.' Wherever that was.

'Yes, I think so.' Luke wrapped his hands round the mug. He had long fingers, with scabs on a couple of joints, from some sort of building work, Alice assumed. No watch. No wedding ring. What did that tell her about him? Was it meant to say something? There weren't as many clues to Luke as there were to label-friendly, open-faced Libby and Jason. He closed himself off.

'You tended to be the last one out most nights,' he added. 'We kept you back, I'm afraid. Me and the lads. Playing darts. Talking rubbish. Sorry. You're not missing much if you can't remember.'

Alice took a deep breath and tried to make it feel as if they were talking about *her* and not discussing some stranger. Gethin. Her boyfriend. The pub with ducks. A life waiting for her, an actual life that she was part of, waiting on hold for her to walk back into so it could restart, and yet . . .

What if she still didn't remember, once she'd been led back to it? What if she had to take up friendships, relationships, that were completely one-sided? Her stomach lurched. What if the memories didn't come back and the last year was completely lost? All her memories and experiences and falling in love, lost like a wiped phone.

It'd be fine, she told herself. Once she saw Gethin.

'Alice?' said Libby. 'Are you all right?'

'Yes.' She tried to smile. 'It's just a lot to take in. I suppose at least you're not telling me I've got three kids and a cat all starving to death in a house somewhere.'

'Well, Gethin must be going pretty mad,' said Libby. 'Wondering where on earth you've got to.'

'You haven't got in touch?' Luke looked surprised.

Alice shook her head. 'I didn't even know he existed until you told me just now. I literally didn't know my own name until a few days ago. No ID. My handbag was lost. Purse, phone, everything – stolen, I guess. It's why the hospital couldn't send me home.'

'The police think maybe Alice was mugged before the accident,' said Libby, topping up Alice's tea. 'Nothing's been handed in – I've been checking.'

'Very unlikely, though.' Margaret had reappeared in the doorway. 'I mean, if someone was attacked in the town, someone would have reported it. Or stopped it in the first place! We'd certainly have heard – everyone knows Alice is here with us.'

'Bad things happen everywhere, Mum,' said Luke.

'No.' She shook her head. 'Not in Longhampton. Your father was on the town council for years and we never—'

'I know, it's a mystery,' said Libby hurriedly. 'But now we've got some leads, let's get on the phone! Poor Gethin – I bet I know what's happened,' she added to Alice. 'Some message will have got lost at the hospital. You know how busy it is in there. It won't be that he hasn't been *trying* to find you; it'll be that some note's got stuck to someone else's file or . . .'

'Now, Elizabeth,' said Margaret, 'the hospital have been *extremely* helpful to Alice, and if someone called—' She stopped when she saw Alice's face. 'Oh, I'm sorry, Alice. I didn't mean that to sound as if your boyfriend wasn't trying to find you. I'm sure there's a very good explanation.' She paused, as if racking her brains. 'He's maybe . . . away with work.'

A brief, uncomfortable silence stretched out in the kitchen, broken only by the distant sound of snoring.

Jason, Alice assumed. Or maybe Lord Bob.

'Where is Embersley?' she asked. 'Is it in Wales?' I can't have been there very long, she thought. If I can't remember where it is.

'No, it's about thirty miles away,' said Luke. 'Other side of the county.'

'What? *This* county?' Libby turned to him. 'You were working in the same county, and you were staying in a pub, and not here? Why on earth didn't you drop in?'

'Yes,' Margaret echoed. 'Why didn't you say?'

Libby was doing a pantomime 'hurt' face, but again Alice's sharp eyes caught something genuine about it. She *was* hurt, she thought.

'Oh ... I reckoned you had enough on your plate,' said Luke. 'Settling into the new job, getting to know the hotel ropes. I didn't think me being here would add to the atmosphere. I thought Mum would be enjoying having you and Jason here to herself.'

Alice glanced between the two of them, trying to read the vibrations in the air. Margaret was trying to conceal her bristling, but not doing very well.

'What an awful thing to say. That's not at all true,' said Margaret, but in a very half-hearted manner.

'Well, you could have called,' said Libby lightly. 'Anyway, sorry – enough about us! Much more importantly ...' She turned back to Alice. 'So! What do you want to do? Go to Stratton and see if we can find your house?'

'Now?' Margaret looked surprised. 'Shouldn't you wait until the morning?'

'Why? No time like the present!' Libby's eyes sparkled, as they had done at the hospital when she'd swept in and organised her out of Marcia's women's hostel. 'This is Alice's *life* she's getting back!'

'We can start at the pub – it'll still be open,' Luke pointed out. 'Have you got a lot to pack? I can drive you, if you want.'

'No, I haven't got *anything* to pack,' said Alice, and suddenly realised that her time here in the Swan was now over. The other life – her own life – was opening up for her even though she still couldn't remember it, and instead of feeling excited, she felt as if she was walking blindfold into a strange room.

This was what she knew, here in the Swan. Libby, and Jason, and Lord Bob, and the daily hotel routine. She wasn't sure she wanted to leave it just yet, not until she knew what she was going back to.

But how will that happen if you don't go and look at it?

'Why don't we ring the White Horse?' suggested Luke, seeing her hesitation. 'They must have an address if they've been paying your wages into a bank account, right? And they'll probably have emergency contact details, so we can get hold of Gethin, let him know you're on your way.'

'I suppose so.' Alice pulled herself together. 'Yes. Let's do that.'

'Brilliant.' Libby slapped her knees. 'You stay there; I'll find the number.'

Alice looked up and caught Luke's eye. He was looking at her with that ambiguous expression, and something in it changed when their eyes met.

Who are you? she wondered silently. And who am I?

Chapter Thirteen

Alice dialled the number Libby found on the pub's website and listened to the phone ringing at the other end. She tried not to think what would happen if they'd never heard of her.

'Hello. White Horse at Embersley. How can I help you?'

The woman's voice – northern, a bit bored – was familiar and Alice's stomach flipped. There was the sound of a busy pub in the background: talking, chinking glasses, music. Then she realised: it wasn't the woman who was familiar; it was the up and down of the phrase, something she'd probably said a thousand times herself. She would normally have been the one answering this phone.

She had a sudden, dizzying panic that another woman had slotted neatly into the space she'd left behind, filling her place, leaving no room for her to return.

'Hello?' the woman repeated, impatiently. On the other side of the desk, Libby raised her eyebrows, eager for new details.

'Hello. Um, it's Alice.'

She held her breath for a moment. If the woman didn't recognise her, if Luke had got it wrong . . .

'Sorry – Alice? I don't know any Alices.'

'I work there. Can I speak to . . . ?' What was the name of the manager? It hovered vaguely at the back of her mind, then slid away as she reached for it. Alice felt her face crumple.

Someone nudged her and she opened her eyes to see Libby by her side, gesturing at her laptop. She'd found the website of the pub and had the 'About Us' page open: '*Tony and Jillian McNamara welcome you to the White Horse . . .*' it said, underneath a photo of a tanned couple in matching white shirts and very dark blue jeans.

'Can I speak to Jillian?' Alice asked, as confidently as she could. 'Or Tony?'

Libby gave her a thumbs-up.

'Jillian's out. Let me see if Tony's around. Who shall I say's calling?'

'Alice.'

'Alice who?'

'Alice Robinson.' It was starting to sound more natural now.

'Hang on.' She clunked down the phone.

'Well done.' Libby gave her arm a quick stroke.

Within seconds the phone was picked up again. 'Alice?'

'Hello?'

'Welcome back! So, how was it?' The voice was deep and friendly. An Essex voice.

'How was what?'

'How was the surprise fortnight in the sun with the boyfriend? You still talking?'

A holiday? Alice wasn't expecting that. She looked up at Libby, who was trying to pretend she wasn't listening in. Her mouth had fallen into an 'O' of surprise.

'So when did you get back?' Tony went on cheerfully. 'We wasn't expecting you until the end of the month. Gethin told us to keep schtum about the whole thing – Jillian nearly went mad not telling you.'

Alice stared at the website page to make sure she got the

names right. 'Tony, I don't remember going on holiday. I was in an accident – I'm still suffering some side effects of the concussion. I've had severe memory loss.'

There was a pause. 'Is this a joke?'

'No. It's not a joke. You can ring the hospital.'

'Oh my God, Alice.' He sounded shocked. 'When? We didn't hear about this! Why didn't you say, instead of letting me ramble on? I feel a right plum. Are you all right?'

'Physically, I'm fine, yes, a bit sore still, but I don't . . .' The words stuck in her throat. Saying them to another stranger made it sound too improbable, when the slow-moving blankness in her head was very real. 'I haven't got any memory of the last year or so. I don't know where I live or what I've been doing, or anything.'

'You can't remember working here? So how did you know to ring?' His tone turned dubious. 'Are you sure . . . ?'

'It's just by some mad coincidence that I've met someone who knows me from the pub. Can you . . . can you help me?' It was so ridiculous that a nervous laugh forced itself out of her. 'I'm hoping you've got my address and bank details and things on the system.'

Libby was making driving gestures.

'I can come over,' Alice went on. 'So you can see it's me. So you're not giving out personal staff details over the phone to a total stranger.'

'Don't be daft, love. Course I know it's you. I'd know your voice anywhere. God, I hate to think of you being in an accident, love. And we thought you was sunning yourself with Gethin!'

The remorse in Tony's voice made her eyes brim. I must be a nice person if he's being so kind, if he's worried about me, she thought.

'You being looked after all right?' Tony went on. 'You need

somewhere to . . . ? What am I saying? Gethin'll be taking good care of you, is he?'

'No.' It came out as a half-sob. 'I can't remember where he lives. Where *we* live. He didn't come to the hospital when I was being treated, and he hasn't tried to find me – the police haven't had any enquiries from *anyone*.'

'You're kidding me.' Tony sounded shocked. 'There'll be a good explanation for that. Gethin wouldn't leave you in hospital if you'd been in an accident – I'd bet my pub on it. No way.'

'Really?' Alice knew she sounded dubious, but it was as if they were talking about a total stranger. What possible explanation could there be for someone you love going AWOL for over a fortnight – to the point where you wouldn't even ring the police? Had they rowed? Would Tony know that?

'So where *are* you?' Tony went on. 'Did they discharge you yet? You need to come here? We can get a room ready . . .'

'No, I'm being looked after. I'm in Longhampton. I've been so lucky.'

On the other side of the table, Libby's round eyes were swimming with tears too now, though her smile underneath was crumpled. She looked like someone watching the end of a particularly satisfying chick flick. Sad, but in a happy, indulgent, 'it's all fine' way.

'I've been so lucky,' she repeated. 'Complete strangers . . . have been so kind.'

'Oh, Alice.' There was some rustling on the end of the phone. 'You get yourself round here and we'll sort you out. I won't lock up till you arrive.'

Alice was tired and confused, not ready to deal with this abrupt shift, this sudden torrent of facts and details. It was all forward motion now, too much for her to process.

'Are you OK?' Libby gently took the phone from her hand. 'Do you need more tea? Or painkillers? Brandy?'

Alice shook her head. 'People are so kind,' she said. 'I can't believe how kind people are. To a complete stranger.'

'You're a nice person. Why wouldn't we be kind to you?'

'How?' It burst out of Alice. 'How can you know that when you don't know anything about me? *I* don't even know that!'

Libby looked at her. Her expression was trusting; it made Alice almost nervous that she wasn't worth that level of trust. That she might let Libby down somehow. 'I know who you are now,' she said. 'You're the first friend I've made here. Come on, let's get you back home.'

Luke was in the sitting room, leaning against the fireplace and flicking through one of Libby's magazines, waiting for them to finish. When they walked in, his head jerked upwards and he glanced between them, but he didn't speak.

'Luke, can you drive Alice over to Embersley?' Libby asked. 'Since your brother won't be driving anything anywhere for at least two days.'

'Of course.' He looked at Alice. 'If you want to go now. I mean, it is quite late . . .'

Alice took a deep breath. 'No,' she said, 'Tony's waiting up.'

'Libby can come too, of course,' he added, and it was only because he'd said it that she noticed the awkwardness of his expression. He knew her well enough to drive her over on his own, and for it to be normal; she didn't know him at all.

'Libby? Do you want to come too?' Alice had the distinct impression that Libby was itching to see the big finish. Ideally, the tearful reunion with Gethin.

She looked over towards the door; Margaret and Lord Bob

were nowhere in sight. 'No, I'd better stay here with Jason – I'm not sure Margaret's really ready for the full drunk-son experience.' She pulled a face. 'Although it is tempting . . . I'd better say goodbye now.'

'I hope it's not goodbye,' said Alice, although it suddenly felt as if it was.

Luke pulled his leather jacket back on. 'We can go and get some details; then if you don't feel up to staying, we can go back in the morning,' he suggested.

'Why wouldn't she want to sleep in her own house?' Libby seemed surprised.

'What if it doesn't feel like my house?' The panic spilled out of Alice. 'I don't recognise Luke, but he knows me. What if I don't recognise Gethin? And why didn't he come and get me? Maybe we've split up? Maybe that was why I was coming here.'

Libby's face fell. 'Oh. I hadn't thought of that.'

'I'm sure there are good explanations for everything,' said Luke impatiently. 'But if we're going to go, let's go now. It'll take us nearly an hour to drive there.'

'Come here,' said Libby, and wrapped her into a big hug. 'I'm going to miss you.'

'I haven't gone yet,' said Alice, into her shoulder. 'I might still be coming back.'

She was joking, but as she spoke, a real memory swam into her head: the fluttering, anxious feeling of being dropped off at school for the first time – knowing what was ahead, but at the same time, not knowing at all.

The road out of Longhampton was quiet. Luke was a fast, confident driver and soon they were on the main road west;

they didn't speak, but a sense of calm filled the dark interior of Luke's work van and Alice sank back into the seat, watching the road signs with the unfamiliar names passing by under the creeping moonlight.

She tried to focus on the now, to stop her brain whirring. The van was extremely clean, the trim, seats and mats all black and spotless. She sniffed . . . It smelled of new car. Not old copies of the *Sun*, crisp packets, unwashed T-shirts, workmen. Luke, she could say confidently, was a meticulously clean workman. What was it he did? Security? That would make sense.

Alice had been trying not to look, but now she glanced across at him. Luke's eyes were fixed on the road, hands gripping the wheel at equal intervals, the shadows of his cheekbones merging with the faint stubble along his jaw.

She wondered when he was going to say something, or whether he was waiting for her to speak first. The silence wasn't uncomfortable, and although Luke wasn't as outwardly friendly as Libby or Jason, there was a determination about him that Alice found reassuring. Why? she wondered. Why was that? Could you trust instincts, if you didn't know people? Or were instincts just a reaction to things people had told you?

Libby seemed to like him, she reasoned. And she trusted Libby.

'Sorry, would you like me to put the radio on?' Luke asked. He didn't look at her as he spoke; she wondered if he was trying not to look at her too.

'No! No, honestly, it's fine. This is the quietest it's felt for days, actually,' she said. 'What with the builders in the hotel, and the phone ringing, and people in and out . . .'

'Not the ideal place to recover from an accident, then,' he

said. Luke's voice was neutral; if Jason was getting his accent back with every pint in the Bells, Luke had lost his altogether.

'I didn't mean . . . That sounds ungrateful. The builders have mainly been stripping wallpaper and pulling shelves out – it's the radio that's the noisiest part. Margaret's on their case about that.'

'I'm sorry I didn't know about the accident.' Luke bit his lip and finally glanced across. Alice's skin tingled as their eyes met. 'I've been in Spain – I decided to take that expat job I was telling you about, the guy with the—' He stopped. 'Well, the job I was telling you about last time I saw you.'

'Which was?'

'About a month ago? Three weeks?' He paused. 'You *really* can't remember?'

She shook her head. Didn't he believe her? 'And everything was . . . fine?' She didn't know why she'd asked that.

'Everything was fine,' Luke repeated, turning back to the road, and Alice realised she didn't know what fine looked like.

She stared out of the windscreen, at the dual carriageway stretching out towards her old life. Villages were passing; the miles were being eaten up; Gethin, the pub, her house were all getting nearer and nearer by the minute. So many questions she wanted to ask Luke, before he dropped her off and left her there.

'Why did I have the hotel address in my pocket?' she asked. 'You said I was looking for a better job than the one I had – was I looking for work there? Did you tell me Jason and Libby were hiring staff?'

Luke didn't answer at once. 'Maybe?' he said. 'We talked about the hotel, the family business, Jason taking over. I probably didn't describe it in the sort of terms that'd make you want to visit, though.'

'Really?'

'No.' He hesitated, then said, 'We talked a fair bit about family – you told me about both your parents dying before you were twenty and how it made you feel rootless, and I was trying to cheer you up, I think, by telling you how having living parents didn't necessarily give you a home from home. I probably told you I had to give my mum a few days' notice before a visit, even though she ran a hotel where dogs could check in no problem.'

'Oh.' It was the most he'd said since they'd met, and Alice sensed Luke was finding the darkness of the van, and the concentration on his driving, easier than the bright lights of the hotel. 'Was I sympathetic?'

He half laughed. 'You're a very good listener.'

'Am I?'

'What do you mean, am I? Don't you know?'

'No,' said Alice. 'You forget that no one's known me for the last couple of weeks. I've been asking myself a lot of questions. There are some things you don't know about yourself till other people tell you.'

'Bit profound.'

'Maybe. Hmm. Am I profound?'

He laughed again and Alice thought, That was familiar. Not the sound of his laugh, but her comfortable slump against the chair, the feeling of relaxing into a conversation with someone you liked.

She struggled to pin down the sensation to a memory, to one night, to a particular conversation, but it slid away and her fingers closed on thin air.

Did it need that sort of memory evidence, though? she wondered. She had enough facts: where it had happened, what they'd talked about, how she'd felt. Wasn't that all a memory was?

They'd slowed and stopped, waiting to turn right. Three, four cars passed; then Luke turned to her. He seemed to be making an effort to keep his expression neutral, but it wasn't completely working; his eyes searched her face for something. 'You really don't—' he started, then stopped, awkwardly.

'What?' Alice held her breath.

'Embersley, five miles,' said Luke, pointing at the sign, and without warning, the warmth gave way to the fluttering anxiety again.

The White Horse was almost empty when they walked in, except for a few late drinkers, and the noisy ducks weren't in evidence. Tony nearly leaped over the bar when he saw Alice, and she was congratulating herself on remembering his deep tan and bouncer's nose, until it occurred to her that Libby had shown her a photo on the pub website.

'Alice! Thank God you're OK. I was imagining you all covered in bandages,' he said, and would have hugged her if she hadn't warned him about her cracked ribs.

He recognised Luke and shook his hand, and made a few quips about darts; Alice watched them both for clues and saw nothing out of the ordinary. Luke had obviously been a good customer; Tony was a model 'mine host' pub owner who remembered everyone's names and favourite beers.

After running through the accident story yet again, more self-consciously with Luke listening, Alice asked for any contact details she'd left, and Tony gave her mobile numbers, hers and Gethin's, and an address in Stratton, which he said was about five miles back the way they'd come.

'You get along there now,' he urged her. 'Gethin'll be over the moon to see you safe and sound. He'll have been going spare.'

'He's not been in here looking for me?'

Tony shook his head. 'No, love. But then I was under the impression you two was on holiday.' His face was creased, confused. Like Lord Bob's when Libby shot the bolt on the swing door.

'I'm sure there's an explanation,' said Luke easily. 'Come on, Alice, we'll give Gethin a call from the car, let him know we're on our way.'

Tony followed them out, and as Alice turned to say good-bye, he slipped her a few folded notes.

'Call it an advance on your wages for next month,' he muttered. 'You don't wanna be rushing back to work, not with a bump to the head. Few mates of mine have had concussion over the years, boxers. It can be nasty. You take things easy, love.'

'Oh! Thanks,' said Alice, surprised by the generosity.

Tony closed his big hand over hers. He wore two gold signet rings, one on each hand. 'You just get yourself well. We want you back here, don't we? Give my best to that fella of yours.'

'I will.' Alice smiled, but with the odd sensation that she was playing a role, not speaking for herself.

Luke was waiting in the van, the engine already idling.

'Tony gave me two hundred quid,' she said. 'Wasn't that nice of him?'

'You're his best employee.' Luke swung his arm round the back of her headrest so he could reverse round a tree and she was aware of his energy: clean, warm, muscular. He paused and looked at her, his arm still resting on the back of her seat. 'That's one for your list. You're good with people.'

'I think I know that,' she said, as they drove out of the car park. 'Libby's put me on reception when she's been dealing with the builders. I don't get as stressed as she does.'

'Probably because it's not your problem. And I bet you've worked out the computer booking system quicker than Mum, concussion or not. Has she offered you a job yet?'

'Libby has, actually,' said Alice. 'I don't know if she meant it. They're not busy now, but her plans are really ambitious. Has she told you about the refurbishments?'

'Nope. Like I said, I don't really have a lot of contact with the place. Wasn't even consulted about them moving back to take over. Do you want to call Gethin?' he asked, tossing her his phone.

Alice hesitated. 'Um . . .' She did, and she didn't. It was late, she was tired, she wasn't looking her freshest, but it would seem odd not to want to see her boyfriend, and they'd come all this way . . .

She opened her mouth to ask Luke if Gethin was the sort of boyfriend who liked a full face of make-up and nice shoes, but then shut it again. Instinctively, she felt she could ask him anything, but Luke's body language seemed to shift between matching her relaxed confidence, and then abruptly closing off.

'Thanks,' she said. 'I will.'

She dialled the number Tony had given her. Her wobbly fingers meant she had to keep deleting and starting again.

'Bumpy road, sorry,' said Luke, without looking over.

Eventually the number was in. She pressed the dial button and held her breath. This is it. I'm going to speak to my boyfriend.

One ring and it went straight to voicemail. A generic

message too, not even Gethin's voice. Alice realised she was relieved.

'No answer?'

She shook her head.

'Never mind – we're nearly there.'

He pulled up outside a house, but apart from a faint light upstairs, it seemed to be in darkness.

'Are you sure this is it?' Alice leaned forward.

'Yes. Well, it's what Tony wrote down – 25 Hazels Avenue.'

Luke turned off the engine and they sat in silence for a moment, while Alice took it all in. It was a small 1930s semi, behind a metal gate topped with a sunburst, and a crazy-paved path that led up to a neat front door, with '25' at a jaunty angle over the brass letterbox.

She stared hard at the unassuming house, tinged yellow in the street light. I'm going to ring that doorbell and Gethin'll open the door and I'll be home, she thought. That's when it'll all come back.

Alice realised she was clutching the seatbelt. Her heart was speeding up, despite her deliberate breaths. She'd hoped and hoped for the moment Mr Reynolds said would come – the sharp click as things fell into place, or the sudden slipping away of the dark curtains covering the old memories – and now that it was here, she wasn't sure she was ready for it.

'Isn't it familiar?' Luke asked.

'No. Nothing is.' She was sure she'd never seen this house before in her life.

'Do you want to ring the bell? He might have gone to bed.' He nodded towards the house. 'It's gone eleven. Bit late.'

'So we're not night owls, then,' she said with a wan smile. 'One for the list.' She was playing for time now.

'Come on. I'll walk up with you,' said Luke, and opened his door.

Alice's legs felt jelly-like again as she stepped down onto the pavement. She made herself notice the other cars parked nearby: normal family cars, nothing too fancy, nothing too old. It was a very average, very nice street that she lived in.

Luke held the gate open for her and she walked up to the front door. Half of it was frosted glass, but she couldn't make out any light behind it, or behind the drawn curtains in the front bay window.

Alice rang the bell anyway, and heard it peal out in the hall. Luke stood a few paces behind her and she wondered if he'd have come with her had there been lights on inside.

Her mind began to race. What would Gethin say when he opened the door? What should she say?

Surprise!

Hello!

Sorry.

Alice checked herself. Sorry? What for?

For disappearing for over two weeks.

Two weeks in which he'd failed to find her. Not a word to the police, or even a notice in the newspaper, or online.

'Ring again,' said Luke. 'He's maybe in the bath.'

They waited for a minute, then another, until it was clear that there was no one inside 25 Hazels Avenue.

Alice peered through the glass, trying to make out any detail that might trigger a memory, but the glass was deceptively blurry and she couldn't make out a thing in the hallway. Not even if there was any post lying on the mat.

'Or maybe he's gone out, looking for you,' said Luke. 'Do you want to leave a note?'

'OK,' she said, and followed Luke to the van, where he handed her a smart leather A4 file.

'My notebook,' he explained, passing her a pen. 'For drawing pictures to explain things to clients. Got to make the right impression when you're selling security. People don't like to see their expensive alarm systems jotted down on the back of an envelope.'

'I see.'

Alice wasn't really listening; she was staring at the paper, and her head felt as if it were full of treacle. Where did you start, in a note to your frantic boyfriend, whose worried face you couldn't even remember?

Eventually, she scribbled, *I've been in an accident. Lost my phone, lost my memory for a couple of weeks – it's been a nightmare. I'm staying at the Swan Hotel in Longhampton. Please ring me as soon as you get this.* She added the hotel's phone number, and after checking with Luke, the postcode and email, then hesitated.

Love, Alice. Kiss?

She frowned. This was ridiculous.

Alice looked up and met Luke's eyes. He pretended to stare out of the windscreen for a second, then gave up the pretence.

'That's fine,' he said. 'Don't try to explain it now – you're tired. Stick it through the letterbox and let's get home.'

It felt reassuring to have all her worries boiled down to that. Alice smiled and went to post it through the door.

As the letterbox closed on her fingers, she had the sense of things tipping into the next stage. She'd started something new. She'd begun to wake up the past.

Chapter Fourteen

When Libby made her way into the hotel kitchen the next morning, her head buzzing with all the questions she wanted to ask Alice, she found Margaret already bustling around, re-wiping the surfaces Libby had wiped the previous evening while she was waiting for Luke and Alice to ring with news.

The bacon was on, and she could smell fresh coffee and toast.

How kind, she thought, surprised. And how nice to see Margaret bustle again. Libby decided she'd forgive her even if she delivered another bacon-cooking lesson.

'Good morning!' Margaret turned and gave her a big smile. She was wearing a pair of Marigolds, and one of the old silk scarves that had been her trademark accessory. Lord Bob was asleep under the table, having, from the look of his muzzle, already enjoyed a scrambled-egg breakfast of his own. 'How are we this morning?'

Libby decided to ignore Bob's illegal presence in the hotel kitchen for the time being, since at least half the breakfast routine had been done for her. In fact, it looked as if Margaret had nearly finished.

'Very well, thank you, Margaret,' she said. 'I thought it was my turn for breakfast today. How long have you been up?'

'Oh, I can't sleep when my chicks are ill.' She flapped a hand, then said, 'Ooh, toast!' as four slices of white toast popped up.

'Is this for room four?' Libby checked the tray that was out on the countertop, already set with a clean glass and cutlery. 'I didn't see he'd asked for room service. I thought he was dining downstairs this morning – did he leave a message?'

'What? Oh, sorry, no, Elizabeth, this is for Jason. Not room four.'

'For *Jason*?'

Margaret put the four slices of bread onto a plate, then turned back to the frying pan, where the bacon was reaching optimum crispness under Donald's bacon crisper. 'I popped my head round the door about ten minutes ago and he said he might be able to manage a little something.'

'Are you sure?' Libby eyed the bacon doubtfully. She'd popped her head round the door five minutes ago and he'd been flat out. The most he'd ever been able to face after a big night was a quadruple espresso. 'He normally just has a coffee and a couple of Beroccas . . .'

'Maybe in London.' Margaret flipped the bacon out of the pan and started to make two bacon sandwiches. 'But I think this'll have him up and back to normal much quicker. He asked for a Mum Special!'

Libby watched her fussing over the crusts, something she didn't even do for guests. It doesn't matter, she told herself. It really doesn't matter.

But it did.

It wasn't so much Margaret's insistence on treating Jason like a teenager, but the fact that Jason would rather choke down a plate of greasy bacon sarnies than tell his mum that he didn't want her making him a fry-up in bed.

Plus the fact that Margaret had got up early to make poor Jason, victim of spiked drinks, breakfast while leaving the job of the actual 'eaten by a guest rating the hotel' breakfast to her.

Not to mention the fact that Margaret had completely ignored the way Luke had rescued Jason last night, then driven all the way to Embersley, then Stratton and back to help Alice, without so much as a 'Isn't he a good lad?'

Libby cringed at her own whiny inner voice and told it to shut up. There was no point Margaret turning her into a stroppy teenager too.

'Can one of those bacon sarnies be for Luke?' she asked. 'He was a real hero last night – I think he deserves breakfast in bed.'

'Luke?' Margaret raised her eyebrows. 'Oh, I could, but . . . I think Jason needs two, and this is going to get cold. The pan's still hot, if you want to put some bacon on. And don't forget room four, dear! They should probably get theirs first, before family.'

Libby ground her teeth, reminded herself this was probably just another Donald-related coping strategy and put on the plain white apron she'd bought for official kitchen breakfast duties.

She'd just got the order from Mr 'Room Four' Harrington in the breakfast room and had ejected a grumbling Bob from her cooking space when Luke walked in, his hair damp, dressed in last night's clothes.

'Morning,' he said, rubbing a hand across his unshaven face. 'Is that for His Lordship?'

'Bob, or Jason? Neither. It's for our one solitary guest.' Libby waved her spatula in the direction of the spare room. 'His Lordship is enjoying a fry-up courtesy of his mother.'

'Ha! I'd like to see him force that down after the state he was in last night,' said Luke.

'Serves him right. You were next on my breakfast list – what can I make you?'

Luke shook his head. 'You're all right. Don't normally bother with breakfast. I didn't realise you *had* guests at the moment.' He leaned against the door frame, well out of her way. 'Don't they mind staying in a building site?'

'Luckily for our cash flow, there's a business park on the outskirts of town and some people have to stay in Longhampton overnight, whether the reception is covered in plastic sheeting or not. Tea?'

'Yes, please.' He smiled as she handed him a mug, and instantly looked less moody; Luke, Libby decided, suffered from Stern Resting Face.

'So, Gethin wasn't in last night?' she asked, unable to contain her curiosity. 'That's a shame. Are you going to go over there again today?'

'No, I'll be off as soon as I've finished this. Got to meet someone in Birmingham about a contract.'

'Work? On a Saturday?'

'Overseas client. They don't tend to bother too much what day of the week it is.' He sounded vague, and Libby wondered whether it was a security thing or because he wanted an excuse to leave. 'Alice left a note, so presumably Gethin'll ring some-time today. You can drive her over, can't you? I wouldn't let Jason behind the wheel for a while. Police are hot on morn-ing-after drivers round here.'

'Of course. You're welcome to come back for dinner tonight, after your job?'

'That's kind of you, but . . .' He made a face that clearly meant 'Mum'. 'Probably easier not to.'

'OK,' said Libby, wishing she knew how to mend the situa-tion. 'But if you change your mind . . .'

Funny, she thought, as he drained his mug too fast, that Luke didn't even want to hang around and say goodbye to Alice. But then if hanging around would mean more sniffing from his mother about his divorce, while Jason got the breakfast-in-bed treatment, she couldn't really blame him.

The hotel as Alice had known it when she'd first walked in had now vanished under a sea of dust sheets, but Libby's mind was clearly focused on the finished rooms. It seemed slightly previous to Alice to be testing paint colours in the first-floor bedrooms when half the walls weren't even plastered, but she could see why it would be keeping Libby sane in the madness.

'I like Mouse's Back,' said Libby, stepping aside to appraise the colours in the easterly light. 'But maybe London Stone would be more neutral. What do you think?'

'To be honest, I can't tell the difference. They're both nice.' Alice was thinking about Gethin's house in Stratton last night. Their house. Had she decorated there? Was Gethin a DIY type?

Her mind slipped to the one person who might be able to tell her. 'Is Luke around?'

'No, he left about nine.' Libby turned and Alice could see she was trying not to look too nosy, and failing. 'He had a meeting in Birmingham. Did you want to talk to him? I've got his number.'

'No. No, Gethin should be ringing soon.' She bit her lip. 'Although, maybe it'd be handy to have Luke's number. Just in case.'

'Just in case what?'

Alice met Libby's innocent gaze. 'I don't know. Just in case.'

'That's probably the last we'll see of him for months now.'

Libby sighed and pushed the lid back onto a tester can. 'Shame. I'd like to get to know Luke better.'

'Is he nice?'

'Not . . . *nice* nice. Interesting. He's travelled a lot. Probably not very domesticated. I sometimes wonder if this security business he's in is a little shady: he seems to work for some very private people, never says much . . .' She looked thoughtful. 'I think Jason and Margaret still see him as an arsey teenager, but I've never seen that side of him. I mean, he's a man of few words, but it's not like he rides into town on a motorbike, making trouble. He's thirty-six, for God's sake. He's probably VAT registered.'

'He's got a leather jacket.'

'So've I. Doesn't mean I've got a flick knife too.' Libby glanced at her, amused. 'I bet you know more about him than we do – or did, before the accident, I mean. I got the feeling you two talked, from what he was saying last night. Do you?'

'He did seem a bit . . . odd about me not remembering things,' she said carefully. Would you feel like that, if all you'd chatted about was darts and ducks?

'Well, I owe him a drink, for bringing Jason home from the club.' Libby groaned and ran her hand through her hair; Alice noted a few silver threads glinting in the blonde. 'I love Jason, but not when he drinks. I just hope he didn't leave his card behind the bar again. Urgh!' She stared around the stripped-back room and her shoulders sagged. 'So much to do . . .'

'You'll tell me, won't you, if there's anything I can help with?' Alice said. She realised she'd feel sorry to leave the Swan before Libby's transformation could take place.

Libby smiled. 'All I want you to do is to be by that phone

when Gethin calls to come and get you. And maybe help me do a couple more testers?'

There was a whole box of them. Alice hadn't even known there were that many shades of grey.

But Gethin didn't call on Saturday afternoon. Or Saturday night. Or first thing on Sunday.

While Alice was sitting in the office on Sunday afternoon, typing up a database of old guest details for Libby, she heard a familiar voice in reception. Two familiar voices.

'Look who's back!' Libby ushered Luke into the office. He was holding a flamboyant metallic bottle bag as if it might explode, and Libby widened her eyes meaningfully at his leather jacket. She looked delighted to have an in-joke.

'Hello again,' said Alice politely, although her stomach fluttered. 'Did you win a raffle?'

'No. Thank-you present.' He glanced sideways at Libby. 'Libby rang me and I was in the area, and she wouldn't take no for an answer. You shouldn't have,' he added. 'Really not necessary.'

'You deserve a *crate* for Friday night.' She squeezed his arm. 'We'll have to IOU you the other bottles till we're up and running.'

'No problem,' he said gruffly. He seemed awkward, particularly next to Libby's easy warmth. 'Tell Jase not to make a habit of it.'

'Believe me, he won't. He's only just regaining the power of speech. I've left him upstairs with the—' She put a hand to her mouth, as if she'd just remembered why Jason might need supervision. 'Oh, nuts. Hang on. I just need to go and . . .'

Libby dashed back up the stairs and Alice and Luke were

left alone. The silence stretched out, tightening the air between them. Alice hurried to fill it.

'And thanks for taking me home.' Should she have given him a present too? 'Bit of a wild goose chase in the end.'

Luke shook his head. 'Please. Don't mention it. Gethin rung yet?'

'Nope. But then a watched phone never rings, does it?' Alice eyed Lord Bob, squashed asleep in a chair too small for him. His back paw was nearly stuffed in his ear, and his rear end was overflowing the edge in a mass of velvety rolls. He'd missed his morning walk, since Margaret was fussing over Jason, and Libby was rushed off her feet, but he didn't seem unduly concerned.

'Maybe you should take the dog for a walk,' Luke suggested, reading her mind. 'Leave the phone.'

'Yes, he needs a walk. It can be my act of kindness for the day.' Alice hunted for her shoes. Not her shoes, she reminded herself, Libby's shoes. Her shoes were behind that locked door, in that strange house. What sort of shoes did she have? Heels? Converse? Doc Martens?

She had a sudden flash of a pair of deep green metallic heels. Green, with gold soles. The feeling of buying them flooded her mind: a bubbling, Friday-night, indulgent excitement. They were glamorous, attention-seeking party shoes. She remembered twirling round in the shop and thinking, Yes. The assistant saying, 'They're so you.'

Luke was looking at her. She blinked. Memories were starting to slip back into place now: bright chunks of experience, slightly over-bright but reassuring.

'Your act of kindness?' he prompted her.

'Oh. Um, I've been trying to do a random act of kindness every day,' she went on. 'There was a board in the hospital

– little things you can do to make the world better for everyone. Walking Bob's an easy one to do. Come on, Bob.'

At the sound of his name and 'walk', Bob performed a graceful backwards slide off the chair and ambled over, wafting his tail from side to side. It didn't wag like a normal dog, Alice thought, stroking his head. It was more like a royal wave.

Luke looked concerned. 'Are you sure you're up to handling him? Your ribs . . .'

'Are on the mend. I've got good painkillers. He's no bother for me. I don't know why everyone makes such a fuss. Anyway,' she added, looking up, 'you can drag him out of bins if need be. You're coming with me, aren't you? For a walk?'

He returned her gaze, not hiding from the question in it.

That was why he'd come, Alice knew. The present from Libby was a lucky excuse. He'd really come back to find out if Gethin had called. To check if she was all right. Why? What was there to worry about?

Or did he want to see her? Her skin prickled with something else she couldn't put her finger on, but it wasn't a memory. It was fresh. Uncertainty.

Then Luke gave his quick, slightly unwilling smile. 'Of course. What else is there to do in Longhampton on a Sunday except go for a walk?'

They didn't talk much, as they followed Bob's swaying rear view down the footpath behind the hotel, avoiding the frothy heads of the cow parsley reaching out of the tall hedge. The morning was soft with May sun, the warmth just beginning to spread through the air, and the gentle roll of the countryside was soothing in its soft greens and golds, dotted with sheep.

One Small Act of Kindness

It felt good to be outside. Not listening out for the telephone was a weight off her shoulders too, Alice realised. The rhythm of walking was a good substitute for conversation; although she felt comfortable with Luke, she couldn't think of a natural way to begin a conversation about such a weird situation, yet it didn't seem to matter that they weren't talking.

Eventually, after he'd heaved Lord Bob over a stile (Bob gazing serenely into space all the while as if it wasn't happening to him), Luke started, 'So what does it feel like, to lose your memory?'

Alice didn't answer at once. She wanted to give him a proper response. 'I'm not sure it's a specific feeling. It's more . . . an awareness of being in the moment the whole time. You can't refer back to anything; you can only deal with what's there. What you actually know. I mean, you know there has to *be* something behind you, but it's no help. You have to trust a lot more, because you don't have any points of reference.'

She glanced at him shyly. 'The more I think about it, the scarier it is, really. It could have turned out so differently. Libby and Jason, and your mum – they're decent people. I'm lucky.'

Luke didn't reply. She wondered if she'd put her foot in it.

'It's not so bad now my memory's coming back,' she went on. 'But the first few days, when I didn't even know my own name, that was scary. I felt . . . I felt as if everyone I met knew more about me than I did. I couldn't actually think about it too much because it made me panicky. I'm pretty sure they gave me medication to stop me thinking about it too much.'

She shivered, remembering. Two weeks ago. It felt like a lot longer. 'Ha!' she said aloud.

Luke turned his head. 'What?'

'That was a memory.' Alice grinned. 'A brand-new one.'

He smiled too, and Alice could believe they'd had long chats; something clicked with him, letting the words stream out without effort. 'So . . .' He pulled a long stem of buttercups out of the hedge. 'When you say long-term memories . . . ?'

'Well, how much of being seven can you remember? Some things are coming back, but it's not like I can check with Mum or Dad, is it? I suppose I won't know until I can't remember something. But it's weird – I keep getting random flashbacks. Like my memory's resending emails by mistake while it reboots itself.'

'Like what? Those ducks at the pub? I can't believe you can't remember the ducks. They drove me insane and I was only there for a few weeks.' He said it artlessly, but Alice wondered if it was loaded in some way, to test whether she could remember their conversations, maybe.

'No, nothing recent.' Alice probed into her mind, trying to pinpoint a time: the green shoes, say. When had she had money to spend on shoes like that? Five years ago? Later? 'The consultant thinks that I might never get the accident memories back. That might be a trauma reaction, as much as a physical injury. They can't always tell the difference, medically.'

'Really?'

'Yep. It'd have been bad enough – the shock, I mean. There were two cars – Libby says everyone was amazed I wasn't more badly injured.'

'*Two* cars?' Luke's voice was concerned and she realised he'd stopped walking. He touched her arm. 'Seriously, you could have been killed, Alice.'

She stopped too. Her arm tingled where his fingertips met her skin. After a second, Luke moved his fingers and she wondered if he'd felt the tingle too. They stared at each other and the silence was so intense Alice could hear sheep in a field beyond the next hedge.

'You look as if you want me to say something,' she blurted out, and Luke seemed about to speak, but then he stopped and shook his head.

'I just want . . . I just hope your memory comes back.' He kept his dark brown eyes on hers, reading her face. 'It must be . . . Well, I can't imagine what it must be like.'

'It's like losing yourself,' said Alice simply, and something answered in Luke's eyes, though he didn't speak.

The moment was broken by Lord Bob tugging on his extendable lead, heading towards a hole in the hedge.

'Poor sod,' said Luke, as the hound duly wedged himself in the hole, leaving half his solid body sticking out in the path, tail curved over his back in blissful contemplation. 'He must get pretty bored up there, fussing about the hotel all day. No, let him have a sniff. We're not in a rush, are we?'

'No,' said Alice. She felt better for the exercise; the clean air and sunshine made her feel fresher. I should ask about Gethin, she thought, while I'm talking to the one person who knows him.

She ignored the sense that she was revising her own boyfriend for a test.

'How long did you say I'd been with . . . with Gethin?'

Luke looked blank. 'Um, I don't know exactly. A year? Bit longer?'

'Because I've got no memory of him. I must be missing the last eighteen months or so.'

'You hadn't been at the pub that long. I remember Tony telling me how quickly you'd picked everything up.'

'Not very flattering, is it? That I can't even remember what he looks like?'

Luke made a friendly 'huh' noise without turning round. He was watching Bob, who was still with concentration, all his focus in his huge basset nose, detecting and processing the complex bouquet of smells in the earth like an expert wine taster.

'You don't know why I was heading for the hotel, do you?' It was easier to ask Luke a direct question when he wasn't looking at her.

'We weren't planning to meet there, if that's what you're thinking.'

'I wasn't thinking that!' Alice blushed. 'That hadn't even . . . crossed my mind.'

'Good.' The smile again. Quick but guarded. 'Come on, Bob, that's enough.'

Bob backed out without a murmur and set off down the hill again. They were almost at the woods now; Alice had done this walk once before with Libby – down to the woods, which in turn led into the town's park, where there was a coffee stand that served doughnuts. Nice doughnuts. If you were Bob, free doughnuts.

'And there's no reason you know of that Gethin hasn't tried to find me?' she asked. She hadn't wanted to ask in front of Libby; something about Libby's eagerness for a happy ending made her too embarrassed to reveal her murkier, middle-of-the-night worries.

'Not that I'm aware of.'

'It's just that . . . two weeks?' It was spilling out now. 'And it's not even like I'm that far away. I assumed I'd come from London or something. How many hospitals *are* there round here?'

'Sorry, Alice. I don't know why he didn't find you. Maybe you rowed?'

'Did we row a lot?'

'Don't all couples row?'

'I don't know.'

He sighed. 'We didn't talk about Gethin in detail. There were always a million and one other things to talk about.'

'Sorry.' Alice remembered that Libby had mentioned Luke's wedding. Two years ago. Oh. Maybe he'd opened up to her about *his* marriage and she'd forgotten. Maybe that was why he was so keen to find out what she remembered. Her heart sank.

Luke ran a hand through his hair and it flopped back onto his forehead. 'You and Gethin were . . . You said he was a nice bloke. Sensitive. You had some mates that weren't so happy with their blokes, asked us our opinions on that, once or twice. One mate whose boyfriend was a bit possessive, like. Not sure we were great agony aunts, to be honest.'

'Oh.' Alice wasn't sure how that made her feel. Pleased? Relieved? Guilty? More friends who hadn't come to find her.

She glanced over at Luke again; his face wasn't giving much away, and the atmosphere between them had shifted.

'I'm sorry I have to ask,' she said, 'but you're the only person so far who can tell me who I really am. Until I remember.'

Luke let out a long breath that turned into a groan. 'It's not healthy for other people to tell you what you're like. I should know. I guess my reputation's gone before me at home?'

'I don't know what you mean.'

'I think you do. As Libby'll find out when she tries to launch her boutique bolthole, Longhampton's a place where things aren't allowed to change much.' Alice had the sense that Luke's observant eyes were seeing more of her mind than he was letting on. It was unsettling. 'But anyway – coffee? I can see a stand down there.'

'Coffee would be great,' said Alice.

They walked down towards the park and took one of the paths round the flower beds to the mobile coffee stand, where Luke ordered two lattes, and Bob helped himself to the water. They were chatting about the park, Luke giving her a surprisingly detailed potted history of the town, when she saw him casually add a sachet of sugar to one cup, and two more to the other. He stirred them, replaced the lids and handed her the two-sugar latte. Something about the gesture felt startlingly intimate.

'That's how I have my coffee?' she asked, staring at the cup.

Luke nodded. 'Yes. Isn't it?'

'It is.' But she'd had to have a couple of coffees at the hotel to remember. *How many coffees have we had together?* she wanted to ask. *Why did you remember?*

'Alice, I work in security,' he said, seeing her expression. 'I notice things. Tell me a phone number and I can't forget it. My brain hangs on to stuff. We were the last ones in the bar every night; we often had a coffee while you were cashing up.'

'Fine,' she said, and waited for the image: over-bright, end-of-the-evening bar, the smell of a coffee machine, cashing up . . . Nothing came.

Then Bob let out a full-throated bellow and she jumped, spilling froth onto her hand.

A volley of smaller, yappier barks issued from across a couple of flower beds. Right on the other side of the park were a pair of dog walkers, each wrestling four dogs, two in each hand. Alice couldn't see the smaller dogs giving out the loudest yaps, as they were hidden behind the splashy bedding, but the two golden retrievers and the collie were making their feelings known to Bob.

'Poor Bob, he always gets blamed for this,' she said, as Luke put himself between Bob and the dog walkers. 'Just because he's got the loudest voice.'

'Bark,' said Luke. 'The loudest bark. Treat him like a dog and he'll behave like a dog. He's never going to cut it as a small human being. It's not fair on anyone, that.'

'Is that profound?' Alice raised an eyebrow.

'Nope,' said Luke. 'I just say what I see. People are what they are, and so are dogs. When you work with security dogs, you don't treat them like they're Sherlock Holmes. Come on, let's head back. Give me Bob's lead – *my* act of kindness,' he added, 'so you can drink your coffee.'

Alice managed a smile. He listens, she thought, logging it in her private mental notebook. Luke listens, and notices. He knew more than he was letting on.

He juggled his own coffee, Bob's lead and his change with impressive control. 'I bet there'll be a message waiting for you.'

'Fingers crossed.' She raised a hand to the dog-walking couple, as did Luke, and followed him back up the path. An hour ago, she wanted a message more than anything. Now, she wasn't quite so sure.

Chapter Fifteen

By the start of the builders' second week in residence at the Swan Hotel, the change was so drastic that when Margaret had gone up to give her opinion on Libby's paint testers, she'd only been able to stand it for two minutes before bursting into tears.

Admittedly, it was a bombsite: Marek's builders had ripped out eight en suites, steamed off more than thirty years' worth of wallpaper, removed the chipped skirting boards and generally stripped the rooms right back. Libby thought it actually had rather a chic deconstructed style now – you could see the honest thick floorboards and solid walls.

Margaret saw it rather differently. As her brave face crumpled, Libby realised, too late, that her mother-in-law was seeing over thirty years' work down the drain. She could have kicked herself. Margaret's improved mood, when she'd had Alice to look after, had fooled Libby into thinking she was more recovered than she really was.

'It'll be beautiful again when the decorators have been in, I promise.' Libby stroked her mother-in-law's arm. 'Look – which of these colours do you like?'

'I don't care. Whatever you think best. I'm not going to look again until it's done.' Margaret had made a gulping noise and hurried downstairs. Jason had had to drive her to the big

Waitrose to restore her equilibrium. He didn't say so, but Libby was pretty sure he'd picked up the bill for the five bags of artisan foodstuffs that later materialised in the fridge. Margaret definitely didn't have the money to pay for organic tiramisu, but then neither did they.

'It's a *good* thing they've got so much done,' Libby pointed out to Alice, while they were checking the latest delivery of baths and basins on Wednesday morning. It was stacked up in boxes in the lounge, nearly filling the room. 'The plumbers are coming tomorrow, and when these are in, it'll look much better.'

She ran her hand round the curved rim of one of the roll-top baths. It was a massive double-ended slipper, more a work of art than a bath. A whole page of the new website was going to focus on the Swan Hotel bathrooms, their signature treat. Glass of wine, big white church candles, Wi-Fi throughout so you could listen to the in-room iPod while you soaked. Who could resist that in the magazine spread?

We could do our own range of toiletries eventually, she thought, imagining the photographs. With a white swan as the logo.

'Is this the Chatsworth double-ended tub?' Alice was flipping through the delivery invoice.

'It is. This is going to be in the honeymoon suite,' she said proudly. 'With a circular shower rail above it, and this stunning lacy curtain I've found in Anthropologie.'

Alice peered at it. 'Which room's that? Will it fit?'

'We're making room five the honeymoon suite and knocking into room six to make the bathroom,' explained Libby. 'Room six was always on the small side. Better to have a really gorgeous romantic suite we can charge more for.'

'OK,' said Alice. 'And the taps for that – are they these?' She indicated a big box, full of bubble wrap.

'Yes, they're amazing, look.' Libby struggled to lift the heavy fittings. 'You need a huge mixer tap and a proper Edwardian shower head with that bath.' They were about the size of a tuba when she finally managed to heave them out of their seafoam wrapping.

She and Alice gazed at the majestic silver contraption.

'Wow,' said Alice. 'And that was separate? On top of the bath? Do I even want to know how much that cost?'

'Don't ask.' Jason insisted that he'd negotiated a good price, and after their showdown about Darren's deal, Libby felt she needed to show she trusted him and his financial acumen. 'It's going to be worth it, though. I've got this vision in my mind of how it's all going to be when it's finished, and I know people are going to be clamouring to stay here. If I would, they will. Why? Is there a problem?'

Alice tapped the paper with her pen. 'According to this despatch note, and your order, only half the stuff's here. You're missing three baths, three showers, four loos and some brackety things.' She compared the lists. 'This is what Jason ordered . . . This is what they've sent.'

Libby rolled her eyes. 'Brilliant. This always happens, doesn't it? If you don't check things . . . Good job we found out before the plumbers did. Jason can get on to the suppliers today. Have you seen him this morning?'

'He was going into town.' Alice looked mischievous. 'He said that if you went mad because he'd gone out, I should tell you that he was shopping for your anniversary present.'

'Oops.' She covered her mouth with her hand. 'Thanks for the reminder. It's on Friday. Five years.'

'I know it's on Friday,' said Alice. 'Margaret asked if I wouldn't mind stepping in to do some cover, so you and Jason could, and I quote, "make a night of it".'

Libby noted that Margaret wasn't 'stepping in' to do the cover herself, but was touched she'd remembered. It couldn't be easy for her.

Or for Alice, she thought guiltily, seeing her eyes drop momentarily to the invoices. Gethin still hadn't called. By now they weren't even jumping when the phone rang.

'Listen, I bet you anything he'll walk in on Friday night,' she said impulsively. She didn't need to say who. 'He'll have been working away all week, back on Friday, sees your note . . . Bam. Round here, bunch of roses, apologies, tears, happy ending.'

Alice forced a smile. 'Yup. That's generally how it works out in Hollywood.'

'And Longhampton.' Libby pretended to look outraged. 'As Margaret is very fond of reminding me, nothing bad ever happens round here. They only keep the policemen on because they've got a nice male-voice choir.'

Libby knew from various 'special meals' of the past that Ferrari's was generally regarded as the graduation/anniversary/birthday restaurant in Longhampton and had been since it opened in the early 1980s. It served a variety of Italian dishes, some of which had been in and out of fashion twice since their original arrival on the menu.

When Libby and Jason arrived on Friday evening, the maître d' arrived to take their coats and make a huge fuss of Jason, whom he'd known since he was so high, and then of Libby, whose hand he kissed.

'How is your mother?' he asked Jason solicitously. 'And her lovely dog?'

'Both very well, Gianni,' said Jason. 'And Mrs Ferrari?'

This was obviously a long-standing joke, as Gianni roared with half-Italian, half-Longhampton laughter.

Throughout this performance, Jason's eyes kept darting towards Libby, as if asking her to be patient, to play along, but Libby's smiles were genuine. She liked the kitschiness of the place, and the sweet way Jason kept up his end of the routine. It reminded her of old times: Ferrari's wasn't unlike some of the cheap dates he'd taken her on before he had much money to splash or knew where to splash it.

They were shown to their table – the date-night table in the corner, with the two red roses in the centre – and Jason held out her chair.

'Very kind,' she said, sliding in.

'Champagne!' announced the waiter, presenting the chilled bottle to Jason with a flourish. 'Sir?'

'You'd better show it to madam – she's the expert,' he said, waving the bottle towards her.

Libby smiled across the table at him. 'Looks perfect,' she said to the waiter. 'Please go ahead.'

The champagne was poured with maximum care and attention, a middle-aged couple dining nearby smiled benevolently at them, and with a final ceremonious lighting of the single candle, the waiter shimmied off.

'Alone at last,' he said. 'Well, as much as you ever are round here.'

'So,' said Libby, lifting her glass.

He touched it with his. 'Cheers. Happy anniversary.'

'Happy anniversary, darling.' She took a sip of champagne,

savouring the tingle of the bubbles on her lips, and instantly the biscuity taste brought memories of all those other nights crowding back into her mind.

'Here's to the next five years.' Jason took a more generous swig and made a 'that's better' face. 'Ah, that's not bad at all, is it?' He checked the label and looked impressed.

It was like old times, thought Libby – happier old times. To watch Jason in charge of a situation, checking wine labels, pretending he knew what he was looking for when they both knew he didn't. She'd forgotten how sexy Jason looked in a suit, and felt a low, dirty buzz of excitement at the thought of later on: cufflinks out, shirtsleeves rolled up, his tanned fore-arms bare. She loved the intimacy of skin revealed under businesslike tailoring. Morning after morning, before she knew his name, Libby had gazed across the packed carriage at the soft gap between the good-looking stranger's stiff white collar and the unruly blond curl at the nape of his neck, and imagined pushing all the commuters aside so she could press her lips against it.

When the hotel was finished, Jason could wear a suit on Fridays, she thought. Dress-up Fridays. So she could trap him in the office, against the partners' desk . . .

'What are you thinking about?' His expression was flirty now too. 'You've got that look on your face.'

Libby let a seductive smile spread from her mouth up to her eyes. 'What sort of look?'

'The "where are we going on after?" look,' said Jason. 'No, I know. Are you wondering what I've got you for your anniver-sary present?'

'No! Since you ask, I was thinking of how this all started. On that 6.53 train. You spilling your coffee over yourself.'

'Oh!' He raised his eyebrows. 'That.'

'That lovely scarf.' She sighed. 'I still miss it.'

'Don't I know it. How many scarves have I bought you to make up for it since?'

When the promised dry-cleaning didn't work – to Jason's mortification – a brand-new cashmere scarf had arrived at her desk. Libby had been dazzled. It had cost the same as two months' salary for her. Too nice to wear.

'You don't need to buy me things,' said Libby. 'It's *you* I want.' She took another sip of champagne and eyed him over the rim of the flute. 'That's all I've ever wanted. You.'

'Oh, so you don't want this?' He reached under the table and slid a small box in front of her. 'Happy anniversary. Now where's mine?'

Libby put her glass down and pulled her bag onto her knee. Jason's beribboned present had only just made it in time. Thank goodness for internet shopping, she thought. 'Open together?'

'OK, go.'

There was the usual theatrical scrabbling at the paper, and when it was off, Libby found herself holding a box from Tanners, the town's jeweller's.

'Oh, now that's embarrassing,' she said, looking across at Jason's box. 'I went for a joke present, for budget reasons.'

'This is . . . perfect.' He held up the Longhampton United football mug, personalised with his name on one side.

'Your old one was on its last legs,' she explained. 'And they've changed their logo twice since then. It was that or the home strip, and I didn't think black and red was really you.'

'No. And I've nowhere to wear it these days. The rugby club tends to frown on people turning up in football kit.'

'I do realise you play rugby, by the way,' Libby added, in case he thought she'd got them mixed up, 'but I noticed your coffee mug and, you know, new start, new team, back home . . .'

'No, I get it.' Jason smiled. She hoped he did like it. She hadn't had as long as normal to think about his anniversary present; it had seemed like a flash of inspiration unloading the dishwasher, but now she wasn't so sure.

'Go on,' he said, nodding at the box.

With a tiny twinge of misgiving, she pushed back the lid. The box was padded inside with red velvet, and sitting on top of it was a pair of diamond earrings. They were tiny – not the sparklers he'd given her in the past – but they were pretty, and real. The sort of thing he used to buy her because all the other wives had wish lists at Asprey, and he didn't think she meant it when she said she'd prefer books or some jewellery she could wear without worrying about losing it.

'Jason!' she said, feeling ridiculously churlish. 'They're gorgeous! But . . .'

'Don't say it.'

'I have to.' Libby swallowed. 'I love them. But you don't need to buy me diamonds when we're on a budget.'

She didn't say *shouldn't*. She didn't want to take away the spontaneous gesture of it. The generosity she'd always loved.

Jason met her gaze. 'I was in town, and I was walking past Tanners, and I remembered how Mum always used to make me stop while we were out shopping, so she could look at the display. And I used to think, When I'm a grown-up and I've got a wife, I'll buy her nice things from Tanners. And now I'm lucky enough to have a wife, a better wife than I ever dreamed of having when I was a kid, and I felt so good, finally coming out with that little bag.'

'Jason . . .'

He reached across the table and took her hands in his. 'I know this last year's been hard, and I know you've compromised on a lot to start again like this. Making breakfasts, and the dog, and my . . . my mother. But I promise you, Lib, I will make this seem like the best decision we ever made.' Jason gazed up at her and Libby felt her heart flip at the hope in his expression.

'I couldn't do any of this without you,' he said. 'I wouldn't *want* to do it without you.'

'Jason, I don't know what to say.'

'You don't have to say anything. Put the earrings in. See if they fit?'

'Course they fit. Diamonds always fit. That's why they're a girl's best friend.' Libby smiled and carefully unhooked her little gold hoops.

He watched as she slipped in the studs. 'You're *my* best friend. And you're more beautiful than they are.'

Libby turned her head back and forth in the candlelight, making the diamonds sparkle, pretending she was modelling them. It felt nice, but she couldn't quite enjoy it. The memory of the conversation with her dad still gave her a bad feeling. And where had Jason actually got the money from? The renovation account? Had it gone on a card?

She caught Jason gazing at her, so proud and pleased at the looks they were getting from the other tables, and she told herself to give it a rest, just for tonight. Tonight wasn't about the hotel; it was about *them*. Their marriage. They might have lost material things, but they still had each other. They hadn't had much when they first met, but it had been more than enough. Accepting these would show that, even if he had stuck them on a card, she believed they'd make enough to pay it off, together.

Libby reached across the table to take Jason's hand. 'I haven't compromised to run the hotel with you, you idiot,' she said, playing with his wedding ring. 'I *want* to do it. I want us to make something real together. It's going to be amazing.'

'Well, it will be now we're not reliant on me faffing around with a sander . . .'

'You were *great* at sanding. You have no idea how much I fancied you in protective eye goggles. But you were right to get Marek in – it's coming together so fast now. It's going to be amazing.'

'You have to take credit for that. Marek says you've got a great eye.' Jason stroked her palm, following her life line. 'Even Mum's going to love those baths, once she sees them plumbed in.'

Libby wasn't so sure. There'd been a slight chill in the air around Margaret since the weekend; she didn't seem to think Libby had paid quite enough attention to Jason's 'alcohol poisoning' and had expressed her disapproval in a series of passive-aggressive comments about the showers. 'Ostentatious', apparently.

Actually, Libby realised, that's *not* passive aggressive.

'Turns out all those spa breaks with the girls were good research.' He smiled. 'I bet Erin's chomping at the bit to come out, is she?'

'She says so.' Libby wavered. 'She might just be being polite. They go to some pretty smart places . . .'

'And the Swan won't be? Come on! Once the website's up and she reads about your romantic boudoirs, the whole street'll be trying to make a block booking. How many thread counts were we supposed to be having? A thousand? Ten thousand? Is that the same as togs? How many togs did you order?'

Jason pretended to look bewildered and Libby laughed at him.

'Four hundred should be fine. But we don't have to . . .'

He raised a warning finger and touched her lips, knowing what she was about to say, then moved it away, before it could feel mean. 'Don't. Just trust me, OK?'

'I do.' Libby gazed into his beautiful pale blue eyes, hoping he could see into her heart the way she felt she was looking into his. 'But none of this is worth more than us. You know that, don't you? I'd rather have nothing and you than be running Claridge's and be . . . and be where we were before.'

'I just want to give you everything,' he said simply. 'You can't blame me for that, can you?'

'The earrings are more than enough,' said Libby firmly. 'More. Than. Enough. Look. Here comes Gianni for our order – do you know what you want?'

'Yes,' said Jason, and the burning, hungry look he directed straight at her, over the date-night-table candles, made her shiver inside.

After the champagne, they put away a bottle of red wine, some homemade ravioli, and shared an ice-cream sundae – which was brought with two long spoons and an avuncular wink – and as they were finishing, two brandies arrived, a gift, Gianni explained, from the older couple they'd seen on the way in.

'Stan and Rosemary. They tell me they were given champagne on their honeymoon,' explained Gianni as he delivered them on a silver tray, 'and they like to pass on the gesture to a young couple in love on their anniversary.'

'That's very romantic,' said Libby. By the door, Stan was courteously helping Rosemary into her smart pink coat, a picture of married bliss. Libby smiled and blew a tipsy thank-you kiss to them and they smiled.

'We should come out more often,' said Jason, turning back to the table. 'I think that's the first time anyone's bought me a drink back here.'

'I'm going to put it on the Tree of Kindness in the hospital.' Libby was feeling quite emotional. Or 'emotion-ale' as Jason termed any booze-enhanced humanitarianism. 'Thank you, Stan and Rosemary, for giving me and my husband something to aim for on our anniversary.'

'What? Still going out for dinner in our fifties?'

'No!' She swatted him playfully. 'For showing us that romance doesn't have to stop once you're married.'

Jason caught her hand and kissed the tender inside of her wrist. 'I can show you that.'

'We should go home,' she said suddenly. 'Or not home.'

Libby glanced outside. It was still quite light, at ten past nine, and a warm evening. The High Street wasn't exactly Piccadilly Circus, but it wasn't quite as dead as she'd expected it would be. A Friday-night bonhomie seemed to have spread over Longhampton – although she was prepared to accept that could have been the wine.

'That bandstand in the park,' she said suddenly. 'Have you been back, since you were a teenager?'

'I can't think what you mean,' said Jason, with a straight face. 'I never went to the bandstand. That'd be my brother you're thinking of.'

'Never too late to be a rebel,' said Libby. 'Shall we get the bill?'

Jason didn't need to be asked twice. He signalled for the nearest waiter, making a scribbling sign in the air. So many dinners, thought Libby, remembering how many times she'd seen him make that gesture. So many drinks, so many taxis home – Jason had always wanted to treat her, look after her.

It must hurt him, she realised, not being able to do that. When the numbers weren't doing what he wanted them to anymore, and she didn't trust him to try.

She felt a vibration in her handbag and looked down. 'I've got a call,' she said, 'from the hotel. Take it?'

'Better had.' Jason sighed. 'Probably Mum trying to change the Sky to John Nettles Gold and getting stuck on *DIY SOS* by mistake.'

'Hello?' Libby pressed the phone to her ear. The restaurant had filled up since they'd arrived and it was quite hard to hear.

'Libby? It's Alice.'

Alice, Libby mouthed at Jason.

He grinned and ran his foot up the side of her calf.

'Sorry to disturb you on your night out,' Alice went on, 'but I thought I should let you know . . . Gethin just called. He's on his way over.'

'Gethin rang? Oh my God! Alice! Do you want us to come back?' She widened her eyes at Jason to convey the exciting news. Thoughts of the bandstand slipped from her mind, to be replaced with the mysterious Gethin.

Libby had wondered a lot about who would come for Alice. Tall? Dark? Blond? Chiselled and moody, like Luke? No, someone reliable, a teacher, or a farmer . . .

'Um, no . . . No, you don't have to come back. I just thought I'd let you know, in case . . .' Alice sounded anxious.

One Small Act of Kindness

'We'll come back,' said Libby. 'See you soon. No, it's no bother. Bye-bye!' She hung up. 'Gethin's just called. He's on his way to the hotel.'

There was a moment's hesitation.

'What happened to the bandstand?' asked Jason.

'Well, what if there's a scene?' Libby's imagination was whirling. 'What if she doesn't recognise him? What if—'

'Admit it – you're just curious,' said Jason. 'That's fine. That's the Libby I married.' The corner of his mouth twitched. 'I've got to admit I'm kind of curious too. Let's get a cab.'

Libby smiled. Gethin had come back. She and Jason had survived their worst year. There *were* happy endings in Longhampton.

Margaret was right. It was all going to be fine.

Chapter Sixteen

It had all happened very quickly, and then, when it was over, Alice sat stunned, struggling to separate what she *felt* from what she *knew*. Before the accident, she'd never realised they were two different things.

She had spent the evening behind the reception desk, turning the old guestbook into a database for Libby. Excel spreadsheets had obviously been a big part of her temping life because the rhythms of clicking and typing had come back to her fingers quickly. She'd enjoyed inputting the data, watching it stack up and knit together to form patterns and trends.

Which counties had the most guests. What the most popular surname was. Who'd stayed the most often. Who were the oldest and youngest guests. Who'd come back with different partners. Alice's brain was hungry for information and liked the feeling of making a contribution to the ordering of the hotel. She clicked 'save' often.

The phone hadn't rung all night, and she'd almost forgotten it was there when it suddenly pealed out. Alice was in the middle of deciphering a scrawly guest information card and reached out with her right hand, without looking.

'Good evening. The Swan Hotel, Longhampton. How may I help you?'

'Is this . . . ? Alice, is that you?'

The voice was quiet, soft. Welsh.

Alice froze. It was him. Gethin. But was that a memory, or because she knew he was going to call, and she knew he would be Welsh? The dark cloud in her head expanded again, blotting out all the details she wanted to grasp.

'Hello?' he repeated, less certainly.

'This is Alice.' Her mouth was dry. 'Is that Gethin?'

'Yes! Alice. Oh my goodness, Alice, what a relief!' He sounded emotional. 'I've just this second walked in and found your note on the mat. I can't . . . I can't understand what's happened. What are you doing in a hotel? Where are your keys? Why didn't you come home?'

Do I know that voice? Alice felt as if she were floating above herself, trying to analyse every detail of her reaction. She'd almost stopped wondering when Gethin was going to call and this had caught her unprepared.

'I'm coming over right now,' he went on. 'I'll be with you as soon as I can. Do you need anything? Do you want me to bring some of your things?'

'No, I'm fine.' My boyfriend's coming to get me, Alice told herself. He sounds upset and worried and confused. She felt like grabbing her unresponsive heart and shaking it, but it wouldn't do anything.

Maybe it was the medication. Mr Reynolds had told her it took a while to get prescription drugs out of your system. It had only been three weeks, after all.

'You stay right there,' Gethin said, as if she were calling from the edge of a cliff. 'And don't you worry, Bunny – I'm on my way.'

He'd hung up.

Bunny. Alice had stared at the phone in her hand for a few long seconds. Her legs felt twitchy even though she was sitting down, as if they wanted to get up and run and run and run.

This is where my life restarts. Like the 'play' button's been pressed again.

Then, with shaking hands, she'd phoned Libby.

When Libby and Jason pulled up fifteen minutes later in a taxi, Alice thought Gethin had somehow managed to get there even faster than she'd thought and at last a swarm of butterflies surged up through her chest.

But it was Libby in her red date-night dress who came hurrying in, high heels scuffing on the tartan carpet. She hadn't even had time to put on her jacket; it was flung over one arm, along with her little evening bag. Her face was flushed with excitement, and her lipstick was smeared where she'd reapplied it in the back of the cab.

Alice noticed the tiny new diamonds in her ears. They were sparkling almost as brightly as Libby's eyes.

'Is he here yet?' she demanded breathlessly, scanning the reception.

'No, not yet.'

Jason hadn't followed her in – he poked his head round the front door. 'Lib, have you got some money for the taxi?'

'What?' Libby frowned, then popped open her bag with some difficulty. Alice could see she was a bit worse for wear. It was quite endearing to see Libby trying to pretend not to be drunk.

'Petty cash,' she said, and opened the drawer with the cash box in it and handed Libby a twenty-pound note. 'Give me the receipt. You were hurrying back for hotel business.'

'You so have a job here.' Libby pointed at her, a little wobbly, and swayed back to give Jason the money.

One Small Act of Kindness

Alice took a deep breath and poured herself a glass of water from the cooler. Libby came back in with Jason and the three of them stood awkwardly round the check-in desk. The long-case clock ticked underneath its dust sheet.

'So . . .' said Jason after a few moments. 'Have I got time to go upstairs and change? What time did he ring?'

'About twenty minutes ago?'

'Oh, we've *ages* yet.' He loosened his tie and undid his top button. 'He's got to get here from Stratton. I'm going to change.'

'Do you have to?' Libby looked disappointed. 'You look so nice in that suit.' She stroked his arm. 'You can take the jacket off if you want. Roll up your sleeves . . .'

'You do look smart,' said Alice. 'Both of you.' There was a different sheen to them tonight, a breath of urban confidence that made them unfamiliar. It wrong-footed her somehow.

'It's Friday night,' protested Jason.

'I know. That's what I meeeeean.' Libby slid her arms round his waist from behind and murmured into his ear. 'Keep the lovely suit on.'

Alice hadn't seen Libby so playful before. Her sleeveless low-cut dress was showing off a lot more of her soft skin than normal, and her usual sensible manner had been replaced with a rather charming kittenishness. Charming because it was quite unexpected. Alice realised she wouldn't have linked this Libby with the Libby making lists for the builders and worry-ing what she'd forgotten.

Jason laughed and kissed her. He seemed different too, Alice thought. Was this how they'd been in London? 'And I thought it was me you fancied, not my tailor.' He peeled her arms away. 'I won't be a minute. I'll let Mum know what's going on – I'm sure she'll want to say hello too.'

227

When he'd gone, despite Libby's complaints, she sank down behind the desk in the chair next to Alice and sighed contentedly.

'Nice evening?'

'Very.' Libby leaned back and surveyed the reception, smiling at something in her head. Then she turned to Alice, all eagerness. 'So, did it all rush back? When you heard his voice?'

'Not really.'

'Oh. Oh well, maybe when you see him. I wonder what he looks like.' Libby swung on her chair. 'I see you with someone . . . quite tall. Dark. With glasses. Sensitive but strong.'

'Clark Kent.'

'No! A nice, normal guy.'

'I don't think it's all that helpful, actually, trying to work out what he'll be like. What if I imagine something he's not? I don't want to be disappointed.'

Libby turned a soulful gaze on her. Her eyeliner was flicked at the edges, proper cat's-eye flicks. She'd obviously taken a lot of time over her appearance this evening. 'Did he sound like he missed you?'

'Yes.'

'Then that's all that matters.'

Alice couldn't disagree with that.

A few minutes later, Jason came back down. He looked more casual in jeans and a blue shirt, but the air of difference still hung around him, like an Instagram filter. Looser, more intensely coloured.

It was the connection with Libby, Alice realised, watching him trail his fingers across her shoulders as he passed. It made them both more vivid. Love. Love did that. When it worked.

'Don't look at me like that, Lib. I put on the jeans you like,' he protested, and they exchanged a private glance that made Alice get up and switch the coffee machine on in the office.

They were still sitting behind the check-in desk, not saying much, when car headlights turned into the drive.

'That's him,' said Libby unnecessarily.

Alice got up, then sat down again. Her knees felt watery. Did she have time to go to the loo? Did she need to? Did she want to be sitting down or standing up?

Libby reached across and put a hand on her shoulder. 'It'll be fine,' she said. 'Calm.'

Jason sprang to his feet. 'One of us should get up or he'll think he's walked into an *X Factor* audition.' He cleared his throat and headed for the door.

Libby reached across and grabbed her hand. Alice's pulse raced. It seemed like an eternity between the sound of the engine stopping, the door shutting, the crunch of feet on gravel and then the front door opening. She got to her feet, her head feeling as if it was only barely connected to her body, and heard Jason's voice, jolly and welcoming.

'Hello, Gethin? Pleased to meet you. I'm Jason Corcoran. Come in, come in . . .'

And then he was there. Gethin. Her boyfriend. Standing next to the cabinet full of local jams and corn dollies, looking for her.

Alice's eyes, sharpened for detail over the past weeks, swept over him. Was he what she'd been expecting? Gethin was shorter than Jason, and stockier, with thick brown hair that curled over his ears and down into his big, puppyish brown eyes. He had an expressive face, clouded with concern until he saw Alice – at which point, a smile spread across it, like the sun coming out from behind the clouds. Small white teeth, nice mouth. Handsome. Gentle.

He looks like a nice guy, but I don't know him, thought Alice, and an icy trickle of fear ran down her back. If her memory didn't reboot when her boyfriend of over a year walked in, would it ever? But he knew her. And he looked so relieved and *happy* to see her that she persuaded herself that this was the next best thing. He'd mirror back who she was.

'Alice!' His smile was so delighted she felt her mouth smiling back automatically. 'Come here!'

He held out his hands and she walked towards him and he threw his arms around her in a bear hug. Over his shoulder, she could see Jason exchanging a soppy look with Libby. Gethin wore a white polo shirt, and black-and-white trainers, and he smelled of clean clothes and coffee, she noted. He had one hole in his earlobe but no earring.

'I've been so worried,' he said, with an extra squeeze.

She winced in pain. 'Careful! My ribs!'

'Oh no! I'm sorry, Bunny!' He sprang away from her as if she were on fire. 'What happened? God, sorry, sorry. What else is sore?'

'Just the ribs. I cracked them. On the wing mirror of the car, they think,' she added automatically.

'The wing mirror . . . Oh my God, what happened? You said you'd been in an accident – was it a car accident?' He looked horrified.

'You've got a lot to catch up on,' said Libby, and Alice felt relieved it was Familiar Libby back again, taking control of the situation, herding everyone where they needed to go. 'Let's go and have a cup of tea upstairs.'

Even as everyone was fussing and flapping about *her*, Alice still felt as if she were hovering over the situation. It would have been more appropriate for them to have gathered in the drawing room for the big denouement, she thought, rather than round the kitchen table, where Margaret was now dispensing sweet tea and gasps of amazement.

She'd clearly decided that she approved of Gethin – he called her 'Mrs Corcoran' and had shaken her hand – and so started running through some of the 'lovely' Welsh regulars, on the basis that Gethin might know them. It was to his credit, Alice thought, that he politely considered the possibilities before admitting that he didn't.

'. . . Now, the Pritchards, I think they were from Llangollen,' said Margaret with a Welsh gargling noise.

'Very good accent,' said Gethin, and sipped his tea, casting a glance across the table at Alice as he did. His eyes twinkled as if he couldn't quite contain his relief to see her, and she smiled back, adding 'sense of humour' and 'nice to mothers' to the list forming in her mind. It was a habit she couldn't break, listing. Giving herself something to refer back to.

She ran through the story of her accident as undramatically as she could, now with the added detail that the police weren't pursuing either driver, as she seemed to have caused the accident and couldn't remember how it happened in any case.

'It's for the best,' Margaret agreed. 'Move on.'

'But you could have been *killed*!' Gethin's big eyes were wide with horror.

Alice had a funny déjà-vu moment that she thought was a memory until she realised that was what Luke had said. When they'd been walking down the hill last weekend. His brooding sideways glance flashed in her mind and she blinked it away, focusing on Gethin instead.

It was funny that he called her 'Bunny', she thought, when

he was the one who looked like a rabbit: all eyes, and soft brown hair, and smooth skin. But handsome with it. There was strength in his arms, and legs.

'But I wasn't killed,' she said. 'Or even seriously hurt. I just don't have any memory of the past year or so.'

'So you don't remember me?' He raised his eyebrows up into his thick fringe, obviously hoping she would say, 'Of course I do!'

Alice hesitated. How could she lie? Even if she wanted to, Libby and Jason would know. Awkwardly, she shook her head and this time saw him flinch. She felt awful.

She grabbed at the feeling. That must tell me something, she thought. That there's a connection, the remnants of something like Libby and Jason's glow.

Libby leaped into the gap. 'I'm sure it's all in there,' she said. 'Quite a lot came back just last weekend, didn't it? You never know, once you get home and put your own clothes on, settle in your own place . . .'

Gethin seemed stunned, then smiled bravely. 'Of course.'

I live with this man, thought Alice. The terrible feeling increased. I sleep with him. We've seen each other naked; we've told each other secrets; we've cried and laughed and touched and tasted each other . . .

Nothing.

'So, if it's not too nosy of me, how did you two meet?' asked Margaret.

'Oh, it's . . .' Gethin glanced across at Alice. 'I don't know if I should say, if you don't remember . . .'

'Go ahead,' she said. 'Unless it was at some dodgy fetish club or something?'

Margaret spluttered on her tea, and Gethin suppressed a smile.

Good, thought Alice. We make each other laugh.

'No, nothing like that. We met on a retreat in Italy. It was for . . .' He twisted his mouth apologetically. 'For people who were in need of a perspective break? It was a really amazing experience. Very spiritual and refreshing. We kept in touch after that, and met up in London, and, well, one thing led to another.' His accent was sweet, up and down, melodic.

A faint memory stirred in the darkness of Alice's mind: a swimming pool with a full moon reflected in it. Floating, floating away. Then it was gone. She blinked again, encouraged. 'And I moved to Stratton?'

'You fancied a change of pace.' Gethin looked round the table, with a wry smile. 'Definitely a change of pace after London. I came down a few times to see you while you were living in Archway. Very exciting, London, but not for me, not long term.'

'Jason and Elizabeth have done much the same thing.' Margaret pushed the biscuits towards him. She'd put them on a plate, Alice noted. 'Downsized for better quality of life. I think it's an excellent idea. So what is it you do, Gethin?'

He ruffled his hair self-consciously. 'I'm a community arts project manager. I'm not an actor myself – I was in a few productions at university, but now I leave it to the professionals. I handle fundraising and getting theatre into schools. Arranging tours and exhibitions, that sort of thing. Every day's different! And it's great working with kids – they're so enthusiastic.'

Alice sipped her tea. A warm feeling spread through her. A community arts worker. That was cool. She could admit now that part of her had dreaded Gethin turning out to be something boring or unpleasant. But a community arts worker . . .

'And what was I doing?' she heard herself ask.

'You were working in the pub,' said Libby, surprised. 'You knew that.'

'No, before that. Presumably I didn't pack in a good job temping in the City to work in a pub?'

'Well, no. You were temping for an agency in Birmingham, but that didn't work out, so the White Horse is something to do while you get yourself back together. Plan your next move, kind of thing.' Gethin helped himself to another biscuit, at Margaret's urging. 'It's nice, though – it means we see more of each other. And you're very good at it, Tony says.'

'I can believe that,' said Libby. 'She made herself indispensable here within days!'

But Alice's attention had snagged on something else. *Get myself back together?* Gethin noticed the slip because a flush spread across his cheeks, and when their eyes met, he looked contrite, as if he'd revealed something accidentally.

He grabbed her hand. 'Alice is like that,' he said, looking into her eyes.

Like what? she wanted to ask, but she focused her mind on the feel of his skin on hers. It was a relief when Margaret offered to refill her tea and she could withdraw it to pass her mug.

'We're really going to miss having you here.' Libby seemed genuinely forlorn. 'You've been such a help. Doing my paperwork, and walking Bob, and helping on reception. How are we going to manage?'

'You will.' Alice pulled her attention back to what she knew. While they'd been talking, Libby had put a cardigan on over her dress, and some of her red lipstick had come off on her mug. The glowing London Libby was fading back into the normal Libby; Alice was secretly relieved.

Gethin finished his tea and shook his head when Margaret offered him a refill.

'I don't want to sound rude when you've been so kind,' he said, 'but we ought to make a move. I've been away all week on a schools tour and I've had about nine hours' sleep since last weekend.'

'Of course, and you've got that long drive back,' said Margaret with a shudder. 'In the dark . . .'

'You can always stay here,' said Libby. 'Oh, go on! Do that! Stay – don't start driving all the way across the county at this time of night.'

Alice stared into her mug, a stubborn childish feeling pooling in her stomach. Now the moment had come, she didn't want to leave.

Don't be silly, she told herself. There would be a first time for lots of things now. What was there to be scared of? She glanced up and – just as she'd feared – Gethin seemed hurt by her obvious lack of enthusiasm to get going.

She smiled, awkwardly, and he smiled back after a second's hesitation.

'Come on, Libby, be fair – I know you don't want your new best mate to go, but Alice probably wants to get back to her own bed,' Jason pointed out. 'After three weeks away from it. And her boyfriend?'

'I know. I know! Sorry. I'm being selfish. I'll help you get your things together, Alice.'

'What things?' Alice gestured at her outfit: all Libby's.

It's all right, she wanted to say, *we'll stay. Let me and Gethin get to know each other here, where I feel safe.*

But Gethin was getting up, and Margaret was clearing away the mugs, and Jason was swearing at Lord Bob, who was lying in exactly the right place for someone to fall over him, and before Alice really had time to think about what was happening, she was standing on the front step of the hotel, hugging everyone goodbye, stunned by how fast it was all happening.

'Call us anytime, and don't be a stranger.' Tears were shining in Libby's eyes. 'Come back whenever you want.'

'I will.' Alice paused. They hadn't discussed that job offer. It had seemed inappropriate, now she was going back to Stratton, to her job at the White Horse, the old normal. 'And you'll tell Luke, won't you? What's happened?'

Libby seemed surprised. 'If you want. But you've got his number? You can tell him.'

I can't, Alice thought. She didn't know why, but something told her that would be inappropriate. That the connection between her and Luke wasn't . . . wrong, because it felt honest, like her connection with Libby, but she had a sense that she shouldn't tell Gethin. Those big, brown, trusting eyes.

She had a sudden flash of Luke dumping the two sugars into her coffee. But he was in security. He noticed details. That was a detail, nothing more.

'Go on,' said Libby. 'Ring me in the morning?' Then she dropped her voice. 'He's a *sweetheart*. He's exactly how I hoped he'd be! I *knew* you'd have a cute boyfriend . . .'

Gethin was standing by his car, a red hatchback. He smiled, less certainly now, and Alice's heart lurched. He was a sweetheart. As she went over, he ran round and opened the door for her.

'Thank you,' she said, as she slipped in.

And then, with a wave, they were driving home.

To her real home.

Chapter Seventeen

The house was in darkness when Gethin pulled up outside and Alice almost didn't realise they were back until he turned off the engine and said, 'Well, here we are.'

It had been a strained journey. Conversation hadn't exactly flowed. As soon as she was away from the familiar atmosphere of the hotel, questions began popping up in Alice's mind, but it seemed rude to ask them outright when Gethin was so happy to see her. Like why hadn't he come to find her? Why had she stopped temping in Birmingham? Why had she been on a retreat for stressed-out people in the first place? Instead, they'd made polite party conversation about the schools tour of *A Midsummer Night's Dream* he'd been doing and what she'd been doing at the hotel.

Now, Alice realised, staring at the dark, blank face of their house, conversation couldn't go anywhere else but back to them.

'Oh God! We've no milk! Sorry, I meant to stop at Tesco.' Gethin had started to undo his seatbelt, but now he hit his forehead with the heel of his palm. 'I literally walked in and out when I saw your note – there's no food in the house.'

'Don't worry about it,' said Alice automatically. 'I'm not really hungry.'

'Do you want to go in and I'll nip out?' He looked anxious.

'I won't be a second. I think the garage up the road's still open . . .'

'It's fine. Honestly.' Alice touched Gethin's hand to stop him flapping; she did it without thinking, but the connection stopped them both. She made herself leave her fingers where they were for a couple of seconds, then patted him affection-ately. 'Let's just get inside.'

She undid her own belt, gathering her small bag of things from the footwell, but by the time she'd straightened up, he was at her door, opening it for her.

'Honestly, you don't have to – I'm not injured,' she said, getting out.

'I know, but . . . I can't get it out of my head.' His expression was remorseful. 'You were in the hospital, on your own! And I didn't know! Can you blame me for wanting to look after you better now?'

'Really, I'm fine. Just . . .' Alice made 'hurry up' gestures and he fumbled for the key and let her in.

The hall smelled stale, like a house that hadn't been lived in for a few weeks. Alice took a few surreptitious sniffs; it didn't smell unfamiliar. The walls were pale blue, with a staircase opposite the door leading to the bedrooms, carpeted with a striking red and gold runner. The radiator was boxed in, and on top of it was a wicker basket of post and some framed photographs.

She picked up the nearest: a selfie of her and Gethin on a shingle beach, their faces pressed close together to get into the same frame. A wild and leaden sky loomed behind them, merging with the iron-grey sea, as they laughed up into the camera lens, their windblown smiles framed by their furry parka hoods like Eskimos.

That's me, she thought. I was there, in that moment. There's a negative of this picture somewhere in my head. The original, with the data trail of words, emotions, sensations attached.

'Where's this?' she asked.

'Oh, Aberystwyth. That was a good weekend. My birthday.' Gethin paused, hoping she might remember. 'In October,' he added, when she didn't. 'The twenty-first. I'm a Libra.' His eyes scanned her face as he stressed the details, and they shared their first rueful understanding that this was how it was going to be. 'We stayed in a hotel on the seafront, and you were particularly taken with the full Welsh breakfast.'

'Really?'

'Really. Extra laver bread and all the trimmings. You finished mine off, which was a novelty.' He grinned.

'A novelty? Why?'

Gethin's grin froze, momentarily; then he recovered. 'Because you don't normally eat breakfast. You normally just have a coffee. The calories. I keep saying you're just perfect as you are, but . . . It must have been the sea air!'

Really? Alice had been eating full Englishes without any problem all week; Libby had been practising her poached eggs on her. Were she and Gethin still in that 'too in love to eat' honeymoon stage? Or had she pretended she ate delicately? She pushed it to one side. 'Did I give you something nice? For your birthday?'

'You arranged the mini-break. It was a surprise – we'd been talking about holidays we'd had as kids, and I'd been telling you about going to Aber with my family. I had no idea you were booking it. It was extremely thoughtful.'

She smiled, pleased that she'd done something nice. And she liked the lyrical way Gethin spoke, the flourishes on certain words, the expressive accompaniment of his mobile eyebrows. 'It looks like we're having fun.'

'Oh, we had a fabulous weekend. We walked along the seafront, until the rain started; then we sat in a café and had fish and chips, and worked out which of the flats we could buy if we won the lottery. We said we'd go back this year.' He paused. 'I like the fact that you and I can have a good time in simple places. It's something we clicked on from the start.'

He was looking at her with a loving expression, but Alice couldn't quite meet his gaze; it was too intimate, too soon. She pretended to be engrossed in searching her own face in the photo for clues. Her eyes were partially hidden by the fake fur on her parka, but her smile was wide and laughing. Was that parka upstairs? Would she wake up in the morning and have that glow of romance about her?

'I'd like to go back,' she said. 'To Aberystwyth, I mean.'

'We can.' Gethin touched her shoulder, gently, and this time she didn't flinch.

They sat at the kitchen table with a can of Coke from the fridge, and Gethin explained that he'd been living here for three years, and she'd moved in about eight months ago.

'I was sharing with my friend Ricky to begin with,' he told her. 'Then we started seeing each other, Ricky moved to Bristol, and you decided you needed a change of scene, so you moved in. It was one of those synchronicity moments – we talked a lot about it on the course, actually. When something's right for you, everything else just falls into place.'

Alice turned the cold can round in her hands; this course was sounding better and better. If only she could remember it. 'And when was this retreat?'

'April last year.'

'And I moved in here . . . ?'

'September the tenth.' He reached for her hand. 'It sounds like we rushed into things, but it's been so good. We . . . we make each other really happy.'

Alice thought of the photo of them on the beach. There were others in the kitchen: her in denim shorts and a sombrero at a campsite, her and Gethin at what looked like a festival. It did look right. It looked like they'd fallen madly in love.

Her stomach contracted with anxiety that she'd had something good, something once in a lifetime, and now not only had she lost it, but she couldn't remember what it had felt like.

She wanted to ask, *What was it that made us fall in love?* She wasn't feeling the special physical pull, but attraction was more complicated than that, wasn't it? It was a collage of coincidences, flashes of wordless understanding, the right words at the right time, shared reactions to moments that had been and gone forever now. Memories. A million tiny shared memories.

'You look tired, Bunny,' said Gethin. 'Do you want to go to bed?'

There must have been something in Alice's face, because he blinked and said, quickly, 'I don't mean like that, but . . . Um, sorry. I meant . . .'

She struggled for the right thing to say. Only three weeks ago, they'd been as close as two people could be, relaxed with each other's skin and taste and smell. Now a complete stranger was suggesting she get into bed with him and all she could think was, No.

'I know what you meant.' He was a decent guy, she told herself. She could read that in his eyes. They looked right together in the photos. They were a couple. They weren't embarrassed about taking cheesy selfies.

It would come back. The memories were all still there, somewhere.

'I'm . . . I'm just going to the loo,' she said. 'Upstairs, I take it?'

'First on the left,' said Gethin. 'And the door jams, so don't lock it.'

'Thanks,' said Alice. 'That'd be a first night to remember, getting locked in the loo! Unless I've already done that?'

Gethin smiled, but didn't say anything.

Alice shut the bathroom door and tried to get herself together to deal with what was coming next: bedtime.

Two blue towels over the stainless-steel towel rail. A white bath. Big white tiles, granite on the floor. Libby would approve of this bathroom. She sat on the closed loo, breathing deeply, staring at volumising shampoo she must have bought, a toothbrush that must be hers, and her eye fell on a make-up bag.

I can't have been running away to Longhampton if I didn't take my make-up bag, she reasoned, and felt unexpected relief. It was a fact. A solid brick of logic on which to build.

Alice got up and tipped the contents quietly into the sink: foundation, eyeliner, concealer, mascara, eyebrow pencil. Nice make-up, some of it expensive. She hadn't worn any make-up for the past few weeks; Libby had offered her some, but she hadn't felt she needed it.

She picked up a blusher brush and stroked it thoughtfully along her jaw. It brought back a distant memory of layering on the make-up she wore for work, waking up hung-over skin with bronzer, layering concealer over dark shadows, putting her face on with her eyes still half closed with sleep. Don't go back, she thought, and her eyes snapped open.

There was a knock on the bathroom door.

'I've got you a clean towel,' said Gethin's voice. 'There should be hot water now, if you want a bath?'

'Thank you!' She waited a couple of seconds until he'd gone and then slowly opened the door. A towel, with a pair of pyjamas folded on top.

Thoughtful. He'd anticipated what she might be feeling. That was a good sign.

Alice had a quick bath, changed and stepped out onto the landing. There were two rooms upstairs, either side of the bathroom; a soft light was on in one and she guessed that was where Gethin was.

Our bedroom.

She took a deep breath and walked in. It wasn't familiar: a king-size bed with a slatted wooden headboard, white duvet, plain bedside cabinet, two big prints of seaside scenes on the walls. Pebbles and sea and sky.

Alice knew she was taking in the details to avoid the issue: Gethin, in a T-shirt, sitting up in bed waiting for her.

'Everything OK?' he asked brightly.

'Yes. Fine, thanks.'

The question hovered between them. She knew she had to take a step forward, or say something, or . . .

Gethin resolved it for her. 'God, I'm sorry,' he said, throwing back the duvet. He was wearing a T-shirt and blue boxer shorts; he had a sturdy body. Warm, thought Alice, trying to imagine it holding her, covering her. 'I don't know what I was thinking. Well, I do know what I was thinking. I thought you'd remember . . . that it'd all come back . . .'

'I don't think it's going to be as easy as that,' said Alice. She paused, wishing she could explain. 'I'm so sorry.'

Gethin was embarrassed, and now she was too. It wasn't that Alice didn't think he was attractive – he was – but theirs obviously wasn't that sort of relationship. It had been forged in some confess-all, soul-baring retreat; they must have connected on a deeper, private level, and she couldn't just . . . pretend.

'I'll sleep in the spare room,' he said, and raised his hand to ward off her protests. 'No, no, I understand. It's . . . I should have thought . . .'

His big brown eyes were so sad; Alice felt awful. She caught his arm as he came near her and he stopped. They stayed like that for a moment, her hand half circling his forearm, and then Gethin moved and wrapped his arms around her, very gently so as not to hurt her ribs, angling himself so there was no untoward groin connection, but still cocooning her body with his.

Alice let him, because she wanted to let him, and because it *was* comforting to be held like that. Baby steps, she thought. He was a good hugger. Her body finally started to relax into his, safe.

'I'm sorry,' he said, into her hair. 'I'm so sorry.'

'What for?'

'For the accident. If I could take that day back . . .'

'What day? What happened?' There was something in his voice.

'Does it matter now?'

'Yes,' said Alice, pulling away to read his expression. 'It does. I need to know what happened. The consultant said I might never recover the memories immediately before the accident – you're the only one who can help me piece that back together.'

Although he wasn't the only one, was he? There was Luke.

'I don't want to start again on a bad note.'

'Gethin, I need to know.'

He took a deep breath, then patted the edge of the bed. They sat down, both facing the drawn curtains. 'Well, we had a row, to be honest.' He picked at a hangnail, awkwardly. 'We were going on holiday in the morning – we'd planned two weeks in France, but I'd actually managed to upgrade that a bit. To a fortnight in Thailand.'

'Thailand? Wow.'

Alice could imagine herself on a beach in Wales. Not in Thailand.

Gethin smiled his wonky smile. 'Well, it was our anniversary. Five-star villa, luxury resort, the works. Not something we'd ever done before, mind, before you start thinking we're globetrotters. Simon . . . Um, Simon's a mate of mine from uni. Don't know if you remember him? No? OK, well, Simon had booked it; then his leave got cancelled, so he offered it to us if I could arrange the flights. I'd got everything sorted – I wanted to surprise you.'

'Oh. And what? Don't tell me I kicked off about a fabulous holiday in Thailand?'

He hesitated, but the way he reached out for her hand said it all. Gethin was too nice to say, 'Yes, you did,' but she'd told him to be honest.

'For some reason, you didn't want to go,' he said.

Alice hadn't expected that. 'Why?'

'Doesn't matter now. We never really got to the bottom of it.' Gethin bit his lip. 'My sister told me I hadn't really thought about it from your point of view. That you'd have packed for a different sort of holiday. "Girls need more notice for five-star beach holidays," was what she actually said.'

'But that's so weird,' said Alice. 'We had a row because I didn't like the holiday you'd booked?'

'I don't know. Like I said, it was a silly argument that got out of hand. We were both tired – it was one of the reasons we were going on holiday.' He rubbed his face. 'Let's draw a line underneath it. It didn't matter then; definitely doesn't matter now.'

She sat for a moment, trying to process this new information but distracted by embarrassment. She'd made a massive, petulant fuss about a very sweet and generous gesture. She'd spoiled it. Why?

'So . . . then what?' Alice asked.

'Um, we argued, you told me to . . . to, er, go on the holiday on my own, and then you left. And in the spirit of full disclosure, I rang my mate Huw and he got a standby ticket and we had a reasonably good time.' Gethin touched her hand. 'Not as good as it'd have been with you. Huw got sick of me moaning on by the third night. I texted you so much he hid my phone.' He shot her a sideways look. 'You never replied. I assumed you were *really* mad with me.'

'Sorry,' said Alice in a small voice. 'I don't know where my phone is. It must have been in my handbag.'

'Don't worry about it. We never argue. This was our first – and I hope *only* – stupid row.' Gethin turned to her. They were quite close now. Not close enough to touch, but close enough for her to feel the warmth of his bare leg near hers. 'But I've got a question for you now – why were you in Longhampton?'

'I don't know. I had the address of the hotel in my pocket, but I don't know why I was going there.'

'No idea?'

'No, none. I must have heard about it from Luke, but I wasn't going there for an interview, because they weren't expecting me . . .'

'Luke?' Gethin looked blank.

I haven't mentioned Luke, thought Alice, and something tightened up inside her. 'Luke Corcoran. Jason's brother.'

'Was he there tonight?' He frowned, trying to remember. 'I thought you said you didn't know these people?'

'I don't. Luke was staying at the White Horse last month – he said he told me his brother and sister-in-law had just taken over a hotel. That they were doing it up. And I guess . . .' She tried to find a better explanation than the one rattling round her head. 'He might have told me to go and have a look around?'

Was I meeting him? Luke hadn't been there, though. He hadn't expected to see her. But other questions were now pushing through. 'When you came back from the holiday and I wasn't there . . . didn't you wonder where I'd gone?'

'Of course! I rang; I emailed; I texted – you didn't reply.' Gethin raised his hands, then dropped them. 'I thought you'd finished with me. I mean, we'd said some things in the heat of the moment, but . . . Well, what could I do, when you didn't phone me, other than leave messages? I was only back here half a day, anyway. Cass – my colleague, Cass? – broke her wrist at the technical rehearsal and I had to take over on the schools tour, so I basically got back from the airport and then went to Yorkshire for a week. I assumed you'd be back here when I got home. Well, I hoped.'

'And you kept ringing?'

'Yes.' He met her gaze with his own open, honest eyes. 'Even though you didn't call me back. I knew you were upset about something, but . . . sometimes you can get quite emotional and I feel like I can't reach you. I thought it was just one of those moods.'

Alice was seeing a version of herself she didn't like much.

247

Was she the sort of person who could sulk for three weeks? Or disappear altogether? 'But I didn't have a phone, Gethin. For the last three weeks I've had no idea who I am, or what's going on. If I'd had my phone, I could have been home in hours.'

'I'm sorry. It's just quite hard to get my head around.' He ran a hand through his mop of hair.

The warm mood was wearing off, and Alice's head ached. She dreaded headaches; she couldn't help worrying it was her brain stopping its secret healing, maybe even going backwards, unpicking the fresh links between her fragile memories.

They sat on the bed, not saying anything.

In the morning, this room will start to look familiar again, Alice told herself, staring at the yellow circles on the grey curtains. The thing that's missing will be here. We'll start again.

She stopped. What was missing? Alice probed her brain; the feeling slipped and slid and finally disappeared. It was a mirage. Nothing was missing. Apart from their old relationship.

Gethin stood up. 'Right, then. I'm going to sleep in the spare room,' he announced. 'You need a decent night's kip. You've probably forgotten about my snoring.' His voice had gone very practical and kind. 'Don't even think about getting up before I bring you some breakfast in bed, please.'

Alice smiled up at him, and he touched her face with his fingers. Still gazing at her, he moved his hand until he was cupping her cheek, stroking her skin very tenderly with his thumb.

'Alice, I can't tell you how good it is to have you home,' he said, and her heart melted. She leaned into his caress, much like Lord Bob had leaned into her ear scratchings.

'I thought . . . I'm so glad you were in an accident, rather than just breaking up with me,' he went on, and almost at once a look of horror contorted his face. 'Oh my God, that sounded wrong. I'm so sorry. God, I didn't mean it like that, Alice . . .'

Alice laughed. The first natural laugh they'd had. The relief was enormous, and when he looked relieved too, she felt the first glimmerings of confidence. This would be fine, she told herself.

And when he said goodnight, and their gazes locked, for a second Alice wondered if she should perhaps say, 'No, come on, sleep in this bed we've shared.' What could be the worst thing that could happen? He was a sweetheart. A gentle soul.

He was already pulling on his dressing gown, a well-loved stripy old thing. Had she wrapped herself in that, the first time she'd stayed?

'Gethin,' she said, 'do you . . . ? Why don't you sleep in here?'

He paused. 'Are you sure?'

She nodded and a look of real happiness spread across his face.

Alice slipped under the duvet and settled herself in, conscious of Gethin's rougher warmth centimetres away. The weight of him on the mattress. He leaned over and kissed her head respectfully; he smelled of minty toothpaste and an unfamiliar shampoo.

'Night, love,' he said, and as his breathing deepened, and he fell asleep, Alice lay staring up at the ceiling, letting thoughts swirl around her head like swallows grouping for their long flight south, whirling into shapes, breaking up to swirl into new, darker, then lighter patterns that scattered before she could take hold.

Chapter Eighteen

G ethin did bring her a cup of tea in bed the following morning, as promised; then at Alice's suggestion, they went out
for a walk. It felt easier to walk and chat than to sit around the
house, surrounded by pictures of herself living a life she didn't
remember. There were only so many times she felt she could
ask what they'd been doing or thinking before Gethin's considerate expression cracked a tiny bit and she felt bad again.

They were just about to start sharing out the dishes of curry
on Sunday night (a treat, from 'their' takeaway) when the
phone in the hall rang. Gethin answered it, and Alice wasn't
surprised when she heard him say, 'Yes, of course, Libby. I'll
just get her.'

'It's Libby, for you.' He covered the mouthpiece. 'I told her
we'd just sat down to supper – she says she won't be long.'

Alice smiled and took the phone.

'Hello, Alice!' Libby sounded flustered. '*So* sorry to bother
you during supper, but I've got a huge favour to ask.'

'Go on,' said Alice. 'Don't I owe you at least one massive
favour?'

'Can you come in tomorrow and give me a hand? We're
getting new broadband installed, but Jason has to take his
mother to the optician's, *apparently*' – Alice sensed that Jason
wasn't too far from the phone – 'and I'm clueless. I know you

understand computers. I don't want to mess up that spreadsheet you'd nearly finished.'

'Of course. I'd be happy to. There's a train, isn't there?'

'You are a *lifesaver*. Thank you so much! How's it going?' Libby's voice dropped, and Alice knew she was eager for the full happy-ever-after ending.

'Great!' she said, conscious of Gethin listening. 'I'll, er . . . I'll see you tomorrow!'

When they'd arranged some details and she'd hung up, Gethin handed her a plate; it had much less on it than his, but she guessed he was trying not to overload her, if she was fussy about food. She could always have seconds. Maybe it had been one of those early date attempts to fake a birdlike appetite that she'd never been able to back out of.

'Smells great!' she said. 'Did you say it was Tibetan, this place?'

Gethin wasn't paying attention to the curry. 'She's not dragging you back there again already, is she?' he asked, and Alice was surprised to see his jaw was set in a defiant way.

'No! She just needs a hand setting up the new broadband. I'm glad to be able to help out. Why? Did you have something planned for tomorrow?'

'No. Well . . . no. It's just that . . .' He looked conflicted, as if he didn't know whether to say what he was thinking.

'What?' Alice paused, her fork raised.

Gethin frowned. 'I hope she's not going to take advantage – of you owing her a favour, I mean.'

Alice laughed, more at the thought of Libby taking advantage. 'It's nothing like that! Why do you say that? You met Libby. She's lovely!'

'I know, she is. It's just . . . You're so sweet, people are always taking advantage of you. Tony was like that, talking you into extra shifts at the last minute. I'm the same . . . It's one of the things we have in common. Oh, sorry, this has come out wrong – I know you hate saying no, so sometimes I feel someone has to say no for you. You do it for me. We're a team.'

That rang a bell somewhere deep in Alice and she felt touched by Gethin's protective instinct. 'Libby's not like that,' she reassured him.

'I'm sure she's not.' Gethin pushed the raita towards her. 'But you're one of nature's givers. Anyway, look, can you blame me for wanting to look after you? After what's happened?'

He smiled, his gentle, boyish smile, and Alice smiled back, albeit with the unsettling sense that he was smiling at someone he knew but she didn't know quite so well.

Libby was waiting outside the station with Lord Bob on a lead next to her. She was texting and creasing her brow, and balancing a cup of coffee from the mobile park wagon, all at the same time.

Bob wagged his tail when he saw Alice coming through the gates and she waved at him. The power of Bob's wagging jolted Libby's coffee hand and she yelped, looked up, saw Alice and a similarly happy expression lit up her face.

'That's a nice welcome,' she said. 'Sorry I haven't got anything for you,' she added, as Bob tried to put his nose into her bag.

Alice had selected the bag from the wardrobe, along with her dress, and her denim jacket. It had been strange looking at her clothes. Some brought back instant memories, like the navy suit from Hobbs she remembered buying for her first office job: her head filled instantly with aching toes, and a Coldplay album she'd listened to every day for months. Others meant nothing to her, like the long black dress Gethin said she'd bought for his work party at Christmas. His favourite dress. Even when he'd produced a photo of her in it – his arm round her, her face lifted to his under some mistletoe – she couldn't remember it.

'I've got your clothes in there,' she added to Libby. 'Washed and ironed. Thank you very much. You've given me a taste for expensive yogawear now.'

'Oh, there was no need! They looked better on you anyway. Sorry about Bob,' said Libby, nodding towards the dog, who was now furrowing his wrinkly brows at a squirrel. 'I took him for a walk to get us both out of the hotel. The builders have only been here ten minutes and they've already knocked down the wrong wall.'

'What?'

'I know. Instead of knocking room five into room six, for the en suite, they've managed to put a hole in room seven.' Libby looked frustrated. 'Jason tried to get Marek to sort it out before he left with Margaret, but Marek's not answering his phone . . . Not a great start to the week.'

'No, but once proper broadband's up and running, you'll feel better,' said Alice. 'Then you can get the website sorted. I'll ring the designers if you want, pretend to be your PA chivvying them along.'

Libby was loading Bob into the back of the car. 'It's really good of you to come today,' she said, pausing with Bob's massive paws up on the bumper. 'You sure you wouldn't rather be at home with Gethin, catching up?'

'He's at work. What am I going to do at home? The sooner things go back to normal, the more likely I am to feel normal again.'

'If you're sure . . .'

Alice got into the car and pulled on her seatbelt. 'I'm sure. Now, let's get back before the builders knock down any more walls.'

Libby shut Bob in and got into the driver's side. 'How's it going? Did you have a good weekend?'

'Fine.' That sounded lukewarm. 'Fine!' she repeated more enthusiastically.

Libby glanced across, eyebrow raised. 'Is that a ring?'

Alice looked down at her hands. She was wearing a ring that she'd found on the dressing table; putting it on hadn't triggered a memory, but when Gethin saw her wearing it, he'd looked pleased and that had told her something.

Her stomach had plummeted, though. She'd thought of Luke, and the secrets she didn't even know if she was keeping. That wasn't the right reaction, was it?

Libby had started the engine, but now she switched it off and turned to Alice. 'Come on. Tell me. Before we get back to the hotel. Or do you want to walk and talk? He's always up for an extra chance to meet and greet his public.' She nodded towards the back of the car.

'Yes,' said Alice. 'Yes, I'd like that.'

Libby unloaded Bob again and they walked out of the station, down the road towards the park.

'The thing is,' said Alice, when she'd explained about the conversation at bedtime and the awkwardness that had hung over the weekend, 'we obviously had – *have* – a serious relationship, but it's clearly a big emotional deal. He keeps going on about how we understand each other. He knows all about my mum and dad dying, so he must have told me some really personal stuff too. Which I can't remember. But the worst thing is . . .' She stopped, blushing.

Libby went directly to what she couldn't put into words, as usual. 'Don't you fancy him?'

'Yes! Well, in theory. He's a good-looking guy, but . . .' Alice bit her lip. 'I remember enough to know I had my fingers burned with good-looking guys in the past. In London, when I was temping. And Gethin's different. Whatever we had is more emotional than that. More . . . subtle.'

'Maybe you need to go on that holiday again. The one where you met?'

'Maybe. I looked it up on the internet – the photos were familiar. Ish. There were lots of testimonials from people who said it put them in touch with who they really were. I don't remember it at all. I know I was stressed, with work, I think, and a relationship that didn't end well . . .' She tailed off. Did she know that? Or was that what Gethin had told her? Same thing. Her memories, just stored by him.

'You can't remember actually being there?'

Alice shook her head. 'That's the point where it all goes blank. I can't remember Gethin, and I can't remember what he told me about why he was there.'

'Urgh, tricky.'

'I'm going to have to ask him. I'm walking on eggshells, worrying I'm accidentally going to put my foot in it, not know-ing something personal he confided in me. It really seems to upset him when I can't remember details about our relation-ship. I think Gethin's struggling, me not recognising him. And he knows everything about me.'

Almost everything. Gethin didn't know why she was in Longhampton when she was knocked down. Or why she'd been so ungrateful about his lovely holiday surprise. Little holes that neither of them could explain, but which Alice felt she could fall through at any moment.

Libby looked sideways at her, her 'problem-solving' expression on her face.

'This is just a suggestion,' she said, 'but why don't you let Gethin court you all over again?'

'That's not easy when you're sharing a bathroom.'

'That's what I mean – don't share a bathroom just yet. Why don't you come back to us for a week or so and have dates with Gethin? Going back there obviously hasn't triggered your memory, so why don't you take the pressure off by letting things develop slowly again? I bet he'd love to court you. He looks the romantic type.'

Alice considered it. It wasn't a bad idea – and Gethin *was* romantic. He had an old-fashioned gallantry about him that was very sweet, and this might give him a bit more control over the weird situation he'd been thrust into. 'I don't want to impose on you and Jason . . .'

'You're not imposing! You'd be doing me a favour. And we miss you. Don't we, Bob? How about it? Run it by Gethin, and enjoy the romance. You already know it's got a happy ending – sounds win-win to me.'

'Yes,' said Alice. 'I think you might be right.'

Gethin's reaction that evening was as Alice had guessed: a flash of disappointment crossed his face when she put it to him, but he quickly rallied.

'I'm going to show you exactly why you and I are made for each other,' he told her, as she packed a bag for herself. 'We're so lucky to get the chance to fall in love all over again. Just wait.'

One Small Act of Kindness

Their first 'date night' was on Thursday. Alice got the train from Longhampton to Stratton, and Gethin collected her at the station. He was wearing an unfamiliar jacket, instead of his usual polo shirt, and seemed to have done something to his hair – the unruly curls were tamed and smooth. But instead of driving into town, as she'd expected, he headed back to the house.

'Wait there,' he said, before Alice could get out. 'I just need to do a couple of things . . .'

She fidgeted while he was gone. Libby had been very excited at the date-night idea and had helped her get ready; they'd both assumed it'd be a meal out, or a film or something, and she'd dressed up accordingly. Before she had time to think how she could downgrade her outfit, Gethin was opening the car door and ushering her into the house.

Inside, the hallway was transformed by a flickering sea of tea lights, and the smell of garlic and herbs drifted through from the kitchen, along with the gentle murmur of an Adele album. The light bounced off the framed photos of the two of them on the hall table.

'Wow,' said Alice. 'This is very . . . romantic.'

'Good! I hoped you weren't going to say, "Have you had a power cut?"' Gethin rubbed his chin. 'I've just put dinner in the oven. Should be about an hour or so.'

'Oh! Sorry – I sort of assumed, when you said you were planning something special, that we'd be going out.' She eyed his jacket and smart trousers. They didn't ring a bell, either.

'Nothing wrong with making an effort.' He held out his hand for her jacket. 'And very beautiful you look too!'

'Thank you,' she said. Libby had lent her one of her own going-out dresses ('You should make an effort! Plenty of time for jeans later!'), and though Alice had scoffed at the

257

tiny black dress on the hanger, it did look very different on. She didn't have anything like it in her own wardrobe, but the shape suited her, fitting her neat curves as if she'd had it tailored. It was *very* tight.

'You should keep that dress,' Libby had sighed. 'I've never looked as hot as that in it.'

'In fact,' Gethin went on, 'you look more than nice. You look *amazing*.'

Alice blushed, and did a self-conscious twirl, ending in a slight wobble. She was wearing the green stilettos she'd found in her wardrobe, and clearly she hadn't worn them for a while because her balance was off.

Gethin put his hands out to catch her and the sudden touch of his fingers on her bare arm startled her. Touching should have been easy and natural, but instead they were both hyper-conscious of every movement they made.

'Sorry,' she said, with a small smile. 'These shoes . . .'

'Ah, I've never been a huge fan of those, to be honest. I don't know how you can walk in them.'

'Well, clearly I can't. They're gorgeous, though, aren't they? Do you wear a suit a lot when we go out? Because you should.' She put a hand on his sleeve jacket. That felt safe. 'It suits you.'

Gethin's puppy-dog eyes widened with surprise, and then amusement. 'No, I'm more of a casual dresser. But if you like it . . .'

'I do,' she said, and finally a flirtatiousness seemed to enter the atmosphere between them. Alice felt her muscles loosen a degree or two. First dates always felt contrived.

'So, would you like to come through?' He gestured towards the sitting room. 'Can I get you a drink, to start with? What'll you have?'

There's a right answer to this, she thought, and I don't know what it is. 'What do I normally have?' she asked, trying to sound jokey.

'You're quite partial to cider, as a matter of fact,' said Gethin.

'Am I?' Alice hadn't felt a yearning for cider at all, but then the consultant had said that some things might change as the brain reset itself. Still, at least she wouldn't have to relearn how to love homebrew or something.

'You're something of a connoisseur,' Gethin went on. 'We went to a cider festival last summer, in Herefordshire? We camped so we could go to an all-day tasting. It was the first time we went away together.' His eyes twinkled. 'Separate tents. You insisted.'

'Did I?' That was a good tick box too. Moral standards.

'You did. And you made me put your tent up too. Sit down and I'll be with you in a second. Just got to check on the main course.' He seemed to be waiting for her to say something; then when she didn't, he ran a hand through his hair, releasing a thick curl from its carefully smoothed neatness. The nervousness of the gesture made something catch in Alice's chest.

'Sorry,' she said. 'Should I . . . ?'

Gethin gazed at her, with a twitch of his mouth. 'No, it's just normally you'd tell me to stop fussing. It's quite nice that you didn't.'

'In that case . . . stop fussing, Gethin,' she said firmly. 'I'm sure supper will be fine.'

He smiled back, grateful, and even though Alice had had to fake it, she was pleased that she'd managed to strike the right chord for him. Familiar behaviour would coax out more famil-iar behaviour. Hadn't she read that online somewhere?

She walked into the sitting room, trying to take it all in by

259

candlelight. By the door was a framed photo of Gethin that she hadn't spotted before, fresh-faced and ruddy-cheeked, in his graduation gown. Where was that from? She ought to know that. Alice peered at the crest. Swansea University. She made a mental note. Swansea. 2004. Gethin Emrys Williams.

There were plenty more framed photos in the sitting room: her and Gethin at a festival. Her on a swing, in wellies and a summer dress. Her and Gethin on the beach at Aberystwyth. The only photos that gave Alice a proper rush of recognition were older ones – her and her dad at Blackpool with candyfloss, her with her first car outside a flat-share in Haringey, her and her mum on a merry-go-round horse called Dana – and they were upstairs in her photo album.

She picked up another photo of her and Gethin standing near a glowing bonfire, their faces spookily lit up with flash as they waved sparklers. Alice had drawn a heart in sparks; Gethin had written a 'G'. Sparks, she thought. Like memories – so bright, then gone.

'Now that was a fabulous night,' he said, and she jumped.

Gethin was behind her, holding two glasses.

'Bonfire night, last year. Very special. There you go,' he said, offering her a cold glass. 'Westons Old Rosie. That is, let me tell you, your favourite ever cider.' He looked excited. 'Have a sip, go on.'

Alice held his gaze. He was clearly hoping she'd have a Proustian moment with the cider. And she wanted to – she really wanted to.

She closed her eyes and focused. The cold glass. The appley smell. She tried to conjure up the tents, the damp grass, the night air – it didn't come, but she smiled anyway, and took a sip.

It was nice cider. It didn't make anything come flooding back, though. When she opened her eyes, Gethin was gazing at her hopefully.

'Lovely!' she said, then without knowing why added, 'A cider festival, you said?'

'It brought something back?' His eyes lit up and Alice found herself nodding. 'Excellent! So!' He steered her towards the sofa facing the large television screen; next to it was a laptop and some cables. On the side tables were bowls of popcorn and nachos and olives – a strange mixture of nibbles and cinema food.

Gethin put down his cider and rubbed his hands. 'Tonight, Bunny, I'm going to take you through a multi-sensory date experience!'

'A what?'

'I'm going to show you our entire relationship through the medium of food, wine, music, photos and finishing up with a film. By which time, I hope your memory will be well and truly jogged.'

Before Alice could speak, Gethin kneeled down in front of the sofa and reached out for her hands, lacing his fingers between hers. It felt a tiny bit too much, but Alice let it happen, because this clearly meant a huge amount to him. 'I know it took *me* back, going through the photos and things. Some really happy times. I hope this works for you. I don't want to be the only one who remembers them.'

Alice didn't know what to say. The more wistful Gethin sounded about their relationship, the more guilty she felt that she might never regain her memory of it. It sounded so happy. Fish and chips, beaches, camping, holidays . . .

'That sounds wonderful,' she said. 'Slightly weird, I've got to admit, but . . . wonderful.'

She settled into the leather sofa and watched him fidget with the laptop.

'Gethin,' she said, 'why don't you take your jacket off? I mean, I'm flattered that you've got dressed up and everything, but if you'd be more comfortable . . .'.

He turned. 'If you don't mind?'

'Course I don't mind.' It was hard enough sitting on the squashy sofa in her tight dress; Alice's thighs were already beginning to ache from the effort of keeping her knees together.

We don't normally dress up like this, she thought, slotting the fact into her new memory. He's making a special effort. To show me how much this means to him.

'Cheers.' He slipped off his jacket, draped it carefully over the arm of a nearby chair and crouched down, his sturdy thighs straining against the trouser material.

'All right. Here we go.' He waved a remote control at the stereo. Adele stopped and Ellie Goulding started. On the television screen was a photo of them smiling up at the camera surrounded by tents, brandishing a bottle of cider each as the sun set. Underneath were the words 'Gethin and Alice'.

'Don't worry,' he apologised. 'It's not all cheesy like that. The slideshow made me do it.'

'It's cute!' said Alice. 'Is that the camping holiday in Herefordshire?'

'Yes!' Gethin looked thrilled, then realised she was remembering something he'd just told her.

He scrambled up and sat next to her on the sofa. 'So . . . I started with some photographs from the retreat where we met,' he explained, as the screen faded up on a picture of some vineyards, rolling in neat lines towards a perfect periwinkle sky. 'You're on the edge of the group there. I'm sitting on the wall.'

One Small Act of Kindness

Alice could just pick herself out of the group – twenty or so youngish people in long shorts and bright sundresses, squinting into the sunlight. She looked plumper than she was now, in a straw cowboy hat.

'Is that me? I've got blonde hair,' she said, surprised.

'Yes, you were blonde when we met. You called it your break-up hairdo.'

That rang a bell. Alice felt something click inside her, a slide slotting into the back of her head. Sore eyes, crying late at night outside a Tube station while people walked past her and not caring if they saw. Aching, aching, aching to talk to her mum, just once more, to bury her face into her chest.

'Gethin, pause this a moment, will you?'

He stopped the slideshow. 'Have you remembered something?'

'Maybe.' Alice squeezed her forehead, above her eyebrows. 'I just need to get it straight, before we go on. What was I stressed about? That I went on the retreat?'

He looked at her and took her hand. 'You worked through it. Does it matter?'

'Yes, it does.'

Gethin breathed in, then out slowly. 'Well, you were at a crossroads. You told me that you felt you should have aimed higher than just temping – you were smarter than some of the people you were working for, but the money was decent and you were worried you'd left it too late to get more qualifications.'

Alice frowned. That sounded reasonable. Her wardrobe backed that up.

'And you'd finished a relationship that . . . that wasn't going anywhere.' He dropped his gaze.

'A married man?' Alice guessed.

'Um, yes. You didn't tell me anything about him. Just that he was married. And you finished it.'

'Oh.' That wasn't a nice thing to find out about yourself.

Part of her felt ashamed that Gethin had known that about her. Still, if he'd known from the start and still liked her . . .

'And I'd just broken up with my girlfriend,' Gethin went on, to make the confession fair, 'and I was thinking about changing jobs . . . We met just at the right time.' He looked at her with his simple, guileless gaze. 'We were each other's fresh start. We were meant to be together. And from the day we met everything started to make sense.'

Alice smiled, but inside she wasn't quite so calm.

He was lovely, and he trusted her, and she'd be an idiot to mess up this gorgeous relationship. But what if she'd done things he didn't know about, and they came back? What then?

Gethin squeezed her hand tightly.

'What?' Alice asked.

'Just thinking.' He smiled. 'How lucky you and I are. You and me, we're meant to be together.'

Chapter Nineteen

Libby didn't know whether it had something to do with the building work reaching a new pitch in the hotel or some kind of early hay fever coming from the garden, but for a few days now both Margaret and Jason had been behaving in odd, and not particularly helpful ways.

Since Alice was now more or less recovered and dealing with any small jobs around the hotel, Margaret's mood had taken a turn for the worse. She wasn't miserable, just critical, picking faults – always excruciatingly politely – about the building work, the frequency of Bob's walks, whether anyone had checked with her before moving various paintings . . . Anything and everything. Libby was grateful for Alice's diplomatic presence in the flat, because frankly Margaret's unpredictable outbursts were starting to jangle her and Jason's already stretched nerves.

'Donald must have been an excellent listener,' Alice observed, after Margaret had spent an entire supper telling them in great detail about Donald's famous tackling of The Guest Who Complained Because There Were No Duvets, a story even Alice had now heard three times. 'Do you think she needs something to do? It must be strange to be here, watching everything changing.'

'She's supposed to be taking it easy,' Libby had replied, but she was beginning to think Alice might have a point. The trouble was, Margaret didn't want to help with any of the changes they were making in the hotel, and Libby didn't know enough people in town to make discreet enquiries about outside projects Margaret could be co-opted into.

Unlike Jason. He'd been out nearly every evening that week, either with the rugby club or his friends, and on the nights he had been around, he'd been on his laptop in the office, 'working on the accounts'. She hadn't wanted to disturb him then, because her worries about the budgets wouldn't go away: the manufacturer still didn't have the entire bathroom order for some reason, and she was having sleepless nights about whether she'd maybe gone overboard with the specifications.

Again, it was a blessing that Alice was around, Libby thought. If it weren't for Alice, and her calm attitude to crashing broadband, and noisy builders, and sulking mothers-in-law, and now Bob's engagement diary, she'd probably go mad.

'You're juggling a lot,' said Alice kindly. 'Bob should have left you a note about his transport requirements.'

'Thanks for reminding me,' she said. 'I thought Margaret was taking him up to the PAT session, but apparently not.'

'Put it on the Tree of Kindness while you're there,' said Alice, swivelling on her chair behind the reception desk, as Libby rushed to get Bob's paraphernalia together. '"Thank you, Alice, for doing a job you really don't mind doing, and in fact used to play at on a regular basis when you were little."'

'I won't be long.' Libby hunted for her handbag. 'Margaret's had to go out somewhere with Jason. Who *had* to take her, apparently.' She glanced up, guiltily. 'I'm being a cow, I know. I've got a feeling it's some sort of minor Donald anniversary, but she *knew* I needed Jason to help me measure up the windows for curtains today. It's like she wants to prove she takes priority. She's making it into some sort of competition, and it's really not.'

'I'm sure she's not doing it on purpose. Well' – Alice twisted her mouth – 'she probably is. But cut her some slack. How long till you can show her another finished room? Not long now.'

Libby found her lanyard and looped it round her neck. 'It'd just be nice if Jason would say something, instead of leaving it to me the whole time.'

They exchanged a weary glance. Jason, Libby had come to realise, was brilliant at avoiding confrontation. He was never at the desk when guests wanted to make a fuss about something or the builders needed a decision.

'Don't rush back from the hospital,' said Alice. 'Have a coffee in town. Forget about this place for an hour. I'll be fine here – it's not like we're busy.'

'Thanks,' said Libby. 'I might do that.'

The roads were clear, and the sun was out, and by the time Libby walked into the hospital with Bob, she was in a better mood. Longhampton wore late spring like a pretty dress: the hedgerows were spriggy and green, distant white lambs speckled the fields, and the freshness in the air felt as if it could clean her from the inside out.

She smiled at everyone they passed in the corridors en route to the geriatric wing, and when Bob made his entrance to the patients' usual delight, Libby felt quite proud of him. He was wearing a floppy velvet bow tie Jason had bought for a fancy-dress party; it gave him a rakish yet academic air.

Bob made a beeline for Doris, the old housekeeper, and Libby dutifully followed.

'Morning, Doris,' she said, when Bob arranged himself at her feet, his noble head lifted for attention. 'How are we today?'

'How do you think a ninety-three-year-old woman usually feels? Happy to be alive, just. How are you, my lad?' Doris was still crotchety at first, but she sweetened up considerably the longer Bob sat there. 'Have I got a biscuit for you? Have I?'

Libby sat down in the chair next to Doris and let Bob do his solemn pat-enduring in return for an illicit custard cream. Across the room, she saw Gina, sitting patiently while two old ladies in wheelchairs talked animatedly to Buzz, her greyhound, who gazed steadfastly between them, his ears lifted as if he were listening to their conversation.

Gina raised a hand in greeting and Libby waved back. Another friend, she thought, and it gave her an unexpected glow.

'How are you getting on with your hotel?' Doris asked, and Libby jumped, since Doris always seemed more interested in Bob than in her.

'Fine, thanks.' Libby seized on the opener. 'Doris, you were going to tell me some stories about when you were there . . .'

'Ooh, we'd be here all day, love. I started working there when the Hannifords first turned it into a hotel. That'd be 1950.'

'What was it before that?' Libby sometimes wondered about the house's life before Donald's tartan takeover. Whether the sideboards had held silver kedgeree dishes instead of plastic cereal containers. Whether the lounge had thrilled to smart parties, rather than the bored rustle of people reading back issues of *Country Life*. What the ghosts of those people made of the glass-eyed stags and avocado suites she didn't like to imagine.

'It was Dr Cartwright's house. Very nice it was too. Not the smartest house round here, but up there. Far too big for one family after the war, once you couldn't get maids to do all that housework, so he sold it and the Hannifords came from Birmingham and turned it into a hotel.'

'And you were the housekeeper?'

'I started as a maid and worked up,' said Doris. 'I learned how to run the hotel from the old housekeeper, Miss Greene. She was a right tartar. She'd been a sister from the old hospital in town. Very particular. Things were much harder in those days, you know. We still had fires in the rooms. The grates I cleaned in that place ... The day Mrs Corcoran had them taken out and replaced with electric fires, I got on my knees and thanked her, so to speak.'

'How funny. We've just taken all those heaters out and unboarded the fireplaces.' Libby smiled. 'How times change, eh?'

Doris looked at her as if she were mad. 'And who'll be cleaning them grates out?'

'No one! I'm going to fill them with pine cones.'

Doris muttered something under her breath and gave Bob's ears an extra scratch.

'So Margaret and Donald took over the hotel when – in 1980?'

'About that time, yes. And with two little babies too. Two under two, she had.' Doris's wrinkles conveyed what Libby assumed was amazement. It could have been mild disapproval, though. 'Very determined, Mrs Corcoran. Never known organisation like it. Took to hotels like a duck to water.'

'She wasn't from a hotel background, then?' Libby knew she wasn't, but Doris clearly enjoyed telling her things she didn't know. Libby knew from interviewing people that was the best way of teasing out gossip.

'Oh no. No, I don't think so. They moved in from Worcestershire. Funnily enough, my cousin Pamela came from the same town as Mrs Corcoran, so when I told her who I was working for, she said, "Oh, that wouldn't be Maggie Jackson as was, would it?" And it was. Pam was at school with her. Same year.'

'Really! Isn't it a small world,' said Libby. She couldn't imagine Margaret being called 'Maggie'. She definitely wasn't a Maggie.

'It is indeed a small world.' Doris's eyes twinkled. 'And—'

Libby's bag beeped and she reached into it apologetically. 'Sorry, that's my phone. I'm expecting the last of the new baths to come today, and the builders said they'd call when they arrived. I can't relax till I know they're here.'

Doris folded her hands in her lap and regarded her with an inscrutable 'old lady knows all' expression.

The text was from Alice's new phone; Gethin had sorted her out with a mobile, which he'd dropped off a few evenings ago. He'd stayed for dinner, of course, and told them some funny stories about his awful school drama tour. Libby liked Gethin; Margaret adored him; she'd invited him back 'anytime he liked'. The only person who hadn't been that keen was Lord Bob, probably because Gethin got his priority spot next to Margaret.

Libby frowned. The message was, **Come back ASAP. Problem at hotel.**

With builders? she texted back, and waited. Nothing came.

'Sorry, Doris, you were telling me about Margaret. Thirty-five years, eh? Maybe we should have a party when the renovation's finished? For the original staff?'

'I'd like that,' said Doris. 'I can't wait to see your fireplaces. With the pine cones.'

'And you have to tell me all your stories about the hotel, so maybe I can put them in a little book.' Libby's mind was racing now; maybe she could make it a present for Margaret? A celebration of the Swan Hotel from 1980 onwards – could she take offence at that?

'Oh, I've plenty of stories,' said Doris, and Libby's phone beeped again.

Big problems with builders and Jason. Please come back ASAP.

'Oh dear,' said Libby. 'I think we're going to have to go.'

Libby knew something was up even before she got out of her car back at the hotel.

Three of the builders were outside loading up the van with their working gear: circular saws, tubs of paintbrushes, dust sheets. And they were doing it about twice as quickly as they'd ever unloaded.

'What's going on?' she asked, in a friendly tone, but they nodded towards the hotel. Libby cursed inwardly; only two of the builders actually had designated speaking roles, and most of them didn't make eye contact with her if they could help it.

She hurried inside with Lord Bob and found Alice hovering around the reception desk, her face clouded with anxiety. Two more builders were dismantling the trestles they'd been using for . . . something or other, and another one walked past with a stepladder.

'Hey,' said Libby. 'That's our stepladder, isn't it?'

Sulkily, he put it back against the wall.

Libby flashed him an 'I'm coming back to you' look and turned to Alice. 'What's happening?'

'I don't know! I'm so sorry to drag you away from the

hospital,' said Alice, 'but I heard Jason and Simon yelling upstairs about half an hour ago, and then the builders started coming downstairs with their gear. I asked Simon what was going on and he says they're leaving!'

Simon was the foreman who made the decisions in Marek's absence; he wasn't completely convincing, and spent a lot of time on the phone checking things with the boss.

Lord Bob was straining to go upstairs and investigate, so Libby pushed him inside the office and shut the door, not even caring about the risk he posed to her good biscuits. 'Why are they leaving?'

Alice widened her eyes. 'I don't know. I heard Jason shouting something about money and being paid, but . . .'

'What?' Libby's heart sank. 'Stay there. I need to find out what's going on.'

Jason was upstairs in room six, which now had ragged holes in two walls, and he was jabbing his finger at Simon, who had his hands raised in a manner that managed to be simultaneously passive and enraging.

'You can't do this!' Jason's face was bright red and he looked as if the situation had left his control some time ago. 'You get that gear back in here right now, and you tell the lads to keep working or I swear I will sue you from here to next week. I know some shit-hot lawyers and they will have a field day—'

'Whoa, whoa, whoa, come on, folks – can't we talk about this calmly?' said Libby, but they ignored her. Clearly things had escalated way beyond calm discussion.

'Instructions from the top, Jason,' Simon replied. 'We're needed on another job. It happens.'

'But you haven't finished *this* one! For Christ's sake!' Jason pointed wildly at the matching holes in the walls. 'You can't leave it like this!'

'It's not going to fall down – they're internal walls. Besides, the boss is really strict about late payments. What can I do? No money, no job. Be reasonable. Do you work for no pay?'

Late payments. No pay. Libby's stomach clenched. There had to be a good explanation for this. She turned to Jason, but he wouldn't meet her eye. Dread rose inside her.

'What can you do?' Jason looked as if he was about to hyperventilate. 'Because I don't believe there's nothing you can do.'

'Jason, can I have a word?' Libby tried to keep her voice calm, but alarm bells were ringing about the hysterical way Jason was arguing. He was an inveterate blame-shifter. He'd managed to blame Bosch for making dishwashers that didn't take Fairy Liquid. The more he tried to make this about the builders, the more Libby's gut instinct told her *he* was at the bottom of this.

Besides, she reasoned, there was no point joining in with his yelling until she knew what they were yelling about.

'In the office?' she added, as he and Simon continued to glare at each other. She had to pull Jason's arm, and then finally, with a glower at Simon, he followed her.

As they went downstairs, they had to dodge a couple of builders carrying more gear towards the front door.

'Can we make this quick before they strip the entire hotel?' Jason said loudly in their direction, and Libby marched into the office and shut the door behind them.

Bob was demolishing the packet of Jaffa Cakes Libby had bought to share with Alice after lunch. Sensing the simmering mood, he abandoned the crumbs and retreated to a place of safety under the desk.

'What's going on?' Libby gestured to the van being loaded outside. 'What did Simon mean, they haven't been paid?'

'There must have been a mix-up with the bank,' Jason started, but as soon as he said it Libby's heart sank, because she knew from the way his eyes slid sideways that there hadn't been.

'Don't bullshit me. Please. When were we supposed to pay them?'

'Friday. But that's not the point.' Jason stuck a hand in his hair and looked evasive. 'I bet Marek had another job lined up all along and he's just using this as an excuse. I knew this would happen . . .'

'*Really?* Friday?' Libby was trying to do calculations: staged payments . . . materials . . . How much did they owe? She kicked herself for not knowing. Was that trusting Jason or being lazy? She knew, deep down, she'd never liked dealing with money. That had been part of the problem. 'That's nearly a week late. How much are we talking about?'

'What? Are you suggesting I'm lying?' Jason demanded. 'Or that I don't know what I'm doing?'

'I'm not suggesting either,' she said. 'But they're walking off the job. They're not going to do that over a few quid. Marek's a reasonable man.'

'Apparently not. Simon had the nerve to say to me—'

'Oh, for God's sake, now's not the time to get on your high horse about builder etiquette,' said Libby impatiently. 'Just pay them, Jason!'

'With what?'

Their voices were rising and Libby made an effort to lower

her tone, not wanting Alice to hear. Or Margaret, if she was back. 'With the money allocated for this phase of building work in the budget.' It came out through gritted teeth and sounded more sarcastic than she meant it to.

Jason stared back at her. The vein on his forehead was throbbing.

'The renovation account,' she said. 'The money from the sale of our house that we set aside to finance this project. I know you said it was tied up and you couldn't get hold of it for that plumbing invoice, but surely you've managed to move things around now?'

He still didn't speak and her heart sank.

Oh no, thought Libby. Please no.

'Are you telling me there isn't any money?' she said. 'There has to be – I saw it in the hotel bank account . . .'

When? When had she seen it in the bank account? She'd been so busy lately that she hadn't been keeping track of the internet banking.

'Bloody hell, Jason, just tell me what's going on.'

He sat down at the desk and put his head in his hands. The gesture sent a chill through Libby's whole body. 'I had to pay some bills.' His voice was muffled. 'Staged payments, and the materials, and the insurance – it added up. And then I found some rate arrears Mum hadn't paid and they were about to go to the bailiffs. She was very upset, obviously, so I paid them.'

'Why hadn't *she* paid them?'

'She didn't know how. Come on, she never paid any bills while Dad was alive. She just put things in the drawer and hoped they'd go away.'

Libby stared. It felt as if this was happening to someone else. And *neither* of them had told her that minor detail? Jason *or* Margaret? It had been *her* money that had gone into repaying Margaret's mortgage too.

'Anyway, that wiped out our cash. Including the money your dad loaned us.'

'What? Oh my God. Then what?' Libby prompted him. She didn't want to know, and yet she did.

Another long pause. 'Then Darren phoned me again. About the oilfields deal.'

'The one I asked you *not* to invest in?' The gaping holes in the walls upstairs flashed in front of Libby's eyes. The unplumbed baths. 'Are you joking? The risky investment opportunity you *promised* you wouldn't risk our only capital on?'

'You know it's not *risky*.' He looked petulant. 'It's a small company that's got a mining licence to—'

'Don't tell me what I know!' Libby wanted to cry, but her eyes felt strangely hot, and dry. 'And don't give me that "you don't understand investments" bollocks! After what you put us through, some people might think that asking you to *walk backwards* for the rest of your life wouldn't be unreasonable, but all I asked you to do, *all I wanted*, so I wouldn't have to worry like that again, was for you to swear you wouldn't do anything with our money without telling me first! How hard was that?' She sank down into a chair, her knees suddenly unable to support her.

'So . . . tell me. That money in the account, from the house. Tell me there's some left.' Her voice didn't sound like hers. A hundred thousand pounds. A safe amount of money.

'No. It's gone.'

'What?' Libby stared. 'Gone? How?' A horrible thought dawned on her. 'Oh my God, this isn't the first deal you've done, is it? Is it? It's just the first one you've told me about!'

He bit his lip and she knew she'd hit the truth; Jason always was bad at hiding his emotions. Libby covered her mouth as a wave of nausea swept through her. The earrings. Of course. That must have been a smaller trade that came off: Jason always liked to treat her when he was flush. She should have known there wasn't a grand down the side of the sofa. You stupid cow, she thought.

'Oh, come *on!*' Jason's voice had turned scornful. 'How else did you expect us to fund the sort of refurbishment you had in mind? It wasn't that much. You knew how much those baths cost.'

No. This wasn't the first secret deal he'd done. 'You said we could afford it!'

'Yeah, and you didn't ask *how.*'

'Why would I? I trusted you when you said it would be all right!'

'And I am! It will be! Come on, I do this for a living! I'm *good* at it!'

'So good your bank decided to let you go for the safety of their investors?'

It was a low blow. Jason flinched. Libby was ashamed, but panic was making her reckless. This wasn't just about the hotel anymore. This was about a betrayal they'd been too tired and shocked to discuss until now, burying it under arrangements and house-move lists. Now, though, every fear she'd suppressed was fighting its way out and there was no way of stopping it. All she could do was try to steer her way through this horrible conversation, on the back of a bucking, destructive anger.

With a momentous effort, she made her face calm. 'OK. Fine. Can you get the stake back?'

Jason stared sullenly at the desk. 'No.'

'Surely you can ask Darren to buy you out, if it's such a good deal?' Jason's stockbroker mates threw their bonuses into these private deals all the time; Jason's stake would be peanuts compared with what they'd put in.

It came down to pride, Libby knew that. But she'd swallowed her pride, going to her dad for money, hadn't she?

Another, longer pause. 'No.'

'Why not?'

'It's not that easy. There's no point pulling out of it now – they could be on the verge of turning over a massive profit. *Massive*. Like buying this hotel a hundred times over . . .'

As Libby looked up, she caught the glint in Jason's eye and she knew, from now on, there was no discussion to be had. Jason was seeing the figures rolling up on the screen, his instant approval, his reward for being right, and daring to gamble. He couldn't see her. He couldn't see the hotel, the people, the bricks. Just the numbers.

The first time Libby had noticed that glint in Jason's country-boy eyes, she'd assumed it was excitement. He was on his laptop in their home office, with some currency screens open – it was fun to watch him doing his job, sexy even, the way his long fingers fluttered confidently over the keyboard. It wasn't gambling, he assured her, showing her what he'd just made while she'd been watching *Mad Men*; it was way more skilled than that. Forward planning, insight, the right moment – his research coupled with a lucky knack had made him a rising star on his team, so why shouldn't he use some of that on his private account? They went on holiday to Necker Island with that glint.

And it was fine, when it had worked. But then – though Jason didn't tell her for a long, long time – it didn't.

Libby's head felt too heavy on her shoulders. One last chance, she told herself, hollowly. 'Jason,' she said, staring at the veins in the scuffed leather of the old desk top. 'Please. For the sake of our marriage, call Darren and get that money back. We have to pay the builders. Unless the hotel gets finished, we're screwed.'

It felt as if the pause was going to go on for the rest of their lives.

'No,' he said, finally, and when he lifted his gaze, he looked furious. 'I won't do that. And by the way, I'm shocked by your lack of faith in me.'

Libby stared at this handsome thirty-something man who'd won her over with his decency and self-deprecation when they were both too young to know how much those things mattered and thought, What's the point? She couldn't trust him. She'd put their marriage above everything else to come here and start again; he hadn't. If he couldn't see what this was doing to her, undermining all the happiness they had, then what chance was there? How much worse would it have to get before he realised?

'I'm trying to trust you, Jason, but then you do things like this,' she said.

'Seriously? If you don't trust me, then we're wasting our time.' He looked outraged. 'I've worked fucking hard – for *us* – and you've got the nerve to tell me it's not the *right* kind of hard work? Do you think you're the only one who's been through hell this year? There's a difference between giving up your Pilates and your handbags, and losing your livelihood and your self-respect!'

'That's not fair. I always worked until—' she started, but Jason was on a roll, still raging from his encounter with the builders.

'I'm not going to stand here and be lectured by someone who hasn't the first idea what I do or how good I am at it,' he snapped. 'You want me to go? Fine, I will. I'm more than happy to.'

He's not going to go, Libby told herself. It's just a stance.

'All right, then,' she said. 'Go. Walk out on me, and your mother, and your responsibilities. I suppose that'll be my fault then, will it? For kicking you out?'

Jason said nothing. Then he turned and walked out of the hotel.

Chapter Twenty

Libby could only watch as the builders continued to dismantle and remove their gear, and by two o'clock, they drove away and silence descended on the hotel.

Alice had managed to get Marek on the phone, and Libby had begged and pleaded with him, but he'd only confirmed what she dreaded: Jason hadn't even paid the whole first stage payment.

'I'm sorry, Libby, but I can't make my guys work for nothing,' he'd said. 'We already made so many allowances because you've been good clients, but Jason . . . Look, keep in touch, yeah? Maybe we can do something.'

She couldn't blame him. Marek was a nice guy, but he was a businessman. She and Jason had been good clients once, but now they were probably on some builder blacklist.

That's the last kitchen I'll ever get fitted in London, she thought.

Libby walked slowly upstairs and stood in the sea of abandoned dust sheets, trying to make her numb brain assess the building work, as far as she knew how. She couldn't even start thinking about Jason, and what they'd said to each other. Whether he was coming back.

This had happened because she hadn't wanted to look at the details, so now she forced herself to look inside each room. Not one of the upstairs bedrooms was finished, and room four, their own special room, was stacked high with boxes and random junk. Four rooms had bathroom suites fitted, but no tiling or floors laid. The others had had their baths and toilets ripped out, leaving ugly broken holes in the en suites. The ground-floor rooms were just the same; Libby couldn't bring herself to look round those.

She bent down to pick up a discarded ball of masking tape, then realised there was no point trying to tidy up. The enormity of what they had to deal with squeezed the breath out of her body. The comfortable, shabby old hotel was wrecked, gone forever. She understood why Margaret refused to go upstairs; the chaos had looked exciting when the end was in sight, but now it felt as if the raw bricks and bare wires were mocking her. *You thought you could manage this? With no experience? How are you going to fix this now? With no money?*

The thought of that lump sum had been a huge comfort, the one thing that had made the move bearable. When Jason had told her they needed to borrow from her dad, she'd assumed it was because that money wasn't easily accessible, in cash. Not that it wasn't there at all. For it to have gone, just like that . . .

Libby stared at the bunch of wires sticking out of the wall above the missing skirting board – were they dangerous? What was supposed to go on there? – and her mind started to form the words 'Jason, what does . . . ?'

But he'd gone too. An involuntary noise came from somewhere inside her. Libby had never felt small or alone before – she'd looked on the bright side all her life, believing that things would work out fine in the end – but she couldn't see the bright side to this. She'd had nightmares less surreal than the scene in front of her. And she felt so sorry for the hotel she'd ruined. For the first time, she saw the bones of the house

– not the slick boutique hotel she'd wanted to impose on it, but the old family home, welcoming and comfortable. What have I done? thought Libby, mortified.

The sun moved in the trees outside, highlighting the patch-work of grey-lilac stripes in the double bedroom, and she saw herself, painting tester patches like Marie Antoinette while Jason played for time, knowing they hadn't a penny left to pay for any of it, gambling with her future.

Oh Libby, said a voice in her head. It sounded a lot like her dad. How could you have been so oblivious?

She turned on her heel and ran downstairs.

Jason didn't reappear that afternoon with a bunch of flowers and a shame-faced apology, as he had on the handful of times he and Libby had rowed before, and neither did he call or text.

Libby wasn't going to text him. She didn't know what she wanted to say. Anger and misery were taking turns to have the upper hand. Fear was there all the time, though – lurking in the background, popping up every time she caught sight of a bill. It was almost too big to feel angry about.

She needed Jason to come back and help her sort out the mess he'd made, but at the same time, Libby had meant the things she'd said about trust and honesty, and now those hard words were out there, she wasn't going to unsay them. They had to be said. Libby just wished, bitterly, that Jason hadn't chosen the worst possible moment to force the conversation.

She sat alone in the office, unable to move or think or speak, not wanting to see anyone. She didn't know how long she'd been in there when Alice knocked and put her head round the door.

'Hey. Are you all right? I thought you needed some time to calm down,' she said. She was doing a brave, if unconvincing, job of covering her concern. 'But then I thought you might need to talk.'

Libby sank her head into her hands. 'I don't know if I want to talk. I just want to walk out of here and never come back.'

But where would she go? Not home. Her dad had been a firm believer in his daughters making their own mistakes from the age of eleven; her mum wasn't a 'there, there' sort of mother. She had her own problems. And her sister was in Hong Kong, getting over an unpleasant divorce to a man much worse than Jason.

The hard fact was, there wasn't anywhere to go. She was trapped. Any money she had was tied up in this hotel, and right now, it was worse than lost – the place was wrecked. Misery paralysed her, and she couldn't even summon the words to ask Alice for help.

Alice waited a beat, then said, gently, 'Fair enough,' and withdrew.

Libby would have sat alone in the office all night, rooted to the spot while her brain whirred in circles, but by six, she was forced upstairs by the dual need for the loo and a large glass of wine.

Margaret was in the kitchen, preparing some lavish supper for Bob, and called out as Libby slunk past.

'Elizabeth? I've been looking *everywhere* for you. Is Jason out tonight? I was hoping he might give me a lift down to Pat Hasting's for gardening club. I see his car's gone. Will he be back soon?'

Libby bit her lip. Obviously Margaret wouldn't have bothered looking in the one place any actual work was done. She might have found some unpaid business-rate final demands. 'I've been in the office all afternoon. Did you knock?'

'Oh, I thought you were upstairs playing around with your paints!' She decanted the contents of the pan into Bob's bowl and put it on the floor for him. 'I saw the office door shut and assumed Jason was doing something complicated with the accounts. Didn't want to disturb him!' The self-deprecating laugh that accompanied this was like nails on a blackboard to Libby's mood.

'Jason's left,' she said flatly. 'As have the builders.'

Margaret straightened up. 'Sorry, dear, I missed that. What's Jason doing with the builders?'

'Nothing, as it turns out.'

Playing with paints? Jason had taken her for an idiot, and his mother's opinion of her obviously wasn't much better.

'He hasn't paid them, so they've downed tools. Walked off the job.'

That wiped the smile off Margaret's face. 'I don't understand.'

'It's quite simple. We had a certain amount of money set aside to renovate the hotel. A small amount went to the builders. Jason used a sizeable chunk of it to pay your overdue business rates. We've also been paying food, electricity, general running costs for us all since we moved in, given that the hotel barely breaks even. And the rest of it – well, what we had left after we'd paid off the debts Jason ran up gambling all our savings on the currency markets . . .' Libby drew a breath and went on, giddy with the elation of saying things she'd wanted to say for months. 'He's invested every penny we had left in some deal. I can't give you precise details, because I was too angry to ask, but the important thing is that that money is no longer ours. It may well be lost altogether, and we have no more. So we're screwed.'

Margaret's face was slack with shock as she tried to take it all in. 'But why has Jason left?'

'Because I can't trust him, apparently. No, not apparently,' she corrected herself. 'I *can't* trust him. Apart from the small matter of him losing our money, he made one promise to me to save our marriage, and he's just broken it. He flounced out, and I'm afraid I didn't try to stop him.'

Margaret sank onto a kitchen chair. 'Are you sure you've got the whole story?' Amazed, Libby could see her struggling to put Jason back in the right, despite everything she'd just said. 'It's only money. He'll have to ask his firm if he can have his job back for a few months.' Margaret's expression brightened: problem solved. 'I know he'd rather be here, overseeing all his plans for the hotel, but I bet his firm would be *delighted* to have Jason back on board for a little while.'

'He can't go back to his old job.'

'Now, don't be selfish.' Margaret looked reproachful. 'It's lucky that Jason has the earning potential to get you out of this hole. In fact, given the costs that you've both incurred with your plans, maybe it would have been better if you both hadn't been so quick to rush to leave your jobs . . .'

This is madness. She thinks this is my fault, thought Libby, reading Margaret's face. She thinks it was *me* who talked Jason into packing in his job, so I could come here to play at being an interior designer. This from the woman who hid bills in drawers rather than deal with them.

The injustice loosened her tongue. Libby had promised Jason she'd never tell his mother the real story, but Margaret's wilful refusal to see any fault whatsoever in her son, who'd dropped them *all* in it, swept away any resolve she'd had.

'Margaret, Jason can't go back. He was *sacked*. And he came this close' – she held up her finger and thumb in a mean, pinching gesture – '*this close* to losing his broker's licence when

286

they found out just how much money he'd lost. Not his clients' money. Our money.'

'What he chooses to do outside work doesn't affect his job . . .'

'Oh, but it does. If you're constantly worrying about how you're going to make up thousands of pounds' worth of personal losses, it tends to take your mind off your day job. Clients notice. And they move their portfolios to a broker who does have his eye on the ball. Eventually, your management team notices, and when, one day, you accidentally email a client with another client's trading details because you're *spread-betting on your mobile phone at the same time*, your managers don't have a choice. You're a liability. You're a risk. You have to clear your desk and tell your wife not only that you've lost your job, but that you'll need to sell the house because you've burned through every penny you'd saved in the bank!'

As Libby spoke, the images spooled across her mind again, and this time she couldn't push them away. Nice handbags or not, she'd never got completely blasé about the sums involved. The carelessness of it made her uneasy. The arrogance. The way it turned a part of her Jason into someone she didn't know; he was bold with other people's money, but it was still money, not just numbers on a screen. That was the glint. The glint that blinded the better side of him, and turned their life savings into numbers too. Not even coming back here could make him ignore that glint. Not his father's hotel. Not her savings. Not her.

'I'm sure Jason was only doing his best,' said Margaret stubbornly. 'Neither of us has worked in that field. We shouldn't judge.'

'I can't judge when my husband gambles away everything

we had? Everything I'd worked for too? No, Margaret – Jason was greedy,' said Libby. 'And it made him reckless, not just with money, but with our marriage, and your hotel.'

There was a long silence. Even Bob had stopped eating; he'd slunk under the table, his ears pulled forward with trepidation.

Finally, Libby thought, watching Margaret fidget with her rings, *finally* it's sinking in that Jason is just as capable of making mistakes as the rest of us. And that this time he's ruined it for everyone. Her shoulders relaxed: the relief of sharing the secret she'd had to carry alone was physical. Margaret had always been so kind to her. Surely she'd understand now why it meant so much to get the hotel up to scratch?

'Well, I blame you,' said Margaret quietly.

'How?' Libby's head bounced up in surprise. 'How on *earth* can you blame me?'

'You've got expensive tastes. He hasn't. He never had. Look at him now, perfectly happy with a pint and some rugby. I think Jason was only trying to make money to keep up with all the things *you* wanted. Just look at what you've done here.' Margaret waved a contemptuous hand towards the door. 'Redecorating wasn't good enough for you. Oh no. You had to tear everything down and start again. Expensive baths. Expensive taps. What nonsense! Silly, self-indulgent nonsense. Jason was quite happy to get it back up and running the way we'd done it for years, but no, you had to do something *better*. I imagine it was ten times worse in London, keeping up with your friends. Jason must have been under enormous pressure trying to work out how to pay for it all . . .'

Libby shook her head in disbelief. 'Margaret, don't defend him. Please. He's let us *both* down. The fact that Jason can't ever accept he's wrong is at the bottom of all his problems. You're just reinforcing that.'

'Have you ever thought *you* might be wrong?'

'Yes!' She laughed mirthlessly. 'All the time! I worry constantly about whether I've done the right thing – not just here, everywhere. But Jason doesn't. He *never* does. He cannot be criticised, by me or work, or anyone, and it comes from never being wrong in this house. And meanwhile poor Luke . . . God, poor Luke works his arse off, builds up a successful business and you haven't got a good word to say about him! I don't know what you *see* when you look at those two.'

'What would you know about parenting?' said Margaret icily. 'Another thing you've been very selfish about, in my opinion. Was that something else you were pressuring Jason to provide for? Private schools? A nanny? Wasn't that why you kept putting him off about starting a family?'

Her words hit a sore spot, and Libby recoiled. Had Jason discussed their family plans with his mother? Had he moaned to her? How many cosy chats about the state of their marriage had they had since she'd given up her life to move in here?

Margaret saw she'd landed a blow and pursed her lips.

'Actually,' said Libby, 'I'm relieved we haven't brought children into this mess. It's their future that Jason's gambled away.' She wanted to be cold, like Margaret, but she couldn't; the reality of what she'd just said made her want to cry.

'Stop saying gambling.' Margaret's mouth twitched. 'It makes it sound so . . . sordid.'

'Currency trading *is* gambling. Just because someone wears a suit to do it doesn't make them any better than the lads down at William Hill betting their rent on the dogs.'

'Oh, for heaven's sake! We're not in a soap opera! I think

you need to calm down, Elizabeth.' Margaret switched tack back to patronising. 'We don't want to say things in the heat of the moment that we might regret. Jason could walk back through the door tonight with everything sorted out. Then what sort of atmosphere would we have?'

You'd like that, wouldn't you? Libby thought. All sorted out, nice and neat, and you don't have to do a thing.

'I very much doubt he's coming back,' she said aloud, instead.

'He will. I know my son. He's probably gone away to think. How can anyone think in this mess? Jason's like his father. He's a coper.'

Oh, the things I could tell you about Donald. Libby's nails dug into her palms. Donald didn't cope at all. He just asked his friend at the bank if he could remortgage – he had all the business sense of a cod.

But she made herself bite her tongue. Donald wasn't here to defend himself. And Libby could already see how that would be repeated to Jason, her spiteful attack on his dead father's memory.

'I wouldn't hold your breath,' she said. 'He's already refused to get his stake back from his mate. Too proud. So he's left us. To deal with his mess.'

'*Your* mess,' snapped Margaret. 'The mess *you*'ve made of *my* hotel.'

'No,' Libby reminded her. '*Our* hotel. My redundancy payment took care of your overdraft. I'm on the deeds, as well as Jason.'

They stared at each other furiously. Libby couldn't decide whether she was angrier that this nightmare was basically down to Margaret's spoiling of Jason or that Margaret held her responsible.

It's Jason's ego that's the problem, pointed out a little voice in her head. *No one made him invest that money.*

'You seem to have given up on him already,' said Margaret, rather dramatically for someone who didn't think she was in a soap opera. 'I'm glad I don't share your lack of faith. When Jason comes back, I'll be in my room. Come on, Bob.'

And she swept out, leaving Libby staring at the shabby kitchen units, too shattered to reply.

The next morning, when Alice tiptoed into the kitchen, there was no one there but Bob, sitting by the fridge waiting patiently for his breakfast.

'Oh good,' she said to him. 'At least someone's acting normally.'

To her extreme embarrassment, Alice had heard Libby and Margaret's entire row from beginning to end; she'd been on the point of stepping in to try to defuse the tension when things had taken a personal turn, leaving her stranded on the squeaky-floorboarded landing, unable to move without drawing attention to herself, but equally unable to go in while they were airing so much dirty family linen.

She'd managed to duck into the bathroom as Margaret stormed out, but when she went in to comfort Libby, she'd been unresponsive and sadder than Alice had ever seen her. She hadn't known what to say, and Libby had gone to her room soon after. Alice had stayed up late, hoping Jason would phone or Libby would emerge to talk, but the hotel was eerily silent for the rest of the night, apart from the heartbreaking sound of Libby stifling her crying.

Bob thumped the floor with his tail, and then thumped the fridge with his mighty paw and looked hopeful.

'Let's go for a walk,' said Alice. 'Breakfast can wait.'

She put Bob on his lead and led him out behind the hotel and down the footpath. It was a crisp, grass-scented morning, and Alice's spirits lifted along with the pale clouds drifting over the treetops. She walked on until they were out of earshot; then she pulled her mobile phone out of her pocket and dialled the number from her notebook.

It rang three, four times, and then he answered.

'Luke Corcoran?'

Relief flooded through her. The sound of Luke's voice, brisk, familiar, swept away the niggling doubts; she'd been right to call. Well, he was the only one who could help, wasn't he?

'Luke, it's Alice.'

'Alice!' He sounded pleased. 'How are you? Everything all right?'

'Ye— No.' She stopped smiling and remembered why she was calling. 'No. The builders walked off the job yesterday, because of some money problem, and then Jason and Libby had a massive row and he's left. Then your *mother* and Libby had a row, and they've both been in their rooms since supper, and . . .' Alice stopped walking, suddenly floored by unhappiness.

The worst thing was, these weren't the people she knew. Kind and snobby Margaret; funny, stylish Libby. She didn't know the catty, angry women sniping at each other. It felt like the ground was shifting beneath her again.

'Alice? Are you OK?'

'Fine,' she gulped, but it came out half as a sob.

Pull yourself together, Alice told herself. Imagine how Libby feels. This isn't about you.

'I probably shouldn't be calling, but I don't know what to do for the best, and I want to help,' she confessed. 'Libby's on her own, and the place is in a right state. Should we try to get new builders? Can you come and advise her? Or get hold of Jason?' The words tumbled out. 'I mean, is it dangerous to leave building work like this? Is it *legal*?'

'OK, stay calm. First things first,' said Luke. 'Are you sure Jason isn't coming back?'

'I don't know if Libby would let him in if he did. She looks . . . like she's either about to cry or punch something.'

'And the builders definitely aren't coming back?'

'Not anytime soon. I managed to speak to Simon, the foreman, as they were packing up and he says Marek's pulled them off the job to do a house conversion in Highgate. He reckons Marek's cutting his losses – he doesn't think Jason's got the money to finish the hotel.' She paused. 'Does he?'

'I haven't a clue. Jason wouldn't talk to me about something like that.'

Alice watched Bob prance happily down the path in the morning sunlight, glossy ermine coat gleaming as his sturdy legs covered the ground in powerful strides, and she felt a vivid déjà vu. Clear air, silent companionship. Morning walks with a dog make me happy, she thought. I've been here before. When?

She struggled to find the memory but couldn't quite catch it. It was there, though. It was fighting to get through the curtain.

'Do you want me to come back?' Luke asked. 'I'm doing a job up in Scotland, but I could get back for . . . Thursday? Is that too late? I'd come sooner, but I'm under contract to be here the whole time.'

As he said it, Alice felt her whole body answer, *Yes, please come back*, but she made her brain take charge. 'I think Libby would appreciate some support,' she said. 'None of us knows much about building, as you can guess.'

'And you? Are you all right? Things going well with Gethin?' His tone was more neutral, which somehow made it more concerned.

Alice hadn't spoken to Luke about the new arrangement with Gethin, or how the date night had gone. Or all the things she'd since found out about him, and herself.

'I'm fine,' she said. 'Thanks. Libby invited me to stay at the hotel while Gethin and I get to know each other again – good thing, as it turns out, eh? So, um, yes. It's going well. It's good.'

That was a mixed message, she thought, despairing of her own intentions. On the one hand, she wanted Luke to know she was back at the hotel, alone; on the other, she needed him to know that things were going fine with the boyfriend who clearly loved her. The loving, supportive relationship she needed to remember.

Alice gazed out over the trees. I don't know who I was, she thought. That's the trouble. I only know who I am now, and I don't think it fits. Why?

'We can talk more on Thursday,' said Luke. 'Can't promise I can fix anything, but . . . we can try. Let Libby know I'm coming, but don't tell Mum.'

'OK,' said Alice, and the weight on her shoulders lifted a fraction. They weren't completely on their own. Luke would know what to do.

The sun was shining over the trees and fields of Longhampton. Maybe it's not that I've been here before, she thought. Maybe this is where I was supposed to be all along. It was a strange sensation, and she pushed it out of her mind quickly, before hurrying back to the hotel.

Chapter Twenty-One

Libby woke the next morning in a panic, thinking that she'd forgotten to get up to make breakfast, but as her bare feet touched the carpet, the events of the previous day caught up with her and she fell back against the pillows as if an invisible hand had shoved her down.

Things looked even more desperate now the adrenalin and anger had worn off. She stared at the ceiling and couldn't find one disaster to be positive about. Jason – *gone*. The builders – *gone*. The hotel – *ruined*. Their money – *gone*. The rock that they'd been pushing up the hill together had rolled back down again, right to the bottom, and the way Libby's entire body ached now, it had rolled right over her.

She pulled the duvet around her for comfort and curled into a foetal position, trying to block it all out.

It was just too much. Libby had no idea where to start, and she had to deal with it alone. No, worse than alone: stuck here with grieving, furious Margaret, who blamed her for the whole thing. The ice-cold look in her eyes as she'd said all those mean things . . . Libby shuddered, because deep down, she wondered if maybe Margaret had a point about most of this being her own fault.

Her alarm went off, but she smacked it down. What was the point of getting up? A lie-in was about the only small pleasure left. After half an hour or so, she heard the bedroom door push open. Since Margaret was hardly likely to be bringing her breakfast in bed, she assumed it was Alice, checking if she was awake.

Libby couldn't face Alice's kindliness this morning, so she pretended to be asleep.

At least Alice was here. She could have gone back to Gethin – he phoned every night to check she was all right, to hear everything she'd been up to – but thank goodness she hadn't. She's so lucky to have found Gethin, Libby thought. A steady, loving, reliable man who adores her.

Jason. Steady, loving, reliable, adoring – two days ago, she'd have said the same things about him. Tears sprang to her eyes again.

Without warning, Libby felt a weight on the corner of the bed, then heard a faint grunt and a solid mass of dog sprang onto the mattress next to her. Well, the back end took a while to slither up.

'Go away, Bob,' she said, but he took no notice. Instead, he clambered over and sniffed her wet face. Libby had never had Bob so up close and personal, but her arms were trapped under the duvet and she couldn't push him away. He smelled of biscuits and sleep. She squinted at him, surprised at how intricate his huge black nose was, the fine white whiskers on his snout. Delicately, he licked the tears that had run down her cheek, drooping his velvety dewlaps over her nose; then with an almost human huff, he settled himself around the crook of her body, using her hip as an armrest and filling the hollow of her legs with his soft body.

'Get off me,' she said, but found she didn't really mean it. There was something comforting about Bob's heavy warmth.

With another grumbly huff, he laid his head flat along her hip, and it struck Libby as such a gesture of trust – she could have got up and sent him flying at any moment – that her heart broke inside her. Bob raised his wise brown eyes to hers, full of hopeful affection, and she thought, So *this* is what those old people up at the hospital find so soothing. That restful, simple, trusting love in his face. Fixing you in the moment.

I've screwed up quite a lot here, she thought, as a lump rose in her throat. But as far as Bob's concerned, I've been all right.

Lord Bob and Libby gazed at each other, and then he nuzzled his head against her and she freed a hand from under the duvet and buried her fingers in his luxuriant folds of warm fur.

'Don't think this is the start of dogs on beds,' she warned him. 'This is a one-off. Because I'm too sad to kick you off. OK?'

Bob grunted happily and closed his eyes.

A while later, there was a knock on the door, and this time it was Alice.

'Libby? Are you awake? I've brought you a cup of tea.'

'Come in,' said Libby, but Alice was already pushing open the door. She had a mug in each hand, and when she saw Bob, she did a double take.

'Off!' she said. 'Off! Sorry, Libby, I've just taken him out for a walk. I didn't realise . . .'

'He's fine.' Libby struggled into a sitting position as Alice perched on the edge of the bed and handed her a mug of tea. Thankfully, it wasn't Jason's new Longhampton FC mug.

'Listen, I heard everything last night,' she said. 'I'm so sorry.'

Libby flinched. 'Everything?'

'Pretty much.' Alice's uncomfortable but sympathetic smile

told Libby she wasn't judging, and it gave her a feeling of relief not dissimilar to Bob's weight on her legs. Better than actual words. 'What are you going to do?'

'What can I do?' Libby closed her eyes, but the images that flared up in her mind made them snap open again straight-away. 'I don't know the first thing about this, really. I thought I did, but . . .'

'Right. Well, who can you ask for help? Are your parents nearby?'

'No. And they're the *last* people I'd turn to.' She flinched; how was she going to tell her dad he wasn't getting his money back any time soon? 'I don't know anyone round here, apart from you, and Margaret's friends, I guess. Doubt any of them are tilers, though. Maybe we could fill the gap in the walls with some really big flower arrangements?'

Alice tapped her mug with a fingernail, then said, 'What about the PAT lady? Gina? With the greyhound? Her card says she's a project manager.'

'You kept her card?'

'Yes,' said Alice patiently. 'That's what they're for. I've started a card file for you in the office. I can't think why there wasn't one before. I was a PA, remember,' she added, when Libby looked impressed. 'It's pretty basic stuff.'

Hope flickered, then died in her chest. 'We can't afford a project manager.' She thought of the man who'd pitched for the job of managing Marek's builders in London; he'd wanted twenty per cent of the budget.

That'd have been enough to get this finished, thought Libby ruefully.

'Well, you can ask. Maybe ask her in front of the Tree of Kindness so she gets the hint?' Alice nudged her. 'You've given up plenty of your time taking Bob to the hospital – if you tell her what a pickle you're in, I'm sure she'd give you an hour of advice. What? What's that look for?'

Libby was cringing. 'Just . . . I hate the thought of it going all round the town what a cock-up we've made. We should have used local builders, shouldn't we? I bet they're already talking about that – Londoners coming here, with their fancy plans . . . Me, putting poor Margaret through the mill, ruining her hotel. That's even before they get wind of Jason leaving. It'll be all over the rugby club before you can say . . . Deep Heat.' She tried to sound light, but inside she wanted to die. And if it got back to London – who was Jason talking to now? Whose shoulder was he crying on?

Alice said nothing, but looked at her in her familiar perceptive way, computing all the tiny details.

'What?' said Libby. 'What are you thinking?'

Alice shook her head. 'Just that I don't understand you sometimes. Why do you care what people who don't know you think? I appreciate that this is a nightmare situation, but really, people aren't going to judge. They're not going to think, Oh, that Libby Corcoran's a right cow – her builders didn't get paid, and her husband's disappeared. Are they? They're going to think, Poor Libby – her builders were unreliable, and now her husband's had to go back to London, probably to work.'

'But . . .'

'But what?'

But what? Libby tried to work out why she was shrivelling inside. It was because she did feel judged by this. Judged by herself. The hotel was going to be *their* thing, the project that'd pull her and Jason back on the same track, and she'd made it sound like the project of a lifetime to her friends, because that's what she wanted it to be. It couldn't just be what it was – a simple little country B&B. Why?

She gripped her mug. 'Everyone Jason and I know either has an amazing career or an amazing house or amazing children. My career was doing all right, but then the company started making layoffs, and then Jason . . . messed up, and I just wanted to prove that we *could* do something incredible . . .'

Something for people to be impressed by. Oh God, I am so shallow, Libby realised. Shallow and glib. Everything I've always hated in other people. I thought I was better than that, but I'm not.

Bob gave another of his expressive sighs and burrowed his head along her hip. Libby could feel pins and needles beginning in her leg, but she didn't care.

'Prove to who?' Alice asked, and her gentleness made Libby want to cry.

'To other people.' Libby paused. That was the truth, but she knew it wasn't the right answer. 'My friends.'

'Your friends whose Facebook posts you ignore?' Alice poked at the duvet. 'Friends who leave me phone messages asking you to call them and you never do? There are only so many meetings I can say you're in, when there are, like, two guests a week.'

Libby said nothing. She knew it was stupid. Every time she saw a message in Alice's neat writing, she couldn't quite believe Erin, or Becky, or whoever it was really wanted to talk to her.

'You don't need other people to tell you who you are,' said Alice, and her face was sweetly serious. 'I've learned that. The only person who matters, the only person who *really* knows you is you. And if you think you're the sort of person who can get back after something like this, and carry on, and finish the job, then you are. You just haven't needed to do it till now. It doesn't mean you haven't been that person all along.'

Their eyes met and Libby felt stronger, just from the sense of absolute belief radiating from Alice.

'You're right,' she said. 'You're right.'

Gina Rowntree, PAT volunteer and Longhampton's premier project manager, it turned out after some cursory Googling, arrived in the afternoon, accompanied by a lanky man with long dark curly hair and a Thin Lizzy T-shirt. He wasn't her husband, she explained; he was her most reliable builder. Which didn't mean she didn't treasure him just as much as Nick, her actual husband.

'This is Lorcan Hennessey,' she said, once she'd greeted everyone and sympathised (briefly). 'He's a carpenter, mainly. He came because he doesn't want you to think all builders are like this lot who've left you in the lurch.'

'Indeed not. Some are worse,' he said solemnly, in a strong Irish accent, then added, 'Only joking.'

Before Libby could react, Gina gave him a mock-horrified look. 'Time and place, Lorcan.' She had a stillness about her when she was with Buzz in the PAT sessions, but here, working, her manner was more like a friendly school prefect – competent, firm, no-nonsense.

'Right now, I'll take all the jokes on offer,' said Libby. 'Even the really bad ones.'

'In that case, Lorcan's your man,' said Gina. 'I only let him play his awful rock music on jobs because it drowns out the jokes. Now, take me to your very worst room. That's always the best place to start.'

After Libby had led them to the horror that was room six, with its two holes in the walls, they inspected the rest of the first floor, with Libby explaining what the plans were, and Lorcan tapping and frowning at the woodwork. Gina listened, and asked questions that made Libby squirm inside: no, she hadn't drawn up a proper contract with Marek for delivery times. No, she hadn't allowed a contingency fund for unexpected extras. No, she hadn't done a business plan. And on and on.

'Are we the most clueless renovators you've ever seen?' she asked despairingly, after Gina had explained yet another basic building shortcut to her.

'No! Not at all. The most ambitious, maybe.' The glamorous baths had drawn oohs and aahs from both Lorcan and Gina, then sharp intakes of breath when Libby had confessed how much they'd cost. 'But you'd be surprised how many couples don't discuss budgets properly when they start these things.' Gina pulled a face over a doorless doorway. 'In a way, it's good because otherwise they wouldn't need to pay me to come in and sort it all out afterwards.'

'But don't you find it annoying?'

'No.' Gina gave her a consoling pat. 'To be honest, the worse the mess, the more satisfying the sorting-out.'

'Good,' said Libby. 'I think.'

After an hour or so, Libby sat Gina and Lorcan down in the kitchen and offered them a cup of tea, with the last of Margaret's expensive biscuits. Margaret had taken herself off somewhere, probably to one of her town cronies to complain about her selfish daughter-in-law.

Gina sipped her tea, then got a black notebook out and turned to a fresh page. Something about the practical gesture sparked a tiny flame of optimism in Libby's weary heart. Tea, notebook, fresh page.

'So, to recap,' she said, clicking her pen, 'you've got a deadline, which is this journalist coming at the start of September. You want to be opening again at the beginning of July. We're now nearly in June. That's about five weeks. Plenty of time. And your budget is . . . ?'

'Minimal. Can we come back to that?' asked Libby bravely.

'No problem,' said Gina, as if it wasn't a problem. 'Lorcan? What's your verdict?'

Lorcan sighed, put his elbows on the table and shoved his big hands into his black curls. 'OK, so . . .'

Libby's forehead creased with dismay.

'Ignore that,' said Gina, seeing her reaction. 'He does that on every job I've ever seen him on. It's how builders think. Brain has to connect with hands.'

'I reckon . . . it's not *quite* as bad as it looks,' said Lorcan. He sat up and met Libby's worried gaze direct; he had disconcertingly denim-blue eyes, with thick dark lashes, and his smile started there and worked down to the rest of his face. 'They've not done the neatest job, but once we've got those walls sorted out, and the rest of the bathrooms plumbed in, it's straightforward tiling and painting.'

Straightforward. It could be brain surgery as far as Libby was concerned.

'And then you'll need carpets.' Gina was making notes. 'And your soft furnishings . . . Did you have an original budget I could look at?'

Libby slid Jason's spreadsheets across the table and watched as Gina flipped through them with an expert eye, circling things here and there.

'Did you say your husband works in finance?' she asked, without looking up.

'Yes?'

'You know he's put no VAT in any of these calculations?'

'Really?' Libby groaned.

'It's no wonder you ran out of cash sooner than you thought. So . . . the bad news is, straight off, I think you're going to have to scale back your plans.' She smiled supportively. 'Again, I say this at least twice a week – you're not the first developer to go over budget; you won't be the last. So my advice is to take control of it. Either focus on getting four rooms really nice and keep the rest of the doors shut or tackle the whole hotel more basically.'

Libby's dreams of Egyptian cotton sheets and luxury detailing were sliding away in front of her eyes. 'When you say basic . . . ?'

'I mean, off the top of my head, sanding and sealing the floors instead of carpeting. Um, going for cheaper curtain material but lining them properly. Painting instead of wallpapering. Getting basic sanitaryware in for the rest of the en suites but decent taps. I can work through your budget and see where savings can be made.'

'But the journalist thinks she's coming to a luxury boutique hotel!' Not just the journalist but all their friends in London, who'd be eagerly flicking through the magazine to see Libby and Jason's fabulous lifestyle change. Something churned inside her. She could almost hear Rebecca Hamilton asking, 'Where's the spa, hon?' in that fake-concerned way she had.

'There's no point going into debt to make *one journalist* happy,' said Gina. 'If you haven't got the money, you haven't got the money. Move on. Change the question to one you can answer.'

Libby stared at her mug, her mind spinning. This week had been full of turning points. She'd always assumed life's turning points would be signposted well in advance, like motorway junctions, so she could prepare for the big swerve towards a new destination, but the reality was that they sprang out at you, you had a split second to react, and then you were heading off in a direction you weren't even sure you'd chosen.

Jason losing his job had come out of nowhere. Now this. A week ago, she thought she knew what she wanted. But now what did she want? And even if she did know, how capable was she of making it happen, with no money and no experience? Right now, even paying for next week's groceries was looking shaky. Was she kidding herself that she could do this alone? Should she just hand over the keys?

The voice in her head pointed out that now she was sitting round a table with two people who were helping her, because they wanted to, and were talking to *her* about what *she* wanted. A first, really, on this project. She had a chance to take control.

Libby's eye fell on Jason's spreadsheets and she had to look away; it sent a shard of pure misery straight into her chest.

'As far as that feature goes,' Gina went on, folding up the spreadsheets without further comment, 'and I'm speaking as a regular reader of those sorts of magazines, I'm way more interested in someone who's put their dream project together on a budget, under mad pressure, than some hedge funder's wife who just threw her husband's cash at some architects, then ram-raided The White Company in order to make a boring hotel the same as all the other boring hotels her boring friends go to. A bit of friction makes it much more interesting.'

'Yes, when you're reading about someone else. When it's you . . .' Libby knew her voice sounded whiny, but she couldn't stop herself.

Gina reached for her mug of tea and gave Libby's wrist a squeeze on the way. It was a friendly grip, but a 'come on, now' one. 'Libby, we've all had moments like this. When you and I know each other better, I'll bore you with my story of how the very best things in my life came out of the very worst moments. Seriously. Lorcan too.'

'Yeah.' Lorcan nodded. 'Life has terrible timing. You wouldn't want it organising a party for you.'

'It's still a great PR opportunity; you just have to decide how to play it,' Gina went on. 'Honestly, this place is such a gem! I love your baths, and the colours you've picked are great . . . So what if you economise? What do people really remember about a hotel? The expensive sheets, or how relaxed they felt when they left? Pick some nice cheap touches to make your own. I've recommended the Swan to visitors on the strength of the dog-friendly rooms alone – that's a really strong selling point, for one.'

Libby opened her mouth to say that wasn't part of her plan, actually, but wisely changed her mind.

'In the end, though, it's your choice,' said Lorcan. He cast a warning look at Gina. 'Easy for *us* to see this as a project – imagine it's more complicated than that for yourself right now. Emotions-wise.'

'Fine, take the emotions out of it,' said Gina. 'Let's get this place finished and then you can put it on the market if you want. But you can't do nothing, right?'

Libby took a deep breath and looked ahead for the turning point. She could do nothing and get nothing, or she could reach out, take some help and see where she ended up. A lightness filled her chest, like a thousand tiny birds lifting her up and up and up. The hotel deserved to be put right. She wanted to be the one to do it.

I'm going to do this, she thought, and I'm going to show Jason he was wrong, that he didn't need to gamble our money to pay for it. And that if it comes to it, I don't need him either.

God, that made her cold and sad. She wanted to take it back instantly, before the universe took her at her word.

'OK,' said Libby, ignoring the ache in her chest. 'How do I do this?'

Chapter Twenty-Two

✕

'... and so Lorcan's getting his apprentices to use the hotel as training to keep the costs down.' Alice deftly moved the chopped clove of garlic into the pile she'd already made. 'Everyone's pitching in to help – Gina's husband, Nick, has offered to do the photography for the website, and another of the PAT volunteers works at a house-clearance charity, so she's stockpiling rugs for Libby for the bedrooms. They're going to give more of a vintage feel, instead of the boutique look.'

She paused, aware that she'd been telling Gethin about Libby's plans for about half an hour, non-stop, and he'd barely said a word. 'But it's going to be a lot of hard work,' she said. 'Everyone's mucking in. I said I'd do some painting, if they need an extra pair of hands.'

'Is that a good idea, though?' Gethin stopped peeling an onion and turned to her, concerned. 'You shouldn't be pushing yourself so hard.'

It was lunchtime, Gethin had taken the day off, and they were chopping vegetables side by side in the kitchen. Tastes were, according to the hospital, good memory prompts, so Gethin had found recipes they used to make together; apparently this was a favourite Thai curry that they both loved and used to make 'at least once a week'.

'Don't worry,' she reassured him. 'I'm just doing easy bits. And making a lot of coffee.'

Gethin tilted his head and gazed at her through his shaggy fringe. 'You were only supposed to be helping out for that one day. I think they're taking advantage now.'

'They're not.' Alice paused. 'They' was really just Libby. Jason was still AWOL, Margaret was barely speaking to anyone, and Luke wasn't coming until the following evening. Something expanded inside her chest at the thought of Luke walking through the front door.

Luke had texted her to check she'd be around when he called in and Alice's stomach had looped over just at the sight of his name on her phone. She wanted to talk to him about the plans, about her memories of her parents . . . About anything, really.

'Libby doesn't know anyone round here: she needs all the help she can get,' she said quickly, to push Luke out of her mind.

Gethin opened his mouth to say something, then closed it.

'What?' Alice recognised the tension that flashed across Gethin's face when he had to remind her of an unwelcome memory, something she needed to know but wouldn't enjoy hearing. It was a miserable responsibility, she thought, that the one you loved most also had to be the most honest with you. 'Go on.'

'I just think you're being a bit naïve. They don't have any money to pay staff, so of course they're going to take advantage of the fact that you're grateful to Libby. I don't want you to get dragged into anything, especially when you're still not completely over your accident. And,' he added, 'maybe it's selfish, but I want you back here with me, not painting walls for strangers. This house feels empty without you.'

'I'm sorry,' said Libby.

Gethin selected another tomato from the pile and sliced it in half, revealing its heart of seeds. 'It's hard, when you've got used to sharing your life with someone,' he said, keeping his eyes on his chopping board, 'and suddenly they're not there.' He bit his lip. 'And it doesn't feel like they *want* to be there.'

'But I do!' said Alice at once. 'That's not fair. I'm just . . . It's just getting used to it all.'

He didn't reply and Alice cast a sideways glance at him. Gethin chewed his lip and looked . . . not quite sad, but almost offended? She supposed he had reason to be.

After that first date night, Gethin had ditched the smart clothes and returned to a more relaxed polo shirt and jeans. She liked his slightly mod look: rumpled and sweet. They'd kissed at the door last time she left – not a passionate kiss, but something lingering, tender, that had caught fire a little at the end, his hands in her hair. Enough to make her hope that, maybe, soon, her body might remember something.

He finally looked up, straight into her eyes. 'When are you going to move back?'

Gethin's sincerity caught her off balance; she hated the idea he could see her doubt, or the more troubling thoughts hovering at the edges of that dark curtain over her memory. 'Soon,' she said.

Alice was saved from saying more by the phone ringing in the hall.

He put down his knife. 'I'll get it,' he said. 'Probably my boss. She doesn't understand the concept of a day off. Won't be a moment.'

'So it's OK for her to take advantage of you, but not for Libby to take advantage of me?'

Alice said it lightly, but Gethin frowned. 'Don't be like that.'

She turned back to the pile of garlic cloves and resumed her chopping. It was nice, this, she told herself. Glass of wine, Gethin's playlist of 'their' songs, summer air streaming through the big doors in the—

Ow. The knife had got too close to her knuckle while she'd been dicing and taken a small but bloody chunk out of her finger. Alice sucked it. One ruby drop of blood had already fallen on the chopping board.

'Gethin?' she started to call, but then thought, No, don't interrupt his phone call.

Where would the first-aid box be in the kitchen? Alice began to open some cupboards at random. Under the sink?

It was stuffed with many, many cleaning products but no handy box of plasters.

She sucked her finger and opened drawers with her other hand. Cutlery . . . utensils . . . tea towels. No sign of anything in the cupboard by the fridge, just the usual Tupperwares with lids belonging to other boxes.

The precious seconds of numbness before the sting were ebbing away, and the iron taste of blood on her tongue reminded her unpleasantly of the hospital. Next cupboard: shoe-cleaning kit, suede protector, dusters.

Why would you make the first-aid kit so hard to find? There was only one cupboard left, above the extractor fan. Alice grabbed a chair and reached up to open it. The door was sticky and she had to yank to get it to move.

Inside were three metal dog bowls, a lead, two red Kongs, a squeaky pheasant, a blue harness.

Alice froze. Dog stuff? Did they have a dog?

She reached up and pulled out the harness. There was a brass tag on the ring: no dog's name, but hers was there, with her mobile number and a different address, 143a King's Avenue.

Alice gripped the webbing and, just as the pendant had brought back a memory in her heart as she held it, suddenly she knew with absolute certainty that she *did* have a dog. She had a small white fox terrier, with a pirate patch of black over one eye and long, straight legs, like an Enid Blyton dog. She was Fido's owner.

'Fido,' she said aloud, and it came out half as a sob. 'Fido.'

Something flashed in the back of her head, and memories shot across her consciousness almost too quickly to register: the concrete run in the North London rescue centre, and the skinny terrier sitting up and begging by the wire grille, pathetically running through all the tricks she knew for every passing visitor – and the unexpected thunderbolt of love that had hit them both at the same time.

Early-morning walks before work, throwing a red ball into the mist rising off the park.

Gladys, the retired nurse in the garden flat below hers, welcoming a wagging Fido inside as Alice headed off to the Tube station for the day.

But mainly her heart filled up with Fido, and her black button eyes, and the white tail that never stopped wagging, and the look of intense devotion she bestowed constantly on Alice, and the feeling of completeness Alice felt in return, not alone anymore, but anchored in the big city by her little dog.

But where was she? Why hadn't Gethin even mentioned her? Alice felt a clawing dread that something bad had happened to Fido and stumbled as she got down from the chair, sending it crashing to the floor.

'Gethin!' she called. Her voice was shaking. 'Gethin!'

'What's the matter?' He came rushing in and saw the blood on her hand, dripping unnoticed onto the white work surface. 'You've cut yourself! Quick, let me run it under the tap . . .'

'No, this.' Alice showed him the harness, the bowls. 'Where's Fido? Why didn't you tell me I'd forgotten her?'

How could I have forgotten Fido? she thought, racked with guilt.

Gethin rubbed his face and looked heartbroken. 'I didn't want to tell you until you were feeling better.'

'Tell me now. I need to know.'

'She's dead,' he blurted out, and Alice felt her face go loose with shock.

'Oh God, I'm sorry. I'm so sorry. Sit down,' he said, and guided her to the table.

Alice's legs wobbled beneath her and he put his arms round her from behind, rocking her gently. She didn't mind the contact now; she barely registered it. Something told her that this reaction was weirdly disproportionate – she hadn't felt this stunned when presented with a man she couldn't remember – but her brain couldn't grip the thought. It slipped and slid away.

'Tell me what happened,' she said.

Gethin rested his cheek against her head. 'You were walking Fido in the park here in Stratton and she was off the lead, having a run around.'

'You were there?'

'No, this is what you told me later. We think the ball must have bounced or something because she ran into the road,

313

and, well, she went into a bus. It would have been very quick.'

Tears flooded into Alice's eyes, blurring the mugs on the table. 'No,' she whispered. 'Why didn't I stop her?'

'I don't know, Bunny.'

'But I always watched her. I threw the ball for her. I never let her out of my sight! Not in London!'

Gethin hugged her, gently, on account of her ribs. 'Alice, this is why I didn't tell you. What can you do now? I really hate having to tell you bad things as well as good things. It's so hard. Maybe you were texting or on the phone to someone or some-thing. You obviously had a lot on your mind at the time – if I'm being absolutely honest, I was worried about you. You hadn't been yourself.'

Alice closed her eyes. Had she been on the phone . . . to Luke? When Fido got run over? Who had she *been* in those weeks? Could a crash have turned her into someone she didn't even recognise now? The evidence was piling up in front of her and she didn't want to see it.

'I'm sorry,' said Gethin. 'I'm really sorry.' He reached over her shoulder and touched the brass circle on the harness that Alice was still clutching. 'We were a little family.'

The word 'family' triggered something deep in Alice's heart and she closed her eyes against another old pain: more memories floating up, old but feeling freshly minted. Barley. Barley the bow-legged Jack Russell who hitched lifts in her dad's coat pocket.

'We had a dog when I was growing up. Fido reminded me of her, of Barley. That was why I picked her: she reminded me of Barley . . .' It was too much. Alice couldn't fight back the tears, and when Gethin pulled her into his arms, she didn't resist.

'Don't cry, Alice,' he soothed. 'I'm here now. I'm here. We're still a family, you and me. You need to stay here, with me, tonight. I don't think you should go back to the hotel.' He pulled away so she could see his face. His doe eyes were fixed on hers. 'Stay here, so we can have some proper time together.'

'But Libby needs me . . .'

'Libby doesn't need you as much as we need to talk,' he said, with a note in his voice Alice hadn't heard before. It wasn't up for discussion. She wasn't sure how to react. He was holding her quite tightly.

'I'm just thinking of you,' Gethin went on impatiently. 'You've got to put yourself first. Put *us* first. Don't you want to get things back to normal? That's not going to happen if you're spending all your time with other people, is it? People who don't even know you.' He paused, and Alice felt relieved when his face softened. 'I just want us to catch up on the sofa. Be together. I need that. I've missed you so much. You . . . and Fido.'

Fido. And Barley. Alice's lip wobbled, and Gethin wrapped her up in his arms again. She buried her face in his shoulder and the sense of being completely on her own faded. Gethin knew her, and him knowing her meant the things she loved hadn't completely gone. Backwards and forwards and side-ways in her life.

True to her word, Gina emailed Libby a rundown of what she thought it would take to put the hotel back together. There was a lot to do, but Gina's suggested timetable made it seem possi-ble. And more importantly, after Lorcan had dropped in on his way to a job to explain each process in beginner's terms, for the first time Libby could visualise *how* it would happen.

It felt even more important that she understood now, and that she knew down to the penny what it would cost. She didn't want to feel this caught out, and vulnerable, ever again.

But even though the revised ideas were going to cost a fraction of Libby's original budget, it was still money she didn't have. She sat at the desk in the office when Lorcan had gone and pressed her thumbs into her temples. Where on earth was she going to conjure it up from?

Normally she'd have turned straight to Jason, but now she couldn't. He hadn't phoned since the evening he'd walked out, three days ago. Libby hadn't wanted to phone him: she knew she'd end up apologising, making it her fault, and it wasn't. For once, she wanted him to take the blame for what he'd done. Meanwhile, the bills needed to be paid. She had to find the money. The simplicity of it was freeing, in a funny way – there literally was no alternative but to get on with things.

Libby made herself think logically. She couldn't borrow against the mortgage; they wouldn't get a loan. So what could she sell? She didn't have an overflowing jewellery box to raid, but she could start with the diamonds Jason had bought her: too painful to look at now, let alone wear, and more about him proving himself at his mother's favourite jeweller's than because *she* wanted them.

Did that sum up their marriage? she wondered bleakly. All show, no substance? How could Jason have lost track of who she was to the point where he didn't realise she'd rather have seen Marek's invoice paid than a pair of earrings? Or had she become that person? She bit her lip. Maybe she had, without seeing it.

Libby picked up her pen. The earrings would be a start, but she needed far more than that. Which meant she was going to have to make a call she really didn't want to make, but right now, pride wasn't something she could afford.

She dialled her father's number before she could start rehearsing the conversation in her head.

Colin Davies picked up on the fourth ring, the exact point at which she always got butterflies and wanted to hang up, but it was too late.

'Hi, Dad. It's Libby,' she said, trying to sound light. 'Is this a good time to talk?'

It was never a good time, but she always had to ask. If she didn't, he'd remind her. The hoops she had to jump through with him increased year on year.

'If you're quick,' he sighed, with audible relish. 'I was just on my way out to the golf course.'

'Good. I wanted to talk to you about the hotel,' she began, but as usual, he talked straight over her.

'Don't tell me,' he said, with an unpleasant chuckle in his voice. 'You've blown through that loan I gave you and you're back for more.'

Libby stared aghast at Gina's notes. 'Um . . .'

'I knew it!' He sounded delighted. 'I said to Sophie, "I bet you ten pounds that money burns a hole in Libby's pocket and she'll be on the phone needing a top-up before the month's out." You really are your mother's daughter, Libby. I can't believe a woman can get to your age and be so clueless about budgeting. I'm surprised Jason hasn't taken you in hand about it.'

'Dad, that's not fair. I—'

'Why don't I just speak to Jason? Or does he not know you've spent it? Maybe this time we ought to think about signing some sort of agreement, if I'm going to buy into this business. Which is effectively what I'm ending up doing, isn't it?'

God, thought Libby. How does he do it? How does he still make me feel like a stupid teenager?

It's because you let him, said the voice in her head. *You let him dictate who you are.*

In a flash of lucidity, Libby saw what a very, very bad idea it would be to borrow more money from her dad. Even after the last pound was repaid with interest, he'd still crow about it. It would fix her forever as The Daughter Who Needed Bailing Out. Always eighteen, always irresponsible. She might change; he wasn't going to.

I'm not going to ask, she thought. It's worth more to me not to tell him; I'll find the money somewhere else. The snap decision sent a soaring, thrilling, panicky rush through her.

'Actually, that's not a bad idea,' he mused. 'Put Jason on and we can discuss this properly.'

'I wasn't phoning to ask for money,' said Libby.

'Oh?' Her father sounded almost disappointed.

'No, I was phoning to tell you how *well* things were going here. How good the hotel's looking. But it doesn't sound as if you want to hear anything positive, so I won't waste your time.' Her mouth was dry. 'I'll give you a call when we reopen. Maybe we can do you a discount on a weekend room rate. Bye, Dad.'

She hung up while he was still spluttering with outrage, and sank her head into her hands. It was the right thing to do, but it left her with another hard phone call to make. Harder, actually. Libby still wasn't sure it was the right thing to do, but her options were limited.

There are no easy ways to ask for money, she reminded herself, as she dialled the next number. That's today's lesson.

One Small Act of Kindness

The phone rang on the other end and then a familiar voice said, 'Hello, stranger! Where've you been?' Erin's voice was warm and Libby felt a gulp of guilt that she'd put off calling until she needed a favour. Some friend she was. 'I was starting to think I said something wrong,' Erin went on, in a more serious tone. 'Did I? It's just that no one's heard from you, and we're all a bit . . . What did we do?'

'Sorry, it's just been mad here,' Libby started automatically. Then she stopped. 'No, actually, it's been . . . Erin, listen, I don't know a better way to put this, so I'm going to jump right in: I need a favour. A really big one.'

Should she tell her about Jason leaving first? Libby wasn't sure she could bear the pity. At least if she framed it as a business thing Erin could still feel able to say no. Her face burned.

'Ask away!' Erin was obviously at a playground from the sound of the laughing and screaming in the background. 'It's Auntie Libby!' she added, for the benefit of an unseen child. 'Can you wave? Wave down the phone? Can you pretend you can see Tobias waving, please?'

Libby squeezed her eyes shut. Tobias was a sweetie. She'd loved being Auntie Libby to Erin's Beans.

'Erin, I need to borrow some money,' she said. 'Just for a few months.'

'Oh, don't tell me – is it the bank?' said Erin. 'Did I tell you how they moved Pete's salary into the wrong account and didn't tell us till we were thousands overdrawn?' Libby could imagine the eye-roll. 'They deny all knowledge, of course. What have they done to you?'

Libby hesitated for a second. Erin was offering her the perfect fig leaf to cover her embarrassment, but she couldn't take it. She had to be honest. It was pretending to be something she wasn't that had led her into this situation. Erin deserved the truth.

'No,' she said. 'It's . . . I need to borrow it to finish off some work here.'

'Right.' Erin sounded surprised. 'How much are we talking about?'

Libby closed her eyes. This was going to make it real. 'Ten thousand?'

There was a long pause at the other end.

'OK,' said Erin slowly. 'It's just that . . . Ten thousand pounds? It's a lot of money, but it's not a *lot* of money, if you get what I mean. I thought you had a massive budget – you sold your house, right?'

Libby stared at the office, its dignified cosiness slowly emerging from the clutter, and realised she could barely remember the details of the house on which she'd spent so much money. It had all been beige and smooth and chrome, not like this hotel, with its cosy corners, and window seats, and unexpected stained glass. Her London renovation had been about adding value to their already overpriced property; this was about bringing a haven back to life.

'Libby? Are you all right, hon?' The background noise had dropped to nothing; Erin had discreetly stepped away from the play area to stop the other mums listening in. It was a thoughtful thing to do, caring about what they might think of Libby, even now. 'Is this really about the hotel?'

I have to tell Erin everything, Libby thought suddenly. She deserves to hear it all before I ask this massive favour, even if it means she doesn't think I'm worth the risk. To her surprise, as the idea passed through her mind, another weight lifted off her shoulders. Not having to pretend anymore. Just dealing with what was here, now, exactly as it was.

'Jason's walked out on me,' she said. Small words for such a big pain. 'Work's stopped on the hotel and it's a building site. And we don't have any money because he's been currency trading again. He's lost everything. Again.'

'What do you mean, again? Oh my God.' Erin sounded stunned. 'Are you all right? Tell me everything.'

Once Libby started, it tumbled out: Jason's losses, his sacking, the real reason for their house sale, everything. It felt to Libby as if she were talking about someone else, in places. A workaholic bloke who never discussed his problems, a stay-at-home wife who thought handbags were a good substitute for conversation with her neighbours. A couple she could barely recognise as the Libby and Jason who'd fallen in love in loud London bars while the rain poured down outside.

When she'd finished, there was a long pause at Erin's end, and Libby felt close to tears at the realisation of what had withered away, without her realising.

'So, there we are,' she finished lamely. 'I guess there's always the option of selling the hotel once it's finished, which means I could return your investment fairly quickly. Before Christmas maybe. But I need to get it finished, however I can.'

'Jeez, Libby.' Erin sounded shocked. 'Why didn't you tell me?'

'I didn't want people to know how badly we'd screwed up. It was just so . . . stupid. To have all that and throw it away.'

'But *you* didn't make that mistake! And it's not like you're boo-hooing in a corner; you've been working like a dog! Listen, for a start, forget worrying about the money. We'll lend you it. No, don't argue! I know Pete would say the same. I've got some savings – they're just sitting in some account earning zero interest; I'd rather they were helping you. Is that all you need? You sure you don't need more?'

Libby winced. Pete had a good job, but he was a designer, not a stockbroker. These were real savings, not Jason's windfall bonuses. 'Are you sure, Erin? Really? I don't have a track record as a hotelier.'

'Libby, it's *you* we're talking about.'

'But—'

'Do you remember the night Pete and I moved into our house?' Erin's voice softened. 'I was seven months pregnant, and the delivery men got lost, and Pete was jet-lagged and kept falling asleep. Then we locked ourselves out and I was hysterical?'

'You weren't hysterical. You were very pregnant.'

'I was hysterical, Libby. But you opened your door and took me in, and Jason phoned his brother to help Pete get into the house, and you lent us clothes and food and wouldn't let me lift a finger till the van arrived? You know, when my friends in Boston try to tell me Londoners are unfriendly, I tell *them* about that night.' She paused. 'You were so kind to us. I've been waiting for years to be able to return that favour, and now I can. I want to. I know you're going to make that hotel a success. Who wouldn't want to stay with you? You make complete strangers feel like friends.'

'Thank you.' Libby was so choked with gratitude she could barely get the words out. Coming straight after her days of blind panic, Erin's simple faith was making her feel almost light-headed. But why shouldn't she believe her? This is who I am, she told herself. Someone people trust. Someone *I* can trust.

'Hey, don't thank me,' said Erin. 'Just make sure that Pete and I are the first people booked in when you relaunch. I can't wait to see it.'

'The first ones,' said Libby. 'I have just the room for you. The bath is amazing.'

'Sold! And listen' – Erin's voice turned as stern as she could make it – 'don't you ever hide problems like that from me again. It *hurts* to think you don't consider me a good enough friend to tell. Promise me.'

'Promise,' said Libby. 'Now, tell me your news. Cheer me up.'

While Erin was talking, Libby heard her phone buzz with a text. She reached into her bag and grabbed it, hoping it would be Jason, and to her relief it was.

But when she read the message – **Coming back for some stuff tonight. Don't tell Mum. Don't want a scene. J** – her heart sank again.

'Darling, get down off the . . . Oh, Lib, you know what, I think we're out of toddler distraction time. I'm so sorry,' Erin apologised. 'Email me your bank details right now, OK? Do it! I'll phone you later!'

Libby said goodbye on autopilot, still staring at Jason's text. Margaret was out at her book group tonight, and Alice was spending the day with Gethin. They'd be alone to talk. Her mind stalled. What did she want to say to him? What did she want him to say to her?

She didn't know. Everything felt different. None of the old reference points seemed to fit. It wasn't just Jason she didn't know; Libby's own mind felt unfamiliar to her, with strengths and opinions and limits she hadn't realised she had until now.

She shivered. **Fine. I'll be in,** she texted back.

Alice texted to say that she'd be staying over at Gethin's – which Libby took as a good sign – and Margaret came in and went out again without speaking to her.

Jason arrived at eight, and from the second he walked into the kitchen, any hope Libby had had that he'd come to apologise evaporated.

His face, under three days' worth of stubble, was stony, and he barely said a word before going upstairs and returning almost immediately with his big wheelie case. The business-class flight tags from their last ski trip fluttered on the handle.

Libby stood at the sink, blank with panic. Too many things jostled to the front of her mind: all she could think was, Please don't go. Please let's start again, but a stubborn pride stopped anything coming out. Jason had got them into this situation; he could make the first move towards fixing it. He could start by apologising.

He didn't. He seemed to be struggling to say anything at all. Maybe he didn't know where to start either.

'Where are you staying?' Libby asked eventually.

'Steven's,' he said. 'For the time being.'

'Steven Taylor? In Clapham?' Steve was an old university friend, another stockbroker, with a huge house, no kids and three Porsches.

Jason nodded. 'Yup.'

Another agonising silence.

Libby's resistance cracked. 'And what are you doing? When are you coming back? Aren't you even going to ask how I am? Or what's been going on here?'

He couldn't look at her. Her heart tore inside as Jason gazed at the floor, the old wall clock, anywhere but at her face. 'You seem to be coping fine without me. I need some time to think.'

I don't have time to think, she wanted to roar. *I'm living in a building site. I'm dealing with your mother. I'm managing our business. I'm trying to cope while you just run away again.*

But it wouldn't come out. Libby's throat was choked with the only thing that mattered to her now: the man she loved was blocking her out. She still loved him, more than she'd ever done before, when everything was easy. He was walking away from every hope and memory and history they'd shared, every plan for the future, and Libby knew she should be strong and angry, but the thought of losing all that drained the energy from her. It was as much disappointment in herself, that she'd got it all so wrong.

Jason finally looked at her, and she didn't recognise the sullen, exhausted man wearing her husband's clothes. There was a glimmer of the old Jason, a ghost of an apology in his eyes, but when he saw her defiance, it faded away, replaced with a hardness she didn't like.

'I'll be in touch,' he replied, and walked out.

A voice in Libby's head, despite everything, said *Good*.

Chapter Twenty-Three

'We're going to be late,' said Alice, tapping her watch. 'Bob's audience don't want their patting time cut short by your inability to decide on the colour of *grout*, Libby.'

'But grout's important.' That was a sentence that Libby never thought she'd hear coming out of her mouth, but after several conversations with patient Lorcan, she found she did care. 'If we can't have the big things, then I want the little things to be exactly right. And you notice that kind of thing when you're relaxing in the bath. Isn't that right?'

Lorcan nudged the long-suffering apprentice, who was holding up ten sticks of coloured grout, waiting for Libby's decision. 'Hear that, Connor? *Someone*'s been listening to me.'

'That one,' Libby decided, pointing at the grey sample. 'It'll look cleanest for longest. And that'll save on Flash.'

The first en suites were being tiled today, and Libby couldn't wait to see them finished. She'd made herself address the budget in brutal detail, and had stayed up until the small hours, planning and replanning to make the most of what she had to restore the hotel to working order. Every pound she saved felt like a triumph. It also distracted the part of her brain that couldn't stop wondering what Jason was doing.

'At last!' said Alice. 'Now, come on. I don't want to be late for the consultant.' She paused, as Lorcan herded his apprentices back upstairs. 'Have you told Margaret we're going into town? Do you think she'd like to come?'

Libby sighed. 'Not if I'm driving. I actually think she's avoiding me now.' Since Margaret's bitter outburst about Jason, she and Libby had barely spoken. Libby had tried to build bridges by telling her about Gina's plans and how they would soon have things back to normal, but Margaret's expression had remained tight.

'I'm not sure what use my opinion would be to you,' was all she'd said, and the polite smile had vanished in a moment from her face to leave it cold and pinched.

It's almost as if she'd rather the Swan went under without Jason than have me sort it out, Libby thought. The irony was that now they were both left to cope without their husbands, something Libby thought might have given them a shared understanding, but no – Margaret clearly felt she'd now lost her husband, her hotel *and* her son, and two-thirds of that was Libby's fault. All the energy that had once gone into holding the family together was now flowing into Margaret's new role, of furious and disappointed matriarch.

Alice patted Libby's arm. 'She'll come round. She probably blames herself for putting you in this hole. And it must be a hard thing for her to see Jason screwing up.'

'She does *not* blame herself. And she definitely doesn't think Jason's screwed up. I suppose the one blessing is that her precious dog doesn't seem to be taking sides. He knows who's buying the biscuits round here. Bob? Bob! PAT time!' Libby went into the office and grabbed Bob's lead. He was supposed to be in his dog bed in there, but wasn't. She marched through the hotel, calling for him, until they eventually discovered him in the unused lounge, curled like a kidney bean on a velvet sofa from which he was specifically banned.

'Off!' snapped Libby, as he slunk down, leaving behind a white hair halo. She turned to Alice in despair. 'Look at that. I know Gina's adamant that dogs are the hotel's USP, but do we have to . . . ?'

Alice raised a soothing hand. 'Libby. Take a deep breath. You can't micromanage everything. Let Bob be the one thing that you let go, all right? People come to hotels to relax. And Bob is the king of relaxation.'

Libby inhaled and exhaled through her nose, the closest she came to yoga these days. Lorcan reckoned it'd take another five weeks, maybe four and they'd be ready to reopen. Things were moving. Slowly, but they were moving. Bob would be on their website: Gina had insisted. And Gina had been right about everything else.

'You're right,' she said, pulling her spine straight. 'Let's go and spread some basset hound love to Longhampton.'

Alice went off to her hypnotherapy appointment, and Libby and Bob strolled down the corridor to the old people's day room. Gina was already deep in conversation with Buzz when they arrived. Buzz wagged his tail when he saw them, and Libby felt touched that he'd recognised her.

Gina looked pleased to see them too. 'I know you're a way off decorating yet, but I've made a list of contacts you might find useful,' she said, reaching into her leather messenger bag. 'Start with Michelle in Home Sweet Home on the High Street. It's a really fantastic interiors shop – people come from all over the county. She'll do you a deal on curtains if you tell her I sent you.'

'Thanks!' said Libby, and her brain started ticking over for ways she could return the favour on her limited budget. 'I was thinking about themed breaks again – maybe I could have a page about shopping in Longhampton? Are there enough independent shops to make that work?' She realised, to her shame, that she hadn't spent any time in the town since they'd arrived; Gina had told her about an amazing bookshop, a couple of great pubs and now this interiors shop – she had no idea where they were.

Gina seemed surprised. 'There are loads of new independent shops . . . You haven't been down the High Street lately? You don't know about the new cake shop? How long have you *been* here?'

'I've been so busy.'

'Too busy for cake? Who in their right mind is too busy for cake?'

Libby shrugged. 'I know. I need to make time for cake.'

'Well, why don't we meet up for a coffee one morning and have a wander round together?' Gina suggested. 'I'll introduce you to some people. It's a small town; you soon get to know who's who. Local businesses like to support each other – offer to have the Longhampton Traders' Association Christmas do at the hotel and you'll have friends for life. Especially if you discount rooms for them to sleep it off.'

Moments like this made Libby feel the tide was finally lifting her off the sandbanks, flowing underneath her and helping her along; Gina could introduce her to some Longhamptoners, who wouldn't just know her as 'Margaret's daughter-in-law'. People she should have met ages ago, if she hadn't been so worried about what everyone would be thinking about her and Jason taking over Donald's hotel.

'Don't be so hard on yourself.' Gina spotted Libby's

self-administered kick. 'You can only deal with so much at once. It's one of life's cruel tricks that the time you need to go out and meet complete strangers is always when you feel most like hiding under the duvet.' She touched her arm. 'Anyway, I'm keeping you back. Doris was telling me she's got something to show you . . .'

Doris was in her usual armchair by the window and seemed delighted to see Lord Bob. She even managed a smile for Libby.

'Hello, young man,' she said, reaching for his velvety ears. Bob lifted his head in expectation of adoration, and/or a biscuit. 'I've got a treat for you. Better distract your owner with this first, though.' She passed Libby a leather-bound book that had been sitting on the side table. 'Here, I looked this out for you. Thought you might be interested.'

'Ooh, is this your photo album?' Libby perched on the chair opposite and opened the old-fashioned album, carefully turning the tissue-paper leaf. Inside, the pages were thick black card, with black-and-white photographs held in by white paper corners. The first one featured a rather familiar staircase. 'Oh!' she exclaimed, delighted. 'Is this the Swan? When you worked there?'

Doris slipped Bob a custard cream. 'It is. Bit different now, I'll bet?'

'A bit. When were these taken?' Libby spotted a young Doris – same squirrelly face, but jet-black hair combed into a beehive – standing with a collection of other women in minidresses, lined up against the reception desk. The decor looked new: the wooden counter gleamed, and the walls were papered in a patterned print, decorated with horse brasses and a spiky sunburst clock. A Christmas tree stood in the corner, and fat

Chinese lanterns hung from the ceiling. All the ladies were holding Babycham glasses self-consciously and pointing their left feet forward in crippling stilettos.

Doris wore flats, and looked cross about it.

'That'd be 1960, so I'd be thirty— I'd be twenty-one again.' Her eyes creased.

'And this was when the Hannifords were running it?' There was another photograph of Doris posing by the frosted lounge doors; Libby had always hated their 1960s tackiness in what she thought should be a smart Georgian entrance hall, but actually, seeing them when they were brand new, they looked all right. They even looked modern, in a space-age, mid-century way. A large bas-relief carving of a swan dominated the wall, and some striking globe lampshades hung in the hall. It was like seeing a younger version of the hotel, as well as a younger version of Doris. Libby warmed to it, and the cheerful bell-bottomed guests marching through in the background.

'It'd be just after they did it up. Hence the photographs. Mr and Mrs Hanniford were very proud of it, you see.' Doris pursed her lips. 'You'll have got it all minimalist now, have you? Still ripping everything out?'

'No,' said Libby. 'Change of plan. I'm not sure minimalism's really going to work.'

Though the photo album was of Doris's family, the hotel appeared again and again, in between the holiday snaps and school uniforms. The lounge for a twenty-first birthday party. The reception area for a baby-faced bride and groom. A cosy back room that must have been the bar, packed with happy faces double-chinned over turtle necks, raising port and lemons while small dogs peeked out from under the chairs. So dogs had been welcome even then, thought Libby.

The black-and-white turned to startling colour as the 1970s rolled in, bringing the tangerine prints of the reception wall-paper to eye-watering life, but the solid wood and friendly atmosphere remained.

'It looks like a popular place,' she observed.

'Oh, it was. It was where everyone went for special occasions in those days,' said Doris, slipping Bob another custard cream. 'That back room of Gerald Hanniford's was famous. Before the breathalyser, of course.'

Ideas were uncurling in Libby's mind. Maybe *this* was the feel she should be aiming for? A sort of comfortable 1960s hospitality – with gentler modern colours behind the old-fash-ioned desk and Margaret's mad tartan carpet, it would look stylish, not dated. That sunburst clock was in the office, wasn't it? In one of the bedrooms, against a plain wall, it'd be a statement piece of art. And was that carved swan the thing under the blankets in the cellar that she hadn't dared look at too closely?

'See, there's Margaret before she got the rod up her— Before she turned into Lady Bountiful,' said Doris, as Libby turned another page.

'Oh!' Libby's decor plans were stopped in their tracks by the startling sight of Margaret in shoulder pads and a curly perm that spilled over her shoulders like a Jacobean wig. She hadn't seen many old family photos of the Corcorans; Margaret was a notorious vetter of pictures of herself, and kept only the framed photograph of her and Donald in full civic-hall eveningwear, celebrating their silver wedding at Ferrari's, alongside her and Jason's wedding group on the sitting-room mantelpiece.

This was a Margaret she definitely hadn't seen before: a

nervous, tired, young Margaret. She had two small boys with her, one hanging on to her skirt, the other standing apart, scowling tearfully at the camera. Jason and Luke, both in red shorts and white T-shirts, Jason chunky and blond like his dad, Luke skinny and dark like his mum. Donald stood next to her, next to Luke, smiling into the lens, looking more like an affable family doctor than an hotelier.

'That'd be right before they started *their* big overhaul job,' said Doris. 'Very stressful it was at the time, I can tell you. Redecorating all through, no expense spared. Madam wanted to set her stamp on things, and Mr C would do anything she asked. He was a lovely man. Put up with a lot, if you ask me.'

Libby knew she should be listening, but something about Margaret's weary yet defiant gaze grabbed her. Margaret must be about the same age there as I am now, she thought. She *knows* what I'm going through. Has she forgotten how stressful it all is? And why does she look so defensive?

Maybe it had something to do with poor string-bean Luke, with his grazed knees, keeping out of arm's reach, hooded eyes slid sideways towards his mum as if he'd just been told off. Maybe it was to do with Doris behind the camera, catching Margaret at a moment when she didn't have everything under control. Maybe it was clingy Jason. Only Donald looked unconditionally pleased with life.

I wish Donald were still alive to talk to, thought Libby. I've been a part of this family for nine years and I still don't understand any of them. So much silence and sulking.

But now she saw the hotel as part of it, looming in the background like a fifth family member – the rackety maiden aunt who'd once been great fun but was now a liability. And Jason had grown up in that atmosphere of stress and silence. Maybe this building project was stirring up different family memories for Jason, she realised. Perhaps not entirely happy ones, going by Margaret's body language.

But she'd thought they could get through this kind of challenge, that there was a friendship at the heart of their love. A respect for each other that would make them try to talk through their problems, even if those conversations were hard. Had she been wrong, all this time, about that?

'Was that of interest?' Doris enquired, as she looked up.

'Yes,' said Libby. 'That was very useful indeed.'

Alice met Libby in the hospital car park, where she was loading Lord Bob into the back of the car and chatting to Gina about where she could get hold of original flying ducks for the bedrooms.

Once Gina had waved goodbye, Alice listened politely as Libby explained her brainwave about the hotel decor, referencing the 1960s heyday – although she did wonder what Margaret would think about Libby reinstalling everything she'd got rid of – and they were halfway back to the hotel by the time Libby ran out of steam and noticed she'd barely said a word.

'Are you all right, Alice?' She glanced over. 'Sorry, I didn't even ask how your hypnotherapy went. Did you remember anything new?'

Alice shook her head. 'Nope, everything still stops about a year ago. We tried to get nearer me and Gethin meeting, but it's still . . . nothing. I told her about finding the dog lead and toys, so we worked on some details about Fido, and Barley, but to be honest, that just made me feel worse. Thinking about my dad, and my mum . . .'

Gethin had found some photos of them walking Fido and

she'd cried on the sofa with him. When she'd talked about getting another dog, though, Gethin had seemed unwilling.

'I know it sounds silly,' he'd said, 'but can I have you to myself for a bit? Before we get wrapped up in another dog?'

It *had* sounded silly to Alice, but he'd seemed serious, so she hadn't pushed it. But the more she thought about it, the less she could make it tally with all the nice things Gethin had said about Fido being part of their little family. He almost sounded jealous of her.

They'd stopped at traffic lights and Libby gave her a closer look. 'What's up? I know it's very sad about poor Fido, but . . . was there something else too? You look awful.'

And then there was the other thing.

Alice bit her lip. Telling Libby things always made them seem more real; she had such a practical way of dealing with problems. Once this was out . . .

'Go on,' Libby prompted her. 'It can stay in this car, whatever it is.'

Alice stared at the traffic ahead. The road to the hospital – the line of trees, the row of villas painted in Neapolitan ice-cream colours, the Esso garage – was calming in its familiarity. A month ago, she'd never seen it.

A month ago.

'I haven't had a period since the accident,' she said, slowly. 'I asked the therapist today if the accident might have any effect on them and she said shock did sometimes disrupt your cycle, but she wasn't an expert.' Alice looked at her hand; she was wearing the ring Gethin had given her, but on her right hand. 'She offered to get a nurse to do a test, but I said no.'

'OK.' Libby looked surprised. 'Why did you say no?'

Alice shrugged. 'She made it feel . . . very medical. Just

another test. I guess I didn't want to find out something like that on my own.'

The lights turned to green and Libby set off. 'Wow. Do you think you might be pregnant?'

Typically, Libby had articulated exactly what was torment-ing Alice. How could you not know something as fundamental as that about your own self? How could another human being be growing inside you and you have no knowledge of how it got there? But then there was so much about herself that she didn't know. Her memory had its own secrets, and now her body had too. It made her feel as if there was nothing at all she could be sure of anymore about herself.

'I don't know what it feels like.'

'Neither do I, to be honest,' said Libby. 'Have you felt sick? Sore breasts? Urge to eat coal?'

'I've felt quite achy, I guess, but I assumed it was just from working. And my ribs healing.'

'I suppose the bigger question is, do you want to be pregnant?'

That was a much harder question to answer. Gethin would be so excited. Alice could see his face now: thrilled, protective, ready to make a playlist to play to the baby. But as she thought of his enthusiasm, Alice felt herself pull back. Even after all his date-night efforts, she still only felt as if she'd known Gethin for a fortnight – and he seemed to know a different woman to the person she felt she was. He knew an Alice who'd lost her dog and behaved strangely and liked cider and didn't have a Facebook account because she didn't trust online security.

It was the ultimate confirmation that she and he were in a happy relationship, and yet . . .

Alice stared out of the window. Who am I? she thought, in

despair. Every time she felt she was starting to work it out, it turned out she was wrong. And if she and Gethin were having a baby, that was a whole other person she'd be. Forever.

And Luke?

Alice felt the funny hum of yearning, the same colour somehow as the yearning she felt for her mum and dad. Not as intense, but similar. *Stop it*, she told herself.

Libby took her silence as an answer. 'Well, there's a simple way to put your mind at rest,' she said, indicating to turn back the way they'd come. 'Let's go and get a test. It'll have to be the Tesco and not the chemist because the last thing I need is Margaret finding out from one of the inner circle that she needs to start knitting.'

Alice recapped the test robotically, flushed the loo and went back into room eight, where Libby was waiting with two cups of coffee. It was surreal, that something so huge could be decided by a piece of plastic.

She put it on the windowsill, result side down. 'You have to wait two minutes,' she explained, and fought the temptation to turn it back over.

'So in two minutes you can stop worrying and get on with your life.' Libby handed her the cup; Alice was pleased to have something to do with her hands. 'I mean, I'm sure I missed a period when Jason got sacked. Stress does that. It's your body's way of saying, "Whoa, now would be a really bad time to have a baby, *schtoopid*!" Now . . . while we're waiting, shall I tell you my exciting yet budget-friendly plans for this room?'

Alice knew Libby was going to talk, non-stop, for two minutes exactly so she wouldn't think about the test, and she was so relieved that she'd waited to find out here, and not in the impersonal surroundings of a hospital cubicle, that she blinked back sudden tears.

'Oh God, they're not *that* exciting,' said Libby. 'I was only thinking lavender walls and maybe a mural.'

Alice managed to smile. 'I'm just . . . It's like it's happening to someone else. Well, it is, in a way.'

'I can't imagine how weird this must be for you,' said Libby. '*Again*. But you know we'll help out, however you want?'

She nodded. 'Thank you. Um, will all the rooms have flying ducks?'

'No! But we could put an old-style radio in every room . . .' Libby rattled through her colour-scheme ideas (all the curtains the same cheap neutral shades, each room a different heathery colour) until she broke off, mid-description. 'Right, that has to be two minutes. Go for it. Unless you want me to look?'

Alice took a deep breath. 'No,' she said. 'I will.'

She made herself pick up the test and turn it over.

The answer was right there, as she knew now she'd known it would be: two blue lines. The blood banged in her eardrums.

I'm pregnant. I'm pregnant and I don't remember. How is that even possible?

When she didn't speak, Libby came across and looked over her shoulder. 'Oh wow. OK. Right.'

Alice had the weird floaty sensation again. She tried to pin down what she was feeling: she'd always imagined this moment would be different. Exciting, expected, anticipated, shared with the delighted father. Not like it was happening to someone else.

She tried to imagine the moment of conception – had it been a romantic night at home, Gethin's strong arms holding

338

her, his compact body locked round hers, his soft voice urgent in her ear, her body responding to his . . . ?

Alice frowned. That sounded more like something she'd read in a book. There was no answering echo in her body. But why was she worrying about that, when the evidence was right here?

Libby looked worried. 'Alice, are you sure you don't want to sit down? Your face . . .'

'Sorry. It's too much to take in.' She forced her attention back to the moment. *Now*. 'So what happens? I'll have to tell Gethin. He'll want me to move back in with him. He won't want me to carry on working here – he doesn't really like me being here anyway . . .'

Move back. Move out of this place, away from everything familiar, her job, her routine. Alice knew what she *should* be thinking, but it wasn't what every instinct was shrilling at her.

Libby was looking at her strangely. 'What do you mean, he doesn't like you being here?'

Alice realised what she'd said and blushed. 'Oh, nothing. He's got the wrong end of the stick. He just wants me to move back. He misses me. Wants everything to return to normal. I can't blame him, really . . .' She paused. 'I just don't know what normal *is*.'

Libby took Alice by the upper arms so she had to look her in the eye. 'You don't have to tell Gethin *anything*, not until you've decided what *you* want. You've got to put yourself first. It must be very early days still – surely it'd have shown up on the blood tests they did while you were in hospital?'

'I suppose so.' That would put it just before the accident. Before that mysterious row. How could you sleep with someone then refuse to go on holiday with them? Had it had something to do with that? Alice's stomach churned.

She realised Libby was looking uncomfortable. 'Don't take this the wrong way, Alice,' she said, 'but when I said, before, about your body knowing whether it's a good time to have a child . . . it was a silly thing to say. I don't know what your beliefs are, but no one would blame you for wanting to be sure you were absolutely recovered before . . .' Her eyes clouded. 'Well, it doesn't mean you *have* to do anything.'

Alice knew what Libby was trying to say. She touched her arm in silent acknowledgement, then picked up the plastic stick, half hoping the two lines might have faded. But they were still there. Darker, like an equals sign. A result. Gethin plus Alice equals . . . this. It was a fact, and Alice had very few of those to go on.

'Ah! You're in there! Can I . . . ?'

They spun round.

Luke was striding into the room, his trainers making no sound on the floorboards, but suddenly he stopped. Alice could see quite clearly from the way he froze, halfway across the room, that he'd taken in the whole scene: her shock, Libby's concern and the white plastic test she was holding in her hand.

Her chest tightened, then expanded, as if a big orange chrysanthemum had bloomed inside her.

Their eyes met and for once his guarded face was as easy to read as Libby's.

Luke looked horrified, and that suddenly made it all real. Alice knew she should say something, but her mind had gone blank, and before she or Libby could speak, he abruptly turned and left the room.

Chapter Twenty-Four

Libby couldn't sleep for worrying about Alice, and when she got up, an hour before her alarm, she found Alice already in the kitchen, staring into a cup of coffee as if it might hold the answer to everything. She jumped, as if she'd been expecting someone else.

'Morning,' said Libby. 'How are you feeling?'

'Not great.' Alice pulled a face. 'Couldn't sleep. I thought I'd take Bob out for an early walk and get some fresh air. Do you need anything?'

Libby didn't, but she could see Alice needed to get out, and walk and think. 'Why don't you plot a dog walk around the town for the website?' she suggested. Seeing the little dogs under the snug tables in Doris's album – and listening to Gina's persuasive arguments about USPs and the price of kennelling dogs while you went on holiday – had finally convinced her that dog-friendliness might be their secret weapon. Just as creating her new budget vintage rooms had made her realise that her glossy boutique dream was never going to work in Longhampton. It would have looked ridiculous – the locals would have been suspicious of the fancy details, and they'd have dated too quickly to be properly fashionable for more than about six months. This had already been in and out of fashion; all she had to do was keep everything spotlessly clean and un-doggy.

Libby grabbed her camera off the kitchen table. 'Take some photos if you can, and see which shops you can take Bob into. I thought we could do a whole page – just like you suggested.

'And don't rush back,' she added. 'There's not much we can do today. Lorcan says it's best not to distract the lads when they're counting tiles.'

Alice smiled wanly. 'Thank you,' she said, and Libby wished she could tell her that everything would be fine. They both knew, though, that it wasn't that easy.

No sooner had Alice and Lord Bob left than Lorcan arrived with three trainees and more grout. Libby had briefed them on the next en suite and returned to the kitchen for her own breakfast when Margaret appeared at the door, dressed in a droopy blouse and skirt, apparently selected to match her mood and face.

'Good morning,' said Libby, determined to be pleasant. How could she ever recreate the friendly hotel atmosphere if there was a permanent frost between the owners? 'Would you like a cup of tea? The kettle's just boiled.'

'Elizabeth, I think it's time you told me what's going on.' Margaret's expression wasn't cold, but it was closed – like Luke's, Libby thought. She tried to see beyond the lines carved by disapproval to the pretty, weary young mum in Doris's photo album, but it was a struggle. That Margaret seemed to have been thoroughly restyled into Margaret Corcoran, Community Pillar, Braced for Disappointment.

'With the hotel? I've told you exactly what's going on,' she said, making a fresh pot of tea. 'Lorcan's going ahead with the revised plans, I've raised some short-term investment, and we're aiming to reopen properly by the beginning of July, which leaves plenty of time to get things perfect for that journalist visit in early September. In fact,' she went on, forcing herself to be inclusive, as Alice had gently suggested on their way home from the hospital, 'I was talking to Doris yesterday about how the hotel looked in the past and I was thinking you and I could—'

'Doris? I'm not sure I'd listen to her gossip, if I were you,' Margaret retorted. 'What's she been saying?'

That you liked getting your own way? That you made life hard for poor Donald? That you, too, did a massive revamp not unlike the one you're rolling your eyes at now?

Libby squashed her thoughts down and said, 'She was telling me that the hotel was *the* place for parties and that there was a little bar at one time. I thought maybe we should look into getting a licence again. We could offer champagne teas, to start with, and maybe christening parties, since we're near St Ethelred's . . .' She paused. 'Margaret, I really want this hotel to work. Not just for me, but for all of us. For the town, even.'

Margaret sighed. 'It all sounds so much *effort*, Elizabeth. I don't know if I've got the energy. The more I think about it, the more I think maybe it would be better to finish this work and just sell.'

'*What?* No!' Libby was surprised by her own reaction. 'Don't you think it'd be a pity to do all this work and let someone else reap the rewards? Anyway, we can't make any decisions like that without Jason here – he's a partner in the business too.'

At the mention of his name, Margaret's expression turned pained. 'That's what I meant when I said I needed to know what's going on. I'm extremely worried about Jason. Where is he? When's he coming home?'

343

Libby stirred the teabags to make them brew faster. At least Margaret seemed to have dropped the combative attitude. That was something. 'He's in Clapham, staying with a friend. He told me he needed some time to think, and that's all I know.'

'I can't believe he hasn't phoned me. His mother.' She looked peevish.

'Well, he hasn't exactly been burning up the phone to me, either. As soon as I' – *his wife*, Libby added silently – 'hear anything I'll let you know. I'm not impressed that he's just walked out on us while we're in the middle of the worst bit. Unlike Luke,' she added. Margaret had barely acknowledged Luke's presence. 'He's dropped some work to come up here and help out.'

Margaret graciously accepted Libby's offer of a cup of tea, but in a way that made it look as if she were doing her a favour. 'Yes, I heard him last night, coming in very late from the pub, I assume. Has he said that's why he's back?'

Luke had gone out shortly after walking in on Libby and Alice – where, Libby didn't know. She hadn't liked to ask. The more she saw Alice and Luke together, the less certain she was about that whole situation.

'Luke's volunteered to sort out the electrics for nothing. He's saving us thousands of pounds.'

'Well, that's a charitable explanation, but I'm not sure I believe it.' Margaret sipped her tea. 'He never lifted a finger before, not when his father and I needed him. No, if you ask me, there's another reason.'

'Really?'

'Yes. I worry about Alice.' Margaret dropped her voice. 'That poor girl is extremely vulnerable, and Luke knows it. I've seen the way he looks at her, and I wouldn't be surprised if he'd been up to something while he was staying at that pub. At least Jason could have had a word if he was here. I think it's high time we encouraged her to move back in with her boyfriend. Gethin seems a lovely boy, and that *is* her home . . .'

Libby widened her eyes. How could you think that about your own son? 'No, Margaret, I think we ought to encourage Alice to take that relationship at her own pace. She needs space to get herself together.'

Margaret stared at her, as if Libby were holding something back. Then she raised her chin. 'Well, there are plenty of mothers in this town who'd agree with me. But since there's nothing useful I can do, perhaps Bob would enjoy a walk. Have you seen him?'

'Alice has just taken him out, actually.'

Her mouth quivered. 'I really am quite a spare part here, these days,' she said in a high voice. 'Not even needed to walk my own dog.'

'Alice needed some thinking time – it's nothing personal,' said Libby. 'I'm sure he'd love another walk later.'

'Maybe you could put me on the waiting list,' she snapped, and before Libby could say something more tactful, she stomped out, nearly bumping into Luke, who was coming in. Margaret gave him a glare as she passed and he recoiled.

'Something I said?' he asked, when his mother had retreated down the corridor.

'No, something I said.' Libby rubbed her eyes. She was beginning to realise how much of a buffer Jason had been with Margaret. 'I didn't want her to feel pressured to help. Now she's acting like I'm leaving her out. I can't win.'

'You get used to it.' Luke pushed his dark hair off his face with a wry smile. 'After about twenty years or so.' He was dressed to start work on the rewiring – battered combats with various screwdrivers and pliers and drill bits in the pockets, and a tight grey T-shirt that revealed his tanned biceps. Libby had only seen him in his off-duty clothes, but in his work gear, he looked extremely competent, in a more interesting way than someone who was just fitting radiators. She could imagine Luke coolly deactivating bombs – or casually scoring tries straight from the clubhouse bar.

Her mind spiralled off momentarily. If he'd been dressed like that to hang around Alice's pub, Libby thought, then she was surprised Alice had managed to fight her way through the locals to get a word in edgeways.

'So, have you made me a list?' said Luke. 'Of what needs finishing?'

Libby shook herself. 'Towel rails. And some extra lights. And can you teach me how to wire plugs, so I can sort out some lamps?'

'What? You don't know how to wire plugs?' He pretended to look aghast. 'No, that's no problem. Have you got the towel rails, or do you want me to get them? I can probably get a discount.'

'That would be so helpful!' said Libby. 'I took a photo of some I saw in . . . Oh. They're on my camera.'

'And?'

'Alice has got it. She's gone out with Bob – I asked her to make up a walk for the website.' Libby saw something cross Luke's eyes and she remembered how quickly he'd turned and left when he'd interrupted them upstairs yesterday. What had he seen? What had he assumed, more to the point?

He hesitated, then asked anyway. 'Is she . . . ? Is Alice all right?'

For a second, Libby wavered over pretending nothing was wrong, but Luke seemed genuinely worried. And he'd been nothing but considerate to her. She couldn't share Margaret's suspicions about him preying on Alice like some kind of dodgy bar hawk.

'She's got a lot to think about,' she said. It was vague enough. 'She's gone for a walk. On her own.'

He didn't reply. Questions swirled round Libby's head, most too awkward to ask. But Luke knew Alice better than any of them, and if she was going to help her . . .

'Alice and Gethin,' she started uncertainly. 'They were all right, weren't they? I mean, I suppose they must have been, if . . . well, if Alice is . . .' She frowned at herself. What was it she was trying to say?

There was a pause; then Luke said, 'She didn't tell me much about him. Just that he was a sensitive soul, and he'd had a tough time. I got the feeling she was quite protective.'

'She's a loyal person,' Libby agreed.

'Very loyal.' Luke fidgeted with a screwdriver in his pocket. 'Listen, I heard some of what Mum said. About me "taking advantage" of Alice.' He raised a hand as Libby started to demur. 'No, I have to say this . . . It wasn't like that. OK?'

His strong cheekbones had flushed pink, and he looked offended.

'So what was it like?'

He frowned at the floor, thinking. This was the most personal conversation Libby had ever had with Luke, and she was transfixed by his energy. He was sharper round every edge than Jason, less predictable, fiercer. For better or worse, he had a determination about him Jason didn't have.

Luke's spent his whole life trying to prove he's not what

people think he is, she thought. Jason's had the luxury of everyone assuming he's a good boy straight off. So much easier. Or so much harder to live up to?

'Talking to Alice was like talking to someone I've known all my life,' he said, then stopped himself. 'You think things are working out, then? With her and Gethin.'

Libby didn't know how to reply; his intense gaze was saying something more than his words. She didn't want to share Alice's secret, but it could give his question a very clear answer.

'I don't know,' she said. 'I guess so. She's stayed over a few nights now . . .'

They stared at each other, the moment lengthening between them as Libby struggled inside. He knew an Alice she didn't.

'Good,' said Luke. He pressed his lips together. 'Good. I'll, er, have a chat with Lorcan about the towel rails.'

'Would you? Thanks,' she said, and as he turned to go, she wondered if she'd actually heard the question he was asking, let alone answered it.

Alice had strolled down the hill, round the edge of town – having taken a nice panorama of the hill, and one of the town, spread out like a child's drawing of steeples and roofs – and was almost into the park when she heard someone calling her name.

She turned and her heart lifted. Luke was jogging towards her. He waved, and she stopped walking to let him catch her up. Bob was oblivious, his head down to the ground, snuffling up a scent, letting the chemicals dance and explode in his huge nose. Something similar happened inside her when she saw Luke jogging nearer, in his work gear.

'Hello!' He wasn't even out of breath. 'I understand you've got Libby's camera?'

Oh. He only wanted the camera. 'I have. Do you need it?'

'Yes, it's got photos of towel rails on it. Very specific towel rails that she saw in some shop. I'm going to see if I can track them down.'

Alice reached into her bag and passed him the camera without saying anything. He turned it over in his hands, then looked up, his eyes cautious. 'Actually, that's only partly the reason I came to find you. I was hoping to catch you on your own.'

'Oh?' Her pulse sped up treacherously and she fought against it. Stop reacting to him, she told herself. Be normal.

'Yes, I wanted to apologise. For bursting in on you and Libby yesterday.' Luke picked his words with care; he seemed determined to say something but in the right way. 'I'm sorry if I interrupted.'

Alice turned back to the path and started walking again. She felt more comfortable when she was moving. One foot in front of the other. Going somewhere. Not having to look Luke in the eye, and risk letting him see all the confusion churning around. There shouldn't *be* confusion. It was so simple, really.

'And you're assuming that was my private moment and not Libby's?' she said.

'Your expression . . . kind of gave it away, to be honest.'

My face, thought Alice. It tells everyone something about me. Doesn't tell me anything.

She stared down the path, where Bob was following the scent in a businesslike fashion, his long ears swinging side to side, in time with his round bottom.

'You didn't interrupt,' she said. 'But . . . don't mention it to anyone, please? I need some time to think about it.'

'Sure.' Luke fell into step, half on, half off the path. His hand swung a few centimetres from hers; he made no attempt to touch it, but Alice was conscious of its nearness. She had to tell herself not to grab it; instinctively she knew his fingers would feel comforting around hers, and that he wouldn't mind, but then what? Almost as if he could sense her unease, Luke stuffed both his hands into his jacket pockets. Silence covered them both like a shared umbrella.

'You don't mind if I walk down into town with you?' he added, almost as an afterthought.

'No, not at all.' Alice made her tone light. 'You think you can find Libby's towel rails in town?'

'I'm pretty sure I know where to look. Wondered if you fancied a coffee? I can bring Bob back, if you'd rather be on your own?'

'No, no, it's fine.' She smiled. 'Quite enjoy his company, actually. Makes me feel athletic.'

Conversation faded away as they walked, but the silence was relaxed. Alice felt suspended in the balance again, somewhere between the person she felt she was and the person she'd been before, the one she couldn't remember. And this new person in the future. Yet somehow Luke's presence steadied things. Quietly, undramatically, he knew exactly who she was.

'How's Gethin?' he asked.

'Fine. He sent me some emails this morning. From when we first met.' He hadn't been pleased about her going to the hotel; Alice had had to make up an excuse about Libby being ill.

'You've got email?' said Luke. 'Why haven't you been checking it?'

'I don't.' Had Luke emailed her? Had she not replied? 'Well, I do, but I can't remember what my email passwords are, and my laptop's password locked.' She glanced over at him. 'So much for modern technology, eh? No, Gethin printed some out and posted them to me the old-fashioned way.'

'Oh. Right. Did they bring anything back?'

Alice shook her head. She hadn't even recognised Gethin's small, neat writing on the envelope when she'd seen it lying on the mat with the hotel post, first thing. Inside, clipped together in chunks, were rambling conversations between them after their Italian retreat: they were her words, and her stories – her parents dying, her loneliness, anecdotes about work, and Fido – but Alice had the curious sensation of reading someone else's mail. They were romantic, hopeful emails, intoxicated with the first thrill of soul-baring, but her eye snagged on details she wished she'd kept to herself. The married boyfriend. Her hangovers. She didn't really like the version of herself she'd confessed to.

But it had proved one thing: she and Gethin *had* had a very emotional, meeting-of-minds connection. They'd fallen in love under an Italian full moon. He sent her poetry. She sent him songs to listen to. She had that ring, his slideshow of holiday snaps, physical proof of the woman he adored when he looked at her.

'They didn't jog my memory,' she said slowly. 'But they're facts. I don't have a lot of them to go on.'

Well, apart from the *huge* fact staring her in the face.

'Did Gethin hack into your email to get them?' asked Luke.

'No, he printed off his replies.' Alice wasn't sure what Luke was getting at. 'Why?'

'Just wondered.'

Alice swung her arms. Gethin's emails were one kind of evidence, but everything her body did when she was with Luke felt like another kind: the relaxation she felt, the ease of their chats, the unconscious way they fell into step as they walked. It was as if her body were trying to present her with a different version of events – but they were only feelings. And what if something had happened between them? Did she want to be a woman who cheated? Had the accident happened just in the nick of time?

'He must be very excited, about the baby,' said Luke. He was looking straight ahead, his hands still in his pockets.

Alice's head swung round. Hearing it from his mouth, so calmly, was a shock, but he carried on staring straight ahead.

She stared ahead now too. 'I haven't told him yet.'

'No?'

'No. I want a day or two to . . . think. I know he's desperate for me to move back. Soon as I tell him, he'll be planning. I—'

Lord Bob interrupted her with an imperious bark that made them both jump. Alice looked over to see what had caught his eye and spotted one of the dog walkers with the multiple leads – one of the same ones whose charges had wound Bob up before. She had six dogs this time, and one of the small white ones was already bouncing up and down, straining to get to Bob for a good yell.

'Oh, not again.' Her head ached. 'I don't have the energy for this today.'

'We'll go this way,' said Luke calmly, diverting Bob up a different path. 'You'll have to tell Gethin soon, though, won't you? Won't he notice?'

It hit Alice: the days were ticking by, whether she willed them to slow or not. Luke would finish the electrics and then he'd leave, and then she'd have to tell Gethin about the baby and that would be it: she'd move back, no more hotel, no more Luke, just her and Gethin. Two strangers and their baby.

'Luke,' she said suddenly, desperate to say something she

couldn't quite express properly, 'you'd tell me, wouldn't you, if . . . if there's anything I should know?'

He stopped walking and looked at her. 'About what?'

Alice's chest felt as if it were being compressed: adrenalin and fear and hope pumping through it at once. *Say it. Jump.* 'About us.'

Luke didn't reply. He just looked at her, and she felt as if she could see right inside his head. His expression was so confused and sad that Alice felt an answering wash of sadness in herself: Oh God, yes, there *had* been something. There *had*.

'Alice, I'm not—' he started, but then Lord Bob lunged forward, all five stone of him nearly pulling her off her feet, yanking her arm painfully in its socket.

She stumbled, Luke caught her, and she barely had time to register the shower of sparks that shot through her whole body as his hands held her before she saw a white blur coming towards them across the grass that you weren't supposed to walk on at this time of year.

Lord Bob was straining on his lead and Luke took it from her.

'This happened the other day.' Alice's voice didn't sound like her own. 'Libby says they're dogs from the rescue over the hill.'

It was a white dog, covering the ground between them like a rocket. None of the other dogs were following it, and Alice could see the walker running after it, shouting apologies while still holding on to the leads of the others. Some of them didn't look that pleased with the enforced trot.

Alice's heart twisted. 'That dog looks exactly like Fido, my old dog,' she said.

'You sure it's not? It looks like it knows you.'

'No, Fido was run over,' she said automatically, but the dog didn't seem to be heading for Bob, as she'd assumed. It was running straight towards her, with a very familiar stiff-legged gait, one dark patch over the eye and a small-dog determination. A dog who'd seen someone it feared had been lost forever.

A dog she'd promised she would never, ever leave. A dog who hadn't forgotten that promise, who'd been hoping, and looking, and longing, and whose strong terrier heart was daring now to burst with joy.

Alice put her hand up to her mouth, too shocked to speak.

It *was* Fido.

The dog was barking now, yapping in uncontrollable delight, and when she was within about three feet of them, she launched herself straight at Alice, bouncing up into her arms, which Alice realised she'd stretched out without thinking.

The terrier was licking her face, barking, then licking, then squealing with happiness, her tail wagging so hard her whole body was almost propelled out of Alice's grasp with each wag, and Alice realised she was crying and laughing too.

'Fido!' she kept saying, over and over, nuzzling her nose into the little dog's warm body. 'Fido!'

Of all the weird and unsettling things that had happened to Alice in the last few weeks, this was the only one that made her heart explode with bright white happiness.

Chapter Twenty-Five

'I am *so* sorry!' The dog walker – a tall, dark-haired woman in a gilet – caught up with them just as Fido had completely covered Alice's face in licks. 'I can't apologise enough. That has literally never happened to me before. Are you all right? She slipped out – look!' She held up an empty collar. 'She must have been really keen to see you.'

'Don't worry.' Fido was nestling into Alice's neck, rubbing her head in delight against her face. 'She's fine.'

'Fido, you are very naughty.' The woman did seem mortified. 'Although I have to say it's nice to see her so excited. Poor little mite's been moping away in the corner of her kennel since she came into us.'

'Fido! How do you know she's called Fido?'

'It was on her chip.' The woman regarded her curiously. 'How do *you* know she's called Fido?'

'Because I think she's my dog.'

'What? You're Alice Robinson? Of King's Avenue?'

'Yes! How did you know?'

She rolled her eyes impatiently. 'Because you went to the bother of chipping your dog, but you didn't update the details when you moved, did you? The vet nurses have been trying to get in touch to let you know she was handed in, but no one had heard of you *or* Fido.'

Alice struggled to process it all. 'The vet's? She's been at the vet's? Aren't you from the rescue?'

The dog walker transferred the leads from one hand to the other and offered her free hand to Alice. 'I'm Rachel Fenwick, and yes, I run the dog rescue at the top of the hill. My husband, George, is the vet. Fido was hit by a car, we think – one of our farmer clients found her unconscious in a hedge and brought her straight to the surgery. Just bruising, as it turned out, but she'd had a shock and was badly dehydrated. If we'd been able to get hold of you sooner, we could have let you know.'

Something cold clutched at Alice's heart. Gethin had said a bus had killed Fido outright. 'When was she handed in?'

'Ooh, not sure. I've been away . . . About six weeks ago? She's been with me since the end of April. We thought maybe being with other dogs would cheer her up, but she's been pining.' Rachel's expression was getting darker. 'Clearly she misses you more than you've missed her. There aren't that many dog rescues in the area. We haven't had any enquiries.'

Luke coughed. 'Alice has been in an accident too. She's still recovering.' He put a protective hand on her shoulder, but Alice was too busy thinking to notice.

'No calls at all?' She frowned. None of this made sense. Why had Gethin told her Fido was dead? If she'd just run off, why hadn't he called round the vets and rescues in the area when she went missing?

Her head ached. Something was wrong and she couldn't put her finger on it. It slipped and slid away, but it was almost there. There were facts in front of the dark curtain now, facts that didn't fit together.

'Oh dear. I'm not sure what to do now,' said Rachel. 'I mean,

I know I should ask you for some ID, but obviously this is your dog. You don't get better ID than that.'

Fido was curled in Alice's arms, eyes closed in bliss. Alice inhaled her familiar doggy smell and thought, That's exactly how I feel right now too. It was an old memory and a new one mixed together: relief, that she and Fido, without a single word of explanation, knew exactly who the other was.

'Thank you,' she said simply, to Rachel. 'Thank you so much.'

Luke offered to drive her and Fido straight back to Stratton, but Alice took the train instead. She needed some time to think.

Rachel Fenwick lent her the lead that Fido had broken out of, and with the collar now refastened – though Fido showed no signs of ever leaving Alice's side, let alone breaking away – they set off from the station back to Gethin's house.

Walking with the terrier trotting just under her peripheral vision, sticking as close to her leg as she could, made Alice realise that her brain had been trying to prompt her while she was walking Lord Bob: it hadn't been déjà vu; she *had* loved walking a dog. It made her wonder what else her brain was telling her when she wasn't trying to remember things. With each street they walked, funny flashes slid across the back of her mind, as if the smell and feel of Fido had released them: Fido's first startled walk in deep snow; a *Big Issue* seller with a sweet, greying Staffie they passed each morning; Dad's dog, Barley, sneaking into Alice's bed; Mum making a tutu for Barley's birthday. Happy, bittersweet memories that no longer made her flinch with shock. Not now she had the beginnings of something solid to hold on to.

But underneath her happiness at finding Fido was the

unsettling fact that Gethin had lied to her. Why had he let her think Fido was *dead*? It was such a huge, strange lie it made everything else feel shaky.

She spent the rest of the afternoon looking again at all the photographs in the house, trying to get into her laptop, wondering what else she didn't know that she didn't know, and at five, she heard the front door open.

Gethin was surprised to find her sitting at the kitchen table. 'Alice! Have you moved back?' His face shone with delight and Alice felt some of her simmering questions slip beneath guilt at doubting his good intentions.

'No,' she said. 'But someone else has.' She moved her chair to reveal Fido, flat out with exhaustion under the table. The scrape of the leg on the tiles woke the dog up, and when she saw Gethin, Fido froze, then barked twice, three times and stopped, her tail wagging at half-speed, uncertainly.

Gethin froze too, Alice noted. Was that a flicker of guilt? Shame? Doubt?

'I found Fido this morning, in the park,' she explained. 'Or rather, she found me. Came racing over.'

'It's definitely her?' He looked stunned. 'I mean, how do you know . . . ?'

'She recognised me. And the vet who found her scanned her chip.' Alice gave him a long look. 'It's definitely her.'

'Of course it's you, isn't it, Fido!' He kneeled down to stroke her, and Alice wondered if he was taking that moment to come up with a story.

Fido sniffed him, glanced up at Alice, then, tentatively, licked his hand. A very polite lick.

Gethin fondled Fido's ears, tickling her under her beardy chin. 'Aw, Fido, it's so good to see you . . .'

Alice couldn't hold it in. What was he *doing*? 'Why did you tell me she'd been run over by a bus? Why did you tell me she'd died?'

'Because . . .' He stood up and shoved both his hands into his unruly hair. 'God, I'm sorry. You must think I'm completely mental. I don't know, it just came out. She ran off while you were walking her, and you were on your phone and you didn't see where she went. We searched and searched. You were absolutely hysterical, blaming yourself – I was so worried about you. I went to report it to the police and . . .' He ground to a halt.

'What?'

Gethin looked sick. 'The police told me, on the quiet, that they'd had a few dogs stolen round here, little ones that gangs were using as bait for fighting dogs. And I didn't want you to even think that might have happened to Fido. I couldn't bear you worrying like that. *I* couldn't bear it. So when you came back and you obviously couldn't remember her, I thought it would be easiest just to hide all her things, instead of telling you she was still lost.'

'But we looked?'

'Of course we looked!'

Alice tried to make it fit. She wanted it to fit. But despite the horrible logic of Gethin's story, something wasn't right. Why was she walking Fido in Longhampton? She hadn't known anyone in Longhampton before the accident. Unless . . . Did she have Fido with her when she was run over herself? But then that would mean Gethin was still lying now. Why couldn't she remember? He was looking at her so sympathetically.

The invisible band round her head tightened. 'The rescue lady said they've had her about six weeks. They hadn't had any calls.'

'She was in a rescue? Where?'

'Longhampton.' Rachel hadn't said where her husband's vet practice was, but surely it couldn't be far from the rescue. 'How did she end up there? Was there a walk we did round there, maybe?'

Gethin frowned. 'Really? I phoned all the local vets and rescues. I'm sure I checked as far as Longhampton. Maybe you *had* gone there. You had been going on quite long walks – not answering your phone. Got me worried a few times. But look, she's back now, and that's all that matters. You didn't lose her!'

Alice felt the nip of guilt. 'It's partly my fault we didn't find her sooner. I hadn't changed the microchip details.' She lifted Fido up onto her knee. 'They could have brought her straight here if I had.'

'You told me you'd changed them.' He looked hurt. 'Didn't you? I was really touched – it was a lovely gesture, given how much you loved Fido. I know she's basically the only family you have, so . . . this was like making me part of it. I wish you hadn't told me that now.'

Without knowing quite why, Alice found herself rushing to apologise. 'If I said I was going to, I'm sure I meant to. I will now. I'll speak to the vet. But you're not going anywhere again, are you, Fido?'

Gethin put his arms about her from behind, locking them gently around her. 'Well, maybe this is a sign,' he said. 'Fido's come home, and now it's time for you to come home too.' He nuzzled her ear. 'Did you get the emails?'

'Mmm.' I wish I could read my *other* emails, Alice thought. For context. She thought of the endless back-and-forth she used to exchange with her mates at work; every date analysed and discussed. Making decisions based on her own faltering analysis was new – and strange. But why did she feel a need to check? Wasn't the evidence all there?

If only she could get into her laptop. Or had her phone, or even Facebook. What had happened that she'd decided to deactivate her Facebook account?

Something stirred in the back of her mind. An embarrassing photograph . . . an office party, maybe? There'd been a few. City drinks. Maybe she'd set her privacy really tight. Maybe because of the ex-boyfriend? The wife? Her heart sank. Oh God, that could be it.

'So?' Gethin kissed her neck and hugged her tight. 'How about you make a decision? We can go over to get your stuff from the hotel right now . . .'

She nearly said yes, but her eye fell on Fido and something stopped her.

'Soon,' she said, and felt shapes moving in her mind, behind the dark curtain.

On Friday morning, in the hotel office, Libby checked the banking screen again, refreshed it, but it was still there: £500 in the business account that she didn't have any record of.

She clicked into the details and tried to find where it had come from. It was her new routine, to check the hotel's account every day after breakfast, balancing it against her to-the-penny budget. The last thing she wanted was to spend money she didn't have, then get a demand to pay it back.

But no, this was definitely in credit. It had come from an account number she didn't recognise . . . Corcoran.

Jason.

She frowned. Jason had walked out on the hotel, and he wouldn't tell her what he was doing, but he was paying money into their account? And where was he getting it from, in chunks like that? He had to be dealing again, on the side. Had Steve let him do some trades on his personal account? Surely that was illegal.

'Nggh.' Libby sank her head into her hands. It wasn't the way for Jason to make it up to her. That would be the worst possible way. He had to know that. She'd rather not have his money at all than have him heading down that road again.

Before she could think, she reached for her phone.

It rang three, four times, then went to voicemail. A few seconds later, she got a text: Can't talk. In meeting.

How convenient, she thought. If he was reacting the way he did after their world fell in last time, he was probably sitting on his own in a cinema, eating handfuls of Revels and crying. Jason had let *her* deal with their friends. She'd had to come up with the explanations, until he'd cheered up enough about the idea of the hotel to bounce back, like Tigger, and tell everyone about their new adventure.

Have you deposited money in hotel account? she texted.

Three seconds later: Yes.

Libby stared at the screen. Could she ask where it was from? It felt so weird to be reduced to texting Jason questions. But she couldn't stop herself comparing Luke upstairs, getting his hands dirty helping her, with Jason, running away, then throwing money at the problem, like that would solve anything.

Although it did, pointed out a voice in her head. It paid for a month's groceries and some electricity bills. It meant she wouldn't have to eBay her last nice handbag. For another month.

Trading? she asked, and was glad the text hid the tone of voice. On the phone, she knew that would be bound to spark an argument. Jason was very sensitive to 'tone'.

There was a pause. No.

Lorcan's van had drawn up outside, and she could hear Alice's voice too, coming back from walking the dogs. The oncoming hustle of the day made her feel stronger, though; she was dealing with it, against even her own expectations. Jason walking out had made this happen. And he was missing it.

Libby heard Alice's voice, laughing with the apprentices, and suddenly felt ashamed of herself. Be kind, she thought.

Thank you, she texted back, and her finger hesitated over the X on the phone.

She missed him so much. What was he doing? What was he thinking? Libby longed to ask, but something stopped her.

She'd always coaxed him into an apology, nudging him until it was easy. This time, she wanted Jason to make the first move, just to show he knew what he should be apologising *for*.

Libby put the silent phone down and got on with her day.

It was funny how Fido was exactly the dog Libby would have guessed Alice would have: old-fashioned, quirky and easy-going. She fitted in very well with the vintage-decor restyle.

'I don't know what I find more surprising,' she said. 'That there's room for two dogs in that basket or that Bob doesn't seem to mind another dog cramping his style.'

Bob and Fido were wedged in the old tartan bed in the office, Fido providing a very small white yang to Bob's glossy black ying. One of Bob's long ears overflowed the side, and Fido's tail was at a strange angle, but neither of them seemed to mind.

'Neither of those is the surprising thing,' said Alice. 'The surprising thing is that you welcomed another dog into the hotel without even mentioning the white hairs. You're sure you don't mind her staying with me?'

'Come on. How could I turn down a miracle dog?' Libby raised an eyebrow. 'It's not every day a dog comes back from the dead.'

'Don't. Gethin won't stop apologising. Do I think he's a psycho? No! Do I think he was trying to wind me up? No! I just think he's a useless liar.'

'It's quite funny,' said Libby. 'It's such a bloke thing to do, blurt out the first thing that comes into his head, then make it worse and worse.'

Alice dropped the stack of invoices she'd been sorting into Libby's in-tray. 'In a way, it's good. I guess this is the point where we get to know each other properly, warts and all. So Gethin says stupid things when he's under pressure. And he's very protective of me.' She stopped, and Libby spotted a tiny frown crease her forehead. 'I suppose that's not a bad thing.'

'Have you . . . told him yet?' Libby deliberately hadn't mentioned Alice's pregnancy for a few days, wanting to give her time to think it through, but she'd worried about it, all the same.

'Not yet.' Alice looked evasive. 'I did another test, one that dates it. I'm still only just eight weeks. That's early enough that, well, things might not work out anyway. I don't want to get Gethin's hopes up, and move back, and . . . all that.' She glanced away. 'It's so final. I wish I knew if we'd talked about starting a family before. If this was planned.'

'You can't ask?'

'I could.' Her face said what she didn't want to put into words. 'But I think I know what he'd say. Oh God. Does this make me an awful person?'

'No! None of it does. How can anyone know what they'd do, in your shoes? But what about those pain meds you were on? Shouldn't you see a doctor to check that wasn't dangerous?'

'Next week.' Alice seemed scared but determined. 'I'll go next week. I promise. I just don't *feel* pregnant. I can't get my head around it. It's like it's happening to someone else. Like it's part of my old life, somehow, and it'll just . . . go away.'

Libby met her gaze. 'It's not going to go away, Alice.'

'I know.' She sank onto the one good armchair in the office and immediately Fido pricked up her ears and disengaged herself from Bob's wrinkly embrace to jump onto Alice's knee. 'I know.'

'Have you thought about—' Before Libby could finish, the phone rang and she grabbed it. At the back of her mind, she always hoped it might be Jason, ringing to apologise, or to explain – anything instead of this silence.

'Good morning. The Swan Hotel. How can I help you?'

'Oh, hiiii,' said a very London voice. 'May I speak with Libby Corcoran?'

'This is Libby.'

'Oh, hiiiii, Libby. This is Tara Brady. I'm the freelancer from *Inside Home*. Coming to visit you for a feature? You spoke with my commissioning editor, Katie, a few weeks ago.'

'Oh, hello! How are you?' She gesticulated at the phone for Alice's benefit, trying to mime 'journalist' by using an invisible typewriter.

Alice frowned and copied her. 'Jools Holland?' she mouthed.

Libby shook her head.

'I'm good, thanks,' said Tara. 'Listen, I hope this isn't going to be a massive pain for you, but my editor's rejigged the Christmas issue and now she thinks a country-house-hotel travel piece would work much better for our October issue. Crisp leaves and cosy walks and new boots, you know.'

'I do. I love autumn features!' said Libby. October issues. They were out in September, weren't they? 'So you'd have to come a little earlier?'

'Yes, quite a bit earlier because I'm going away on a three-week trekking thing for most of July. Um, I was really hoping I could come . . . the week after next? I'd need to file copy by the end of this month. Are you going to be ready then? We'd need to do photographs too, if you could rustle up some autumn atmos from somewhere.'

She laughed, and Libby laughed too, even though she didn't feel like laughing at all. Her stomach had dropped as if she were on a rollercoaster.

The end of June was the week after next. *Fourteen days.* She stared at the calendar on the wall in front of her and blanched. They hadn't even started sanding the floors, let alone painting the walls, and none of the new rooms had beds in, let alone soft furnishings. Could you get paint dry in that time? What if they poisoned the journalist with . . . floor preserver, or whatever it was? There was still room four, but they could hardly put her in one room, and keep every other door closed . . .

'I mean, if that's going to be a problem, then I understand—' Tara started, but Libby didn't even let her finish. She couldn't let this opportunity slip. They'd just have to do it, somehow.

'Not at all. We'd absolutely love to see you, um, the week after next.'

'Week after *next*?' Alice mouthed, in horror.

'Thank you so much! You are a star. I was *so* hoping it'd be all right – Erin was really excited about your project when I spoke to her. I think she's jealous I'm staying before she is!'

Shit. Libby's hard-nosed *Apprentice* attitude melted abruptly. She'd forgotten that Erin had probably told Katie, who had commissioned Tara, to expect Soho House with cider. That definitely wasn't what she'd be getting now. It was more knitted hot-water-bottle covers and homemade shortbread, to draw attention from the basic linen and refurbed bedside cabinets. Would she pull out if she knew? They couldn't afford for that to happen.

Alice's huge eyes were so wide Libby could see the white all around the brown irises. Libby had to turn away in case her panic transmitted down the phone.

'We're looking forward to seeing you too, Tara!' she said, with a touch of the old London Libby. 'I've got your contact details – I'll pop a welcome email over to you, and if you could confirm a date, we'll have your room all ready!'

Welcome email. That was another thing she had to do.

On the chair, Fido and Alice were both staring agog at her. Lord Bob, unwitting star of her website design, carried right on sleeping like the delegator he was.

'What was that about?' demanded Alice.

'Change of plan,' she said, putting the phone down and immediately turning on the coffee maker. 'Journalist now coming in approximately fourteen days.'

'What? I thought I'd misheard that. Did you find a time machine in the cellar or something?'

'I know. But what could I say? We *need* that feature.' Libby sat down, then stood up again. Her misgivings were growing. Blithely agreeing a new timetable without checking with Lorcan was bad, but misleading Katie about the hotel style . . . 'Should I have told Tara we're not going for that *Grazia* luxe experience anymore? Oh God. She's going to walk in and ask where the massage and sauna are, and all we'll have to offer is Bob sitting on her knee with the heating turned up.'

Libby put her hands on her cheeks and pulled her face down into a *Scream* pose. 'You don't think she'd turn round and leave straightaway, do you?'

'Not without having a cup of tea. It's a long way to come to flounce off. Anyway, you're going to send her your welcome email, aren't you? Surely that'll give her a rough idea of what to expect.'

'But . . . she's probably been briefed that the Swan Hotel is a little piece of Soho in the middle of the apple orchards. What if that's her human-interest story? Trendy London couple standing on a tractor?'

Alice looked awkward. 'In that case, I'd be more worried about the fact that Jason isn't here.'

'That's a very good point.' Libby stared at the big oil painting of the lonely stag – she'd been spacing out Margaret and Donald's melodramatic Scottish collections throughout the hotel, which was now painted in paler, calmer colours, and they all looked much better in isolation than they had in a gloomy herd. Maybe the misty drama would be peaceful against a cream wall, rather than this blood-red wallpaper. You'd see the rolling hills, rather than the doomed stag. 'How am I going to get round that?'

'I suppose you could say he's shy?' said Alice. 'Lock Luke in one room and pretend he's Jason, and he's got himself stuck? Hint that he's away?'

Libby raised her hands helplessly. 'She's bound to ask. And what about Margaret? I mean, I'd love reading about "Sisters Doing It for Themselves" – if it was happening to someone else.'

'But you are doing it without Jason. You're doing it on a shoestring, without your husband . . . to keep his family business going.'

'That makes it sound like he's dead.'

'Well, if you're Gethin, that'd be a perfectly acceptable explanation to give her.' Alice frowned. 'Just bring him back to life when he conveniently reappears.'

Libby laughed, then put her hand over her mouth. 'Sorry. I shouldn't laugh.'

'No, laugh,' said Alice. 'It's what Gethin and I need. Running jokes.' She looked wistful. 'They're what glue you together, aren't they? Running jokes and memories.'

'Yes,' said Libby. She hated making the bed on her own. It *was* quicker with Jason at the other end of the duvet, being stupidly competitive with the buttons. 'But come on, let's focus on the hotel. We need to break it to Lorcan that he's on borrowed time. Bring Fido.' Fido, it turned out, reminded sentimental Lorcan of his girlfriend Juliet's white terrier, Minton. 'He can't say no to anything when you've got Fido with you.'

Fido wagged her long tail.

'We all earn our keep in this hotel, Fido,' said Libby, and grabbed her notebook.

Chapter Twenty-Six

Lorcan was supervising the final tiling of number seven's en suite, which had reached a critical stage, but he took the news that he only had fourteen days left to finish the entire job with his usual equilibrium.

'What? Are you sure you're not filming this for some television yoke?' He rubbed his stubble doubtfully. 'First you cut your budget; then you halve our time . . . What are you going to do next, Mrs Corcoran? Bring on some celebrity plasterers? Should I expect David Hasselhoff with a trowel tomorrow?'

'No, I'm going to have you working blindfold,' said Libby. 'Seriously, can we make it? Tell me what I need to do and I'll do it. I'll paint all night, if you want me to.'

'Ah, come on, now. That'll add about another ten days, if you don't mind me saying.'

'I mean it about the painting,' she said. 'Though it might be quicker if you don't have to redo things in the morning.'

Lorcan lifted his broad shoulders, then dropped them, making his curls bounce. 'Sure, we'll get it done. Somehow. Have you told Gina?'

'I thought I'd tell you first so you could give me the real answer, before she makes you say yes. She won't say no, on principle.'

'Ha!' He pointed at her. 'You're learning fast. Anyway,

sooner you're up and running, the sooner you'll be earning money and we can all get paid. Besides, I'm sure you'd much rather be behind that reception desk dealing with guests than slapping on primer upstairs.'

'Exactly.' Inside, Libby's confidence wobbled. She hadn't thought past the moment of finishing the building work. Actually running the hotel on her own was something else again. But she dragged her focus back to the moment.

'I've made a list,' she said, waving her notebook. 'One thing at a time, right?'

'My best advice is, phone Gina.' Lorcan patted her shoulder. 'She's never met a deadline she couldn't destroy in a morning and four coffees.'

Gina swung into action with a barrage of suggestions and lists, and Libby found herself working and planning and making decisions from the moment she got up to the second she fell asleep. Decisions, it turned out, were easy when you didn't have time to agonise over them.

The web designers were based in the same warehouse conversion by the canal where Gina had her office; unsurprisingly, the draft version magically turned into a ready-to-go-live version several days ahead of schedule. It was uncomplicated but stylish; they designed a simple new logo for the hotel, and a pencil drawing of Lord Bob wandered across the special page devoted to canine guests. Libby had borrowed Doris's photo album, and, with her permission, used some of the old snaps of the hotel alongside the new photographs taken by Gina's husband, who managed to make the place look far more finished than it was, and agreed to take his payment in the form of a weekend break in the honeymoon suite.

Libby was getting very good at bartering.

While the decoration was going on at a frantic rate upstairs, Libby shut herself in the office and wrote the reservation email to go out with all bookings – starting with Tara Brady's. It was an idea she'd borrowed from a romantic hideaway Jason had taken her to for their third anniversary; she couldn't match the complimentary champagne, but at least a bit of charm was free. It was a friendly email, welcoming the guest and outlining the Swan's routines and cancellation policies, along with a printable location map and suggestions for nearby places to eat, since they didn't offer food. She set up a template so she could add seasonal local events and other little ideas that would make a guest's stay as easy and pleasant as possible.

Libby checked and checked and rechecked until Alice, arriving with some lunch for her, finally lost patience and clicked to send it to Tara; the second it swooshed from her outbox, they exchanged excited looks.

'No going back now,' said Libby, and her stomach tightened with nerves. They were down to seven days and counting.

To make doubly sure everything finished on time, Lorcan had pulled in some extra pairs of hands from his ex-roadie mates. After a worrying moment when Libby was convinced the hotel was actually falling down as the floors were being sanded by two bald men in Metallica T-shirts, the rooms started to come to life. Colour crept up the walls in soft heathery shades of lilac and thistle and cream, picked out by Gina's interior designer, Michelle, who provided them with curtains in a sturdy oatmeal fabric for a generously discounted rate. A chunk of the miniscule budget was reserved for decent bedding, and everything else had to be sourced in more creative ways. Gina arrived one morning with a van full of old 'magic carpet' rugs from the house-clearance charity, which she instructed Lorcan's apprentices to shampoo back to life in the garden, while Libby raided the local charity shops for vintage wall clocks and mirrors, leaving notes with all the organisers to save any spiky sunburst decorations for the hotel.

They worked late and started early, fuelled by Alice's supply of coffee and sandwiches, and Lorcan's equally constant supply of soft-metal mixtapes. Gethin wasn't thrilled about Alice's overtime; he'd taken to arriving on his way back from work to collect her, making pointed remarks about her health, and one day she hadn't come in at all, because he'd insisted she needed a day's proper rest. But apart from that, the atmosphere in the hotel was like nothing else Libby had ever known at work. Everyone was determined to get it done, happy to help out wherever they could. Whenever she tried to thank someone – Margaret's old part-time receptionists who dropped in to polish mirrors and clean windows, or the nearby farmer calling with breakfast samples and a new deal on fresh milk and vegetables – they just waved away her gratitude.

'It's all good for the town,' was the comment she heard again and again, and it made her realise that the Tree of Kindness wasn't just something the hospital had made up. Longhampton wasn't home, but with every kind gesture, it felt more and more like somewhere she was proud to belong. Libby was just sad Jason wasn't there to share it with her.

The only person not caught up in the dash to get the place ready was Margaret.

With Jason still sulking, Libby had made a superhuman effort to involve her in all the decisions she could think of, big and small, but whatever she tried was met with a stubborn lack of interest. Libby couldn't believe Margaret really felt nothing, not when the hotel was starting to look so amazing, and it hurt her to think that all the work she was doing to save the family business somehow wasn't as good as it would have been had Jason been there.

'Maybe you should check with Jason,' she kept saying, and when Libby explained that it was *her* opinion she wanted, Margaret just sniffed and muttered something about being out of touch with what people wanted. She still seemed to be taking Jason's absence more personally than even Libby.

But as the day of Tara's visit got nearer, unexpectedly Margaret started to take more of an interest in what was going on. Libby was upstairs, arms aching as she hung yet another pair of curtains, when she sensed Margaret behind her. A cloud of Yardley Lavender, basset-hound hair and disapproval.

'Do you like these?' Libby asked. 'They're double-lined, to block out the light for a good night's sleep. More important than posh material, I thought.'

'They're quite plain . . .' Margaret rubbed the fabric between her finger and thumb.

Well, yes, thought Libby, compared to the floral madness that was your colour scheme. People had gone insane in plainer bedrooms than Margaret's.

'. . . but they seem well made. I suppose this rustic look is in now, is it?'

'Simple quality is the idea.' Libby climbed down from the stepladder. 'Was there something I can do for you?'

Margaret was gazing around the room; it was one of Libby's favourites, painted thistle green with a pristine dark wooden double bedstead she'd found in a charity house-clearance shop, with bedside chests and dressing table to match. A bargain for the hotel, a couple of hundred quid for charity. Libby had put a thank-you on the Tree of Kindness for the person who'd donated that from their nan's spare room.

Libby waited for her to say how nice it was, but the compliment didn't come. Instead, Margaret said, 'I was talking to Timothy Prentice from the round table, and he was saying that it might not be a bad idea to get an estate agent over to value the place, once it's finished. Just to get an idea for insurance,' she added, stroking the radiator for dust.

There was no dust. Libby had cleaned it herself.

'But we're not going to sell,' she said. 'I thought we discussed this. I've worked on a plan for the coming year – Gina and I brainstormed ideas for expanding our appeal locally.'

'I do understand why you'd feel like that, dear, but it's a lot of work. You can't possibly know how draining it is. And if Jason doesn't come back . . .'

It hung in the air between them, more acrid than the fresh paint.

'Jason will come back,' said Libby, though she wasn't sure she believed it. 'He's just . . . working through some things. We can't do anything without his say-so, anyway, not legally. He's a co-owner.'

Margaret tilted her head. 'You've been saying that for a while, and he hasn't come back. And if *I* haven't heard from him, I have to ask myself if you really know what's going on.'

Libby had really, really tried with Margaret, but she was rapidly coming to the end of her rope. Luke was right: she shifted the goal posts constantly; it didn't matter how you tried to please her, you could never win. Donald must have been a *saint*.

'I appreciate what you're saying, but can't this wait? The journalist is coming at the end of the week and I want everything to be right for her. And I don't want everyone who's thrown themselves into helping us this week to feel we were only doing it up to sell. Just . . . be positive.'

'I *am* positive. Whatever gave you the idea I wasn't?' Margaret looked outraged and turned to leave. 'Oh,' she added over her shoulder when she was almost out of the door, 'you haven't fixed the final ring to the end of the pole.'

Libby looked up. She hadn't. She'd have to start again.

Bollocks.

Tara Brady arrived in a brand-new Range Rover just before lunch on Friday.

'She's here!' Alice announced, peering through the net curtains in the office. 'And . . . it looks like she's brought a dog with her.'

'How big?' Libby glanced at Lord Bob and Fido, sprawled long back to small back in a patch of sun. 'Small enough for Bob to squash?'

'It's in a bag.'

'Oh God. A really small one.' Libby felt her coffee repeating on her. 'She didn't say she was bringing a dog.'

'That's good! It'll be a test for my dog hostess trolley.' Alice's special trolley was parked outside the four rooms Libby had designated dog-friendly: it was stacked high with Bonios, wipes, bags, Febreze, red towels, spotless water bowls and a spare lead.

Libby clapped her hands, without thinking. 'Right, action stations.' She hadn't been able to sit down since her breakfast at 6 a.m., stalking from one room to another, tweaking cushions, hoovering corners, checking loos for hairs. Lack of cash at least meant there were fewer things to tidy up.

'Calm down – you're making me nervous,' said Alice, just as Luke popped his head round the office door.

'I think your woman's here,' he said.

She noted the way Luke's eyes slid across to Alice, lingered for a moment, then self-consciously returned to her. Lorcan had had to leave for another job, so Luke had come back to be on hand in case of any practical emergency during Tara's stay.

Margaret, naturally, didn't see it like that. Libby found she no longer cared what Margaret thought.

'Let's go, then – Alice, are you set?'

Alice, the Swan's official new receptionist, was dressed in a plain navy suit with a high-necked blouse. Libby was surprised: it seemed more formal than her usual clothes, but Gethin had apparently chosen it; he liked her in simple styles, she said. Libby wanted to suggest something a little less puritan might fit the hotel – and Alice – better, but not today. Later.

'Good luck, Libby,' she said, and gave her a quick hug. 'You're going to be fine. This is just the beginning.'

She didn't mention Jason, or the fact that he hadn't called, or that Margaret had announced she would be 'out all morning'.

'Yes, Libby,' Luke added. 'Good luck.' He raised two crossed fingers. 'Never seen this place look better. She'd be mad not to love it.'

Libby took a couple of deep breaths, nodded her grateful thanks and marched out to welcome Tara to the new-look Swan Hotel.

* * *

'. . . Obviously we haven't fully opened yet, and you're our first guest, so please bear with us if there's anything we've forgotten . . .'

I should shut up, thought Libby. My impression of a confident hotel owner isn't even convincing me. She'd shown Tara upstairs to room three, a dog-friendly one with a view of the garden and a wall full of round mirrors from the charity shop. Luke, rather charmingly, had carried Tara's bags up without being asked. She noticed a stray wrapper from the creamy blankets delivered only last night from Michelle's shop and grabbed it while Tara was examining the biscuits on the tea tray.

But Tara didn't seem to notice any rough edges. She was looking around with a surprised smile playing on her lips, running her gaze over the fresh flowers on the dresser and the lavender bags on the pillows. Her Yorkshire terrier – Mitzi – had given the room her seal of approval by going to sleep in her carrier.

'This is so lovely,' she said. 'Really peaceful. I love how there's no television. Or is it hidden?'

'No, we decided no televisions.' Libby nodded as if that were the plan, rather than because they couldn't afford them. 'It's all about decompression,' she said, glad she'd put her own Roberts radio on the dressing table. 'Back to old-fashioned relaxation.'

'Perfect! Right, so my room is adorable, but what I'd really like is if we could go back to that nice lounge, have a cup of tea and a chat about you. How you came here, what your story is. Can we do that?'

Libby's heart, which had slowed down as she'd shown Tara the bathroom (room three had one of the good baths), now sped up again. The lounge had only been cleared of debris the night before; Lorcan hadn't really had time to do more than give it a quick lick of paint and move the sofas back in.

'It's not really ready . . .' she started, but a voice in her head told her to stop drawing attention to the negatives and focus on the positives. 'But of course,' she said. 'Follow me.'

Gina's carpet cleaners had done a miraculous job removing all traces of Lord Bob from the lounge, and Tara curled her long legs under her on the big velvet sofa, sinking into its depths with an appreciative sigh.

'You'll have to imagine that fire on,' said Libby quickly. 'Bit hot for June! And we can make this room very cosy with a Christmas tree. Oh, thank you!'

Alice had come in with a tray of tea and biscuits. She cast a hopeful glance between the two and Libby raised her eyebrows a tiny fraction to show things were going fine so far.

Tara put her phone on the table next to the teapot to record the interview. 'So,' she said, 'tell me how you came to be here.'

Libby took a deep breath. 'Well, my husband Jason's parents ran the Swan for thirty-five years until his father sadly died last year and we decided that it would be a good time to move home and let his mother take a back seat.'

If Margaret had agreed to talk about this interview, she thought, she could have asked her how she wanted to set it out, but she'd refused, point blank. 'None of my business,' she'd said, looking like a martyr in search of a bonfire.

'So it's a family concern,' said Tara. 'I like that.'

'Yes, Luke, who took your bags upstairs, he's my brother-in-law. He helped with the wiring. We all pitched in. Lord Bob, my mother-in-law's dog, you might have seen on the website.'

'Ah, yes. Tell me about the dogs. That's unusual!'

Libby talked carefully about the hotel, her plans, getting in all the details she'd bullet-pointed in preparation, skirting round the tricky topics of Jason's absence and Margaret's contribution, until Tara put down her teacup and broached the subject Libby had hoped she wouldn't.

'If you don't mind me saying, this is totally different from the hotel I had in my brief.' She raised an eyebrow. 'I suppose I was expecting something a bit more . . . upmarket? That's probably the wrong word.'

Upmarket? Libby's face flushed with the old skin-crawling uncertainty she used to feel surrounded by the wealthy stockbroker wives in London, before she learned the fashion singular language of statement bags and investment cashmere. But then, looking away to hide her blush, she caught sight of Alice at reception, typing away under the stag painting. By 'upmarket' did Tara mean slick? Seamlessly metropolitan? Because she was proud of the *personal* contributions on show. Lorcan had stayed past midnight one night to get the reception area finished. Alice had spent a whole day polishing the reception desk with beeswax. One of the cleaners had actually brought her some original 1960s lamps. They'd turned a drab and tired hotel into something warm and stylish and ready to *grow*.

A bit more . . . upmarket? What did that even mean?

Through her nervous exhaustion, Libby felt a twist of indignation on behalf of the hotel.

'Well, that was my original plan, that boutique feel,' she began. 'But when I'd been here a while, I realised that would be all about *me* and not about the hotel. An indulgent hotel experience isn't about stupidly expensive sheets or carpets; it's about being treated with care, feeling like nothing's too much trouble. Being surrounded by comfort and kindness. I only really understood that when I saw some old photographs of the hotel in the 1960s,' she went on, realising how much she really meant it. 'The guests seemed so relaxed and happy – that wasn't because of the Italian marble in the bathroom, but because of the staff, and the atmosphere. That's why we took the 1960s feel as our starting point and mixed it up with modern comforts. But the old-fashioned service is our touchstone.'

'You sound very passionate about it.'

'I am,' said Libby. Maybe it was the gallons of coffee she'd drunk to stay awake this week, but affection for the Swan was rushing out of her. 'It's been such a learning curve, not just about running a hotel, but about myself, about my friends, about the town, everything. We had . . . we had a major setback with our first builders that made me want to pack it all in, to be honest, but I was just overwhelmed by the help I've had locally. They made me believe this would work. I didn't know anyone when I came to Longhampton, but the way people have rallied round us, to make sure we kept going . . . it's made me change the way I look at everything.' She could feel tears rising in her throat and had to battle to stop them filling her eyes.

'So you're planning to stay?'

'Definitely.' Libby nodded. 'I'm only just getting to know Longhampton, but it's as if I've been waiting all these years to come home. I'd love to pay that back by making the hotel successful, and supporting the businesses that have supported us.' She smiled, because suddenly she knew it was true. All she needed now was for Jason to come back and see what she'd done. Her heart lurched.

'Aw,' said Tara, visibly moved. And she didn't look the sort of journalist who was easily moved. 'This is going to make a *great* story. Is your husband about? Can he tell us some of the builder nightmares? Readers love a builder nightmare.'

Libby faltered. She didn't want to lie, but at the same time, she couldn't bear to say that Jason had walked out.

'Unless that's . . . a problem?' Tara's sharp writer's eyes spotted Libby's discomfort.

'Jason's working away during the week.' That was true enough. 'But he's very supportive of me. I don't think I'd have stepped up and done this if he'd been here – I'm definitely not the person I was when I left London.'

'Really? You seem very capable to me. I wouldn't have guessed from your welcome email that this was your first hotel.'

Libby considered it. 'Maybe that's it – you don't know what you can do till you're doing it.'

Or who you are until someone tells you.

Come back, Jason, she thought sadly. Come back and see what I've managed to do.

'Well, that's a great hook for the feature,' said Tara, reaching for a biscuit. 'So often you read about these ex-City types who buy up hotels for nothing, then just sell up and sod off once they're profitable. I love the idea that you've found community support and want to give something back.'

Libby nodded. 'That's it. We've got a lovely function room that's still mothballed that I'd love to do up for christening parties and charity teas and—'

There was a knock on the wooden frame of the lounge door and she looked up to see a middle-aged, balding man in a shiny suit standing there, a hopeful smile playing beneath his moustache.

'I'm looking for Mrs Corcoran,' he said.

Libby rose to her feet. 'Hello. I'm Mrs Corcoran.'

'Hello, hello.' He hurried over, juggling his file and his phone to shake her hand. 'Norman Connor from Connor Wilson. Pleased to meet you.'

'Pleased to meet you too,' said Libby politely. Connor Wilson – were they a supplier? A solicitor? 'I'm sorry – I'm not quite sure what . . . Did you want to make a reservation? Our receptionist would be delighted to help.'

'No! Goodness me. No, I'm your estate agent. I have an appointment to meet with yourself to value the property.'

Libby felt herself freeze; then a hot flush flooded her cheeks. He'd stressed the words 'value' and 'property' with loud relish. So loud Tara couldn't help but hear. 'I think there's some mistake. I definitely didn't arrange . . . I mean, we're not thinking of selling. We've barely relaunched!'

She glanced back at Tara, who wasn't even pretending not to be listening. And it was all going on her recording.

'It was definitely today,' he insisted. 'I've got a message here from my secretary – Mrs Corcoran, Swan Hotel, two thirty. Valuation, possible view to putting on the market. I'm so sorry to interrupt your tea,' he added to Tara. 'My apologies.'

'Not at all,' said Tara. She didn't look very impressed – as she wouldn't, thought Libby, if she believed I'd just spent the last half-hour *lying through my teeth*. 'I think you must have spoken to my mother-in-law,' she said, with grim politeness. 'We definitely aren't thinking of selling, but she's perhaps got her wires crossed with—'

'Ah! Hello! Is that Norman?'

Now three heads swivelled as Margaret appeared at the frosted-glass doorway. She was wearing the pale blue suit she saved for special occasions – Jason jokingly called it her Margaret Thatcher tribute number – and her hair had recently been coaxed into soft waves around her head, the new silvery threads softened back into her usual chestnut.

So that's where she'd been all morning while they were rushing around frantically polishing everything in sight: at the hairdresser's. Ready for her big moment.

Libby's head throbbed with fury and embarrassment. She's done this on purpose, she raged inwardly. This is to show me she's still in charge. That I can plan all I want, but ultimately, I'll be somewhere down the pecking order after Jason, Donald's last wishes and probably Bob.

Norman Connor was delighted to see Margaret. He swapped his files around again, shook hands and introduced himself; all the while Libby was praying that Margaret would see Tara and explain that this was a mistake.

Libby gazed at her, pleading with her eyes. If she prompted her, it would look as if she was trying to cover it up.

Margaret didn't say anything of the sort. With a look of petty triumph, she smiled at Libby and Tara, and said, 'So sorry to have interrupted, Elizabeth! Do excuse us.' Then she turned back to Norman, and as they left, Libby heard her saying, 'We should start with the bedrooms. They've been recently refurbished.'

Their voices faded away and Libby was left feeling as if she'd just been kicked in the chest.

Tara reached out and turned off the recording on her phone with a withering glance.

Chapter Twenty-Seven

Libby looked across the coffee table at Tara and wondered if there was anything at all she could say to recover the situation.

'My mother-in-law,' she stammered. 'I really have no idea what—'

'You should have said.' Tara's face, so sympathetic a moment ago, had hardened, and Libby realised she didn't know how to brazen this sort of thing out anymore. Any office wiles she'd ever had had deserted her.

Before she could speak, there was yet another knock and another interruption.

'Hello! Sorry to interrupt!' It was Alice, sporting her brightest hospitality smile. 'Just wanted to say that one of the services we offer our guests with dogs is an afternoon walk before tea. I'm happy to take Mitzi for a spin round the park if you want to put your feet up, Tara, or you're very welcome to come too? Perfect plan for an autumn weekend. We have several walking routes, and one goes past some wonderful independent local shops . . .'

For a moment, Libby thought Tara was going to announce she was off home, but she drew in a resigned breath and got up. 'Well, since I've come all this way . . .'

'Great! Do you need a lead?' Alice was full of solicitous

care, escorting Tara out and leaving Libby with the remains of their cosy tea: a battered silver teapot and hot-water jug from the original hotel. Her face looked scratched and warped in the reflection, and that was exactly how she felt. Every niggle she'd been suppressing, trying to ignore, forgiving, writing off to Margaret's grief, burst through the worn-down banks of her self-control. There was no other way of looking at it: Margaret had staged Norman's arrival on purpose.

The hot tide of fury that swept through Libby's chest was weirdly refreshing.

The moment Libby heard the front door open and close, signalling Tara and Alice were safely out of the hotel, she pushed herself off the sofa and marched out of the lounge.

'Hey, hey!'

She nearly bounced off Luke, coming down the stairs. He held up his hands. 'Where are you going in such a hurry?'

'I'm going to have it out with your mother,' she said. 'I've had enough. She did *nothing* to get this place up and running again, and now I've managed to turn things round, she asks an estate agent in, *today*, and makes me look like a total liar! If Tara scraps the feature, I'm blaming her. And I'm leaving.'

Luke put his hands on her arms and looked at her, his eyes calm like a soldier's. 'Libby? Libby, listen to me. Listen. Don't go storming up there. That's not going to help.'

'No! I'm sick of this family never talking about anything.' She shook herself free. 'She needs to hear it, and I need to say it. It's about bloody time.'

Margaret's sales tour of the hotel had reached Libby's prize honeymoon suite, where to her intense annoyance, Margaret was showing Norman Connor the luxurious bath and fabulous shower head – the only spectacular one she'd managed to hang on to when half the order went back.

'. . . has the wow-factor for any potential investor,' he was saying, and Margaret was preening as if she'd plumbed the bloody thing in herself.

Libby's fury peaked. So her ruinous choice of bathrooms was to blame for the collapse of her marriage, but it was fine to use them to flog the hotel?

'Margaret, can I have a word, please?' she said tightly.

Margaret turned round. 'Right now?'

'Yes, please.'

She touched Norman on the arm and said, 'Remind me to ask you about that colleague of yours who played golf with Donald,' then glided out of the room.

Libby strode down the corridor to the furthest room, then closed the door behind them. 'What the hell is he doing here?'

'I decided, on the advice of a friend, to go ahead and be guided as to the hotel's current value.' It sounded rehearsed, as if she'd been prepared for Libby's reaction and had decided on her moral defence.

'But I asked you to wait. Until after this feature, at least!'

Margaret lifted her chin. 'You're not the only one who can make decisions round here, Elizabeth. You're not the sole owner.'

'I might as well be!' Libby's eyes boggled with frustration. 'I'm the only one who's doing anything to keep this place going. You haven't lifted a finger since we arrived. Jason dropped us both in it, then buggered off and you blame *me*. Luke's worked his socks off, for no thanks from you, and Jason's done nothing. Jason thinks sending a few hundred quid now and again is the extent of his obligations when it's his fault we're here!'

'Jason left because of *your* decisions,' Margaret snapped back. 'You ripped this place apart. Everything Donald and I built up, you destroyed on a whim! Why shouldn't I sell? This hotel means nothing to me now. Thanks to you.'

Libby tried to ignore the sting of guilt.

'Fine. So I made mistakes! I've admitted I was wrong! But the hotel needed updating – you couldn't stay stuck in the past. Didn't you ever look to see how much money you were losing, or did you expect us to bail you out forever?'

Margaret drew a shuddering breath and played her trump card. 'Donald would be horrified to see what you've done.'

'Would he? Really? I don't think so.' Libby stuck her hands in her hair and made herself modulate her voice to a reasonable level. 'I came back here because Jason convinced me this was a family business. So far, all I see is one son who can't deal with being in the wrong, another son who can't do a thing right in your eyes and a mother who's happy for someone else to carry the can and do all the work, so long as she gets to be in charge.'

She glared at Margaret. 'I'm sorry Donald's not here: I miss him, and I am sorry for your grief. But right now, I don't think it's me Donald would be horrified with, do you?'

And she turned on her heel and marched out, so Margaret wouldn't see her tears of frustration and disappointment – and shame.

Luke was waiting for her at the bottom of the stairs.

'Just don't.' She raised her hands before he could speak. 'I've said some mean things, but they needed saying. We can't go on with—'

She didn't finish because Luke was propelling her into the

office. He steered her towards the comfortable armchair, pushed her into it, pulled a hankie from his back pocket, then went back to the door and closed it.

'There's something you need to understand about Mum,' he said.

Libby wiped under her eyes where her mascara had smudged. Her heart was still racing painfully, as if she'd just done a spin class. 'I know what you're going to say – she's still grieving. I'm not a monster. But it's like she's decided this isn't going to work! She wants us to fit into her version of reality, in which she and Jason are perfect, and you and I are selfish egomaniacs. I don't understand her obsession with the hotel being a family business when she only seems to like half of her family! Seriously, how do you cope?'

Luke pinched the bridge of his long nose, as if he was struggling with something inside. 'It's not that. There's something you need to know about Mum that I would never tell you in a million years if I didn't think there was more than just the hotel at stake here. I don't want you to leave. Mum doesn't want you to leave, not really. Jason definitely won't. I'd bet everything I've got that he's desperate for you to be here when he finally hauls his sorry arse back home.'

'If he does.'

'He will. He's his father's son.'

'Yeah, but so are you, Luke. In fact, the way you've helped me, I'd say you're *more* like Donald.'

A shadow passed across Luke's face. 'That's the whole point, though. I'm not. I wish I was, but . . . I'm *not* my father's son.'

'What?'

He came to sit down on the chair nearest to hers. 'The

389

reason Mum is so uptight about this hotel, and about Dad, and what matters in the town is . . . Donald wasn't my dad.'

Libby stared at him. 'I don't understand.' She'd been braced for some revelation about Margaret losing money on the horses, or maybe having a secret sherry problem, but not this.

'He's Jason's dad, but not mine. Mum was pregnant when she and Dad got married, and one of the reasons they moved here and took over the hotel was to give themselves a fresh start where no one would know.'

'You're kidding.'

Luke shook his head. 'Nope. It was a shock to me, I can tell you. But it suddenly made a lot of things make sense.'

'So who is your dad? And who told you?'

'Dad told me. Donald, I mean. The funny thing was, it wasn't in anger. He didn't throw it at me. He told me because he wanted me to understand why Mum . . . was as she was.' Luke stared at the floor, then frowned. 'I was naughty when I was little. Like lots of little boys are naughty. But Mum was always so down on me that it turned into something else. I couldn't do anything right, so I stopped trying. Course, now they'd say it was a case of any attention being better than none, but I was just an angry little boy, and it didn't help that Jason literally could do no wrong. I got up to all sorts I shouldn't have at school because I knew someone would have to come and get me, and I got an afternoon at home. And of course that escalated as I got old enough to get into proper trouble. Mum used to go absolutely spare – how could I be so selfish? Didn't I care about Dad's reputation? – but Dad never reacted. He just picked me up, said nothing, but I knew I'd let him down and that was worse than Mum kicking off.'

'So when did he tell you?' Libby was struggling to imagine

tweed-jacket-and-cords Donald even initiating such a *Jeremy Kyle* conversation, let alone how it might have gone.

'I'd been dragged down to the station by a copper who thought I could give them a name for some burglaries.' Luke picked up a pen from the desk and started rolling it between his fingers. 'I didn't know anything about any burglaries, but it was definitely my last warning. Dad got a tip-off from one of his mates in the Force and came and got me, but Mum had said one more incident with the police and I was out. It was upsetting Jason's A-level revision, apparently. I thought we were going home for a bollocking, but Dad drove me to the big supermarket – it was deserted, like in a film – and said we needed to have a chat. Proper man-to-man chat.'

Luke glanced up. His eyes were sad. 'I'll never forget how knackered Dad looked. He said, "I'm going to tell you something you need to know about your mother, and I'm trusting you, on your honour, to keep it a secret. And I'll know if you break your word, and that'll be the end for you and me." I said, "Go on," thinking he was going to say she was bipolar or something, but he said that, well . . . he and Mum met when she was a secretary in the law firm his dad owned in Oxfordshire and he was a junior solicitor. Mum was a real looker in those days, and though she went out with Dad a couple of times, I'd guess she was really looking for someone . . . better.'

Libby thought of the photographs in Doris's album: tired, pretty Margaret with her curly dark hair and shoulder pads and nice legs. And Donald next to her, a bit older but handsome in that cricket-whites-centre-parting way.

'Better than your dad?' she asked. 'I can't imagine you could do much better than him. He was a gentleman.'

'Well, exactly. One morning he comes into work, she's in

floods of tears, and when he asks her what the matter is, it comes out that she's in trouble, as he put it.' Luke raised an eyebrow. 'She'd "been seeing" the star player on the local football team. He was only in town on a loan and then conveniently got a transfer to Newcastle and was never seen again. I think she met him in the office. When he was getting some legal advice about a speeding ticket.' He huffed, amused. 'Dad gave him the advice. Swapped it for a season ticket.'

'I find that quite . . . hard to picture,' said Libby slowly. 'Margaret getting herself into trouble.'

'She wasn't born into the WI, you know. And it's not just easy girls who make bad choices about men. Nicer they are, the worse decisions they make.' He moved swiftly on. Too swiftly, Libby thought. 'Anyway, Dad proposed. She said yes. And rather than stick around in town and have people put two and two together, he bought a run-down hotel three counties away, and lo and behold less than twelve months after I was born, Jason came along and they've got a ready-made happy family.'

'And very happy you were too,' said Libby. 'Look, I don't want to rewrite the past, but your mum and dad adored each other – you could tell. I don't think he made her do anything she didn't want to. And he loved you.'

Luke looked away, then straight back at her. He was handsome, thought Libby. Footballer handsome. 'I know. That's one good thing. But Mum was worried about what she might have made Dad take on with me. What unpleasant traits might emerge. Dad reckoned that when she was giving me a hard time, it wasn't about me, but about *her*. She wanted to nip any potential love-rat behaviour in the bud.' He twisted his mouth. 'Didn't help that I *was* a bit of a player when I was a kid. Always had a few girls on the go at the same time – you know what it's like. But I never got anyone pregnant. I never hurt anyone. But it's why she's so worried about Alice now – habit of a lifetime and all that. She's worried that my inner love rat's come out and ruined poor Alice.'

'Oh, but that's ridiculous!' Libby was outraged. How could Margaret be so . . . medieval? 'You don't inherit *behaviour*. You are who you are.'

'Well . . . are you?' Luke looked up, his eyes dark and questioning above his sharp cheekbones. 'I sometimes wonder. I Googled my real dad once.' He winced. 'Three wives, washed up at fifty. Made me feel sick. No,' he added, before Libby could ask. 'I never wanted to get in touch. As far as I'm concerned, Dad was my dad, and that's it.'

Silence fell between them. Libby had too many questions to know which to ask first. But before she could order her thoughts, Jason was speaking again.

'I know Dad wanted me to understand that Mum did love *me*, deep down, and I see why he thought it might help me cut her some slack, but it knocked me for six. And it meant Jason would always have something I wouldn't. I could never be Jason, in their eyes. So I joined the army, where no one knew me. No history. No expectations. Course, it wasn't enough for Mum, but by then I didn't care as much. And things have worked out OK.'

He stopped flipping the pen. 'When I'm not here.'

Libby rolled this new information round in her head, not wanting to say the wrong thing. Luke had been right: it did change everything. Well, it didn't change anything, but it explained a lot. Jason, the swiftly conceived reward for Donald's gentlemanly rescue. Luke, the ticking time bomb of irresponsibility. And Margaret, constantly worrying – about Luke's inheritance, about her own character, maybe even if Donald would one day throw the favour he'd done her in her face.

'And does Margaret know you know? Or Jason?'

Luke shook his head. 'Nope. Neither of them. I made a promise to Dad. And I was angry for a while that *she*'d told this huge lie yet was down on me for stupid teenage things, but as I got older, I realised why Mum was the way she was. All because of one mistake.'

'You're not a mistake,' said Libby. 'You've given them both so much to be proud about. If Margaret can't choose to show it, for whatever reason, then I know Donald was proud of you.'

Luke shrugged; he wasn't used to taking compliments, she could tell. 'I don't know. But I'm only telling you now for the same reason Dad told me – I don't want Mum's hang-ups to drive you away from Jason, and from the hotel. She needs you. We all do. So swear to me this goes no further than this office.'

'Of course, but . . .' Libby turned her palms up. 'Is it healthy, sweeping this under the carpet? I understand why Margaret would feel ashamed thirty-odd years ago, but does it matter now? The knock-on effect is much worse. Jason can't deal with failure, and it's come from Margaret treating him like some infallible prince. You know it took him three days to tell me he'd been sacked? He left the house in a suit and went to his mate's rather than tell me. His wife.'

'You're kidding.' Luke looked disbelieving.

'I wish I was.' That had almost hurt more than the bigger betrayals. 'I don't even know what he's doing now. He keeps putting five hundred quid in the account every week. I told him I don't want the money if he's trading again. But I reckon he's been bailing out the hotel for years – I went through the accounts and found loads of mysterious deposits, usually to stop the mortgage defaulting.'

'Well, some of those were mine. Don't tell Mum – she doesn't know. I did it for Dad.'

'What? Seriously.' Libby let out a long breath. 'You lot really need to start talking to one another.'

'I know. But this has to stay between us, right? I've never told a soul. Not even Alice.' Luke caught himself, but not before his expression had given him away.

'Not even Alice?'

He seemed to be about to deny it, then shook his head as if it was a relief to let it out. 'I wanted to, because Alice is the only person who might have understood – she used to talk about wishing she knew whether she took after her mum but there being no one to ask. Whether having to be your own person was a blessing or a burden. I could talk about anything with her. She's the most extraordinary woman I've ever met. We talked about things I didn't know I felt until she winkled them out of me.' He shook his head and Libby saw his lips had curved into an unconscious smile. 'Probably a good job she can't remember some of the deep and meaningful conversations we had.'

So had it been a crush? A local holiday romance? Whatever, it must have been hard, Libby thought, seeing Gethin come back, sweeping Alice away. Especially if Luke felt the pressure to be decent, not to live down to his reputation and steal some-one's girlfriend.

'Alice is amazing,' she said. 'It sounds like you had a real connection.' She paused, then said, since they were being honest, 'Well, it's obvious you still do. Even if she can't remem-ber any of those things you told her.'

'You know that feeling that you've met someone before? I think it's more that they're so similar to you that you feel you already know them. Like looking in a mirror. You're on the same frequency.' Luke glanced up. His face was vulnerable and Libby saw a much younger Luke in his eyes. The one who was scared of who he was, what he might become. 'The baby . . . do you think she's going to keep it?'

It was pointless pretending; clearly Alice had told him. 'I don't know. She and Gethin might have been planning a family. They'd been together a while. And she says Gethin's keen to settle down; she's wearing that ring he gave her . . .'

Why did I say that? Libby could have kicked herself. *Is it yours?* she wanted to ask. *Could it be . . . ?* But how did she ask that? After what he'd just told her?

'Guess so.' Luke pressed his lips together. 'Anyway, none of my business. So! Is there anything else you need help with before I pack my tool case and bid you a fond farewell tomorrow?'

'You're not going so soon?'

'Job in Surrey all next week. Top secret.' He tapped his nose and Libby suspected he'd just made it up. She felt she had to play along, though, for the sake of his dignity.

I'm turning into one of them, she thought. Please, no.

'Sure I can't persuade you to hang about for dinner?' she said. 'A thank-you meal for all you've done? I was going to break out the takeaway leaflets the instant Tara's breakfast plates are washed.'

He shook his head. 'I'd better make a move. Anyway, you're more than capable of running this place single-handed.'

'I don't know about that.' Libby was flattered, but she wasn't kidding herself. 'I've had a lot of help. It's not something I ever thought I'd end up doing, but . . . it's surprised me, I suppose.'

'Well, that's the thing. How do you know what you're good at till you do it?' Luke got up, and arched his eyebrow at her. 'As Dad used to say, hotels are easy. It's the people in them that are the pains in the arse.'

Yes, thought Libby, and I've just managed to stir up a hornets' nest with the only person living here permanently.

Chapter Twenty-Eight

When Alice got back to the hotel with Tara, after a walk around Longhampton, during which she'd extolled the virtues of Libby, Jason and the community spirit that had brought the hotel together to the point where it almost sounded as if bluebirds had made the beds and woodland creatures had chipped in to finish the tiling, she was surprised to find Gethin waiting for her outside in his car.

'Come to take you both home!' he said with a big smile for Fido.

Tara, who'd started off frosty but had warmed up to chattiness by the second deli, seemed charmed. Gethin introduced himself, asked some sweetly baffled questions about women's magazines, and then before Alice had really had time to let Libby know she was off, they were on their way home.

In all the fuss about Tara's visit, she'd forgotten it was a date night.

'Are we going somewhere special?' she asked, as they headed out of town towards Stratton.

'Don't you want to stay in? I've barely seen you this week.'

'Sorry, it's been so busy with—'

'I know.' Gethin didn't take his eyes off the road. 'That's why I thought it might be nice to spend time relaxing together.'

When she didn't answer, he added, more solicitously, 'As

you seem so tired. After all your hard work. You need to put your feet up.'

'Oh.' Alice felt guilty. 'I'm not that tired, if you'd like to go out – it's nothing a quick coffee wouldn't fix.'

'We've got loads to catch up with on series link. And I can't think of anything nicer than a whole evening on the sofa with you, a pizza, a bottle or two of cider . . .'

'And Fido,' said Alice.

'And Fido.'

Once they were settled onto the squashy sofa with the dog in between them, a pizza in the oven and six episodes of *Homeland* lined up, Alice made a conscious effort to stop wondering what was going on back at the hotel and to enjoy her evening in. Because it was nice. Settled, and cosy, and quiet.

Gethin had just started the first episode when the phone rang, and as usual he sprang up to answer it. Alice fed Fido a couple of Pringles, but Gethin was back before she had time to run through her 'paw' routine twice.

'Who was that?' she asked.

'Oh, no one.' Gethin settled himself back on the sofa, slipping his arm round her.

'It must have been someone.' Alice wasn't sure who, though. She hadn't spoken to his workmates since she'd come home. Or, it occurred to her, anyone in Gethin's family. He said he'd told his mother and sister what had happened – the edited details: he didn't think they needed to know about the row – but they hadn't called her or sent 'get well soon' cards or anything. It was odd, considering how motherly Margaret had been, but then Gethin didn't seem to like talking about his family.

He looked at her strangely. 'Why are you so bothered?'

'Because I thought Libby might have rung to say how things were going with Tara. I suggested some places she could go for dinner tonight with her.'

Gethin's expression flickered.

'*Was* it Libby?' Alice asked.

He looked annoyed. 'Yes, actually, it was.'

'And she didn't want to speak to me?'

He frowned and unpaused the television. 'If you must know, she wanted you to go in tomorrow to help out, and I said we were doing something.'

'What?' Alice twisted round on the sofa to look at him. 'Why?'

'Because she can't just snap her fingers and expect you to jump.'

Alice was surprised by the flat line of his mouth, the unsmiling stare he was directing at the screen. 'Gethin, I think you've got the wrong end of the stick about Libby. This is a big weekend for her. She needs Tara to be wowed by the hotel, and there's only her, Luke and Margaret there tonight. Of course I want to go in and help her if she needs me!'

'Luke?'

She tried to control her face. 'Yes, he's on standby for any building issues, I think.'

Gethin's gazed locked with hers for a few uncomfortable seconds. Then he turned back to the television, flicking the volume up a notch. 'And what if I need you?'

'But you don't need me,' said Alice, trying not to sound frustrated. 'Didn't you say about ten minutes ago that you wanted to stay in and get some jobs done around the house tomorrow? It's only for this weekend.'

'There are different kinds of need.'

'Oh, Gethin, *please* don't turn this into some kind of competition between you and my job.'

With that, the nagging doubt crystallised into a certainty in Alice's mind. There's no way I can move back in with him, she thought. If we're arguing about work already, then surely we must have argued the whole time about the hours I worked at the White Horse . . .

Without warning, Gethin muted the television and turned round, his face contorted with hurt. 'Be honest. Is it that you don't love me anymore?'

'What? No!' The answer ricocheted out of her.

'Are you sure? Because you're not really acting like you do.'

His eyes were sad, but there was an unsettling anger behind them that woke a coiling anxiety inside Alice. It slithered in the pit of her stomach. 'Can you even imagine what it feels like to meet someone you've waited your whole life to be with, then after just a few weeks apart, they're looking at you like they don't even know you?'

'I . . .'

'I'm sorry if that sounds hard, but you're breaking my heart.' Gethin winced, as if he was making an effort to control his emotions. 'I've been trying and *trying* to help you remember, but now it's starting to feel like you don't want to.'

How had he gone from sulky to distressed so quickly? Alice panicked. What was she missing? What had she said? 'Please don't say that.'

Gethin seemed visibly upset. 'You know I'm not going to mess you about like those other men. You don't have to treat me badly to prove anything. I'm not like that. You told me I made you understand what love felt like. I can't believe that's just gone.'

It was her. Not him. *Her.* Alice flinched: she knew she hadn't been an angel in the past; she didn't want to be that person again. Lonely, too eager to trust, rebounding from one disappointment to the next. Gethin had stopped her from doing that. Not just in his words, but it was all over his face: he loved her, and she'd loved him.

'I'm not saying I rescued you. We rescued *each other*,' he continued. 'I was in a bad place when we met, the worst I'd ever been. I was having panic attacks, I was on anti-depressants . . . You changed that. I don't know where I'd be now if we hadn't met. Seriously.'

'Don't say that.' Her voice wasn't much more than a whisper.

Gethin reached for her stiff hands and Alice let him take them: it seemed much easier than working out what to say. 'I hate having to tell you stuff like this, because it's not who I am now, and I don't want you to think I'm some kind of nut job, but I need you to see how being together's changed us *both*. You know why? Because we're perfect for each other. Life without you would be . . . Well, I wouldn't want to go back to how things were. I couldn't.'

'Definitely don't say *that*,' she said, trying to introduce a lighter note in her voice, but Gethin carried on gazing at her, as if he didn't want to put something terrible into words. Yet still wanted her to remember.

The silence lengthened and a chill ran over Alice's skin. It felt as if he were putting his entire life into her hands, and the responsibility was paralysing.

She sat immobile with panic until an easier, more familiar smile warmed his eyes. 'But enough of that. Talking about sad stuff on a Friday night! That's not what you moved back for, is it?'

Alice started to form the words 'I haven't moved back' but found she couldn't. Not while he was looking at her like that. And when she didn't speak, Gethin's expression changed slightly, as if he'd won a small but important victory, but wasn't going to make a big deal of it.

'Can I get you another drink?' he asked, seeing her empty glass. 'Might as well, while the telly's on pause? I'll check the pizza.'

'Um, yes, please,' said Alice. 'I'll just . . . go to the loo. Don't start without me.'

He grinned, and when she got to her feet, her legs trembled slightly.

Upstairs, Alice shut herself in the bathroom and dialled the Swan on her mobile. Hearing Libby's familiar voice sent a welcome ripple of reassurance through her.

'Libby, it's me, Alice.'

'Oh.' Libby sounded surprised to hear her. 'I'm so sorry about calling earlier! Gethin made me feel as if I'd interrupted you . . . you know. In bed! Sorry!'

Alice blanched at the thought. 'God, no! We were just watching *Homeland*. I'm sorry about tomorrow. I can come in the—'

'Don't worry. It's not that we're busy – it was more your advice I was after,' Libby sighed. 'And before you say it, I'm not going to tear you away from your romantic date night now.'

The more Libby talked, the more Alice could detect a strain in her voice.

'What's happened? Is it Tara? She seemed happy enough when I left.'

'I don't know what you said to her, but it worked. She's just having a bath. I'm taking her to that new burger place in town for supper.' Libby sounded flat, and weary. 'I've just . . . I had another row with Margaret today, Luke's left, and I need to talk to Jason. He won't answer his phone.'

'Then text him. Life's short – you could be hit by a car and lose your memory tomorrow. Get things sorted out.' Alice strained her ears – was that Gethin coming upstairs?

'But should I, if he refuses to communicate?'

'Libby, he's proud. He knows he's screwed up *and* dropped you in it. Just tell him you need to talk. And then clear the air with Margaret.' Alice was speaking too fast, gabbling to say all she needed to before Gethin heard her. 'She's really unhappy too. And proud. You can see where Jason gets it from.'

'Are you all right? You sound . . . stressed.'

'I'm fine.'

Gethin was calling her from downstairs. 'Alice? Alice, are you nearly done? Pizza's ready!'

'Really? You don't sound fine.'

Alice caught sight of herself in the bathroom mirror. She didn't look like herself. She looked jumpy, and pale.

What the hell am I doing making secret calls to my friend, worrying about what Gethin might think? she wondered. Who exactly am I? Who *was* I?

What am I going to do?

'Alice?' Libby's voice came at the same time as Gethin called up the stairs.

The sense of time pressing down on her made Alice weak inside. She wanted to come up with a strong, confident answer to her own question, but her mind was loose with a confusion that hadn't been there when she'd left the Swan that afternoon.

'I've got to go. But I'll see you on Monday,' she managed, and hung up.

Back in the hotel office, Libby stared at the phone and wondered if she *had* interrupted Gethin and Alice in bed: Alice sounded very odd.

She was right, though. Life was too short to wait for Jason to make the first move; it could take months, and Libby didn't feel like playing games anymore. After what Luke had told her that afternoon about their childhood, Jason's hang-ups about failure made a sad kind of sense. No wonder he couldn't deal with disappointing people, she thought, if he'd been unwittingly shouldering Margaret's ambitions for cast-iron respectability his whole life. It was just as cruel a burden to put on a child as Margaret's equally unfair fears for Luke's moral compass.

Before Libby could change her mind, she texted, I want to see you – we need to sort this out. Let's meet on Sunday lunchtime, and pressed 'send'.

She stared at the phone for five minutes, but nothing came back. She tidied the office. Nothing. Eventually, four hours later, after she'd taken Tara Brady out for dinner, turned down her room, put out Mitzi the terrier's goodnight Bonio and gone to bed herself, Jason finally replied, OK. Meet halfway, Sunday lunch. Will book somewhere.

Libby was about to text, *Why not the hotel?* when she realised she didn't care. She just wanted to see him.

It had been over three weeks since Jason had marched out of the Swan without a backward glance. As Libby drove to the gastropub where he'd booked lunch, halfway between Longhampton and London, she tormented herself with what he'd been up to in London while she'd been working all hours to get the hotel ready. Nights out? Drinking benders with Steven? Flirtations with women who didn't give him a hard time about VAT receipts?

But when he walked into the bar of the Wheatsheaf, Libby's heart turned over, first with relief to see him, despite everything, then with concern at how he looked.

Jason seemed to have aged ten years in mere weeks. His cord jacket looked a size too big for him; his lank hair had lost its healthy thatchiness; his eyes were sadder than Lord Bob's. And droopier, and more bloodshot. Libby had to fight an impulse to gather him up in her arms.

'You should have come to the Swan,' she said, unable to hide her concern when he returned from the bar with their drinks. 'I'd have made you a decent breakfast. Isn't Steven feeding you?'

'Not sleeping much.' He rubbed a hand over his chin. Jason was always meticulous about shaving; the sight of his stubble jarred with Libby. 'Or eating.'

'Oh, I see. Back to bachelor ways.' She meant it lightly, but it came out wrong and he winced.

'Don't,' he said, and the refusal to rise to any argument nipped her more than a snappy retort would have done. Jason looked so wretched that there was no point even asking if he was sorry; it was written all over him. She'd been expecting some defiance, a bit of the old 'everyone else is wrong' attitude, but there wasn't any. Quite the reverse.

'Why didn't you want to meet at the hotel?' Libby could hear the jolly positivity enter her voice; she sounded like her mum, covering up the spikes in one of her dad's moods. 'It's looking great. You know the journalist came this weekend? I think she liked it. Fingers crossed, anyway.'

'I know. I've seen the finished website.' Jason managed a smile. 'You've done a great job. Seem to be managing fine without me.'

'Well, I haven't done it on my own. I can't believe how generous people have been, rallying round us.' Libby meant it; sometimes, in her knackered state, Gina's spontaneous ideas and Lorcan's patient overtime made her feel dangerously weepy. 'It's amazing how everyone's got behind the hotel. We should have asked for help months ago.'

'And Mum? Has she been scrubbing the floors and polishing the silverware?'

Libby drew in a long breath, then let it out. At least if Jason didn't know about Margaret's plans, they hadn't been having cosy mother–son chats behind her back. 'Not really, no. She had an estate agent round on Friday. She's talking about selling up.'

'You're joking.' Jason paused, his shandy halfway to his mouth. 'But it's her life, that hotel. Her and Dad's life's work.'

'Not anymore, apparently. I've ruined it. It's only the fact that you're not there that's stopping her from putting it on the market.' Libby braced herself; she had to say the tough things. 'It's not helping me or Margaret, the fact that neither of us know what you're doing.'

He put down his glass and looked defensive. 'Oh, don't start . . .'

'I *have* to start, Jason. I've got people depending on me. We've got guests booking in, suppliers to pay, shifts to arrange. I need to know what you're doing. I don't even know if you're working. Are you?'

'I'm talking to people. You know, putting feelers out. It's complicated.' He was being deliberately vague and it irritated Libby. There wasn't time for snobbery about the 'right' firm, or a job he felt befitted him.

'Just tell me what's going on. I appreciate the money you've been sending, but I worry, Jason. I worry that you're getting back into that . . .' Her voice trailed off and she gazed at him, choked by words she didn't want to hear coming out of her mouth.

How had it come to this? From cosy weekends-in-bed in luxury hotels in Paris to strained conversations in an anonymous pub, in less than a year? Even a month or so ago, they'd been toasting their new start in Ferrari's, still able to finish each other's sentences and read each other's minds, but now Libby had no idea what Jason was thinking. The blank greyness of his dejection made him unreadable, a stranger.

The idea of a future without her golden, loveable Jason was suddenly real to Libby and it took her breath away. Her life, his life, rolling away in different directions. Existing, aging, seeing things without each other. Meeting other people. Their little clutch of happy years vanishing into the past.

They stared at each other, winded by the coldness of their thoughts, until finally Jason spoke.

'I'm so sorry, Lib. I screwed up.' He looked lost, as if he still couldn't believe it had happened. 'The only thing I had to do, make some money for us . . . I screwed up.'

'Everyone screws up once or twice. It's human.' She reached for his hands.

Jason shook his head. 'But I did *stupid* things. Like the renovation money.'

'What about it?'

'There was never as much as you thought, right from the start. By the time we paid solicitor's fees, and the removal costs, bills here and there ... It just kept going down and down; every time I checked the account there was five grand less. But I'd talked you into the hotel idea, and it seemed like that was the only thing keeping you going, believing that we had that safety net – I couldn't tell you. I was going to do a couple of quick deals so I could top it up before you noticed, maybe double it.' He flattened his hand against his forehead. 'But I put it off and put it off, and then I got nervous, and I ballsed up a few trades. And once you're out of the rhythm . . .'

Jason paused. 'And Dad, you know. I kept thinking, I should tell Dad, but then remembering he wasn't there ... And that ... I don't know. I should have told you. But I couldn't. You'd been so good about it all. I couldn't let you down again.'

'Oh, Jase.' Libby felt her heart contract. Of course he was grieving too; that was so much more important than money. Why hadn't she noticed? Why had she let her panic about his job blind her to what Jason must have been pushing down inside?

'Why didn't you just tell me? You know I wouldn't have spent so much money on showers.' Libby rubbed her eyes; she was worn out after the last few weeks' late nights and early starts. It hadn't made any difference in the end; the hotel had still, somehow been revived, with twice as much character for half their original budget. 'I'm not blaming you for the whole thing. I should have paid more attention.'

'Why?' he asked bitterly. 'That was my job. Looking after our finances.'

'No, come on. We never divided the jobs up anywhere else. We made the bed together, didn't we? We both took out the bins. It wasn't *just* your job to be responsible for money – I should have asked.'

'Stop being nice,' said Jason. 'It's not making me feel any better.'

'I'm not trying to make you feel better. I'm trying to stop you feeling so sorry for yourself – we don't have time for that now.'

He turned his glass round on the beermat. 'I keep looking at Steven's house and thinking, We had this. And now we don't . . . That life. I ruined it.'

'So what? I mean, it was lovely, the house and the treats and the money, but . . .' Libby tried to make him look up at her. 'I'm not a labels person, Jason. It was only ever something to talk about. I miss the *holidays*, maybe – that exploring we did together. And maybe I miss the decent gin. And the taxis. But I don't miss the handbags.'

A quick, humourless smile, more an acknowledgement of her effort than an indication he believed her. 'Cheers. But I mean our marriage. I spoiled it.'

Jason was being maudlin now, and it reminded Libby of Margaret. Ironically enough. It was harder for Jason, falling from so high up, she told herself. He'd never had to pick himself up before; this was new, this shock of failure.

'It *could* have spoiled our marriage,' she persisted, 'if we'd thrown in the towel and let it, but we didn't, did we? We chose to do something different. Together.' She stretched out her hand across the table, desperately wanting some of the bumptious Jason back. She'd never known him self-pitying like this, so unsure of himself. 'How does anyone know how strong their marriage is if they never test it? We're testing it now. It's not broken until one of us gives up.'

One Small Act of Kindness

She paused, suddenly aware she'd gone out quite far. So far she had to ask the next, unwelcome question. 'Unless . . . You don't want to give up, do you?'

Jason couldn't meet her eye, and something shrivelled, high in Libby's chest. *Don't say it*, she begged silently. *Please don't say it.*

'I don't know what I want anymore,' he said quietly. 'But you deserve better.'

'I think I'll be the judge of that, thanks.'

He hung his head. 'I'm not the man you married.' If Jason didn't look so stricken, Libby thought, she'd definitely shake him. 'I don't recognise myself. I do things I didn't think I'd do. It's fucking weird. It's scary.'

'I know it's scary, but that's life,' she said. 'You don't know *who* you are until you have to be that person. Listen, I begged Erin for a loan. I negotiated fifty per cent off our original deal with the tile supplier. I even gave your mother a piece of my mind.'

'What?' Jason glanced up in surprise.

'After she pulled her stunt with the estate agent on Friday.' Libby could feel heat returning to her cheeks. 'I couldn't let it go. She's been impossible since you left, blaming me for everything, making out I drove you away, that all this is my fault. I told her she needed to take a hard look at herself too.'

As Libby heard her own words, she cringed with remorse. She'd actually lashed out at a grieving woman, still floundering without the man who'd been her whole life? I'm going to have to apologise, she thought. I really am. But, at the same time, observed a voice in her head, what she'd said to Margaret was true, and maybe it was time to start being honest. How could this stubborn family heal otherwise? It was like the damp and the cracks in the hotel bedrooms – you could only fix the walls once the paper was stripped back. And Libby *wanted* the

Corcorans to mend their cracks; she knew Luke did too, and Margaret, deep down.

'Oh my God.' Jason looked stunned. 'And what did Mum say?'

'That I had no right to talk to her like that, that I'd ruined her hotel.' Libby bit her lip. 'I'm going to say sorry, obviously. But I did mean it.'

She wasn't sure if Jason was going to take Margaret's side, but he didn't say anything. He sank his head into his hands.

'I feel like I've let her down too.' His voice was muffled. 'And Dad.'

His voice caught, cracked, as he said, 'Dad', and Libby ached to hold him.

'You're only letting them down now by running away,' she said. 'So you're human: you make mistakes. Come back. Make things better. It's what your dad would have wanted you to do. And I need you. *We* need you, Jason.'

'Do you? Really? You've done all the hard work in that place. I can't even get the books right. Luke's given you more help than I can. I've only made more problems.'

Libby closed her eyes, and tried to keep her voice level and calm. 'Shall I tell you what I need?' she asked. 'I just need a man who does his best. A man who is who he says he is. A man who wants to share a life with me. I'm not asking for more than that. You *are* all those things. Jason, I know this isn't just about the money – and anyway, I promised to stick it out for richer or poorer, remember? We can sort all this out, together. But I need to know where I am with you.'

He left a long pause. 'I don't know where I am with me. I mean, who am I? If everything I thought about myself turned out to be bollocks?'

'Oh, Jason, I can't answer that question for you,' she said, finally exhausted. 'You've got to work that bit out for yourself.'

He didn't reply, and his shoulders rounded.

I could stay another three hours and tell him how much I love him, how much I believe in him, thought Libby miserably. But it's not going to make a shred of difference. He's somewhere else. There's nothing for me to do now but leave.

She felt a crack of misery deep in her heart, and pushed her chair back from the table. 'I've got some clothes for you in the car. In case you needed them. Suits and things.'

'Are you going?' He looked devastated. 'Don't go yet.'

'I don't want to go.' Libby gazed at his stubbly, tired face. 'But I've got so much to do, to get things ready for reopening.' And who am I doing it for? she wondered. Him? His mother? Me? The bank?

She'd been so fixated on finishing the renovations, then on Tara's visit that she hadn't thought beyond those deadlines. But now the reality of life running the Swan, alone, rolled out in front of her. The joy had rubbed off, leaving only the dull morning-to-night responsibility rising up in a series of alarm clocks, fried eggs, and accounts. A hard, hard job, not an optimistic joint project. And what did *she* want? For the first time Libby wondered whether Margaret was right to sell. It wasn't Margaret and Donald's hotel anymore. Maybe it wasn't going to be her and Jason's hotel either.

If they did sell it, split what money was left over, where would she go then, to start again alone?

Dread pooled in the pit of Libby's stomach, and she had an unexpected lightning flash of how Alice must have felt when her memory was blank. Blindfolded, but forced to move forward into a silent, formless future. Without Jason.

'Please,' said Jason.

Libby sat down again, more out of shock at the intense sadness that had surged through her, and when he smiled, relieved, her heart twisted.

'We're having a garden party to relaunch the new rooms,' she said. 'Next weekend. Surely that's enough time to get your head straight? You always worked best to a tight deadline.'

Jason gazed at her and pressed his lips together. He didn't reply, but he didn't say no.

'This is our future, Jason. Not just yours. Mine too. If you love me, you'll at least give that some consideration.' One last desperate attempt. Libby forced herself to smile. 'Can I tell Margaret you'll be back for the party?'

He took a deep breath, and she searched his face for the man she'd fallen for across the train carriage. The haybale sunshine of his self-confidence glowing among the drab, coffee-breathed suits. The smooth skin she'd fantasised about reaching out and touching. The smile.

'You know I love you, Libby,' he said, but it didn't answer her question.

Chapter Twenty-Nine

When Libby got back to the hotel at five o'clock on Sunday afternoon, the reception area was deserted. Although it looked beautiful now the green tartan carpet wasn't competing with mad red wallpaper, and the freshly scrubbed stone fireplace in the hall hinted at wintry cosiness to come, she couldn't summon up the enthusiasm she knew it deserved.

All Libby could think of was whether she and Jason would be here by Christmas, to see a fire crackling in the hearth. She honestly didn't know what he was going to do. That was what hurt the most: seeing the stranger looking back at her, over that pub table, not knowing what he was thinking, not being able to reach him to help.

Libby stared at her hazy reflection in the deep, polished reception desk and ached. She let herself ache. She no longer had the words to pinpoint how she felt when sadness made her whole body feel like lead.

Keep moving, keep moving, she told herself, pushing on through to the back office. There was the ad to put in the local paper in the morning for the open day next weekend; there were emails to send, website updates to write, the beautiful photographs taken by Gina's husband, Nick, to ping off left, right and centre, so everyone could see what a transformation they'd wrought on the hotel.

She also had to apologise to Margaret.

Libby wasn't particularly looking forward to that, but she knew she had to do it. She'd been mean. That wasn't who she was, no matter what rocks life was throwing in her path.

Her eye fell on Jason's cashmere jumper. One she'd bought him for Christmas a few years back, when he'd taken up golf for about three weeks. Libby picked it up off the floor, remembering how they'd laughed about the ridiculousness of the club, how he'd packed it in by February. Since no one was around, she sank onto a chair and swung her feet up onto the desk, pressing her nose into the soft fabric. She inhaled Jason's familiar smell with a hungry gulp and it sent her back into their airy sitting room, into their old bed, into a world of memories she couldn't bear to lose.

Somewhere in the distance, Libby heard the office door push open over the pile carpet and didn't bother to turn round; it sounded exactly like Lord Bob on one of his stealth biscuit raids. Or as stealth as a five-stone basset hound could be.

'Bob, I'm not in the mood,' mumbled Libby. 'Go and bother Margaret if you're looking for biscuits.'

There was a very un-bassety cough and Libby jerked to attention, nearly falling off the chair.

'Elizabeth. Is this a good time to have a word?' It was Margaret, her chin raised in a determined expression Libby had never seen until she'd moved in, but now knew all too well.

Oh God, she thought. It's either going to be my marching orders or one of those non-apology apologies she's so good at. Or maybe Jason's called her.

'Of course it's a good time – come in,' she said, feeling awkward about Margaret's asking to come into her own office.

Margaret stepped inside and sat down on the same chair

Luke had occupied a few days ago; she and Luke perched on the edge in the same anxious way. Libby tried not to think about what Luke had told her, but it was impossible not to search for traces of that story in her face. Young, pretty, feisty Margaret seemed a wholly different person to the uptight, faded and lonely Margaret in front of her. But then *this* Margaret seemed a very different person to the plump-cheeked, generous, kindly fusspot who'd welcomed her every Christmas since she'd known Jason. She'd gone too.

Libby sprang to her feet. 'Would you like some coffee? I'm just going through the plans for—'

Margaret raised a hand as if she just wanted to get it over with. 'I want to apologise for interrupting your interview on Friday,' she said. 'It was . . . it was insensitive of me. I'm sorry. I should have been more considerate of the situation. I should be thanking you for all the effort you put into getting the hotel ready.'

The apology was there. Only a tightness in her face undermined it.

'Alice is really the one you should be thanking,' said Libby. 'She walked Tara round town telling her what an amazing family business it was. I mean, still is. By the time she left, she'd more or less persuaded Tara how much we all love this place.'

Margaret stared hard at something on the desk. Libby wondered, wearily, if it was the absence of the outmoded filing cards that had sat there for twenty years, doing nothing other than acting as a place to put a cup of tea.

'So did you come to a decision? About selling?' she asked.

'As you say, it's not my decision to make, is it?' There was a martyrdom in Margaret's voice that reminded Libby of Jason's wallowing indulgence and it stretched her already flagging sympathy. 'I don't have a role here anymore.'

'Margaret, that's not true . . .'

She looked at Libby and they both knew it was. Libby struggled to find the right way to say, *Stop punishing us. Let me help you*, but she was tired and, if she was honest, hurt by the lack of appreciation. She wanted to apologise but wasn't sure, now, there was anything she could say that wouldn't be taken the wrong way.

They stared at each other, beneath the baleful glare of the lone, doomed stag over the mantelpiece.

'So . . . I've said what I came to say. I'll leave you to it. You probably have lots to be getting on with.' Margaret got up, but as she went to leave, she laid her hand unconsciously on the back of the chair by the door that Donald had always thrown his tweed jacket over when he came in; the automatic tenderness of the gesture pierced Libby's heart.

How many times had Margaret sat in the office with Donald, one either side of the partners' desk, presiding over their empire of daily routines? The guests came and went, but they opened and closed each day together, thousands of morning coffees, thousands of Donald's perfect breakfasts, thousands of goodnight kisses. And now the routines were changing, Donald had gone and Margaret was left alone in a hotel that was no longer hers. Missing his smell, his touch, his tweed jacket thrown on that chair. A ghost in her own life.

And Jason was making a fuss about losing his job at thirty-five.

'Margaret,' she called out, and when she turned round, Libby saw her pale blue eyes were shining with tears. 'Margaret, don't go.' She sprang to her feet and crossed the office in two paces, holding out her arms to her.

Margaret stood stock still for a moment, too proud to

submit straightaway, and then Libby gave her no choice, hugging her mother-in-law to her chest not only to comfort her, but for the comfort she needed herself. They were both lost, both bewildered by grief for familiarities that had vanished in the space of a breath.

'I'm sorry,' she said, as Margaret's body shook with a silent sob. She was so much smaller than Libby remembered, her bones sharp and fragile through the wool of her cardigan. The last year had worn her down, and Libby felt ashamed that she hadn't made more time to understand properly, that she'd let her own worries and panic blind her to how unhappy Margaret was. How much smaller she was getting under the layers of drab clothing, how the colour had drained from her.

And then slowly Margaret's arms went around Libby, her head resting on Libby's shoulder as she hugged her and swayed.

They stood holding each other in the silence of the office, broken only by the ticking of the longcase clock in the corner, and Libby felt tired, and young, and old, all at the same time. But she didn't feel as alone as she had when she'd walked in, half an hour ago.

'I'm so sorry, Elizabeth,' said Margaret, eventually. 'I've been no help to you whatsoever. Silly old woman, finding fault with everything.'

'No, we came to help *you*,' said Libby. 'That was the idea.' She held Margaret at arm's length, her tear-stained face rueful. 'And we didn't really help at all, did we? Not in any way that you actually needed. We made things worse. I'm sorry.'

Margaret sighed and sat down, pulling a small white hand-kerchief from her sleeve. 'You did what you thought was best. You couldn't give me my old life back.'

'We tried. Please believe that, Margaret. No matter how cack-handedly we went about it, we honestly did try. We just didn't . . . couldn't think beyond the practicalities. We lost sight of what the hotel meant to *you*.'

'Well, you had your own problems to worry about.' She stared at the desk and wiped her eyes. 'I didn't realise until you told me what the situation was with Jason's job. I don't know if I'd have let you invest so heavily in the hotel if I'd known that.'

'It was what we wanted to do. It's what we still want to do.'

Margaret didn't answer and Libby wondered if she really did understand what Jason had done. It wasn't her place to tell Margaret about the lies he'd told. But then would she believe her if she did roll them out? Libby was almost beyond caring herself now – it was what he did *next* that was important.

'I'm so sorry about Donald,' said Libby quietly. 'I've often wished he was here, to ask his advice, or just to hear him tell me something that's bothering me doesn't really matter. I can't imagine how much you must miss him.'

Margaret was staring, half smiling, half sad, at the filing cabinet, as if Sunday afternoons of years past were being projected onto it like ciné film. 'It's funny, I can manage the day-to-day things on my own, I always did,' she said. 'But I miss having someone to chat to in the garden. Having someone notice when I've had my hair done.' She glanced at Libby. 'Having someone to tell me when I'm being a ridiculous old trout. Like this weekend.'

'You're not being . . .'

Margaret fixed her with a more familiar beady look. 'Donald would have taken me to one side and asked me what I was *really* uptight about. What I was pretending not to care about while I was making a fuss about silly things like estate agents.'

'And what's that?' Libby readied herself to be told that she needed to get on with grandchildren, or that she should have been supportive of Jason's financial woes.

The melancholy in Margaret's answer took her by surprise. 'When I see you behind that reception desk, it feels like I was never there. You've taken to it so naturally, and you're making this hotel your own – which is only fair, since you two have paid for it and got it up and running again. No, really, let me finish . . . But where does that leave me? I'm not a wife anymore. I'm not a mother, now the boys are grown up. I thought I might be a grandmother – that'd give me something to do – but . . . that hasn't happened.' She looked bereft. 'And now I realise that's partly because Donald and I got this place into such straits that you and Jason have to work night and day to pick up the pieces.'

'Well, I suppose you did it with two small children . . .' Libby began.

Margaret stopped her. 'I was very tired, Elizabeth. If I'm honest. I was very, very tired. And I had no choice. You do.'

There was a lot of Jason's self-laceration in what she'd said, but Libby detected a strength in Margaret – a desire to find her identity again, even in the middle of her bewilderment at what was no longer there.

'Margaret, you'll always be a part of this hotel, and you haven't *stopped* being any of those other things,' Libby pointed out. 'You're still a wife – thirty-five years of marriage doesn't just cease to have happened because Donald's gone.'

'That's very sweet of you to say,' said Margaret.

'But it doesn't. He's everywhere in here. The carpet in reception, for a start. Whenever I see that Black Watch tartan, I think of him.'

Margaret managed a smile.

'And look at how much support we've had in the past few weeks – that's not about me,' she went on. 'That's about *you*. The standing you've got in the community. If people didn't care about you, and want your business to pull through, they wouldn't bother. Donald was obviously very important to Longhampton, but you are as well, Margaret.'

As Libby carried on talking, a brighter energy was rising through her. It wasn't just that it was true, everything she was saying, but she felt better for saying it, better for channelling something happy and honest and positive, and seeing the grateful recognition dawning in Margaret's face.

'This could be the start of a new chapter for you, now I'm covering the fried-egg duties,' she went on. 'You're a wonderful organiser, and a networker, and a fantastic hostess – all those qualities are still inside you; the town's your oyster.'

'Maybe . . .'

'And you'll never stop being a mother.' Libby paused, unsure whether she should tell Margaret about her meeting with Jason, and her frustration with him. She didn't want their tentative new understanding to be spoiled with a row about Prince Jason.

'I don't know.' Margaret's face stopped brightening and she looked sad. 'I did my best, but . . .'

'Luke and Jason will always need you. They miss their dad. That's why they want to support you. It's not because they think you're not capable or you need help – they want to do what he'd have done. Jason *and* Luke.'

'I do love them,' she said 'My little boys.'

Their gazes locked, and Libby wondered if Margaret might be coming round to opening her heart to Luke, at the same time as opening her eyes to Jason, with all his faults and gifts. Donald must have tried in his own gentle manner, but until Margaret saw it of her own accord, how equally flawed and perfect her sons were, neither of them would get beyond the teenage boys they still were in so many ways.

This was about Margaret forgiving herself first, Libby realised. That's what had led to Luke doubting his own ability to love and stand by a woman, and left Jason terrified of letting her down. Margaret projecting her own fears about herself.

'They're good men, and they both love you,' said Libby. 'Exactly the same.'

'I know. I might not show it well, but I do. I love them both.' There was a long pause; then Margaret added, 'And you.' She held out her hand to Libby. 'It's been so hard, these past few weeks. Feeling I might lose you too. The daughter I always wanted.'

'Oh, Margaret.' Hot tears rushed into her eyes: Libby hadn't expected that.

Margaret nodded. 'I know people say no woman's ever good enough for a mother's son, but I couldn't have wished for a better daughter-in-law, Elizabeth. You're kind, and patient, and you've stood by Jason, after he . . .'

Libby held her breath.

Margaret seemed to be bracing herself. 'After he let you down like that. I haven't been able to stop thinking about what you said. It was foolish of me to dismiss it. And selfish – I love Jason very much, and I suppose I see a lot of his father in him. It's not easy for me to see his bad points, but . . . His not calling me is very poor. I'm disappointed in him, and I never, ever thought I'd say that.'

'I saw him today,' said Libby, unable to bear it. 'I met him outside Oxford to talk.'

Margaret's face lit up. 'Did you? How is he? Is he all right?'

'He's fine, but . . .' No, he wasn't fine. No white lies. Libby started again. 'Jason has never had to deal with failure until now. He doesn't see it as an unavoidable part of life – he sees it as a reflection on himself. He's let us down; he's let himself down; he's not the infallible creature he was brought up to believe he was. He thinks he's not worth loving if he's not perfect.' Libby let a tiny pause sink in; Margaret didn't reply.

'This is a turning point for him,' she went on. 'If he can drag himself up and start again, then he'll conquer the world. If he carries on thinking his whole identity is based on being perfect, then we're all in trouble.'

'You think it's my fault?' There was a hint of defensiveness in Margaret's voice, but Libby didn't blame her.

'I think you're the only person who can make him see how unconditionally he's loved,' she said. 'Whether he realises what's at stake and chooses to sort himself out is really up to Jason.'

And that's the most important job of all right now, she wanted to add, but didn't. Maybe Margaret wouldn't want to do that. It was, after all, as good as admitting that her parenting had failed with Jason as much as with Luke.

'I love him,' she said. 'More than anything in the world. But you're his mum.'

They sat in the quiet office, surrounded by paintings and filing cabinets and knick-knacks given by long-forgotten guests. It was the last room Libby planned to renovate, and although it was a lot tidier than it had been in Donald's day, in appearance it was still the closest to the old hotel.

'And you?' Margaret looked at her over the desk, more briskly than she had in a long while. They were looking at each other in a different way suddenly. 'What if Jason doesn't come back?'

The question was left wide open, and Libby could hear various different shades in it. Stay? . . . Go? . . . Divorce? . . . Run the hotel with Margaret?

Libby didn't know the answer. 'Let's just see,' she said, with a brave smile.

Margaret's answering smile was sad, but it wasn't as defeated as Libby had feared.

Chapter Thirty

The week between Tara Brady's visit and the open day to relaunch the Swan passed more quickly than any Alice had spent in the hotel so far. She was busy from the moment she arrived until she left for the day, organising the weekend's party and starting to take bookings for the new bedrooms now the website was live and attracting attention. Each phone call took ages because Libby couldn't stop herself describing every available option to make sure the guest booked the perfect room.

'You might like room eight,' she'd say enthusiastically. 'It has a beautiful view of the garden. But room three has the rainfall shower head, and a feature bath, so if it's a romantic weekend . . .'

It all felt very real now. A half-page ad had gone into the Longhampton paper, with one of the new photos of reception next to Doris's old snap of the same, announcing that there would be an informal open afternoon on Saturday, and all were welcome to see the new-look Swan. Alice had sent out specially targeted emails and updated the website with chatty news. She had a proper job title: head receptionist, with responsibilities for social media. (Translation: she ran @LordBobOfficial's Twitter account.) Even though it was just her and Libby in the office – Margaret had left for her sister's for a few days on Wednesday 'to think about things' – the atmosphere never felt stressed or panicky.

All in all, Alice was really happy. The only fly in the ointment was that Gethin wasn't.

Even Libby commented wryly on Gethin's new habit of collecting her and Fido on the dot of five o'clock, a compromise they'd reached about her continuing to work at the hotel when she'd 'promised him' she wouldn't. He'd started sulking whenever she mentioned work; he'd even queried whether she'd given him enough notice to make the open day on Saturday.

Alice had noticed Gethin was fidgety about plans; their supermarket deliveries were already marked on his kitchen wall-planner, and he hated last-minute changes to anything.

'I take it you haven't told him yet,' said Libby, as they sat in the office on Friday afternoon, folding fliers as a gentle July breeze floated through the open windows, drifting the scent of roses in from the garden.

'Told him what?' There was a lot Alice hadn't told Gethin about: the cells slowly knitting into a baby inside her, her worries that she wasn't the person he'd fallen in love with, her growing doubts about him. The way her thoughts still kept straying towards Luke. She'd had to delete Luke's number from her phone to stop the constant temptation to call him.

Libby gave her a look. 'Alice, you *have* to tell him soon. He's going to notice. And he needs to know.'

She let out a long breath. 'Sorry. It's just . . . hard to make it feel real. When I'm there, it's like I'm in a different world. The one I was in before the accident.'

'That sounds a bit weird.'

Alice struggled to put it into words. 'It is. It feels like Gethin knows a different version of me, and I'm trying so hard to *be* that person that I can't go forwards, if you know what I mean. I'm always second-guessing myself.'

Libby seemed surprised. 'But you are who you are. Were you really so different?'

I was in love with Gethin, thought Alice, running her nail down a crease to make it crisp. I wrote him those needy, soppy emails he keeps showing me. They don't feel like me now. But I did write them.

'Maybe love makes you a different person. Then when it wears off . . .'

The words hung in the air and Alice hoped she hadn't put her foot in it. There was still no sign of Jason; Libby hadn't said whether he'd be at the relaunch or not. She wished there was something she could do, but Libby had her determined, cheerful face on most of the time, and she didn't like to ask.

'You're going ahead, though?' asked Libby. 'With the baby?'

Alice nodded. 'I started this bit of my life like this. I just feel it's right. He or she's with me now.'

'Even if you don't know if you want Gethin?' Libby frowned. 'Are you sure that's logical? Or sensible? You'll be tied to him forever.'

'I can't explain. I just know it's right.' Alice had gone back and forwards over and over her instincts until they were worn smooth; just a flat certainty remained. She wanted the baby. It was cast in her head, a solid fact of her future.

'Then you definitely have to tell him,' said Libby, conclusively.

The thought sent a greenish shiver of panic through Alice, and Libby raised an eyebrow. 'What?'

'I don't think he's going to take it very well,' said Alice. 'He already thinks I'm behaving oddly, compared to normal. He thinks I'm still readjusting. Gethin's very sensitive,' she added.

'I . . . I found some anti-depressants in the bedroom. He said he's been on and off them for a while. I don't want him to go back on them because of this.'

He hadn't been lying about how she'd 'saved' him from depression, then. It made Alice wonder what else there was to find out.

'Then you'll have to tell him in stages.' Libby's attitude had reverted to its friendly bossiness. 'Tell him you've got a new job with key responsibilities here, which you have, no lie, and it comes with accommodation. You have to live here during the week.'

The relief that flooded through Alice as Libby said that took her by surprise. 'He won't like that . . .'

'Alice, you're trying to break up with him, aren't you?' She gave her a direct look, and Alice couldn't deny it. Again, the relief of hearing Libby say it in such a matter-of-fact way was extraordinary.

'Fine. So then when you're safely moved out,' Libby went on, 'tell him calmly about the baby, and that you hope you can work out a way of co-parenting him or her together. As good friends.'

'You make that sound so simple,' said Alice. She was already haunted by Gethin's face, bewildered and angry; how could she hurt him, his big soft eyes seemed to say, when he was making so much effort, sacrificing so much of his own feelings?

'But it is simple.' Libby stopped folding paper and looked at her over the desk. 'It's very sad that you had this accident but it's changed something. You can't force someone to love you, not if it's not there. If your memory comes back and you remember Gethin's the love of your life, then great. But if not . . . Even if you'd *married* him, you could still leave. Staying isn't worth anything if one person doesn't want to be there.'

Alice smiled sadly. 'I'll tell him after the open day.'

'Tell him *at* the open day,' said Libby. 'Then you can stay here. He won't make a scene, but if he bursts into tears, Margaret can take him off for tea and cake – you know she likes Gethin. Then you won't have to find the right moment at home, or deal with any embarrassing leaving logistics.'

Alice hoped Libby was right about the lack of big scene. She had a worrying feeling it wasn't going to be that easy.

Libby didn't sleep at all on Friday night. She watched the morning of the open house creep around the edges of the curtains – which weren't as beautifully lined as the ones in the hotel – and checked her phone in case a text from Jason had somehow appeared without her noticing.

It hadn't.

She blinked and made herself focus on the morning ahead. A lot of people had RSVPed, nearly everyone she'd invited. Margaret's contacts made up most of the list, but it was nice to recognise her own new friends, as well as Erin and Pete, driving up from London to be their first guests of honour in the 'honeymoon' room. Either people were eager to come and see what they'd done or they'd picked a quiet weekend: the local paper was coming, plus various great and good, many of the local traders chivvied along by Gina, all the old staff, Lorcan and his entire building team . . . Luke had generously offered to 'sort out' the champagne, and Lorcan's wife, who it turned out was a caterer, was doing some nibbles. It was shaping up to be a nice day all round.

There was only one person missing. Jason.

The thought of him sent a spike through Libby's heart.

She'd texted him again on Wednesday about the party, but

hadn't had a reply. She'd almost texted him another reminder on Friday, but the moment she was about to press 'send', Margaret had walked back in from her mini-break, in such a good mood and with such a startlingly flattering new haircut that Libby had been distracted.

She smiled at the mental image of Margaret 'modelling' her haircut in the office, patting her shorter, lighter curls with a touch of modest pride. It was a tiny step, but one that Libby hoped meant Margaret was starting to emerge from the shadows of her sadness, not quite as her old self, but a new one. The transformation was partly down to Jason's Auntie Linda, who had taken Margaret off to her hairdresser in Banbury and insisted on treating her for the launch.

'No point our hotel looking nice and me looking like a wreck,' she'd said, and Libby loved her for the 'our'.

Then when Margaret told her she was thinking about standing for the town council 'to do something about those awful wind farms up on Wergins Hill', Libby hugged her, mainly to stop herself cheering.

Margaret hadn't mentioned their conversation about Jason again. Another £500 had landed in the hotel account, but there had been no message. No text. It was small consolation that Margaret told her she hadn't heard anything either. What could she do? Was this really it? Didn't he want to make the effort to restart their life together?

Libby lay back in bed, stared up at the ceiling and let the darkness spread through her. She'd been keeping it at bay with tasks and lists and bright hotel smiles, but once she was alone, her misery seeped through the cracks. Everything about the hotel reminded her of Jason. Their hopes, their plans. Their fresh start, when they honestly believed they were making one. If he wouldn't come back . . .

I don't have to leave Longhampton, she thought. But maybe it'd be better to draw a line under this place and start a chapter of my own. She'd found new strengths, new friends, a sense of purpose she hadn't had till now.

The thought made her so sad.

But first she had to make the hotel work. Libby threw back the duvet and headed for the shower.

The first curious visitors began arriving on the Swan's gravel drive just after ten, when the trays of mini croissants were circulating the reception.

Alice and Libby – with Lord Bob and Fido – were also circulating, answering questions, passing out cards and information, and feeling justifiably proud of the way everyone walked in, then stood stock still, taking in the transformed entrance. Each member of the gardening club had sent a box of flowers from their gardens for Margaret to arrange, and the cottage-garden scent of sweet peas, roses and peonies filled the air, mingling with the wood polish and newly cleaned carpets, lemon slices and fresh cakes.

Gethin had agreed to come along about lunchtime, as he had 'things to sort out'. Butterflies were already massing in Alice's stomach at the thought of the conversation she needed to have with him. Even as she rehearsed it in her head, she wondered if she was making a mistake. He could be so thoughtful, so sweet and sensitive . . . Was she rushing into a decision based on nothing but her weird instincts? And hormones, weren't they supposed to mess with your head?

If Alice was being completely honest with herself, there was only one person she wanted to see today at the open day, and that was Luke. She wanted to talk to him, even if she didn't know what she was going to say. A certainty was taking shape, just out of reach of her reasoning, that seeing him would somehow make every loose thought fall into place, like a magnet dropped into iron filings. She couldn't explain why, but even thinking about him seemed to calm down the swarm of buzzing questions in her mind.

Fido was coping very well with the crowds, although she didn't have Bob's experience, and Alice had just shut her in the lounge for a brief moment of quiet time when Libby caught her arm.

'Gethin's here,' she said, and nodded to where Gethin was standing over by a painting of a mournful stag. He wasn't talking to anyone and was holding a glass of champagne nervously.

'Will you come with me?' asked Alice, and hated the way it came out.

'Of course.' Libby met her eye and said quietly, 'There's nothing to be afraid of, Alice. You've done nothing wrong.'

Libby walked straight over, and when Gethin saw them approaching, he smiled – his sweet, 'like-me' smile – which instantly made Alice worry that Libby would think she was mad.

'Hello, Gethin!' said Libby. 'How nice of you to come!'

'Thank you for inviting me,' he replied, sliding an arm round Alice's waist. 'You've done an incredible job. Congratulations.'

'I've been very lucky to get so much help,' said Libby. 'Alice has been indispensable.'

'She's brilliant, isn't she?' Gethin squeezed her proudly and Alice thought it was rich, given the way he grumbled about her overtime, and Libby 'taking advantage'.

'So what are you up to at work at the moment?' asked Libby in her cocktail-party voice. 'Any tours coming up? Ah, one second – here's Luke. I need a quick word.' And she waved him over.

Alice felt a moment's panic, then told herself not to be so stupid. It would be fine. It would be fine.

But her instincts were saying something else.

Luke had put on a suit for the occasion. Alice had never seen him out of his work clothes or his jeans; the suit made him seem more serious but also handsome in a sharp-cheekboned, actorish way. It was well cut, and the pale blue shirt was unbuttoned at the neck. Somehow, knowing there was an apple tattoo hidden under the dark cuff made her skin prickle.

'Hello, Alice,' he said, and she wondered why he sounded so formal, but then his eyes slid to Gethin.

'Luke, is it right that you and Gethin haven't actually met?' said Libby. 'Gethin, this is my brother-in-law, Luke. Luke, this is Gethin.'

They shook hands awkwardly. Or rather, Alice thought Gethin seemed tense and Luke looked like he'd rather be somewhere else.

'It'll have changed a lot since you were last properly inside, won't it, Gethin?' said Libby.

He was about to answer when Libby's face suddenly lit up, as a couple approached. Alice didn't know who they were, but from their very stylishly casual outfits, and the way Libby bounced forward to meet them, she assumed they were old friends from London.

'Erin!' she cried, flinging her arms open wide. 'Erin! You made it!'

The woman responded with a squeal and a hug too, and then Libby hugged the man, and turned back to Alice and the others. 'These lovely people are my friends Erin and Pete . . .'

'Who are *so* thrilled to be here,' added the woman, in an American accent.

Libby made the introductions, then touched Alice apologetically on the arm. 'I must get these two a drink, and show them their room. I'll catch up with you all. Have some champagne!'

That left Alice alone, with Gethin and Luke. And Bob.

Bob had been sniffing Luke's ankles, and now he waved his tail.

'No show without Punch, eh, Bob?' said Luke, bending down to scratch Bob's wrinkly head. 'You're the real family host. Aren't you?'

'You'll have heard the news about our little family?' said Gethin conversationally, and Alice's throat tightened. What did he mean by that? The baby? Had he guessed? Was he putting her on the spot, in front of Luke?

She saw Gethin was looking at Bob and reassured herself. No, he meant Fido. Fido was their little family.

Luke straightened up, and his face was unemotional. Then he smiled, but it was so unlike his normal smile that Alice almost cried out.

'Congratulations,' he said. 'You must both be thrilled.'

'Cheers! Although I'm not sure it's really something to congratulate us on,' said Gethin. 'It was more one of those amazing coincidences. It's lucky Fido ended up in the same park as Alice was walking your dog in.'

'Oh! Sorry, I thought you were talking about the baby.' Luke glanced between Alice and Gethin.

Alice felt the floor drop from beneath her.

'Whose baby?' Gethin frowned.

'Yours.' Too late, realisation flashed into Luke's eyes and he squeezed his brows together. Too late.

'Alice?' Gethin looked at her and she couldn't make her mouth move to reply.

'I'm so sorry,' said Luke. 'I really thought—'

'Don't apologise, mate.' Gethin still seemed stunned. 'That's . . . that's amazing news. Listen, um, Alice and I need to have a chat . . .'

Luke raised his hands. 'Of course. I'll leave you to it.'

There was nothing she could do but follow as Gethin grabbed her hand and led her towards the lounge, which was set up ready for the afternoon tea. Alice could see Fido in there, napping on one of the sofas, a ball of white fur.

Behind the dark curtain of Alice's memory, something began to stir. A feeling of déjà vu. A flicker of images: red tulips. A tea towel with blackbirds on it. The kitchen, in Gethin's house. She hadn't seen that tea towel since. Where had it gone?

'Gethin, can you let go of my wrist, please?' she said. 'That hurts.'

He was gripping her so tightly the metal strap of her watch was cutting into the tender skin by her bone.

'Sorry,' he said, but didn't let go until they were in the lounge, where he shut the glass door behind them.

Fido jumped off the sofa at once when she saw them and Alice bent down to stroke her, to buy herself some time. What could she say? Deny it?

This is the moment, she thought. Tell him. *Go.* But something was holding her back.

'So come on.' Gethin sounded excited. 'What's this? You're pregnant? Has Luke got the wrong end of the stick?'

Alice nodded slowly.

'Oh my God! That's amazing! That's absolutely *amazing*!'

His face glowed and he hugged her tightly to him, too happy to notice her lack of response. 'Why didn't you tell me? Have you just found out?'

Tell him. Alice nodded. He was thrilled – how could she puncture that? It felt as if his joy were backing her into a corner, defying her to contradict it.

'But . . .' Gethin's eyes ran up and down her body. 'No wonder you didn't know – you're not showing at all. You must be five, six months along.'

'Five or six months?'

'Yes.' He flushed. 'That would be the last time we . . . you know. Your birthday, in February. Things hadn't been great on that front, to be honest, but maybe that's why.' His expression brightened. 'That would explain how moody and weird you were. Why you didn't like being touched. I knew there had to be a reason.'

This isn't right, thought Alice. Something really isn't right here. Was he telling the truth? February? They hadn't slept together since *February*?

'I was going to wait until you'd moved your things in properly, but now we need to make this official . . . You know I'm an old-fashioned romantic.' Gethin began to drop to his knee and finally something snapped in Alice's brain.

'No!' Her voice was sharp. Too loud to be polite.

'What?' Gethin looked up from his uncomfortable position on the floor. 'Come on, I'm trying to do this properly . . .'

'You're not proposing, are you?'

'I certainly am. You're the mother of my child – I think the least I can do is make an honest woman of you.'

Alice heard herself say, 'I can't marry you.'

'Why? I don't care about what happened in the past. Forget

437

that.' His eyes had never seemed so huge, gazing up at her. 'We're meant to be together. I said that from the start.'

'But I don't *know* you.'

Gethin's face crumpled. 'What? Alice, what do you mean, you don't know me? How can you *say* that? You *saved* me.'

Blood hammered in her ears. That was too cruel, she thought. The words slid into her head from nowhere. What has he got if I don't love him anymore? He's going to threaten to kill himself, and it'll be my fault.

Wait. He hadn't threatened to kill himself, had he? Was this déjà vu? Something about the words passing through her mind was weirdly familiar. I've been here before, thought Alice. But I can't have been.

She stumbled on, trying to remember what Libby had said, when it sounded so reasonable. 'I'm sorry, Gethin, but whatever we had . . . it's not there now. I can't marry you. I hope we can be friends, and try to make the best of this, but . . .'

'But the baby – you can't just walk away from me. From us. You don't know what you're saying. It's the hormones.' He got up, standing very close to her now. 'Maybe we should go home and talk about this.'

By her feet, Fido started whimpering.

'I don't want to go home.' Alice's voice was firmer than she felt, but something in it made Fido whimper even harder.

'Shut up, Fido,' snapped Gethin. He took a step towards Alice and Fido's whimper changed to a low growl, the growl of a much bigger dog.

'Ssshhh,' she said, but while she was looking at Fido, trying to reassure her, she felt a sudden movement near her face. Gethin had gripped the hair at the back of her neck; from outside the door, it would look as if he was affectionately caressing her neck, prior to a tender kiss, but he'd twisted her hair round his fingers and was pulling tightly, so much that she had to lean back her head.

'Is this some kind of game you're playing?' said Gethin. Despite the pain he was causing her, he seemed bewildered and hurt. 'Are you treating me like those other boyfriends you told me about? Being mean to me to keep me keen? Is that it? Is that what you want me to do? Because I'm not going to give up on us, Alice. We were supposed to find each other. No one's ever going to love you like I do.'

Something was moving behind the curtain in Alice's mind, memories pushing and jostling to the surface, clicking together in a chain that was starting to make sense. She could smell curry, for some reason. Curry that she hated the taste of, she'd eaten it so much. Their curry.

She had a sudden jolt of fear for Fido, a foreboding feeling that made her dizzy. Too many things were pushing around in her head, as the pathways of her brain flooded with too many images, too much to process. She could taste something metallic. She had a vision of tulips. Tulips scattered on the white kitchen tiles. Trying to run in flip-flops, trying to carry Fido.

Fido carried on growling, and as Gethin tightened his grip on Alice's hair, and she yelped in pain, Fido barked, twice, three times in protective fury, jumping up around his leg.

'No, Fido, no,' Alice begged, but Gethin didn't even speak. Without warning, he kicked the little terrier hard in the stomach, sending her flying across the room, where she landed with a thud against the sofa.

Alice gasped, her heart too light in her chest. And in that instant, her memory came back in a tumbling, sickening flood.

439

Chapter Thirty-One

Alice stood frozen to the spot, her head spinning and tight with frantic mental activity. Jumbled images flashed in front of her mind's eye, but faster and harder than when she'd found Fido's stuff in the cupboard. These were darker memories, fear and panic, memories that made her chest light with adrenalin.

The curtain had gone. Now when she reached out, her mind found memories, old feelings, clicking and linking.

She hadn't planned to leave that day. She'd decided to give Gethin notice that she'd be moving out, because it just wasn't working with them sharing a house, as flatmates. It was over, and he would move on much more quickly if she wasn't around. One of them had to face the fact that they were friends, not lovers (and even then Alice knew she was being kind).

'You'll find someone else,' she'd told him. 'You're a lovely guy.'

And he was. A lovely guy. Just not for her. Not when she wasn't full of Italian wine and sun and New Age hopefulness.

The betrayed expression in Gethin's eyes came back to her in a flash. He hadn't accepted it. He hadn't accepted their relationship was over when she moved into the spare room. She'd been there for months. She'd only shared his bed for six, seven weeks, until she'd realised the chemistry wasn't right between them, and she'd liked him too much to pretend. But even then Gethin had refused to give up. They had a special connection, he insisted; they were soulmates; it wasn't just sex. But his love drained something out of her; the more he needed her, the more exhausted Alice felt.

She'd tried to leave before. Alone in a new place, not enough money to move out, with Fido to look after, a job to hold down – and Gethin reminding her how much he needed her around She'd caved in. After that, he'd seen it as a sign that she secretly wanted to stay, and occasionally reminded her that he saw something in her that her other boyfriends hadn't. Then not so occasionally. Then regularly, until Alice had started to think maybe he had a point.

But that morning . . . Alice had had a reason to leave at last. A very good reason that made the words flow where they'd stuck, guiltily, in her throat before. She'd met someone else. Someone who didn't make her feel faintly ashamed of herself. Someone who sent sparks of white-hot joy through her whole body. She'd fought it for a while, wary of making the same mistake twice, but he was different, and she wanted to be free to admit what she felt.

Gethin's reaction had been worse than she'd expected. Tears, yes. Not this outrage. The force of it took her by surprise.

'How can anyone love you like I do?' he'd demanded, and the shine in his eyes had turned Alice's indistinct worries into something sharp. 'You can't go. We have to talk about this.'

You can't go. The grip on her wrist. The low growl from Fido.

It flashed in front of her eyes now like a film she couldn't stop.

The tearful attempt to kiss her. Her pushing him away. More growling from Fido.

Then the shaking, the angry grab as she tried to shut down the conversation. Fido barking. Barking, barking, barking.

Horrified, Alice closed her eyes, but it only made the memories clearer. Gethin lashing out at Fido, snarling at her viciously.

That had been when she realised she didn't know Gethin at all. When she had no idea what he might be capable of.

That had been when she'd scrambled to leave, with only what she had in her pocket, and her whimpering dog under her arm.

That's when he'd told her about the 'surprise' holiday he'd booked for them, and she'd run, run out of the house.

Alice let out a cry and tried to go over to Fido, who was motionless against the sofa, but Gethin still had hold of her hair.

'Let go of me!' Alice yanked herself free. She didn't even feel the sting on her scalp as she pushed him away.

Gethin covered his mouth with his hands, his eyes wide with shock above them. 'I didn't mean it! You made me do that, Alice. I just care about you so much. I'm sorry . . .' He made a move towards her, but she held up her hands, warning him off.

'Lay a finger on me and I will scream this place down,' she said, and meant it.

Where did you look for a pulse on a dog? Alice didn't know. She didn't know where to touch her, in case she accidentally hurt her. Fido's eyes were two fine lines on her narrow face; she could have been sleeping, but Alice knew she wasn't.

She felt sick with panic. Fido was only protecting her, doing what she could . . .

Gethin took another step closer, his head tilted to one side. 'I'm sorry, Alice. I'm so sorry. I don't know what came over me. It's been so weird, you not recognising me, not remembering us

– I feel I've lost everything. You made me feel complete, and now you say you don't remember – it's killing me . . .'

He's lied from the start, she thought, as newly released memories spilled randomly through her mind. Meeting him in London. That beach in Aberystwyth, so cold and salty. A tent, kisses and crushed grass. What was real? All those photos, the slideshow, the playlists . . . No wonder they all stopped at my birthday – that's when I told him it wasn't working. Gethin had let her think the relationship was still going on, and she'd believed him. Bile rose up her throat. She'd have stayed, her and the baby forever. Wondering why she couldn't remember anything, getting trapped deeper in his web of neediness. Turning into his version of her, losing herself.

'Get away from me,' she said, as evenly as she could.

Gethin reached out and grabbed her hand. 'You owe it to us to talk about this.'

'I've got nothing to say.' She shook him off, anger flooding her. 'I was leaving! You *know* I was leaving! You lied and lied . . .' Fido wasn't moving. 'You told me Fido was dead so I'd feel bad about losing her – you *knew* I didn't lose her! You're sick!'

Alice pulled herself away from him, looking towards the glass door. While they'd been talking, more guests had arrived, and now the reception was full of people enjoying the happy atmosphere and Libby's triumph – she couldn't drag her dirty linen through there. She couldn't leave Fido with him either.

'Go and get some help, please. Quick.'

Gethin positioned himself between her and the door. 'No, let's get this sorted out. I want to go out there and tell the world our news – you can't deny me that, surely?'

'What? No! There is no way you're announcing anything.'

Someone was approaching the door – a guest probably,

wanting to see the new lounge. Alice's heart thudded with relief, but Gethin saw her head turn and moved quickly to open the door, using his body to block any sight of the room.

'Sorry, mate,' he said, in his affable Welsh accent, devoid of the earlier rage. 'We're just sorting out a few things here – can you give us a minute? Special moment in a couple's life, isn't it . . .'

'I've got to check the lights, apparently. Boss's orders.' It was Luke. Luke! Alice felt a rush of absolute relief. She was safe with Luke.

'Give us a moment, mate.' Gethin started to close the door, but Alice jumped up.

'Luke,' she gasped, 'Fido's hurt. Gethin kicked her! We need a vet, quickly!'

'Kicked her?' Gethin laughed, as if surprised. 'Why would I kick Fido? She's having a nap. Seriously, are you feeling all right, Bunny?' He glanced at Luke. 'Is there a doctor here? She's . . .' He didn't finish but raised his eyebrows.

'Please,' she begged. 'Is Rachel here, the lady from the rescue? Her husband's a vet.'

'The big bloke? Yes, they're in the garden, talking to Bob.' Luke didn't move, but stood there taking everything in, and Alice felt as if something that had been suspended was moving again.

I was leaving for him. She didn't have to think. When she reached for memories now, they were already in her head. *I was leaving because I wanted to make things clean and honest for Luke. He needed everything to be straight. He insisted. After that one* . . .

Alice took a sharp intake of breath as the memory flashed across her mind. Luke met her gaze and she knew he had felt it too: it was there in his face, in his concern. And yet he hadn't said anything; he'd been waiting for her to remember. Now she

444

knew why, in a collage of moments: the smell of old beer, Luke's long fingers playing with a coffee spoon, his eyes resting on hers, the light of the bar shading his cheekbones. They'd talked, about his past, about his bad teenage reputation, the way his family assumed the worst every time and how he had to work so hard not to fulfil that.

He'd been booked in for a fortnight, with his team. They'd shared their stories; they'd still liked each other despite them. The tension, building, building every evening, as the conversations got longer and the tiny electrical links between them built into a web of attraction, pulling them closer. Secrets, glances, coincidences, music, the smell of each other, the irresistible tug from the core of her whenever she saw his dark eyes watching her, knowing her and liking her anyway. The moon outside, growing bigger each night, into the full opaque disc. That night. They'd watched it rise over the trees.

Luke looked at her now and Alice knew what had happened.

'I've remembered,' she said. Her voice was too high. 'I remembered everything.'

His eyebrows lifted, more in hope than in question. 'Everything?'

And at last Alice did remember: the missed bus, the bottle of wine, her hands on his leather belt, his hands tangling in her hair, the sense that this was so right, so natural, just a continuation of their conversation but with their bodies, his mouth against the soft skin behind her ear, breathing raggedly as something lifted her out of her own body, his contrition afterwards, and her decision to make things right for him. So he could feel like the decent man she knew he was.

'Everything,' she said, and felt Luke's heart expand in his chest, even though she was nowhere near him.

'What about the dog?' said Gethin petulantly. 'What does he look like, this vet? I'll go and get him . . .'

'No, I think you should stay here,' said Luke. The warning tone in his voice was just enough. 'I'd like a word with you. Alice, you go. Run – Rachel said they couldn't stay long.'

Alice's legs stumbled as she got up, adrenalin still coursing through her veins, and she didn't know how she made it to the door, but she did.

Libby thought the party was going very, very well.

She'd done an interview with the paper and had her photograph taken with Margaret behind the reception desk. When she made a joke about them both being Sybil, Margaret had said, 'Ooh, I *know*!' in the most spot-on Sybil Fawlty impression she'd ever heard. The unexpectedness of it made her laugh out loud.

The photographer had shown her the photo on the back of his camera: her head thrown back with delight, Margaret gazing solemnly at the camera, perfectly aware of what she was doing. Libby loved it. It summed up everything she wanted people to think about the hotel: happy, elegant, friendly, a little surprising. A family business.

Margaret had asked if she could give a speech and Libby had said of course. She didn't mind about giving Margaret her moment in the spotlight. It was better, she reckoned, to say thank you personally to all the people who'd been so kind to her. A speech was really about her, not them. And so many people were here: Michelle, lapping up the praise for the decor; Lorcan and his caterer wife, Juliet, who'd arrived with trays of fondant fancies that she said she'd be happy to supply for afternoon teas; all Lorcan's apprentices, scrubbed up in clean shirts and looking like babies, with their tattoos covered up. Even Doris had been brought over by one of the carers from the hospital; she was sitting by the reception desk, holding court and telling everyone outrageous stories about the old Longhampton sherry circuit. Libby wasn't sure what Margaret made of that.

And Erin. Erin's amazement at how gorgeous the hotel was, how proud she was of Libby, how honoured they were to be the first official guests – it made Libby want to cry with relief and gratitude. She did have friends. Maybe the silver lining to all this mess was finding out exactly how good friends they were.

From worrying that no one would turn up, there was now a real risk that the champagne Luke had had delivered might run out, and that cars would have to spill over into the next field. But Libby had another reason to keep moving, thinking, smiling – so she couldn't dwell on what had happened just after she'd opened the doors to the first guests.

Secretly, she'd been daydreaming about Jason coming back for the party, walking in and seeing what she'd done. His face would be suffused with admiration, love and apologies, in that order; he'd beg to make a fresh start, a proper one this time. Every tweet, every Facebook post, every website update about the party had been done with him in mind; Libby wanted to believe he was out there, reading about them.

Then, just as she was handing the mayor and his wife a drink, her phone had buzzed. She'd pulled it out of her pocket with trembling hands and – yes! – it was a text from Jason. But all he said was, Good luck for today.

That was it. Not *I'm coming*. In fact, it might as well have said, *I'm not coming*. Libby's disappointment had been so bitter she could taste it. But this is still a good day, she told herself. It's a good day. Donald would be pleased.

Margaret's speech was due to take place at twelve in the garden, and at a quarter to, Libby thought she'd better round up Lorcan, Alice, Gina, Luke and anyone else Margaret would be thanking. She was making her way slowly through the milling people when she nearly bumped into Rachel's husband, George, coming out of the lounge with something wrapped in a bath towel. A brand-new white one, from her linen cupboard.

'Whoa!' she began, then saw Alice right behind him, her face streaky with tears, and Luke and Gethin following. Luke's face was tight and purposeful, and Gethin seemed to have been crying too.

'What's going on?' she asked.

'It's Fido,' Alice gasped. 'She's—'

'She's had an accident,' said Gethin.

To Libby's surprise, Alice turned on him. 'No, Gethin. It wasn't an accident. Stop lying!'

'Quiet, the lot of you. We don't have time for this,' said George, and carried on marching towards the door.

Libby took a step back to let him through. 'Fido?'

'Gethin kicked her.' Libby had never seen Alice angry, but now she was almost trembling. 'He kicked my dog and now George thinks he'll need to X-ray her for internal injuries. And he's lied to me about *everything*.'

'Alice . . .' Gethin began, but Luke was moving him towards the door too. He was barely touching him, but Libby could tell he had some kind of invisible army moves going on.

'I think it's time you left,' he said mildly.

'No! I . . . There's been a massive mistake.'

'No mistake,' said Luke. 'Now, if you wouldn't mind . . .'

'Can one of you open the bloody door?' demanded George. 'Can't you see I've got my arms full?'

'I'll come with you,' said Alice, but he shook his head.

'There's nothing you can do apart from wait in our surgery upsetting the other clients. I'll call you as soon as I know anything, but please don't worry.' His face softened. 'Rachel would never forgive me if anything happened to this one. But for God's sake, update your identity chip in future, all right?'

Luke gave Gethin another prod, and Libby watched as he escorted him out of the front door.

She turned to Alice, baffled. 'You're going to have to tell me what happened there. I feel like I've missed something vital.'

'Me too,' said Alice grimly. 'But now I've caught up.'

Margaret stood in the middle of her perfect garden surrounded by thirty or so of the guests and blushed when a spontaneous ripple of applause greeted her as she got up onto the hastily set-up stage (two catering crates with a tablecloth draped over them). Behind her, bees bumbled from rose bush to rose bush, and the clean-laundry scent of honeysuckle floated from the big tree in the corner. The garden was entirely her own creation; it was the star of the Longhampton Open Gardens weekend, but now Margaret looked shy.

Libby had never noticed Margaret being shy before, but then she'd always been there with Donald, tucked happily next to him, a step behind. This was her appearing on her own for the first time. Good for her, thought Libby. Although she *is* totally going to steal my thunder.

'Speech!' called someone, and Margaret said, 'I'm waiting for some quiet!' and everyone laughed.

Luke slipped into the space next to her. He was smiling in a

449

dazed manner, and his whole face was lighter than she'd seen it. 'Has she started?'

'No, you're just in time.' Libby raised an eyebrow. 'What the hell was that about? With Gethin?'

'Alice told you, then?'

'She said Gethin had completely invented most of their relationship to make her stay.' Libby widened her eyes. 'It's always the quiet ones. Did you know he was like that?'

Luke shook his head. 'No. She once said she was worried about some mate with a possessive boyfriend who refused to take no for an answer and I suppose I . . .' The smile faded. 'I suppose I knew, but I didn't . . .' He wiped his face with a hand. 'I'm not brilliant with the female mind. I gave her the address of the hotel, and told her if her mate needed to get away, there'd always be a bed for a mate of mine there.'

'So she was run over on the way to us then? Was she leaving for you? Why didn't you say something when she came back?'

'I didn't know what she'd said to Gethin. I mean, yes, there *was* something, but I told her she needed to sort things out before it went any further between us.' Luke's expression shifted between guilt and relief. 'I *wanted* to say something when she came back, but Alice didn't remember me, and I didn't know what was going on. She's very loyal . . . If she couldn't remember about us, and things were OK with Gethin, I didn't feel I had a right to ruin things.'

Libby watched Luke struggling with himself; once, she'd have rolled her eyes and thought, Commitment phobic, but now she saw Luke in a new light. His dad. His genes. His free will. 'But you're staying now?'

Luke glanced down, and when he looked up, there was a sweet determination in his dark eyes. He had a chance to right an old wrong, Libby thought. A chance to be the man his biological father hadn't been – instead, to be the rock his real dad *had*. 'I'm not going anywhere,' he said. 'I'll be whatever Alice wants.'

'Did I hear my name? Am I too late?' Alice wriggled her way into a gap next to them. 'Sorry – I was clearing up.'

She hadn't been, though. Libby noted her fresh make-up, the damp curls where she'd splashed her face with cold water. Luke put an arm round her, and Alice leaned back into him; silently, he moved so she was in front of him and wrapped both his arms tightly round her, fitting their bodies together as if they'd been made as a pair. They both smiled at the same time, at nothing, at everything.

Libby opened her mouth to say something, then decided not to. There would be time later.

'Ladies and gentlemen,' Margaret was enunciating carefully, in an accent a shade posher than normal. The prompt card in her hand trembled, but she didn't glance down at it. 'Guests past and present. Friends old and new. And of course, dogs.'

'She's missed out family,' Libby muttered to Luke.

'Of course,' he muttered back.

'This won't be a long speech, as public speaking isn't really my forte. I'm delighted to see so many of you here this afternoon, and thank you for all the kind things you've said to me about the renovation. I'm very sad Donald isn't here to see his hotel looking so beautiful, but I know he would thoroughly approve. Something fresh has been brought to the Swan and yet it still feels like the hotel we all know and love.'

'Hear! Hear!' someone murmured.

'However, I can't take credit for it, and nor do I want to.'

She was growing a little less formal as she went on. 'It's all been the work of one person – my very talented daughter-in-law, Elizabeth . . . Libby. Ably assisted by many of you here today, including Alice Robinson, our receptionist . . . and my son Luke.'

Libby hadn't been expecting that. Her eyes filled up as Margaret glanced in their direction with a tentative smile.

'One thing my husband always used to say to me was that it was best to be the first at the party, but not the last to leave.' Though Margaret's voice was strong, her eyes seemed misty. 'And this seems like a very good time for me to leave this particular party and hand the reins of the hotel over to the next generation. Thank you all, for the years of support you've given me, and I hope you'll continue to love the Swan in its marvellous new incarnation.'

Spontaneous applause broke out and Margaret had to wait a moment or two for it to die down enough to speak. Her face was wreathed with a sort of startled pleasure, as if she'd surprised herself, as well as been surprised by the reaction from the guests.

'Now, as president of the gardening club, it seems only appropriate for me to hand out some bouquets. Happily, I found an assistant who is just as keen as I am to acknowledge the hard work that Libby has put in, to the hotel, and to our family.' She stepped back and Libby realised someone was standing at the back of the crowd behind Margaret.

It was Jason. He was wearing a white shirt and jeans, his hair washed and cut shorter. He was gazing at her with a mixture of wonder and pride. And he was holding the biggest bunch of home-grown tea roses she'd ever seen.

* * *

One Small Act of Kindness

'You know my mum's never been to London on her own before?'

Jason and Libby were sitting under the jasmine trellis in the garden, away from the crowd of guests tucking into Juliet's afternoon tea.

'She came to see us,' Libby pointed out. 'When we were first married.'

'Yeah, with Dad. And we had to see them in their hotel. Which they accessed by a series of black cabs. I don't think Mum's feet actually touched London pavements the entire time.'

'Your point being?'

Jason gazed into her eyes. 'She came to see me at Steven's house. In *Clapham*. She said that what she had to say to me wasn't something she could tell me over the phone, and that she needed to know I'd heard it.' He looked down and plucked at the grass. 'She's never yelled at me before, either. Mum told me that unless I pulled my finger out, I'd lose you and she'd never forgive me. And that you'd done an amazing job on the hotel, and if my dad were here, he'd give me a right earful for putting you through the last year.'

A week ago, Libby would have found that impossible to imagine. Now, after Margaret's speech, and the new hair-cut . . . maybe.

'And what did you say to that?'

'Well, I pointed out to her that I wasn't exactly sitting around crying into my beer. I was going to work every day . . .'

'Where?' This was news to Libby.

'In the marketing department at Sanderson Keynes. It's not a brilliant job, but it's . . . a job. Have to start again somewhere.' He pulled out more grass. 'Bit embarrassing, having to go

453

through the whole "So why did you leave Harris Hebden?" thing, but . . . I told them I was willing to work hard, and I got some good references.'

'From Steven?'

'No! From my old boss. Everyone's allowed one mistake, apparently. Even Mum.' He looked up, and from the serious way he met her gaze, she knew Margaret had told him her own one mistake, the one she'd turned round into a great life.

'Well done,' she said. 'That takes guts.'

He moved his hand so the edge of his little finger was touching hers. 'I've never minded working hard. You know it was never about the money for me? With the stockbroking? I only ever wanted to make some cash, come back here and have a nice life. With a nice girl.'

'That you could buy presents for in Tanners.'

He grunted. 'Mmm. Did you take the earrings back?'

'I tried. I told them they didn't suit me.' Libby winced at the memory of that awkward conversation. First with the assistant, then the assistant manager, then the manager. 'Apparently I could have a credit note, but I didn't think I could use that to pay the electricity bill, so . . . they're still upstairs.' She paused. 'Let's give them to your mother, for Christmas. It'll make a change from bath oil.'

Jason took her hand in his. 'I'm an idiot, Lib. I put you through all this, and it took you, and my mother, to make me get a grip, and it scares me how I nearly screwed up all our lives. I know it's easy to say I want to try to make this better, but . . . I can only show you. Because none of this means anything to me without you to share it with.'

She looked at him and saw a new Jason. Not the man on the train, but a weathered man, with a few laughter lines and a different set to his jaw. Libby could imagine growing old with him, like Margaret and Donald had, curving round each other's strengths and weaknesses like the apple trees in the garden, growing towards the sun, resisting the rain, and her chest ached with how much she loved him.

'Jason?'

'What?'

She put her hand gently on his chin and turned his face up towards her. 'You know why I've put up with you? Because you're that man on the train who spilled his coffee and ruined my scarf. A decent man. Who can also cook pasta and deal with blockages,' she added, for clarity. 'The rest . . . the rest just comes from that.'

Jason touched her face with a reverential fingertip, running it over the slope of her nose, the curve of her cheek. It came to rest on her lower lip.

'I have a confession to make,' he said solemnly.

Libby's heart, which had been beating faster on account of his familiar smell, and the soft hollow of his throat, so close to her now, gave a low thud.

'Another confession?'

Jason nodded and sighed. 'I spilled my coffee on purpose.' He stroked her soft lip with his thumb. 'I had to get your attention somehow. My chat-up lines were appalling. But the rest . . . fair enough.'

Libby leaned forward, keeping her eyes fixed on his as their mouths came closer, closer, close enough to feel his warm breath on her skin. And then she closed her eyes, and her head filled up with jasmine and honeysuckle and shaded sunlight, the taste of Jason's mouth and the scent of his skin, and a single thought: I've come home, and I never knew I'd been away.

To Libby,
Thank you for rescuing a stranger on your doorstep
and for making her your friend.
Love,
Alice x

To Alice,
Thank you for bringing your heart into our home.
Sometimes it takes a stranger to tell us who we really
are.
Love,
Libby x

Acknowledgements

I'm lucky to be surrounded by some truly kind people, and this seems a good time to thank some of them for their big and small acts of kindness to me during the writing of this book – all of which made my world a better place!

Here's what my own Tree of Kindness would have on its branches . . .

Francesca Best, my amazing editor, for being patient and encouraging, arranging all our meetings at my favourite café, Honey & Co, then sharing puddings.

The team at Hodder, particularly Naomi and Véro, for the creative support, inspired marketing, beautiful covers, and infectious enthusiasm.

Lizzy Kremer, for letting me believe I thought of her genius suggestions by myself, and for being the kindest, wisest advisor on everything, ever.

Harriet Moore, for her inspiring, eloquent and thoughtful first read, and an editorial letter I re-read frequently to cheer myself up.

Chris Manby, soignée queen of the wine list, for making me laugh daily, in various ways.

Hulya Mustafa, for the cards-at-the-right-moment, and generally just being fantastic.

Dillon Bryden, for sorting out my computer crisis, fixing my car, and finding the kindest light for author photos.

Didrikson, for making a dog-walking coat with a hood that never falls down, and plenty of pockets.

James and Jan Wood, for being the sort of friendly, caring neighbours you only expect to find in Longhampton.

Sandra Allen, for the last-minute basset sitting and the best free-range eggs ever.

Christopher Columbus, for introducing chocolate to Europe.

My writer friends, for their sound advice and support, and for their generous honesty.

And as always, my mum and dad, for being at the end of a phone, and dealing with mousetraps, respectively.

Most of all, thank you to **all the readers** who are kind enough to take the time to write reviews, tweet me, or leave messages – it only takes a few words to brighten a writer's whole day, and it really does mean the world. Thank you very, very much!

Lucy Dillon

grew up in Cumbria and read English
at Cambridge, then read a lot of
magazines as a press assistant
in London, then read other people's
manuscripts as a junior fiction editor.
She now lives in a village outside
Hereford with two basset hounds,
an old red Range Rover,
and too many books.

one small act *of* kindness
is Lucy Dillon's sixth novel
for Hodder & Stoughton.
The people are made up,
but the basset hound,
unfortunately, isn't.

🐦 @lucy_dillon

f /LucyDillonBooks

one
small
act
of
kindness
can make the
world a better place…

Tell us about the acts of kindness
you've observed or been involved in,
and you could **win a spa day**
for you and a friend.*

Submit your story at
onesmallactofkindness.co.uk

*Competition closes 31st May 2015,
but feel free to share your acts of kindness after that date too!
Terms and conditions at onesmallactofkindness.co.uk

Here are some real-life acts of kindness you've already shared:

Mum and I noticed an old lady looking at the flowers outside a florist's – nothing fancy, just daffs and tulips. The lady would get her purse out, look inside, then at the flowers again as though she couldn't make up her mind or was trying to work out what she could afford.

Mum said she'd just be a second, went inside the shop and as I watched she came out with a bunch of spring flowers, said something to the lady and poked them out the top of her shopping bag.

The lady looked like she'd been given a million pounds. I remember her holding my mum's hand and beaming.

I'll never forget that. Never forget that lady's face or my mum's generosity, as we didn't have a lot ourselves.

Lesley

Once when my daughter was a newborn, and I still lived in London, I thought I'd take her out in her buggy on the bus. Except I didn't know how to fold the buggy *and* hold a baby, and the longer the angry busload of people waited for me to struggle with it, the more flustered and confused I got. I will never forget the kind older gentleman who got off the bus, folded the buggy, help me get on, gave me his seat and a clean hanky to blow my nose on.

Rowan

During a recent hospital stay, a nurse noticed my Kindle on my bedside tray and asked me what I was reading. At the time I was very poorly and wasn't reading anything but once the medication had started to work, I was moved to another ward where the same nurse was working the night shift. I told her I'd been able to read a little that day, and she asked me about it and even recommended me a book. Personal touches such as these can make an unexpected hospital stay much more bearable. I would love to see her again and thank her a) for the recommendation and b) for her kindness.

Vicky

When I was applying for a place at university, the teachers at my state grammar school – The High School For Girls in Gloucester – gave up their lunchtimes to give me extra tuition to get me through the Oxford entrance exam. It's only as an adult that I realise what a generous gesture that was. I wish I'd thanked them much more profusely for that big act of kindness which made such a huge impact on my life.

Chris

Backpacking by myself after uni, I got lost in the middle of Singapore one morning, hunting for the bus station. A man in his late twenties pulled up in a big 4x4 beside me, asking if I was ok. Nervously, I ignored him and carried on walking, but he was persistent and friendly, kept driving beside me saying he would take me to the bus station – and eventually I was won over and (I know, I know) got into his car. As we were driving he said he would take me all the way over the border into Malaysia (a couple of hours' drive) to the next leg of my journey. I refused – both out of politeness and wariness – but he was insistent that he was going that way anyway.

We chatted all the way into Malaysia. I found out his name was Zack, he told me about himself and his family and – despite my protests – bought me lunch, my bus ticket and saw me safely onto the right bus, standing there waving me off like an old friend.

It sounds ludicrous to other people that I would do something so silly, alone, in the middle of an unknown city but I now look back on the risk I took and am so grateful for Zack's pure kindness and goodness. It reminds me not to ignore my gut instinct, and also not to judge people. I later heard from other travellers what a nightmare their convoluted bus journeys from Singapore into Malaysia had been, and felt even luckier.

What breaks my heart slightly is that Zack gave me his number, asking me to call to let him know I got to Kuala Lumpur safely, but I lost the bit of paper and was never able to call to say thank you and let him know how much his kindness and help had meant to me.

Katy

My dad died, five years ago. It was very sudden and I was in Italy for work; I returned to the UK hours before it happened. I was due to be in work for a day and then off for two weeks' holiday. The holiday turned into arrangements for the funeral and looking after my mum. I had to just get on a train and head north to Lancashire to sort everything out for her.

Two very lovely things happened. My boyfriend (now my husband), drove the length of the country at five in the morning, so instead of arriving 'at some point' during the days following, he was there as soon as I got up. He supported me and my mum for two weeks when we were falling apart.

The second lovely thing was on my return to work. People fended off 'did you have a lovely time' questions about holidays and protected me from having to explain over and over again. But someone I worked with said nothing, just gave me some yellow roses which I took for remembrance, and which I kept on my desk and dried when they were finished. I still have the petals. It was a small, cheering, thoughtful gesture, which I think of every time I look at them.

Mandi

I was a bridesmaid to an old friend many years ago. I had no family of my own and didn't drive so went on to the reception in one of the wedding cars. The reception was about an hour from home and I assumed I would get a bus or train back later.

At the end of the night I realised I didn't have enough money on me and it was very late. The groom's mother, whom I had only met that very day, kindly paid for a taxi to take me all the way home. I thought that was amazingly kind of someone I barely knew. She wouldn't even let me pay her back later.

Gill

Jane, a local ceramicist, has given her time and smiles to me as I have asked all sorts of questions over the last few years, and I have just returned from another session with her. I'd like to thank her for her encouragement and advice as I embark on a new life / direction.

Fiona

Last week I took my coat to be dry-cleaned. It was chucking it down outside and obviously my main coat was taken! (I was wearing a rubbish non-waterproof one.) The guy serving me in the shop – a young man of around twenty-five – lent me his umbrella and said to hold on to it till it stopped raining. I thought that was so sweet.

Katy

When my parents bought their house, they inherited the lodger, a wonderful retired lady who became a sort of godmother to me and my sister. She hadn't had children but she loved us like her own. Over the years, my parents have returned that love by taking care of her, visiting her in her residential home and generally making sure she knows how much she means to us all – their quiet kindnesses have been a real example to me.

Victoria

Pets As Therapy: a note from Lucy Dillon

Could your dog (or cat! Or donkey!) bring some Lord Bob-style sunshine into new people's lives? There are currently 4,500 registered Pets As Therapy dogs, and 108 PAT cats, delivering their own kind of waggy-tailed medicine via half a million visits a year. If your dog is calm and sociable, fully grown, and can rock a fluorescent vest, why not consider volunteering with him/her?

Pets As Therapy is a national charity founded in 1983.

We enhance health and wellbeing in the community through the visits of trusted volunteers with their behaviourally assessed animals. We provide a visiting service in hospitals, hospices, nursing and care homes, special needs schools and a variety of other venues all across the UK.

Our therapeutic visits:
- Enhance lives in our communities by providing companionship and friendship and helps to tackle loneliness.
- Improve the lives of people suffering from debilitating mental and physical health conditions and illnesses such as strokes by including animal assisted interventions as part of a holistic approach to treatment.
- Improve literacy in children by developing their confidence, interest and enjoyment in reading.

You can find further details about registering as a PAT volunteer, and having your dog assessed at their website, www.petsastherapy.org, or by calling 01844 345 445. You can follow the PAT team on Twitter at @PetsAsTherapyUK. Be prepared to have a happy cry at some of the beautiful stories, and photographs!

Has Lord Bob stolen your heart?

For more from
One Small Act of Kindness's canine hero,
follow him on Twitter at

 @LordBobOfficial

And if you have a special pooch
that deserves recognition, head over to
lucydillon.co.uk.

You can enter your dog into Lucy's Dog of the Month,
and you could even get his or her name
in the next Lucy Dillon book*!

*For a limited time only.

LUCY DILLON

A Hundred Pieces of Me

Shortlisted for the RNA Contemporary
Romantic Novel Award

Letters from the only man she's ever truly loved.
A keepsake of the father she never really knew.
A blue glass vase that catches the light on a grey day.

Gina Bellamy is starting again, after a few years she'd rather forget. But the belongings she's treasured for so long don't seem to fit who she is now.

So Gina makes a resolution. She'll keep just a hundred special items – the rest can go.

But that means coming to terms with her past and learning to embrace the future, whatever it might bring.

'Bittersweet, lovely and ultimately redemptive; the kind of book that makes you want to live your own life better.'
Jojo Moyes

HODDER

LUCY DILLON

The Secret of Happy Ever After

When **Anna** takes over Longhampton's bookshop, it's her dream come true. And not just because it gets her away from her rowdy stepchildren and their hyperactive Dalmatian.

As she unpacks boxes of childhood classics, Anna can't shake the feeling that maybe her own fairytale ending isn't all that she'd hoped for. But as the stories of love, adventure, secret gardens and giant peaches breathe new life into the neglected shop, Anna and her customers get swept up in the magic too.

Even Anna's best friend **Michelle** – who categorically doesn't believe in true love and handsome princes – isn't immune.

But when secrets from Michelle's own childhood come back to haunt her, and disaster threatens Anna's home, will the wisdom and charm of the stories in the bookshop help the two friends – and those they love – find their own happy ever after?

'Lucy Dillon's voice is gentle and kind throughout . . . perceptive and well handled. A heart-warming piece of escapism for long winter nights.' Red

HODDER

LUCY DILLON

Walking Back to Happiness

Juliet's been in hiding. From her family, from her life, but most of all from the fact that Ben's not around anymore.

Her mother **Diane** has run out of advice. But then she insists Juliet look after her elderly Labrador and it becomes apparent that **Coco** the dog might actually be the one who can rescue her daughter.

Especially when it leads to her walking dogs for a few other locals too, including a spaniel, **Damson**, who belongs to a very attractive man . . .

Before she knows it, Juliet realises she has somehow become the town's unofficial pet-sitter. A job which makes her privy to the lives and secrets of everyone whose animals she's caring for.

But as her first winter alone approaches, she finally begins to wonder if it's time to face up to her own secrets? To start rebuilding her own life? And maybe – just maybe – to fall in love again?

'Witty, heart-warming and a very real tale
of loss and redemption' *Stylist*

HODDER

LUCY DILLON

Lost Dogs and Lonely Hearts

Rachel has inherited a house in the country, along with a rescue kennels. She claims she's not a 'dog' person. But then she tries to match the abandoned pets with new owners, with some unexpected results . . .

Natalie and **Johnny**'s marriage hasn't been easy since they started trying for a baby. But will adopting **Bertie**, a fridge-raiding, sofa-stealing Basset Hound make up for it?

Meanwhile **Zoe**'s husband has given their kids a Labrador puppy, and left her to pick up the mess, literally. She's at the end of her tether, until her pup leads her to handsome doctor **Bill**, whose own perfect match isn't what he was expecting at all.

As the new owners' paths cross, and their lives become interwoven, they – along with their dogs – all find themselves learning important lessons about loyalty, second chances and truly unconditional love.

'Heart-warming, fun and romantic.
Marley and Me fans will love it.' *Closer*

HODDER

LUCY DILLON

The Ballroom Class

When three couples join a new ballroom class, they're all looking for some magic in their lives.

Lauren and **Chris** are getting married, and Lauren's dreaming of a fairytale wedding with a first dance to make Cinderella proud.

Not wanting to be shown up on the dance floor, her parents **Bridget** and **Frank** have come along too. They normally never put a foot wrong, but Bridget's got a secret that could trip them up unexpectedly.

Meanwhile **Katie** and **Ross** are looking for a quick-fix solution to their failing marriage, even though neither is quite sure who's leading who anymore.

As friendships form over the foxtrot, the rumba rocks relationships, and the tango leads to true love, all the students in the Ballroom Class are about to face the music and dance . . .

> '*Strictly Come Dancing* with added off-floor love,
> betrayal and glitz makes Lucy Dillon's dazzling
> debut a must for ballroom fans.' *Mirror*

HODDER

When one book ends, another begins...

Bookends is a vibrant new reading community to help you ensure you're never without a good book.

You'll find monthly reading recommendations, previews of brilliant new books, and exclusive features on and from your favourite authors. We'll also introduce you to exciting debuts and remind you of past classics.

There'll be a regular blog, reading group guides, competitions and much more!

Visit our website to see which great books we're recommending this month.

welcometobookends.co.uk

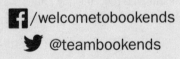